NIGHTSHADES

Also by Tanith Lee

Heart-Beast
Elephantasm

NIGHTSHADES

Thirteen Journeys into Shadow

Tanith Lee

HEADLINE

First published in Great Britain in this collection in 1993
by HEADLINE BOOK PUBLISHING

10 9 8 7 6 5 4 3 2 1

British Library Cataloguing in Publication Data

Lee, Tanith
Nightshades
I. Title
823.914 [F]

ISBN 0 7472 0877 8

Typeset by
Letterpart Limited, Reigate, Surrey

Printed and bound in Great Britain by
Mackays of Chatham PLC, Chatham, Kent

HEADLINE BOOK PUBLISHING
A division of Hodder Headline PLC
Headline House
79 Great Titchfield Street
London W1P 7FN

Contents

THE NOVEL

NIGHTSHADE

Nightshade

In 1974, DAW Books of America accepted my fantasy novel, **THE BIRTHGRAVE**, *and liberated me into the world of professional writing.*

I had already written three fantasies by then, with no eye to publication anywhere. They were the previously mentioned **BIRTHGRAVE**, *and* **THE STORM LORD**, *and the* SF *novel* **DON'T BITE THE SUN**.

Strangely, the moment I got my break into fantasy writing, I conceived the idea of the following book, **NIGHTSHADE**. *I knew it would not be suitable for DAW, but couldn't resist it. Although set 'somewhere' in the Mediterranean, and 'some-time' in the late Sixties (probably) it was and is what I would class as a contemporary novel.*

But then again . . . It certainly has some exotic and wildly fantastic elements.

There is the Dionysos theme: this god, generally dismissed as the deity of wine – he is much more – has always intrigued me. The master of inner terrors and truths, the breaker of chains, his power passes through the freeing medium of drink, or any strong excitement, including madness.

There is, too, the character of the anti-heroine, Sovaz.

Elizabeth Taylor, surely one of the most beautiful women in the world, is proof that a beautiful human being may also possess great talent and character, and a fully operational soul. And yet I confess a fascination with those great beauties, male and female, who are, operationally, soulless. One glimpses them now and then, usually briefly. What, if there is no warmth, is making them tick? What, aside from beauty, has vampirized them? Some of this I have tried to investigate in the form of the pale, red-lipped icon of Sovaz.

3

ONE

It was seven o'clock; the sun was dying on the sea. The water, like the sky, was glazed by a smoky glare, which diluted at its edges before smashing itself delicately on the beach.

The house stood on the highest point of the cliff overhanging the bay, the shoreline, and the wide sea falling away before it into the mouth of the sunset, the levels of the city falling away behind into shadow.

The house was sealed from the city by a high wall, reminiscent of a jail, broken only by a pair of oriental wrought iron gates. The wall mostly shut off the elevation of the cliff, and the induced gardens which clothed it, yet a scent of roses, oleanders, peach and lemon trees filtered occasionally into the streets below. Rising from the gates, a hundred shallow stone steps, indented at their centres as if from age and great use, led in four tiers to the house. On each landing stood two marble columns with horses' heads.

The house itself had a strange decaying look, the stucco of its balconies and arches purplish-brown as if steeped in incense, erupting into growths of vine and tamarisk.

The first lamps and neons were spangling across the city to the south. The polarized windows of the house, losing the stain of the sun, became black.

Sovaz stood at the window, telling the chain of pearls like a rosary, listening to the sounds that her husband made, putting on his clothes in the dressing room. Such immaculate, precise sounds: now the rustle of the linen shirt, now the icy clink of a cuff-link lifted from its onyx box. Presently he came into the room.

'You aren't dressed yet.'

'No.'

'It's very dark in here.'

Kristian touched the discreet electric bell. The door opened almost at once and the black girl, Leah, crossed the room and let down the drapes of the three tall windows without a word. Light came obediently, spreading from the master switch at the touch of Kristian's hand. Sovaz' suite was mainly black, the lamps gold or green silk with crystal pendants on jade stands. A scented joss stick was burning in an antique bowl of bronze.

Sovaz glanced aside at Kristian in his perfect white dinner clothes, the little cold fires of emeralds winking on his cuffs. He was forty-eight: a very handsome man of excellent physique, his hair a rich blue-black which led women who had failed with him (most women) to suppose aloud that he had it dyed. His face was arrogant, remote. His eyes, a light but definite blue, seemed extraordinarily intent by contrast with the eyes of Sovaz which, even as she looked at him, appeared unfocused. She stood in her slip, playing with the pearls absently.

'Leah,' Kristian said, 'help my wife with her dress.'

The black girl lifted the dress from the bed and quickly, deftly, slipped Sovaz into it. Like the room, like Leah herself, the dress was black.

'Were you intending to wear those pearls?' Kristian said. 'Where are the rubies? They would be more suitable.'

'If you think so,' Sovaz said.

Leah, who had already opened the ivory box, brought the rubies and proceeded to fasten them in position. Sovaz let go the chain of pearls; they fell into the rugs. (Leah bent immediately to retrieve them.) Sovaz went to the arrangement of mirrors. She touched hesitantly at her neck.

'I look as if I had had my throat cut.'

'If the rubies don't please you, then wear the sapphires. You have plenty of jewels.'

The black girl, her tasks accomplished, perambulated silently about the room and out of it. Sovaz stared after her with that remarkable, apparently abstracted gaze.

'Yes, I do, don't I?' The door was shut. Sovaz returned to her own image and extended the tip of one finger to her reflected face. 'So white.'

'You should use your sun-lamp.'

He himself was tanned to a healthy, satiny finish, like wood, from use of a lamp. She, who lived mainly by night, sensed her element. The sun-lamp obscurely frightened her; she was psychologically afraid it would scorch her blind. She did not answer but leaned to adjust the low neck of the black lace dress, then picked

5

up a lipstick and slowly coloured her mouth.

'Why do you burn this disgusting cheap rubbish?' Kristian said. He reached in and extinguished the joss stick.

'They sell them in the night market on the quay,' she said irrelevantly.

He took out his cigarette case and lit a cigarette.

She had bought the joss sticks in the city three months before, the last night she had spent with her last lover to date, a boy twenty-two years old. Sovaz was twenty-five; the ages of her lovers had ranged from twenty-three to nineteen. There had never been anyone older. These amours did not offend or distress Kristian; if anything they fitted into his scheme of things, as a hobby which kept the woman in the background of his life. Always, though indirectly, he vetted the young men. But their high standards of physical perfection, their sound health and good manners were symbols for him, for others, of his own opulence and taste, not pleasures he sought for her. The wife of Kristian might have only the best.

He himself had not been to bed with her in four years. She had never interested him particularly except for a week or two at the start of their marriage, when she was virgin, novel, and unexplained. Now she was a convenience and an ornament, a showcase for his wealth and aesthetics, like the carious grandeur of the house.

They had been married for seven years. She was the daughter of a friend, a librarian and scholar, a man a few years his senior, to whom Egyptian and Greek manuscripts were brought for translation.

Kristian had seen the girl reading under a green and red stained window, the panes casting gems on her white skin, and her black hair down her back. Her eyes were so large, like coals, her body slender as a stalk, with a woman's breasts. He had been stirred by that picture. He did not know what she was reading but had hoped for some of the father's intellect in the child. She disappointed him. She gorged herself mainly on bizarre modern fantasies by writers with inelegant names, among the gracious ancient dusts of the great library.

The old man (Kristian composedly thought of him in this way; although virtually contemporaries, physically they were quite unlike) became sick, and tuberculosis was diagnosed. He refused to leave his books to be cured, dismissing medicine as preposterous. 'I shall soon be better,' he would say. Kristian found his illness distasteful, like a bad smell. Presently the old man's lungs haemorrhaged and he died. Kristian, going to witness the aftermath, now acceptably clean and sterile, found Sovaz wandering like a lost pet animal among a welter of stacked furniture. The old man had died a pauper. Everything would go to bury him and to settle his debts.

Kristian found the mess agitated him, a last unhealthy odour. He paid off the debts and took the girl into his house. Despite her vulgar leanings, the vile books and records she brought with her, her presence did not jar. She did not, for example, cry. She seemed a void that might be filled. He became fascinated by the task of remodelling her, forming her into his own creation.

She was not precisely rebellious but he found he made no headway. The culture he wished to impose slipped off her surface.

One night she found sleeping tablets in his dressing room and swallowed most of them. It was only three months since her father had died. She was eighteen.

At least nothing about the affair had been public. Kristian's valet, finding her with the last tablet clenched in her hand, had forced an emetic between her teeth, and compulsorily brought her back to life. Five days passed before Kristian could bring himself to see her, however. When he did, he was startled by her quality, like a rare porcelain. She sat behind the house, looking out over the garden and the sea, the warm night wind, perfumed with jasmine, lifting up strands of her dark hair and setting them down again.

He had not expected to find, after the sordid thing that had happened, something so exquisite.

'I imagine you want me to go,' she said. 'I shall.' And again he sensed in her the unfilled, empty room.

'My dear child, where do you propose to go to? You are quite untrained, unfit for anything, except possibly for factory work or prostitution.'

'That then. Does it matter?'

'I doubt very much if you would enjoy either. The work is hard and wages low.'

7

'I shall have to bear it then, shan't I?'

He felt a flicker of alarm. It was no secret she had been with him, here, in this house. If she deliberately left him for the filth, petty crime and squalor of the back alleys and doss houses of the slums, she would leave a smear of this dirt on his own life.

'I suggest you think again, Sovaz. You're not a little girl. You have a brain, I believe. Attempt to use it.'

He did not keep a watch on her then. Before dawn she was gone.

It had taken him three days to find her. Tenacious as a lover, he had gone to a great deal of trouble and expense to do so. His hands were clammy with a dungeon sweat. He was afraid the besmirching quicksand had already swallowed her. Prescott, the Englishman, had finally hunted her down.

Evening on the quay, the wharves rife, active. A stink of rotting fish, oranges, cheap hashish, the rancid oil in the lamps bobbing and coruscating their moons on the glutinous black water below. Men waiting, smoking and spitting, alert for work on the smacks of the midnight fishermen, the pleasure craft with their fringed canopies. Kristian's valet pushing open the canvas door of a leprous overhanging tenement. A whore putting her hands on him, Kristian striking her off; some trouble with the pimp, settled by Prescott. The long climb up the broken stairs, the tang of urine on the treads, fumes of inferior opium and zombie laughter from small black holes passing as rooms.

It was the attic, rafters sloping, lamplight and waterlight cast up on them, and a battered chaise-longue, where a girl was lying, smoking a green cigarette. It took Kristian some moments to realize this was Sovaz. Her hair was bleached, her eyes sticky with mascara.

Prescott and the valet drew back beyond the door. Kristian crossed to the open window, and turned, staring at the creature which confronted him.

'You look already like a hag seventy years old,' he said, 'riddled by disease and sick with opium. Is this the life you prefer?'

She murmured: 'The madam is bringing a man here. Of some importance, she said. She has told him I am fifteen, but well developed for my age.'

'No doubt.'

'You had better be going, Kristian. You might meet him on the stairs otherwise.'

'How many men?' he asked abruptly.

She started. 'Do you care? Oh, none so far. This will be the first.'

'Get up at once,' he said, 'you're coming with me.'

'Leave me alone. You don't want me,' she said bitterly. Her eyes were very dull. He tapped his fingers impatiently. He wore gloves.

'Get up,' he repeated, 'or I shall have Prescott fetch the police.'

'I have chosen what I want.'

'You talk like a melodramatic schoolgirl.'

'You know,' she said, meeting his eyes suddenly, 'that I am in love with you. You, for your part, have scarcely ever exchanged a word with me that was not a criticism or an instruction. I am sorry to have failed your ideals so dreadfully. I am certain you see I can't possibly return with you. Now go. Please.'

Outside a man was strolling by, harnessed with cages full of twittering birds.

It had not before occurred to Kristian that the young girl might think herself in love with him. Yet she was impressionable and without anchor, the logic of it struck him now. Love. A clinging, cloying emotion. He found it almost offensive to be the object of her desires. If she had said she passionately admired him it would have been different. But love – it was too familiar of her, impertinent almost.

Nevertheless, the filthy room, the weird light and smells, the hopeless laughing and twittering of the damned below, snapped his nerve. He must get out and she with him, for she had come to belong to him – her ingenuous confession only branded her more irrevocably his property.

He went to her and pulled her up. Even in her tart's costume she was beautiful. At first he thought she would lean on him and be still, quiescent as before. But abruptly she began to fight him, using even her nails and teeth, putting him in mind of a white fox one of his father's gamekeepers had once trapped, which had immediately gnawed through its manacled foot in order to be free.

Kristian began to sweat in earnest. The situation became immense and intolerable. Already his face and neck were streaked by her nails; disgusted panic took hold of him.

'Stop it,' he rasped, afraid to speak more loudly for the valet and the agent outside the door. And then, uttering the first promise that came to him to quieten her: 'I intend you to be my wife.'

The effect of his words was not as he expected. Though she ceased fighting, she began instead to laugh.

Nevertheless, he was able to propel her slackening body to the door.

'As I thought,' he said coldly, 'there has been some mistake.'

The two men accepted the ridiculous statement without comment. The woman and her customer were late in coming, it seemed; they passed no one on the stairs, but got down to the limousine without incident.

Prescott stood at the street corner watching them drive off, his eyes impersonal behind green-tinted glasses, his hands thrust deep in the pockets of his rumpled jacket.

As a boy, Kristian had been brought up on his father's large European estates. It seemed to him in retrospect that those years were very nearly perfect. He had not precisely loved either father or mother, but he had respected them, a fastidious man of great erudition and intellect, a woman of elegance and finesse. It was easy to recollect the huge white house, burning from within all the long hot nights of summer, the indigo sky, the coloured lamps flickering across the slowly moving couples on the lawns, the black swans sleepless on the lake. To remember also the hunting parties at dawn, his father a faultless shot, and the beautiful guns, clammy with the dew, and the white brandy in the silver hip flask burning on his throat. In those years life had been confined to certain compartments, each item in its place, ready to be taken up when needed, to be replaced when finished with, like ornaments from a box. Times for dinner engagements, for shooting, for riding, for music, for literature. Everything was there to hand. Even women, if he wished for them, would come discreetly to his room, ask nothing except to please him, and never importunately, departing when he desired, gracefully and without question.

The estates were a kingdom of sorts, in some ways rather more. His father presided at curious little courts of justice set up to contain disputes among the tenants and workers of the land. It was tacitly understood, too, though never demonstrated in Kristian's time, that the power of life and death belonged also to his father. There were a couple of stories, one being that three months before Kristian's birth his father had hanged a persistent poacher, the other that once, years earlier, he had shot a stranger caught at midnight trespassing in the grounds.

In this environment and from this soil Kristian grew, observing the feudal pyramid at its most explicit all about him, the workers beneath, the landowner above, and, elevated just beyond the rest, the images which represented God.

For religion, like everything else, had its seasons and observances. Though it was quite clear to Kristian from the earliest that his father did not believe a godhead to exist, the symbol and the ritual – the motions of the censers, the candles and the exquisite singing – these were all-important. At forty, the milk-white faces of the icons still stirred in Kristian cool thrills of pleasure, and the light through coloured windows. It was too intimate a delight to be shared with any rude intrusive deity.

Perhaps there had been a half vision in Kristian's subconscious of the milk-white face of Sovaz lit similarly by coloured windows, as he had once found her beneath the panes of the library. Nevertheless, he was inspired to marry her in the office of a registrar with a handful of acquaintances looking on, the only hymn the distant external wailing of a street musician's flute.

That marriage. It had surprised everyone.

When he brought her back to the house from the tenement attic her laughter had been stopped. Indeed, he did not see her laugh much after, except sometimes, now and again, across a room full of guests and smoke. He had her hair dyed to its original shade, her face wiped clean in readiness for expensive cosmetics. She was now extremely docile. Kristian discovered in himself a sudden quickening, almost of desire or lust. He had rescued her, barely in time, from the filth of the waterfront night, from the nights of disease, ugliness and ennui which would inevitably have followed. Had rescued himself, more important, from a foul memory, a stinking leper of a ghost in every angle of his house that she had occupied.

Just over a year later, when all vestige, even all travesty of communication had flickered out, she told him.

11

She had begun to paint by then, small exact paintings which he abhorred for their theatrically gesturing participants and their raw colours. Moths were fluttering like rain against Sovaz' lamp as he came out of doors to smoke his Turkish cigarette. Sovaz, looking up from her canvas, had said: 'Didn't it occur to you, Kristian, how lucky it was we never met the madam and her customer on the stairs, when you came for me that night?'

He did not wish to speak of it. 'I don't recall the night in question.'

'The night you found me on the waterfront, I told you the madam was bringing a man up to me. Do you remember now?'

'There is no point in discussing this.'

'I lied to you,' Sovaz said.

He did not turn, but kept his eyes on the descent of the gardens and the black sea below.

'Wasn't that foolish of me?' Sovaz murmured. 'I thought it would force your hand, make you aware of me in spite of yourself, if you imagined that I'd despaired enough to do that – but really, the moment you came into the room I guessed it would be useless. I should never have told you that lie. Are you disgusted at my deceit? Disgusted enough to divorce me?'

'I suggest this conversation has come to an end,' he said. He finished his cigarette. 'You understood, I thought, that divorce is out of the question.'

She said nothing, but, taking up her brush again, began to work upon her picture.

Presently he went inside.

Sovaz had remained at the mirrors, still fingering the rubies round her throat. It was extraordinary to Kristian that she should use on her canvases such garish hues, when she would only clothe herself in black or white, and baulked even at the coloured jewels in her box.

He said: 'I'm going down. I suppose you will be following shortly.'

'Yes. Of course.'

'Very well,' he said. He went out.

In the dressing room she could hear the valet busy among Kristian's things, setting them out, pure as brides, for his return.

Beyond the blinded window came the eternal soft disintegrations of the sea.

TWO

Prescott, finishing his drink alone on the terrace, saw the young American come out of the open double windows leading from the ballroom, and take a swift surfacing deep breath of night air.

Prescott automatically ran over him a quick, mercilessly thorough glance. The Greek pearl merchant's protégé, some youthful itinerant New Yorker named Adam Quentin. Mikalides, it seemed, had at some time known (in whatever sense) the American's mother. Finding Quentin adrift on the unsafe currents of the city, he had taken him up, and now brought him here with an intention as transparent as when he praised his latest pearl.

How old was the boy? About twenty, probably. What you expected perhaps of a young American male, lean, athletic, gold-coloured skin and sun-bleached hair and eyes, very white teeth, and too broad-shouldered to look particularly elegant or at ease in a dinner jacket. His clothes were correct but had a look to them that suggested to Prescott they might have been hired for the occasion. There was no cunning in the boy's face. He stood at the balustrade, clear-eyed and ingenuous, for either he was an opportunist like the Greek, or else naive.

Prescott had already inadvertently memorized the face. He now found it turned to him.

'Good evening,' Prescott said.

The American smiled.

'It's a beautiful night,' the young man said softly.

Just then the Greek, pausing at the threshold of the room, called the boy back to him like a man whistling a dog.

Prescott put aside the feeling of compunction that had come on him. No doubt he would be seeing something of Quentin in the future.

The Englishman set down his glass and left the terrace for the garden. A few couples were strolling in the dark. Their different accents and the scents of their cigarettes and perfumes came drifting across the ambience of the lemon trees.

It was indeed a beautiful night, but not an extraordinary night, for mostly nights were beautiful in this climate.

A man and woman passed him, going towards the terrace, their arms lightly linked. Prescott paid little attention to them; the woman's soft voice, a snatch of French: 'Je veux aller à la plage . . .' Only the flash of the small diamonds in her ears recalled Sovaz to him, for Kristian's wife must by now be on the stairs.

The marble staircase cascaded, shining, down into the old ballroom, between ranked candelabra. The space below was full, as it was always full on the occasions of Kristian's receptions and dinners, and men and women had also placed themselves at various junctures on the stairs, falling apparently unconsciously into the harmonious shapes the room seemed to expect of them.

Long ago, Sovaz had wondered that he should invite so many people, permit even, though at the reception only, the uninvited companions of guests to invade his sanctum. Yet nothing could touch the house, the great jewel box lying open and all the jewels laid out. The enchanted visitors, like ghosts, went swiftly by, unable to dirty or profane with their insubstantial hands and voices, until only the house remained.

Sovaz came along the wide gallery and set her foot on the topmost stair. It was ten minutes before nine, ten minutes before the dining room would be thrown open, the room in which at all times, other than these, Kristian dined alone. She had come late, yet she paused and looked straight down the dazzling vista of the staircase to the spot where Kristian was standing. Sovaz took little notice of the group about him, a swarthy Egyptian, a tall woman with hair the colour of ice, one or two others. Although no longer aware of Kristian as an object of love or desire, she had remained, nevertheless, acutely aware of him as a live presence. She knew that immediately he saw her he would approach her, take her arm and lead her among his guests. He would expect nothing of her save the gracious manners and mannerisms he had seen to it she practised. Envious and evaluating, the eyes of his guests would follow her wherever she went.

She was noticed now. Heads were turning to look at her black and white figure and the scarlet glitter round her throat.

14

Like blood, she thought again, suddenly, for no reason. *Priceless life blood. I'm bleeding to death.* And just then she caught a fragment of conversation, someone nearby speaking analytically of a murder in the city.

She came down the stairs, and Kristian moved to take her arm. Once, six years ago, at the theatre, when his slightest touch still had the power to excite in her the most extreme of emotional and physical reactions, he had taken her arm, and she had undone the diamond brooch from her shoulder and, pretending to place her hand over his, had thrust the pin deep under his thumb nail. He started violently, his mouth whitened from the pain. She thought he would curse or strike her but he did nothing, said nothing, waiting even until their party was seated before staunching the surprising flow of blood with his handkerchief. When some acquaintance leaned across to inquire what had caused the wound, he said, 'I can't imagine.' Returning alone together to the house an hour before dawn, he said to her, 'You were careless this evening. Don't let it happen again.'

The Egyptian had kissed her hand. They were passing on. Other lips on her skin, other faces and other names floating like the thickening light of the room across her eyes and mind. She was now so adept that she could react perfectly to them, and at the same moment stay within herself, looking out, through their transparent bodies. Afterwards she would remember neither what she had done nor what she had said to them.

At the far end of the room the great windows which gave on to the terrace were wide. The moon was snowing on the sea.

Suddenly a black shape appeared between the windows, extinguishing the moon like an eclipse. Sovaz glanced up. Kristian stood talking at her elbow to Mikalides, the man who controlled half the pearl fisheries based on the waterfront.

'Madame Sovaz is welcome to call at my office on any evening she cares to name. I can show her the queen of our recent catch – a large pale green pearl with, nevertheless, a peerless orient.'

The shadow still blotted out the moonlight. A man. A man too tall and too slight to be Prescott.

'Why not pay Thettalos a visit, Sovaz? It would be a pity to miss something so rare, wouldn't it?'

'Oh yes,' she said automatically. 'If you think so.'

The shadow moved, turned a little. The brightness of the room passed like a summer lightning across his face, and was gone. She caught only an impression, like a plaster mask, no detail except a pair of eyes, very dark, like her own, looking directly, demandingly, at her. At once a burning electricity ran up her spine and spread across her shoulders. She did not know why. Then the path of the moon was clear again on the water, and the shadow had stepped aside into the night.

She felt a violent prompting to run to the windows, go out, shouting into the darkness: 'What do you want?'

But she found she was instead being given the hand of a very beautiful young man, with a gentle uncertain American voice.

'Are you sure, Madame Sovaz,' Adam Quentin said to her, 'that there hasn't been some kind of a mistake?'

'I don't think so,' she said.

'But surely, Madame Sovaz, to seat me next to you. Do you think someone has the places mixed?'

'Why should I think that?' she said.

'There must be thirty people here more important than me. It looks like some kind of a mistake.'

'Well, we shall have to make the best of it.'

He smiled sideways at her, grateful, perhaps, for her tolerance. Sovaz marvelled absently at his wonderful teeth, so even and so white. She made conversation as a sleep-walker takes steps, but more proficiently.

'I guess I'm nervous,' he confided to her. 'I quit my job in New York about a year ago. I've been travelling since then, living pretty rough.'

She smiled. 'What an adventurous thing to do.'

'No, not really. I wanted to write a book . . .'

'Yes?'

'But I never did get the ideas together –' Aware of the writer's compulsive urge to communicate his dream, which threatened to overwhelm him like an attack of coughing, he broke off and began to eat the consommé.

'Forgive me, but you are so very young, aren't you?' Sovaz murmured, touched in a sentimental way by his youth, to which she had abruptly become sensitive.

He flushed faintly. 'That sounds kind of strange, Madame Sovaz.'

'Why should it?'

'Well, you don't seem much older. You couldn't be.'

'How chivalrous, Mr Quentin.'

'Please call me Adam. I'm not trying to be chivalrous.'

'Then how very charming of you.'

He glanced at her, his eyes wide, bemused by the poised denying quality of her voice, the careful sophisticated utterances of a woman of forty.

Servants slipped between them, removing their plates. The wine had gone to his head; he sensed something without understanding it, and dropped his eyes. The rubies round her neck cast a transparent fiery mesh across the curves of her breasts, which were pulsing very slightly to the beat of her heart. The surreal atmosphere of the dinner seemed every moment to grow stronger, like the scent of jasmine now pervading the whole house. He stared at the fresh course that was in front of him, and, like a swimmer way out of his depth and valiantly drowning, he began to eat.

Poor boy, she thought mechanically.

Thettalos Mikalides, seated lower at the long table, had stolen a look at them. The pearl merchant was also a pimp. But it did not matter.

Her eyes moved along the length of the table. Few of the people in the ballroom for the reception had been invited for the dinner, the scalpel of Kristian's snobbery. For example, the shadow she had seen between the windows had not materialized into a dinner guest. Some stranger, he too had been exiled and was already gone. No doubt she had imagined the demand in his eyes.

When the meal ended, people drifted in twos and threes from the table.

The young man, who had grown silent and constrained – what had they said to each other all this while? – now stood up. She lifted her head and saw Kristian, the icy-haired woman still at his side. Sometimes Kristian showed an interest in other women, though never for very long.

'I have arranged for you to visit Thettalos tomorrow, Sovaz. Have the pearl if you want it.' Kristian turned to Quentin. 'I wonder if you would do me a very great service. I am unable to take my wife to the theatre tomorrow evening.'

17

Sovaz heard the boy stammer slightly, trying to be courteous and gallant, not knowing how to refuse.

'Thank you,' Kristian said. 'I shouldn't like Sovaz to have to miss the play. I'll see the tickets are sent round.'

Sovaz began to walk slowly through the room, into the ballroom, letting Quentin follow at his own pace.

Reaching the terrace windows, she hesitated.

The night was cool, smelling of darkness, yet below, the jagged glitter of the broken moon persisted on the water, and for no reason she stared about her at the empty space, before crossing it. She set her hands on the balustrade, and gazed away from the sea. To the south, a million lights lay like fallen stars across the city; sometimes the wind would bring a distant twang from the bars, or the mooing of car horns.

The American emerged suddenly from the ballroom behind her and, as if unable to withstand the cliché, cleared his throat.

'It's very kind of you,' she said, 'to agree at such short notice. I hope you had made no other plans.'

'No,' he said. He came forward, searching her face, troubled. It was a look she had grown accustomed to. It filled her with boredom and obscure pity. 'If you'll excuse me, Madame Sovaz, I'd better leave now.'

'So early? A shame. But I shall see you tomorrow evening, shan't I, Adam?'

'I guess you will.'

She held out her hand to him. He looked at her hand, then came to her and took hold of her fingers. He was a little drunk. She only said: 'Yes, you're so tanned. I think I should burn dreadfully if I stayed in the sun so long.'

'Is this some game?' he whispered, bending over her through the moonshade of the jasmine plants. She said nothing. 'You're so – and you act like you were some rich old woman – and your husband asking me to take – what the hell does he know about me?'

'Quite enough, I imagine.'

'Yeah. So I gather. I didn't believe this.'

'Oh, didn't you?'

His face was stiff and angry. Perhaps it was his good looks that somehow saved him from seeming absurd to her.

'Please don't distress yourself,' she said. 'All you have to do is stand me up.'

'And then what? Someone else?'

He dropped her hand and his whole body tensed for some wild action.

She smiled, and glanced away.

'Perhaps, Adam, you should go now,' she said. 'Don't try to be generous to me. Don't think about it any more. I shan't expect to see you tomorrow.'

She could hear the unspoken words hovering on his mouth, then a group came strolling on to the terrace from the golden room, talking, bringing with them the scent of Turkish tobacco and patchouli. The young man turned and immediately left her.

She felt a dragging downsurge of disappointment. Possibly it was the certainty of success which so depressed her spirits.

She let go of the balustrade, and began to walk along the terrace to the spot where steps led down between the oleanders. The group of men and women were murmuring and laughing together, discussing Strindberg. She understood that once she had descended into the dark, they would begin to discuss her with equal posturing vehemence.

Yet what could there be of interest to say about her?

The house, its sounds and lights, faded behind her. The garden closed her round. A melancholy night fragrance clung to every leaf and stem. Her mind emptied itself. She could hear the sea breathing on the beach below, and between each breath a resting soundlessness.

It was midnight.

By three o'clock the house was void of its guests, and the tide coming in to shore.

On the seaward perimeter of the gardens, a narrow oriental iron gate stood open in the high wall, and steps fell down the cliff to the shoreline.

Sovaz was walking on the beach.

The sound of the returning tide had strangely alarmed and aroused her.

The moon had set hours before. The water was impenetrably black except where its breakers hit the rocks like the unravelling silver fringes of a great shawl. The shore became a bowl of silence. The city and the house ceased to exist.

19

She walked eastwards, holding her evening shoes in one hand.

The beach below the house was for several miles generally deserted, only police patrols going by at irregular intervals. She had never encountered them. She might have walked till dawn. She had done so before.

But instead she made out a woman's long scarf trembling in short eddies along the water's edge towards her.

Sovaz stopped still. The scarf, moving as if half alive in the night wind, was somehow threatening. She drew away as it slithered by. Then, looking up, she saw the outline of a woman and a man stretched together on the ground, curiously unified by the darkness both with each other and with the surrounding sand. She thought they were making love; their stillness undeceived her. Only the woman's long dress was fluttering with the same motions as the scarf.

Precisely at this moment the man raised his head.

His eyes were for an instant glazed and withdrawn, seeing nothing, but Sovaz knew him at once. The sense of recognition had nothing to do with his physical appearance, which she had scarcely registered.

The starlight was very dim. It faded yet did not clarify the shadows. The pale elliptoid of the man's face, turned up to hers, so resembled a mask that at first the painted quality of the mouth did not surprise her. Then, she saw it was blood.

As his eyes focused on her, she made an instinctive attempt to avert herself, uselessly, for immediately her image seemed to have been snapped into storage in the brain behind his eyes, as if she had touched the trip-wire of an automatic camera.

Everything had taken place in silence, the great sea-silence on the shore. Even now, she felt no impulse to cry out.

She began to take irrational paces backwards, towards the surf. The man watched her, making no move.

Their recognition was now mutual and significant.

The sea, reaching for her, laved her feet suddenly with cold. She ran.

She did not, somehow, expect him to follow. He did not. But the shadow had fallen on her so that where she fled it fled with her, ubiquitous as the night.

She reached the cliff steps and began to stumble up them.

She had lost her shoes, the hem of her dress was torn and clinging cold. Finding the wrought iron gate, she clutched it, and, having got inside, thrust it shut, bolted it, and lay against the frame.

What now? she kept thinking shapelessly. *What must I do now?*

She forced herself to go through the garden, up the avenue of lemon trees towards the house.

Finally she was on the terrace. She was trembling to such an extent she could not at once push open the unlocked windows. Her whole body ached, as if from fever.

The ballroom was empty.

One of the candelabra still sluggishly burned half way up the marble staircase.

She began to climb the stairs, slowly. Great festoons of solidified wax poured from the candelabra. Something about the wax nauseated her. As she passed them the last lights smoked out.

'Leah,' she called, or thought she did. Her voice made no impact on Kristian's house, and the black girl did not answer.

She came into the gallery and paused with her hand against the wall. She felt intolerably ill and listless, as if in the grip of mal de mer.

The doors of the library stood ajar.

Sovaz went to the doors but did not go in.

The aroma of Kristian's books was powdered thickly on the air. Everything was dark, except for the open windows where the balcony hung at the far end of the room. A lamp flickered there among the rustling vine.

The woman with the winter hair was leaning at the rail, as Kristian caressed her. There was no urgency or apparent pleasure in his movements, or in hers. The connoisseur, a statuette of valuable jade in his fingers.

Now, for the first time, the need to scream aloud overcame Sovaz. She could make no sound.

She turned away from the library doors and moved quickly towards her own, feeling her way with her hands.

Her room was empty, the bed opened, the lamps shining in their green and golden shades, her combs and brushes and cologne laid out for her, everything unchanged. Beyond the wall, in Kristian's dressing room, the accessories would lie in ranks,

21

like well drilled soldiers. The first time he had been with a woman after their marriage, she had gone into his dressing room and smashed the mirrors and the bottles, torn open the drawers and chests and torn out the pages from the books lying by the window. The library had been locked, otherwise she would have gone there too. Yet he never spoke to her about what she had done. The valet had replaced the articles as if by magic.

Now, she did not think to go near Kristian's rooms. She went into her bathroom, turned on the taps of the bath and tore off the lace dress and silk underclothes and left them lying under the roaring, steaming water.

And, staring down at the swimming garments, she expected blood to run out of them.

Presently she turned off the taps and went through again to lie on the bed. Reaching out, she touched the master switch and blackness flooded her eyes.

She was floating, disembodied.

She had felt this sensation before, seven years ago, when she had swallowed all the sleeping tablets in Kristian's bottle, this same unanchored lightness. Who would find her this time? This time, surely, no one.

THREE

Sovaz woke in the heat of late afternoon.

Already the room was becoming real, her vision sharpening. Too late to sleep again. She leaned from the bed and pressed the bell. Would Leah come? Last night she had called Leah, and Leah had not answered – no, that was absurd. Of course Leah would come.

The door opened. The black girl came through.

'Leah, please open the windows and see to the blinds. Then run a bath.'

At the inrush of air, perfumed faintly from the garden flowers below, the room seemed to hollow out. Sovaz sighed, lifting herself up in the bed. She could hear the black girl doing something to the bath, a sound of sodden garments dripping. Sovaz got to her feet and put on a wrap of Chinese silk, and seemed to activate, by doing so, a little gold and crystal clock which chimed thinly: four thirty. She crossed to the arrangement of mirrors.

Her face surprised her. There were still traces of cosmetics on her lips and eyes. She leaned forward, and saw, between the black silk revers of her wrap, the scarlet drops of the rubies lying on her throat.

Sovaz stood back. Her eyes widened.

'Leah!' she screamed out. 'Leah! Leah!'

The black girl came running.

'What is it, madame?'

'Leah!' Sovaz screamed. She threw back her head.

'Madame – what's wrong? Have you hurt yourself? Madame –'

The girl sprang at her and took Sovaz' shoulders in a practical, restraining grasp. Sovaz was trembling convulsively. She ripped at the jewels around her neck. Leah, moving to help her, undid the clasp efficiently and in seconds.

'Get rid of them,' Sovaz said. She had stopped screaming and shut her eyes.

'I'll put them in your box, madame –'

'No. I told you to get rid of them. I don't want to see them again. Do what I say.'

Leah's face was impassive. She slid the gems into her pocket. She would take them to Kristian.

In the silence Sovaz heard the sea break on the shore. She sat down, and the horror went out of her abruptly, like a gush of blood. She did not open her eyes.

'I'll bathe now,' she said, very evenly. 'I can manage, thank you, Leah.' She sensed the girl hesitating, distrusting her. 'I shall want orange juice, fresh figs, black coffee. In half an hour, say.' Her incongruous normalcy seemed to reassure Leah, or at any rate to bribe her. Sovaz heard her turn and go out.

Sovaz rose, remembered to open her eyes, went into the bathroom. The drowned clothes had been removed, the bath was filling. Sovaz stood staring down into the water until it brimmed over and ran out upon the floor.

At half past five Sovaz entered Kristian's library. This time he sat alone, reading, in the chair of Italian carved mahogany.

'Kristian,' she said.

He did not look up.

'The limousine is waiting for you,' he said. 'Don't forget you are going to look at the Greek's pearl. I hope Mikalides has now provided his young friend with a better dinner jacket.'

She had forgotten the pearl, that she was going to the theatre with the boy, Adam.

'Kristian, last night a woman was murdered on the beach.'

He did not immediately reply. His distaste at discussing such a topic hung thickly in the room as the odour of books. But he was not surprised. It was his habit to glance at the evening papers, a dutiful, contemptuous glance. If death was in them, he would have seen. Presently he said, 'So I believe.'

She said slowly, 'A man cut her throat. No, it was worse than that. I think he was drinking her blood. There was blood on his mouth.'

'Not a subject to deliberate on, do you think?'

'I saw it,' she said.

She checked at once. It was too unequivocal. She should not have put it in this way.

After a moment, he did look up at her. His face was blank.

'Saw what, Sovaz?'

'I saw the dead woman on the sand, and the man lying on her. His mouth was covered in blood; I thought at first he was hurt. Then I saw her throat. I ran back to the house. He didn't follow me, though he was here earlier, before dinner. I came to tell you but you weren't alone.'

His expression did not change. He said nothing.

A thrill of pure horror went through her.

'Kristian, what am I to do?'

'Do?' He set aside the book. 'You will go down to the car, and Paul will drive you to Mikalides' office. When you have looked at the pearl you will meet the young American and go to the theatre.'

Sovaz swallowed and said, 'You don't understand me. She was lying on the beach and the man on top of her. I thought they were making love – but the blood – I was walking, Kristian, do you see? And I found them –'

'This will stop, Sovaz. Do you expect me to believe this rubbish? You came here last night and I was with a woman. I am sorry you were distressed, but you are not a child. Now you have

24

heard a news bulletin and made up a ludicrous fantasy. What do you suppose you will gain by it?'

'But it's true,' she said, 'it's true.'

'You forget,' he said, 'there have been other occasions on which you have lied to me.'

She pressed her palm over her mouth.

Kristian had turned away from her to open the balcony windows, as if her words had introduced too much carbon dioxide into the air.

'You had better be going,' he said, 'otherwise you will be late.'

She stood inside the doors of the library.

She thought: *Perhaps I heard some radio in the house, half awake, perhaps I fell asleep again. Perhaps I dreamed it. No*, she thought, *perhaps I invented it, and now believe it to be true.* Her mind seemed full of shadows. She searched them. Yes, there was the long scarf blowing on the rim of the sea, and there was the woman on the sand, and the creature crouched over her. Now he looked up, and now – the plaster mask face, the bloody mouth, the optic discs, and yet –

Remembering the landmarks of the man's face, she could not recapture his appearance.

She had not known him by his looks, he was collective, symbolic. He had no face, after all.

In the gallery she experienced again the urge to scream. She leant against the cool wall, and presently the spasm passed. She began to walk on.

She had forgotten where she was going, but Kristian's chauffeur, Paul, was waiting for her, he would know.

Outside the house, the mature sunlight fell over the garden walks, the parched stone of the hundred steps, the chess piece statues.

The chauffeur handed her into the limousine.

The quay at this hour was mostly deserted. A fisherman sat mending his net, the idle ships rocked indolently at their moorings. The ceiling of mazarine sky phased to lilac on the horizon like the smoke from the distant burning galleys of some antique war. The American, Quentin, leaned at the rail in his sun-bleached denims – the uniform of the youthful foreigner – watching a great black beetle creep along the deserted road from the north. He had been scribbling notes; now, diverted by the limousine, the paper hung dead in his hand.

A block away the limousine went sliding down among a complex of side streets. Pushing the incomplete notation (the description of a woman) into his pocket, the American followed.

The car had slowed to a disdainfully careful pace. Its windows were of a black-green vitreous, impenetrable. He had never seen Kristian's car, neither been told its make, yet he had known it at once. It was inevitable that the rich aristocrat should possess only such a car, of a gliding, subtle oiled quality . . .

Now it had moved aside into the open space before the pearl merchant's offices. The engine stopped.

Adam too stopped, watching the car. His guts tightened. A chauffeur appeared from the front of the limousine and opened the left hand door.

The woman got out. Her hair was long and very dark, loose on her shoulders. She wore a white voile frock, no jewelry.

The chauffeur stood back against the car. The woman began to walk towards the buildings. The little embryonic breeze of sunset fluttered her filmy dress and hair, making her look weightless, incorporeal.

Adam started after her. He passed the chauffeur but the man's eyes did not follow him, the face betrayed neither interest nor boredom.

'Madame Sovaz.'

She halted at once and turned. At first she seemed to look straight through him, as if she were indeed a ghost, or he. Then her eyes apparently focused. Adam felt himself flush. She appeared bewildered, genuinely at a loss. She did not quite say: 'Who are you?' It was not pretence, or any kind of cruel playfulness. He was startled.

He drew the two theatre tickets from his shirt pocket, as if to identify himself. Her eyes went down to them then up again to his face.

'Last night,' he said, 'your husband asked me to take you to a play – I said a few things I wish I hadn't. Look, I just brought you the tickets. They came round by mistake, I guess.'

'Adam,' she said.

'I'd like to apologize to you,' he said. 'Would it do any good?'

'Adam,' she said again.

The breeze still moved her hair and dress. It blew across the space from the buildings to the giant lizard of the limousine, unchecked, except where it encountered their two bodies.

Her face, though beautiful and beautifully made up, was grey, her large eyes leaden. Six months ago, sick with food poisoning in some nameless hospital, he had seen this same look of blind struggle in the eyes of amnesiacs or men dying of cancer. As then, he was consumed by sensations of helpless frightened horror. He could not see how he could go to her aid, and he was half afraid to touch her.

'Something's wrong, Madame Sovaz?'

She stirred. She smiled at him. She was attempting, listlessly, to reassure him.

'Oh. Just the heat. I can't bear the heat.' Still with the smile nailed on her mouth, she turned away towards the limousine. 'I don't think I'll bother with Thettalos' pearl. Kristian wants me to have it anyway. Paul,' she called. The chauffeur discarded his pose and came over. 'Please go up for me and say I should like the pearl. My husband will see to it. Then take the car back to the house.'

The chauffeur gave a little bow and went wordlessly off.

'Do you drive, Adam? Of course, all Americans drive.'

He was choked by the need to undermine this dialogue and come at the truth. He discovered himself saying, with atrocious banality, 'I haven't got a dinner jacket.'

'It doesn't matter. It will take twenty minutes to get there, by the hill road,' she went on. 'Will that be all right? The performance begins as the sun goes down, doesn't it?'

He said, 'You want me to come with you.'

'Why not? Oh, yes. Of course you must come.' Her eyes flashed a desolate brightness. He felt a child in her presence, nine years of age, and she an old woman. He was presented with a frightful vision of Miss Havisham in *Great Expectations* screaming, her swirling white bridal dress alight, and he trying to beat out the flames, while the disturbed beetles and spiders ran away over the floor.

Driving north-east through the outskirts of the city into the hills, they sat unspeaking, the American turning the wheel in his hands, she lying back on the dusty seat of the ramshackle little hired Ford, the voile dress spreading round both their feet and the gears of the car.

The road ascending was crowded by olives growing on the slopes, a landscape now darkening as the sun sank. By contrast, the whole sky, even the east, was vivid with an exceptional bronzen red.

The theatre was constructed in the old style, weathered by sun and rain and by the emotions of joy and tragedy conjured on the stage at its core, travelling up its tiers like thrills along a complex series of nerve endings. It appeared to be and felt of enormous actual age. Though in fact, built ten years before, time, as if recognizing a good copy, seemed to have consented to the deception. On the top terraces of cheaper seats men and women clustered like pigeons over bottles of wine, baskets of cheeses, figs and sausage, and children ran about like dogs. The spell of the play was not yet cast on them, the occult masked figures on the skene below, the voices of gods and doomed kings manifested by loudspeakers with terrifying intimacy even on the highest benches.

Kristian's tickets of course belonged to those rows where men in evening clothes smoked cigars and women with diamonds in their ears murmured over fans and programmes. Adam Quentin, feeling conspicuously undressed-up, took the seat beside Sovaz. He was appalled and fascinated that they should be sitting to watch a play by Euripides with all this burden of unsaid things between them.

A gong roared somewhere beneath the stage. Immediate soundlessness responded from the upper tiers. Prepared for magic and superstition, the opening of hearts and minds was almost audible. Below, the intellectuals composed themselves differently, stubbing out their cigarettes.

The palace of a Hellene king, a ruined altar with smoke stirring on it. Quentin saw Sovaz' eyes abruptly flicker, as if in recognition.

The *Bacchae*. It would be performed in its intended Greek, so he would pick up one word in ten. Three years since he had read the play in translation, a minute here and there, in a drawing office in New York.

A flute sounded in the sunset's scarlet stillness. The god was coming. The young man felt the atmosphere, with no warning,

28

overwhelm him. He dimly realized the unfruitful communion with the woman beside him had quickened and made him ready, on these chill and flame-drunk hills.

The sun left the incredible sky. Soon the evening would creep down the slopes to follow Dionysos, the shadow precious to his worship, and torches would flash, and Selene's altar-fire spring up. The god would come to the city of Thebes to establish his divinity. The Theban women, who had scorned and refused his gift of wine, he would send mad to the hills, to dance with wild beasts and to rend cattle with their teeth and nails. Pentheus, the king, who would attempt to imprison and humiliate him, Dionysos would send after them to spy on their rites, where, discovered, the king would be torn to pieces, and Agave his mother would wrench off his head.

He came out with a deadly grace, an animal tread. The god. A sigh like a gust of wind surfed across the benches.

The masks were in the true style, very lifelike. Dionysos' face, framed by supernatural hair, jet black yet somehow catching a gold highlight on every grape-cluster of curls, seemed living, though exalted. A pale, beautiful, unhuman face, matching exactly the almost naked body, dark white and slender, which, even in its fawnskin loincloth, breastless and male, was oddly hermaphrodite, an enticement to either or any sex.

The demon.

Sovaz sank back against the seat. The world seemed to go from under her.

Dionysos. The features, which in her memory comprised no face, came suddenly together. A white mask with kohl-ringed, impenetrable eyes, its lips stained with wine, or blood.

The headlights burst on the road before them. Objects seen beside the road, trees, walls, the abandoned corpse of a motorcycle, appeared to leap forward at the window.

Suddenly Sovaz put her hand on Quentin's arm.

'Stop the car.'

She did not speak loudly, her touch was light, almost impersonal, yet a surge of adrenalin shot through him. He found he had jammed on the brakes as if a man had run into their path.

The car stilled about them with small subsiding noises. The night came closer. Crickets ticked in the grass. He switched off the headlamps. He heard the door open, the rustle of her dress as she got out. Presently, opening his own door, he too came out and stood on the slope. He caught a glimpse of her face, pale as the dress, expressionless yet intent, before she turned. She began to walk up the slope. He followed her slowly, his mouth very dry.

Wild olives clambered and clustered. Sovaz stopped in front of him. The shadow of the leaves, dappling her, gave her frock the strange look of a leopard skin, a Bacchic image, a maenad. As he came nearer, she moved round and caught his hand. Her own was icy and narrow.

'You're cold,' he said, acutely aggravated at the idiocy of his own remark.

'Yes.'

She stood staring up at him. Her eyes did indeed contain terror, he could see it now.

'Do you want to go back?' he said hesitantly.

'Where? To Kristian's house? No.'

Her hand slipped from his. She began to unbutton his shirt, then slid her arms about him. The touch of her cold, cold fingers burned on his skin. But her mouth, following, was warm.

'Adam,' she said to him, as if to be certain who he might be. Her whole body was trembling. He caught her need inevitably, abruptly, like catching fire. Shadows, grass, the smoke of her hair; the dark roped them together inexorably. Yet, even as she clung to him, there seemed no energy in her, no fierceness or real intention. Lying down with her, the folds of her dress spread away from them over the uneven ground, shifting slightly in imitation of their movements. Her hands clutched his flesh in a drowning, strengthless motion, she cried out softly, and let go. She was one of those women who in orgasm seem possessed by a devil, which expels their reason, shakes and worries at their bodies.

When, in a few moments, she opened her eyes and gazed at him, it was with a dull, amazed and bewildered expression.

'And so you see,' she said, as if they had been speaking of it all along, and had paused only briefly, perhaps to admire the view, 'that everything you accused me of on the terrace, everything you thought of me, was quite correct.'

His own eyes were wide open on her, by contrast very clear.

'Sovaz . . . that doesn't matter any more.'

30

'Poor Adam,' she said.

'Sovaz –'

The wind brushed over the tops of the olive trees.

She shut her eyes. She lay void and joyless. The clamour of panic had faded. Now only the white mask hanging in her brain, the beautiful god with his dark gifts of blood and wine, and the human youth shipwrecked on her body, and the whisper of the wind in leaves.

At about four thirty in the morning, strolling across the sprawling waterfront night market, Prescott found Adam Quentin seated on a bench beneath a canvas awning, among a row of derelicts smoking the cheap hashish sold on the quay.

Prescott sat down opposite, and pushed away the old man who came immediately scampering to him, offering a pipe and squeaking.

The rest of the market, having scented the dawn like a scurrilous and night-preying animal, was now in the process of packing itself up and sliding away down into the rat-hole crevasses of the city to hide from the sun. Lamps guttered out. Men cried hoarsely to one another. Canopies were dragged free and folded, charcoal stoves extinguished, goods thrown back into crates. All along the shore the pleasure boats were returning stealthily, black-winged across the moonless water, like vampires seeking their tombs. Only here and there the occasional island of humanity still unstirring – the brothel door, the booths of the opium eaters, the sellers of night flowers, the astrologer beside his crackpot telescope and tarot cards, placidly chewing a lemon.

Adam looked up. The fact of seeing the Englishman did not appear to disturb him.

'This isn't the place for you,' Prescott said quietly. 'Here you will be cheated, robbed, probably followed afterwards, attacked or even killed. It's a popular theory that certain kitchens in the vicinity obtain their meat from dubious quarters.'

Adam laughed.

'I can recommend several establishments,' Prescott said, 'where you would be safe, and where the quality of the goods is also above reproach.'

'Great. I guess the price matches the goods.'

'Yes. We'll come to that presently. I'm surprised you've chosen

31

this form of amusement. Have you enjoyed yourself?'

'I surprised myself,' Quentin said. 'It's been a surprising night. No. It's been a night that was surprisingly unsurprising.' He looked at Prescott. 'Is that what I mean? No, I didn't enjoy it.'

A man next to the American muttered and spat on the ground. Prescott spoke to him in the slum argot. The man's gaze darted and watered.

Prescott rose and pulled the boy up, unresisting, by the arm. They walked into the wider open streets north of the market.

The boy was unused, Prescott imagined, to the unclean mixed hashish of the old Arab's stall. His eyes were swimming and dreamlike.

'What time is it?' he asked, without interest.

'Almost dawn. Where are you living?'

Adam leaned against a peeling wall.

'I forget. Nowhere special.' His eyes swam leisurely across the sky. The eastern edges of faint clouds were beginning to become visible. 'You're the rich man's agent, my mother's Greek jockey says. Did you follow us tonight?'

'Follow? Whom?'

'You know damn well whom. Who. Sovaz. You're paid to keep tabs on her for him, aren't you?'

'Did Mikalides say that too?'

'Maybe he did.'

'Then maybe he was right.'

'And now your boss told you to keep me out of trouble. Oh, man, I can believe it.'

'I am authorized to offer you a sum of money,' Prescott said. 'Your inclination may be to refuse it, but you should consider first. The companion of Kristian's wife will need ready cash. She's used to the best.'

Adam Quentin, still staring up at the sky, said, 'He's very generous, your *master*.'

'Not exactly. You must remember the life style Madame enjoys; people know whose wife she is. Her reputation is valuable to him.'

'Caesar's wife,' Adam said. 'But not above suspicion.'

He eased himself from the wall and began to walk on, unsteadily. Prescott was oddly struck by the curious gracefulness of the young man's naivety. Here was a creature which was still openly amazed, moved, wounded by what took place about it, the somehow tragic aura of the young. A quality Sovaz had never possessed.

'I shan't bother Caesar's wife any further. So forget the money. And forget seeing me to my door, will you?' Adam said abruptly, 'In the morning I think I'll take the goddamned train out of this place.'

Prescott fell out of step with the young man, allowing him to proceed alone.

The sky above the hills was turning to the colour of steel.

How many of Sovaz' lovers had behaved in this fashion? Perhaps a third. Some actually escaped the city, then came back, like the addict.

Prescott was not generally given to flights of fancy, yet in respect of Sovaz, highly coloured images sometimes suggested themselves to him. He supposed he too was not quite immune to the perfume, like that of some poisonous night-growing plant, that clung about her. He still vividly remembered finding her in the tenement attic, lying on the rotting French sofa, her hair burned a chemical yellow, her eyes eaten by night. In some extraordinary way she put him in mind, as she lay there, of a succubus, or the rakshas of Indian mythology. A stupid notion. She was then a pathetic and inexperienced young girl, without hope or common sense.

Dawn had not yet touched the house, or the sea.

Behind the sightless windows, the woman was lying on her bed, Stravinsky playing from the gramophone, the dark discordant harmonies washing over her, as the tides below washed over the rocks and sands and other detritus of the beach.

Presently the record came to an end, though the turntable continued to revolve with the mindless beat of a mechanical heart.

Sovaz opened her eyes. The room was all shadow, only the faint smoke rising from the joss sticks burning in the bronze bowl.

She lifted herself on one elbow. Across the room, catching the angle of the mirrors, she saw her own face looking back at her, a mask, set with two black glass gems to give an illusion of sight. She touched at her face with her hand. Her eyes fell on the array of combs, perfumes, the crystal tray with its boxes of powder and sticks of kohl, the ivory jewel casket.

Sovaz left the bed. She crossed the room (her feet were bare; the thick carpet had a feel of life, the pelt of some creature, lying supine). She set her fingers on the clasp of the ivory box. Heat burned up in her as she did so. She drew back her hand.

She went out into the gallery. The house was breathing to itself like an animal.

The smell of the library in the dark was heady, despite the open window. The balcony lamp was extinguished, yet there was light in the sky, for the room faced eastwards.

In the rack of carved cedarwood stood the evening papers, neatly folded by Kristian's valet. Each sunset they were removed and replaced by fresh ones.

Sovaz picked up a paper, turned it to the east.

A woman had been murdered on the beach. The time of death was estimated at about three o'clock in the morning. She was twenty-nine years old, the wife of a minor official attached to the French consulate; she had had many lovers and was not particularly discreet. Her throat had been slashed, but she had not been robbed, the little diamonds were still in her ears and the garnet rings on her fingers. There was no sign of a struggle, or of sexual assault. The police patrol had found her. There had been in the city an identical case two months before, unsolved. And earlier . . .

The light, falling on to the paper, was turning molten now.

Below in the garden, birds were singing.

Sovaz wrenched the page out of the paper.

Going back to her bedroom she lifted the needle from the record. She opened the jewel box and placed the sheet of newsprint, folded very small, in the lowest compartment.

She felt exhausted and did not properly know what she was doing. She took up the silver-backed brush and began to use it on her hair. There was light now too in the western windows.

Somewhere in the city the American boy was walking or sleeping. She remembered now, only faintly, the wild olive grove in the hills. She did not at all remember parting with him, his eyes painfully searching her face for clues, the limousine materializing from shadow, the swift drive along the shore road.

She did not want to sleep, could not bring herself to it.

There was fresh blood inside the jewel casket.

The black girl, presumably on Kristian's instructions, had

34

replaced the rubies in the box. Sovaz lifted them out.

Holding the necklace in her hand, she left the room a second time, went down through the house, descending blindly the marble stairway into the ballroom, opening the doors of the terrace, and stepping out.

The scent of the sea, overriding the scent of the garden trees. She reached the narrow Moorish gate and thrust it wide. Below, the beach, the agate layers of water, stained now by the rising sun. At the horizon, like a flock of black gulls resting on the waves, the boats of the night fishermen.

The dawn with its floods of light and colour, its avowal of radiance and heat, made her afraid. The shrill bird song was full of menace. She flung the rubies from her – down, beyond the steps, towards the beach, out of sight.

The sea would take them away with the tide. Or some urchin searching for crabs would grab them up. You could not throw out rubies on the perimeter of the hungry city and hope to find them again. And yet, the small diamonds in her ears, the garnets on her knuckles . . . Perhaps it might have been better, driving on the fringes of the slums, to have tossed them into some filthy court, and seen the beggars and the sick tear themselves and the necklace apart.

There was a man standing among the lemon trees.

Her heart leaped up, choking her. She stumbled. He came quickly and caught her arm. It was the Englishman.

'Are you quite all right, Madame Sovaz?'

'Yes, thank you. Perfectly.'

There was something she must eventually ask the Englishman. What was it? It had to do with Kristian's dinner party, the moon-drenched terrace.

The Englishman held open the nearest terrace window for her.

'Thank you,' she said, and passed through, out of the rays of the sun.

FOUR

One warm evening, when he was twenty-three years old, Kristian had seen his parents' car plunge off a mountain road and fall three hundred and eighty feet into the ravine below.

They had been going to the theatre, he behind in the second car with various acquaintances, his father and mother alone in the first, the chauffeur left behind and his mother at the wheel. She had been wearing, he recollected after, a frock of amber silk, an Egyptian jade scarab ring on her right hand. Her thin mocking figure elegantly imposed on the last traces of the sunset, the cicadas buzzing, the darkening whiteness of the house against the backdrop of the great estate. She had said, he remembered, that she did not particularly want to see the play.

There had been no warning. The Daimler was perhaps half a mile ahead of them, going quite fast. The final orange flash of the sun swelled like a spotlight across the road. Abruptly the great car seemed to swerve, as if at some unexpected obstacle, then swung on in a fluid motion, a sort of horrid gracefulness, crashed through the railing and was gone.

The second car braked at once and disgorged its passengers in time for them to see the last of the Daimler's spinning descent. A ghastliness of predestination seized Kristian; the space of seconds seeming almost a full minute before the vehicle made impact below, those moments of time during which the occupants of the car still lived, screamed in the extremity of terror or possibly even hoped for some reprieve. Presently the car struck the rocks. Another instant of stasis followed. Then the explosion of the petrol tank, the blot of sound and colour on the porous paper of twilight. While figures ran back and forth along the road, Kristian sat beside the railing on the ground, watching the pyrotechnics alternately flare and fade, like a sleepy eye on the gathering night.

Later he learned that his mother, at the time of the car accident, was dying of cancer. There was, after all, no inanimate obstacle on the mountain road from which she might have swerved. Certainly no small animal life would have disorganized her progress; once, driving back from a shooting party, proudly yet negligently displaying her bag, she had added: 'I have also littered the road with dead hares and foxes.' Kristian came to believe that his mother had chosen not to wait. The burning petrol took on fresh symbolism. She, in her beautiful clothes and jade jewelry, lying in the Daimler like a warrior in his finery and chariot, her consort, either willing or unwilling,

36

consumed at her side. He could visualize her, indeed frequently did so, letting go the wheel, her hands in her lap, perhaps smiling.

In the muddled aftermath of the 'accident', Kristian discovered grey-faced grey men like gathering ravens at his door. His father's debts were numerous. Like all men who live hour by hour by means of their own reputation, he had left only chaos and unfinished business behind him. It became clear that the northern estates must be sold. Walking about the grounds, in those last days, among the vast stretches of pines, beside the lake, through the familiar house with everything now stacked up in crates or masquerading under sheets, the death which had precipitated it all became of necessity elevated, unique.

Finding one night the empty bottle of sleeping tablets in his dressing room, Sovaz hidden away, the valet wiping his hands on a towel, Kristian had fallen prey once again to a compulsion which he did not recognize. He must in some way elevate, he must simultaneously eradicate and deny, the thing which repelled and drew him. Experiences are initial: whether exact or distorting, all later situations are only mirrors of what has gone before.

Kristian wrote his signature over the final batch of letters. His secretary, a self-effacing young man, took up the correspondence neatly and silently and went out.

The previous night, coming back to the house at about midnight, Kristian had heard the gramophone whispering softly through the walls of his wife's bedroom. Both doors were shut. The music moaned, the records were occasionally changed or else played over and over. Sometimes water ran into the bath. Once Leah had been called to fetch her the fruit and black coffee that Sovaz habitually took on rising. Yet Sovaz lay on the bed, the turntable of the gramophone whirring ominously, the cigarette box half empty, a scattering of sketches for some new painting cast indiscriminately about the floor like fallen leaves. The black girl was not adequate to the task of describing to Kristian the subject matter of these drawings. She imagined she had seen one or two of an animal resembling a panther running with a white cloth draped loosely across its body. Despite her lack of descriptive power, a faint look of fear came over the black girl's face when she spoke of this, a fear so subterranean that she herself did not seem to be aware of expressing or even feeling it.

Sovaz had now been shut in her suite for thirty-nine hours.

Kristian rose. The items on the escritoire were meticulously arranged, the inkwell of black onyx, the Persian paper knife which had once actually tasted blood when some woman of past acquaintance – this time not Sovaz – had picked it up and flung it at him in a cataleptic fit of rage. The blunt little point, thrown with such force, had torn through the sleeve of his shirt and nicked his flesh before it fell back exhausted on the rug. The woman had fled. Going upstairs to change his shirt, he had discovered the empty tablet bottle lying face down among his brushes, and presently his valet had come through from Sovaz' bathroom, a towel in his hands.

Now, mounting the stairs, Kristian was not unaware of a distasteful unease building in him with each step. For six years his wife had been unassertive. Yet suddenly, once again these curious and hysterical lies, this demanding seclusion. The little bottle reappeared with a sharp perfection of detail in his mind's eye.

Prescott had told him the American boy had taken the train inland. Perhaps this might be the root of her behaviour, only some trite quarrel. A small package had come for her this evening and been left with Kristian's mail beside the fresh newspapers in the cedarwood rack. The valet had mentioned to him that, on removing the papers yesterday, he had discovered a page had been torn from one of them.

Outside her door, Kristian waited a moment. The gramophone, not playing yet still active, throbbed. He did not like her records: Stravinsky, Kodály, Prokofiev – these seemed to pierce his ears like burning wires – neither Rachmaninov, whom he found impure and cloying.

He knocked. She did not answer. He tried the door, which opened.

She lay on the bed, smoking. The room was wreathed in smoke, smoke from her cigarette, smoke from the burning joss sticks he abhorred. She had on no make-up, which had the peculiar effect of making her appear excessively young to him, and yet, about the eyes, very old. She had lost weight. He did not like this look of her.

'Are you unwell?'

38

'Yes. But it's nothing.'

'Do you want me to telephone Florentine?'

At the mention of the little doctor, she abruptly laughed, but almost at once was again lifeless. She made a small loose gesture with one arm.

'If you like. But it isn't at all necessary. I shall be perfectly all right tomorrow.'

He caught sight, through the half open bathroom door, of steamless water held unused in the bath. He crossed to the gramophone and, lifting the needle, set the arm on its rest. One of the drawings Leah had reported lay on the table.

Kristian took up the sketch. A panther, caught in the midst of a statuesque static leap, filled in jet black with a heavy and merciless lead pencil. The lack of subtlety that always offended him in Sovaz' paintings prompted him to discard the paper at once. Nevertheless, he became aware that the white cloth Leah had described as draped across the animal's back was in fact an unconscious woman, her head dangling, her tangled hair trailing on the ground.

'I have something for you,' he said, producing the small package. 'It came with this evening's mail.'

'Oh, leave it there,' she said, immobile, uninterested. 'I'll open it later.'

As she spoke, the crystal clock suddenly sang out eight chimes like a tiny soprano.

The voice of the clock galvanized him. He set the package down beside her and was turning to go out, when she asked abruptly: 'Who brought this?'

He glanced back at her. She was all at once sitting up, holding the thing, unopened, in her hands. She looked excited, feverish.

'I don't know. Why not unwrap it and find out?'

Perhaps the American had sent her some cheap, paltry and emotional token. Yet she did not undo her parcel.

Kristian opened the door.

'Please,' she said, 'wait a moment.'

He paused impatiently.

She pulled at the paper ineffectually. It appeared to come away only in despite of her. Her face which had been white now burned as if a fire was concealed in the wrapping. Sovaz thrust the contents, the paper, everything, from her. Blood seemed to splash out on to the black carpet. A pool of rubies. He knew them immediately, and crossed to the bed.

'He was watching,' Sovaz said. 'He saw me. He's sent them back.'

'What are you talking about?'

'The necklace. I threw it away, threw it down on the beach.'

'You're talking nonsense,' Kristian said, 'I don't understand you.'

A small fragment of paper still adhered to the coverlet. Kristian picked it off, for he could see a single line of writing on it. The words were part of a quotation from Virgil: *Nos cedamus Amori* – we must yield to love. He held it out to her. When she would not take it, he let it fall beside the jewels on the carpet, and went out.

Going into the library, he closed the doors, and presently telephoned Florentine.

The doctor arrived at the house in the late afternoon. As on previous occasions, the hundred steps had left him breathless. In his black coat and white shirt, both still formally buttoned despite the heat and the climb, holding the apologetic cliché of his bag beneath one of his short arms, he resembled perfectly a penguin.

There was a tired gentle eagerness about the doctor, a nervous compulsion to ease pain, alleviate fear. He seemed to beg his patients to get well, if only for his sake. Standing in the foyer, upon the tessellated floor, it was plain that Kristian's house overawed him, not by its wealth or magnificence, but because of the emotions and aims so apparent in it.

Ushered by the black girl into the bedroom of Kristian's wife, oppressed by the sombre furnishings, the sombre sunlight soaking through the polarized windows, Florentine's psyche responded nevertheless to the isolated figure of the woman seated there. Her white silk robe, the loose hair, seemed to increase her appearance of youth and defencelessness. The doctor found himself falling into a stance – half avuncular, half conspiratorial – which he adopted with sick children.

'Well, Madame Sovaz. And how are you feeling today?'

'Quite well. It was nothing at all. A migraine.'

'Ah yes, but they can be unpleasant. Have you had any vomiting?'

'No. I am quite well. I can't imagine why Kristian should call you.'

'A husband worries.'

Silence greeted this.

She let him take her arm and wind around it the serpent he used for checking blood-pressure. Unexpectedly she laughed.

The little doctor smiled at her encouragingly, cocking his eyebrows, asking to be let in on the fun.

'I was only thinking,' she said, 'how absurd it was that you should suppose Kristian might worry about me.'

Dr Florentine dropped his eyes, embarrassed, and was unnerved to see suddenly that she wore about her throat the mesh of rubies Kristian had told him of.

He took her pulse; her flesh was cold. She seemed too entirely relaxed, relaxed to an extraordinary degree, as if drugged. Peering into her eyes, he was reminded of an oriental belief that women have no souls. Discouraged by this idea, which sprang from racial memories he at all times attempted to suppress in himself, the doctor packed up his bag and perched before her, with his prescription pad.

'Well, I don't think there's anything much the matter. These tablets should help.'

'In what way?'

'Oh,' he dismissed the question softly, 'a mild stimulant, nothing drastic.' He finished writing and pretended to have trouble with the spring of his pen. 'I'm so glad that you recovered your jewels, Madame Sovaz.'

'Yes. It was very lucky.'

He waited, but she said nothing more. He put away the pen and glanced up at her. The alteration in her demeanour was strikingly obvious after her lassitude.

Her cheeks were slightly flushed. Her hands, formerly loose on the arms of her chair, were twitching. She was a young girl of seventeen, a virgin, or a woman pared of her youth, unloved and unkindled for seventeen years, seeing her lover advancing for the first time towards her bed. On her face there was briefly such an amalgam of vulnerable innocence, fear, longing, bewilderment and desire, that a complementary sweat started out on the doctor's forehead.

'And did you really throw such lovely things down to the

41

beach?' he asked her, with the rusty playful air he used sometimes on the very old, unbalanced and ailing, in his care: *Did you
really swallow all those pills? Did you really poison the concièrge's
little dog, after she had been so kind to you?* The usual response –
'I *did*, I *did*' – was not forthcoming. Sovaz' face paled serenely.

'How strange you should think that.'

Kristian had told him what she had said. In Kristian's opinion,
she had no doubt mailed the rubies to herself, including the note
– written in a palpably invented hand. Understanding that he had
been employed more as detective than physician, the doctor now
did detect, in her cool denying volte-face, the sinister rational
stealth of the truly insane.

A little later, standing in Kristian's study, he observed painfully, 'I don't think I am qualified to treat this condition.'

Kristian's cold face made Dr Florentine afraid in a general,
unlocalized way – perhaps of inhumanity.

'This is a confidential matter,' Kristian said. 'I don't intend it to
go further than yourself.'

'Well, of course, I am always discreet – it is my duty to my
patients to be so. But the sort of attention your wife may need –'

Kristian was not listening, only politely waiting for him to
finish. Dr Florentine began to say the things Kristian would
tolerate from him. *A clockwork mouse*, he thought. *He winds me
up, I must perform as I am meant to.* The key in his back was real
enough: Kristian's generous promptness in the matter of bills, his
donations. *One of my few paying patients.* Well, if one could not
live by bread alone, certainly one could not live without bread.
But what should he say? *Love your wife.* A simple cure, as
possibly the cure might be for sclerosis or cancer, once it was
discovered.

Going down between the savage horses' heads of the stairway,
he saw again the scatter of leaves across her black bed, which he
had surreptitiously observed as he moved about the room. Press
cuttings concerning a murder, smudgy photographs of a stretcher,
the Frenchman weeping and trying to shield himself from the
flashing eyes of the cameras – it was the killing of the Gallier
woman on the beach.

So many cuttings.

In her current mood, the crime might have obsessed her for any
number of reasons. Perhaps she was afraid. Near the edge of the

bed lay a sketch, unfinished. It filled the doctor with a sense of enormous horror, a horror he could not translate at all into cohesive thought. The drawing, surely, was a sibling to the cuttings. A leopard straddled a gazelle, tearing at its flesh. Underneath had been written the word μαινάς (maenad).

The bar was hot and humid, alive with the buzzing of flies, the cursing of a card game, the ineffectual noise of two electric fans whirring in a trance from the ceiling. The girl who had served him his drink had chattered to him with a spontaneous bright chatter, like a little bird. Her English, obviously learned from tourists, was spoken with an unintentional accent as American as his own. She was a pretty gentle girl, a girl plainly not of the city. Ten years maybe before the city stripped her down to greed, vulgarity, envy and despair, ten years or five, or two, or less. Yet now she fluttered her eyes at him sweetly. Adam Quentin, longing to become involved in the mayfly tragedy of her life, could think only of Miss Havisham in the crumbling white dress, Miss Havisham with her vampire eyes, not sweet at all, only starving. This girl's eyes were also black, yet a superficial warm blackness, a shallow river, containing uncomplex instincts, quite animal, even understandable.

And yet, when he stood up and left her, he saw on those eyes the first stoical scars, the adult tiredness . . .

The number of the house he had seen about a week ago in Mikalides' book of numbers, which the Greek carried with him as a magician carries his trick cards, and for similar reasons of deceptive magic.

Adam telephoned. Then, the receiver clicking in his hand as if with radioactivity, depressed the cradle.

The girl, polishing glasses at the bar, no longer watched him. Adam took up the receiver a second time, dialled, and presently stood once more waiting, at a loss. A servant answered.

'. . . Madame Sovaz . . .'

'Who is calling, please?'

'My name is Quentin. Q-U –'

'One moment. I will see if Madame is able to receive your call.'

Three days. He had taken the inland train. He had worked one day at erecting administrative buildings of white cement like guano, on the river. He had worked one day at unloading the

43

cargoes of fish, oranges, melons, the tourist-bait of enamelled blue alligator skins, the aphrodisiac tusks of rhino. The second night, lying with a girl, empty of anything except Sovaz – the smell of her, the touch of her flesh, her hair, her premature oldness, her cold hands and burning mouth, her vacant hungry eyes. Again the train. The night train. Families asleep, children sobbing fitfully, rattling into the city over tracks reverberating like machine guns.

The telephone clicked against his ear.

'Adam,' the telephone said.

He could only stammer. He had not, after all, expected her to speak to him.

The line was poor.

'What?' he asked her.

'Help me,' she said faintly. 'I'm going mad,' she said. It was only a whisper. 'I must leave here – help me – help me –'

'Sovaz? You know I'd do anything –'

'No. You won't do anything. No one can help me. Why did you call?'

The line blanked suddenly out, and began to sizzle. She had cut him off, or else her handsome pale-eyed husband, intercepting, had cut them off, or else the erratic wires had played a joke on them, or else the city had abruptly broken in two, and one half, crowned by Kristian's house, had vanished into the sea.

He dialled again, then hung up. He went to the bar and stood there, indecisively.

'You want another beer?' The girl looked out from her tired dark eyes. She no longer flirted with him. He had been appraised.

'No, thanks.'

He went out.

He began to walk along the shore road. He did not want to. His muscles ached, his belly was leaden.

The sun lay smashed on the water. A meeting of flame and liquid that produced no smoke. Eastwards the sky spread great lammergeyer wings. He could reach the house in half an hour.

He felt no pity for her. He was apprehensive of her. And yet her voice in the telephone, the voice of a terrified old little girl, impelled him towards her as if by sorcery.

The day fell below the sea. A torchlight redness faded over the waves, leaving them the colour of the night. The crickets began

44

their eerie irritation in the scrub at the roadside. Two or three battered cars passed him, going south, and a donkey cart loaded with pale flowers.

Finally he was staring up at the façade of the enchanted castle, towering above its prison wall.

The shadow of it, the scents of its garden disturbed him, but he had expected nothing else. Waiting to be admitted, he noted his own shabbiness, impartially. Like an armour the stained denims, the bleached shirt, a charm to keep him safe from the spell of the house.

Presently all the lights sprang into golden life along the four tiers of steps. He could see now the chess piece marble horses snarling on the landings among the vines. A faceless man – truly, all Kristian's servants seemed faceless, or robots – came down to the oriental gate.

'Madame Sovaz is expecting me,' Adam Quentin said.

The lie, unpremeditated but obvious and essential, seemed to release him from heavy chains. The dehumanized servant stared for a moment out at him through the iron lattice, then activated the electric switch in the wall. The password presumably was correct. The gates slid open.

Adam stepped through, waited for the servant to close the gates, then followed him up the hundred steps into the house.

The scent of jasmine clung in the foyer, reminding him of the dinner party. After her entreaty to him he half expected some hint of upheaval or of fear to have manifested itself. Seeing nothing out of place, nervousness overtook him, some unease that he had imagined the swift, half inaudible torrent of her words, or misunderstood some flippancy.

At this moment Kristian emerged to his left from between a pair of polished wood double doors. Rather than reinforcing, by his arctic faultlessness, the illusion of balance, his presence seemed to Adam Quentin to make entirely possible Sovaz' hysterical anguish.

Kristian overawed him, as he overawed and intimidated most of those he met.

'You have come to see my wife,' Kristian stated.

'That's right. Do you think you can stop me?'

'I see you are in melodramatic mood, Mr Quentin. Of course, I have no such intention. Why should you imagine that I have?'

45

Kristian moved aside, graciously motioned Adam to step into the room behind him.

'Like you told me, I'm here to see your wife,' Adam said.

'But first I should like a moment of your time. If you would be so good.'

Despite everything, Kristian's impeccable manners overpowered him. Adam Quentin's age sat, in that moment, so lightly on him that he felt almost unborn. He went past the older man, into the room. It was so obviously Kristian's, the Persian rugs, the escritoire with its onyx penholders, a case of silvery duelling pistols and other guns, an icon with a white unliving face. Adam seemed to discover himself suddenly standing in the midst of it all like a bedraggled beaten dog.

Kristian had come in, closing the doors behind him.

'Now, Mr Quentin. I believe you telephoned my wife earlier tonight. Am I correct?'

'Why ask? I reckon you must know what goes on in this house.'

'Yes, Mr Quentin, I do. Which is quite reasonable, do you not agree, since it is my house.' Kristian paused. 'I may assume, I think, that your conversation gave rise to some concern. Which is why you have come here so promptly.'

Adam found his responses could only free themselves through a defensive angry boorishness, which in its turn further disabled him.

'I only know she wanted to get out of this goddamned place.'

'As you say, Sovaz may wish to spend a few days in other surroundings. Are you willing that she should also spend them with you?'

Aware of being manipulated, Adam said nothing.

'You are grudging of your time, Mr Quentin. If you answer my questions as I ask them, you would waste a good deal less of it.'

'OK. Yes. I'm willing.'

'Good. In that case, I recommend that you return tomorrow. I shall by then have made all the necessary arrangements.'

'What the hell are you talking about? If she wants to leave, it's now –'

'I doubt it. I believe you will be sleeping in a dosshouse in the slums. Did you intend to take my wife there?'

'You surely know everything, don't you?'

'I know enough, Mr Quentin. Let me suggest you do as I say.

By tomorrow afternoon I can provide you with a car, accommodation, and money.'

'I don't want your money.'

'Probably not. But I am merely providing for my wife's comfort, which you, you recall, are unable to do.'

'Perhaps she feels the same way I do.'

'Yes. Perhaps at the moment she does. I suggest therefore that you tell her the money and car are a loan from Mikalides. Also the beach house you will be taking, about forty miles outside the city.'

'All right. I'll go along with it for what it's worth.'

'Splendid,' Kristian said, without inflexion.

'And now I want to see her.'

Kristian opened a box of Chinese jade and extracted a cigarette which he slowly lit, by this gesture finally demonstrating his power over the American, who stood intolerably still and silent, as if turned to stone, during the procedure.

'Yes, Mr Quentin. As I assured you earlier, I shall not attempt to prevent you. But I would point out that my wife is at present in an unsettled state of mind. She is a highly strung woman, a victim of her temperament. It will be good for her to get away for a while. However, since you can as yet do nothing, does it occur to you that to return tomorrow, with every means at your disposal, would be better than simply to exacerbate her mood unnecessarily tonight?'

Adam felt a wave of guilty release sweep over him. He would not after all have to see her until the following day. He cleared his throat.

'Do you know something,' he said, 'you make me sick.'

Kristian's cold face did not change. Only the cigarette smoke moved past his eyes as he exhaled.

'Regretfully, Mr Quentin, I find your opinion of me entirely immaterial. And now, I would not dream of detaining you further. My chauffeur will see that the hired car reaches you, also the money I spoke of, and any essential documents.'

Adam turned towards the door. 'Does it strike you she might not come back to you?'

'No,' said Kristian, 'it does not.'

'You didn't buy her,' Adam said, 'like the furniture.'

'Oh, but that is exactly what I did,' Kristian said. 'And like my beautiful furniture, my beautiful wife fully understands and appreciates her position in my house, whatever notions she may entertain from time to time. She is playing with you, Mr Quentin. And the pure and doubtless estimable ideals of your youth and inexperience are blinding you to that salient, unalterable fact.'

At midnight, lying awake among the ranks of restless, groaning or snoring men, his fellow occupants of the run-down dortoir, Adam felt this conversation turning like a great wheel in his head. He was indeed sick, sick to his stomach with a depressive dread. Like a fly caught in a web, struggling in the sticky substance over which it has no control, for which it can find no name, but which it vaguely ascertains means death.

The spitting and farting and weeping prayers of the human creatures about him were all that stood between him and the day, and the woman.

Kristian entered her room this time from the dressing room, and found her seated in a chair. She had, as usual, the unawakened look so familiar to her. Ashtrays were littered with dead cigarettes. He noticed with distaste that her hands, normally exquisitely manicured, were yellow with patches of nicotine.

The interview with the American had also been distasteful, unpleasant. Never before had it been necessary to spend so much time on one of Sovaz' amusements. The telephone conversation had been reported to Kristian by his valet, a silent third party on the line.

'Sovaz,' Kristian said, 'please get up. I want you to come downstairs with me.'

It surprised him when she did at once as he said. She had looked immovable. As she rose, the silk robe slipped away from her left shoulder. Against the whiteness of her skin, through the darkness of her hair, he glimpsed the bloody fire about her throat. She drifted to the mirrors and stood, apparently aimlessly, before them. Then took up a slender phial of scent and began to dab it on her flesh.

Kristian went out of the bedroom door into the gallery. Presently, she followed him. He saw that, despite her acquiescence, she carried in her hand one of the grey press cuttings from her bed.

Below, Kristian opened the doors of polished wood for her.

She went inside and stood, much as the American had done, roughly at the centre of the room. In fact, what he had to say to her would have been said as well in the black chamber above, yet he felt a compulsion to speak to her away from the fumes of a room choked with her mental smoke as well as that of her cigarettes.

The study, his room, seemed able to hold her at bay.

Without asking her, he poured a little cognac into a glass and gave it to her. She lifted the glass and drank.

'Sovaz, you can't possibly continue in this way. You are making yourself ill.'

She said clearly, 'Oh, yes.'

'I should like you to go away for a few days. Longer if you wish. I think it would do you good. The young American was here earlier. I believe he has some plans for you both.'

'And do you have no plans for me?' she said.

'I plan that you should regain your health and your self-control.'

'Do you?' she said. She smiled at something her blind eyes were seeing. Then the smile slid back into her mouth like a snake. 'My father,' she said, 'never imagined he could die. He thought all the while he would get better.'

Kristian turned away from her to light a cigarette, and noticed the stub of a previous cigarette.

'The night he died,' Sovaz went on, 'there was a storm. He must have been calling to me, and I didn't hear him for the rain. When I went in, it was only by chance, because I had seen his lamp was still burning. He was working on a translation of Plato, but there was blood all over the page, the book, the top of his desk. I ran to him and he caught my hand. He looked terrified. But he only said very calmly, "I think I'm rather worse tonight. Will you go to the doctor's house and ask him to come?" I let go his hand and rushed out, but I heard his head fall down on to the papers before I reached the door.'

'This is pointless, Sovaz.'

'Yes,' she said, 'quite pointless. I shall, naturally, do whatever you say. When am I to leave?'

'Tomorrow.'

'And when do I come back?'

'When you are ready.'

'Suppose,' she said, 'that I never come back to you.'

'I don't think that you will be so foolish.'

'I am foolish enough to stay, why not to go? Why,' she said softly, 'why didn't you let me go when I was able?'

'If you are speaking of divorce –'

'No. That would be very stupid of me, wouldn't it?' He glanced at her, but her eyes still seemed blind, yet a polarized blindness, appearing dark only to those who stood outside. She said: 'Kristian, I opened the door and there you were. Everything was in crates and boxes. I had to sell all his books, and I thought I would be jailed because there wasn't any money left . . . I thought I should have to steal food, and they would catch me . . . And I opened the door and there you were.'

He said: 'I think you should go upstairs.'

'Yes,' she said, 'of course.'

She turned and went without another word. But he saw that she had left lying on the rug the grey press cutting.

Kristian retrieved it. A cold feverishness had come over him; he found he was repelled even by an object she had been holding. He saw for a second the headline as he balled the cutting in his hand. Igniting the desk lighter, he set fire to the smudgy wad, and let it fall into an ashtray to burn. It was a dramatic gesture, a gesture alien to him.

The paper flared with a cleansing flame. It reflected brightly in the case of pistols, as the rising sun had once reflected on the beautiful guns, and the birds had rained from the sky, and the deer crumpled with the grace of ballerinas between the tall stalks of the pines.

FIVE

The slender white sports car sprang eagerly southwards. Leaving the cement towers, the minarets and spires of the city behind, it rattled down the shore road, between landward banks in mourning with cypress groves, and the tumbling western edge, which in places dropped sheer to a glittering afternoon sea.

The road, tortuous, caked red or white with powdered clay, owed its existence to various empires. The Persians, the Romans, the Americans had all had a hand in it. It was a polyglot, mongrel construction, an aggressive bastard of a road, and given to practical jokes (a dead cow lying around the bend feasted upon by clouds of flies, a flock of ragged sheep spilling across between broken fences from one field to another, an abandoned cart on its side).

Old farms dotted the eastern heights. Goats galloped away, pretending that the car was still a unique anachronism on this ancient time-locked landscape – that, meanwhile, swarmed at certain periods of the year with cars and buses fleeing from the summer heat of the city, and which had burst consequently into little red gas stations like an eruption of acne.

The slender vehicle was open, a golden young man driving it, a black and white woman at his side, partly concealed beneath a wide-brimmed black straw hat.

The journey was not long. They did not speak.

The robot chauffeur had handed to him relevant keys, receipts, a manilla packet. Sovaz had appeared on the steps, moving between the chess pieces like another chess piece, the Black Queen, in her inky frock and hat, a trailing of black and white chiffon about her neck.

She looked altogether too dramatic, coming towards him, and he had a ghastly sort of Sunset Boulevard impression of her, an aging insane actress, dolled up to the nines. It was a shock to see, when the sun struck suddenly on the triangle the hat left free of shadow, how young she was.

He said to her awkwardly, 'Do you have everything you need?'
'Yes,' she said, 'thank you.'

Two small suitcases, packed by her maid, lay already in the boot.

He opened the door for her. She got in. Claustrophobia welled in his chest as he shut both of them together into the car, despite its state of rooflessness.

He was near to hating her, for he hated himself. He could not even now comprehend how he had become entangled in this incredible act. Somehow the train had run away downhill before he could get out. Now, left clinging to its trembling superstructure, he could only stare about him at the fall in disbelief.

He was to say Mikalides had lent him money and a villa so that they could be together. No doubt, other men had absorbed Kristian's money without reluctance and lied graciously when needful. Yet surely she must know? It was obvious she had only come with him because Kristian had so instructed her. That he, Adam, had only come to take her because Kristian had so instructed *him*. Of her earlier cry for help nothing seemed to remain. She was polite and soulless. The situation was laughable, pathetic and revolting.

She sat beside him and said nothing. They were two strangers summoned to a hanging. There seemed to Adam no way out of it.

The quality of the afternoon altered. Veils of heat obscured the sinking sun. They drove through a little town with the obligatory number of gasoline pumps, a café or two and tiny shadowed shops and alleys. The road ran up then down. In the hot grey dusk, bumping along a track between the dunes, they reached the white beach house so carefully indicated on the chauffeur's map.

The breakers buzzed softly far out on the shore.

The interior of the villa was neatly designed, the walls regardlessly whitewashed. It was an acceptable, almost elegant setting, though not imaginative. A pang of reluctant admiration went through Adam, for it was so very much what the Greek merchant would have arranged for him, as he had arranged the evening clothes to be worn to the dinner party.

A freezer lurked in the stone-flagged kitchen, its gut stuffed with food. Green and gold idols of wine and spirits glinted in a wooden comb. A woman and her husband from the town came and went in the day, he had been told, to clean, and to prepare meals if necessary. Everything had been taken care of. Even a cold supper had been set out for them beneath covers, which neither approached.

Now the sound of the car had left them, as once before, their silence seemed to grow. The dull resonance of the sea, muffled by a sky of low cloud, did nothing to dispel it. Sovaz sat in a high-backed chair, motionless and unspeaking, still in her Swanson-Garboesque hat.

His mind went back to a beach party three years before on Long Island, trying to warm itself at those red fires, now ashes, among the beer cans, now further wreckage polluting the Sound, and the tanned young bodies and thoughtless hopeful silly happy laughter, now stifled for ever by experience.

He extracted a bottle of wine from its melting ice, and opened it.

'Do you want a drink?'

'Why not?'

The words fastened in his brain like a code of conduct. Why not? Why not?

He handed her a glass of the wine, and drank his own rapidly. Very quickly it warmed him. He felt a surge of anger and dislike.

'Well, here we are,' he said. He poured himself another glass and sat facing her. 'Why don't you take off your hat, Sovaz? There's no sun in here. I can't see you.'

'Does it matter?' she said.

'Sure it does.'

She put up her hand and drew off the hat, then held it on her lap with the untouched wine.

'Do you remember what you said to me,' he said flatly, 'when I called you at the house?'

Her eyes flickered and dilated.

'That was stupid,' she said. 'I don't know why I should have said such a thing.'

'You said it because you meant it.'

He felt something at her confusion, for he could see he was confusing her. Mixed together in him now were interchangeable desires to help or harm.

'Sovaz,' he said, 'stop running away from it, whatever it is. If you tell me, maybe we can work something out.'

'I was foolish to speak to you as I did. You can do nothing.'

'OK,' he said, 'OK, Sovaz, if that's what you want.'

He got to his feet again. He took up the half empty wine bottle and its companion from the table, and went straight out of the villa on to the beach.

The sea was stealthily abandoning the shore. He walked after it, a bottle in either hand.

He finished the first bottle and slung it out to sea.

He was, after all, leaving her. He could travel all night and fetch up God knew where and get some train and beat it, and this time not oh Christ not come back. He pulled the loosened cork of the second bottle. *Dionysos*, he thought, *god of wine*. He had eaten nothing all day and was already drunk.

Abruptly there was a noise of war in the sky overhead.

53

Lightning shrilled across the ribbing of the waves. Rain fell to meet them.

All at once he visualized her seated alone in the beach house while the storm tore at it. The cold water slapped him across the face as if trying to sober him. 'Help me,' she had said to him. He recaptured suddenly how she had clung to him in the wild olives, how she had looked in the aftermath of sex, as if she had fallen from a great height and lay dashed on the ground. A wash of pity did after all well up in him.

He turned and half ran up the sand to the villa.

The room was deserted. Her hat lay on the ground where she had let it fall, the wine stood pristine in her glass on the table.

'Sovaz!' he shouted.

She did not answer.

He went to the wooden stairway and ran up it. A whitewashed bedroom exploded in the bomb blast of the lightning.

He went through the door. She stood brushing her hair at a glass, long rhythmic strokes.

He said hoarsely, 'Didn't you hear me calling you?'

She turned. She seemed strangely puzzled.

'The rain,' she said, 'I didn't hear you above the rain.'

The relief of finding her, engaged in such a relatively normal action as brushing her hair, made him feel ill. He leaned by the door and waited for the feeling of illness to abate. The storm was already dying, but lightning still flashed on and off inside his head.

Then looking at her, he saw the most extraordinary phenomenon of weeping he had ever witnessed. For her wide-open eyes seemed to fragment in tears, and the tears themselves gushed forth like the water that falls from the urns or breasts or dolphins' mouths of fountains.

At sunrise the tide returned gently to the beach. The waves, each overtaking the other, ran up into the morning, and opened in slow platinum fans, like the glissandi of successive harps.

Dawn woke Sovaz, dawn softly rupturing the parchment blinds of the villa windows. Opening her eyes, she was for a moment unnerved by the pale window spaces, by all her surroundings.

She lay quite still, faintly hearing the harp notes of the waves, and watching their reflective patterning cast upwards on the ceiling by a freak of angle and light. Memory came into her conscious brain in similar gentle rushes, one upon another, and, like the beach, she received them.

How strangely easy it was now to look back into yesterday, at all she had felt and done, unmoved, as if looking at some other person. But then, each sleep being a sort of death, each waking therefore a definitive of birth, yesterday's Sovaz was indeed no longer herself. That woman, sloughed like the skin of a snake, might be observed without prejudice. The new Sovaz, reincarnated, was at her beginning.

Never before had she experienced this sense of absolution and hope. A creature of night, she had seldom woken to sunrise.

Yet something in her warned her how fragile the moment was. She lay still, afraid of cracking the delicate glass that encased her.

Yesterday she had been an old woman.

She had moved through a terrible timelessness, that anaesthetic suspension which before had sometimes overcome her for an hour or so, which all at once had swallowed her whole. Events and people had beaten on her numbed flesh and spirit like hail on stone. She did not precisely know what had happened to release her. A storm – she had begun to cry. She had not cried, had she, for seven years.

Then the presence of the young man made itself known to her. Of his troubled and uncertain comforting she was not conscious, nor of his murmured entreaties that she stop crying, tell him what was wrong, let him in some way help her.

The last orchestral violence of the storm faded over the sea. The storm of her pain faded also. Soon the need to comfort and be comforted exchanged itself in both of them and merged with an inevitable progression. Not speaking, they made love, and presently slept, only to wake again to each other thirstily at intervals through the black, sea-breathing night, sleeping still locked, as if they were indeed only a twin machinery of desire. In this manner, she lost her identity, her sense of past or role. She woke at dawn, the old skin seeming sloughed, to a day seen through crystal, a day for the moment novel as the first morning of the world.

Later, the light upon the blinds turned golden.

Sovaz rose on her elbow. She had fallen asleep once again. The

55

magic of the dawn was over; now she could move without shattering the glass – the warmth of the sun had melted it.

Adam lay, still asleep, turned on his side towards her. She studied him gravely, as if seeing him properly for the first time.

Sleep had both accentuated his youth and curiously dispensed with it. He too had a timelessness. She was put in mind of the marble statues of renascent Italy, the slumbering heroes carved on mausoleums. Having accepted sleep in its aspect of death this did not chill her.

As she leaned looking at him, as if responding to her mood even in sleep, he opened his eyes. At once he smiled at her.

'Sovaz . . .'

She put out her hand and stroked his hair, and he lay, still smiling, his eyes shut in pleasure at her touch.

She lay down and drew him into her arms. His sleepy happiness seemed to soak into her, by a method of osmosis.

He turned suddenly and sat up, looking down at her as she had looked at him.

'You are so beautiful,' he said to her, 'and you look like you were about fifteen years old.'

He seemed as if about to speak to her with an earnest seriousness from which she withdrew.

'Adam,' she said, 'open the blinds, the sun is so lovely, and it's not even hot yet.'

A shadow crossed his face. Then he grinned, and swung out of bed. The blinds flicked their tassels like the tails of obedient horses and ran up the windows.

He stood looking out at the sea and sky.

Watching him, the play of gold on his blond hair and amber skin, entranced by his physical splendour and prepared abruptly to adore him for it, she felt young indeed, perhaps for an instant even as young as he had said.

With all her lovers she had sought youth. Thinking it to be their youth she sought, she herself felt, with each of them, far older than she was. The image of the rich and desolate matron with her creased skin, her toppled breasts, and her gigolo, lay always in her mind's eye. She had seen these women years before through the green and ruby windows of the great library, walking in the squares below. Painted wizened monkeys with their handsome boys strolling like expensive dogs at their sides. Now an emerald monkey, tapping her cigarette on its green metal case, now a scarlet dog rearing acrobatically on its hind limbs to light it for her.

It had never occurred to Sovaz, until this moment, that it was not after all the youngness of her lovers that attracted her to them. It was her own youth she hankered for, freely expressed, untrammelled, in their bodies. She was a victim of the bizarre juxtaposition which made a woman imagine she had fallen in love with a man, when in fact she had actually fallen in love with the masculine facet of her own self as projected in this man's image. The heart of the timid and puritanical virgin was inflamed by the daring and libidinous pirate in the universal myth. But the cutlass thrust through his belt was as much the symbol of her own unrealized potential, of the castration of her mental bravura, as it was the emblem of the male phallus. In reality she did not yearn for the pirate's embrace, she yearned to *become* the pirate. The frigid strength of Kristian then was something Sovaz had not worshipped but jealously burned to possess for herself. For herself the anchor of his wealth, his iron and impervious will, what she saw as his emotionlessness. Kristian would always perhaps be her torment. She could not devour him.

But Adam, Adam who, more than all the others, was her beauty, her sweetness, her youth, Adam it seemed she could love, at least for a little space.

The woman came from the town. They heard her, in a hoarse voice, singing snatches of *Tosca*.

When they went down, she brought them hot rolls, peaches, and fresh coffee, to a table laid for them on the veranda. The man, whistling tunelessly, had begun to clean the white sports car. He gnawed used matches as he worked and, occasionally emerging to cross in front of the veranda to the side door of the villa, would grin at Adam a macabre grin of filbert teeth and matchsticks protruding between them like the limbs of tiny prey.

The beach house, in the honey sun, was warm and friendly, the stretching glittering sand like powdered topaz, the surf rolling in in lazy gusts of white smoke and blue fire.

Sheltered by a bay, the villa was remote, without another habitation nearer than two miles away. The shore blazed, deserted under the sun. After they had walked leisurely along the rim of the sea for a while the house was out of sight. Adam discarded his clothes and swam out into the silken water.

Sovaz, who could not swim, seated herself. The sand was voluptuously warm, even so early. The sun, the caress and colour of it, soothed her, seemed to penetrate into her bones. She stretched and dreamed in it, unafraid. And although she had put on again the black straw hat, the black and white chiffon was now tied about it. She wore a knee-length white dress, which also left her throat and arms bare.

(She did not recall how Leah had taken off the rubies in her black bedroom, and then locked them in the ivory box. How Leah had looked doing it, how she, Sovaz, had stood in petrified terror at this omen. No doubt Kristian had given instructions. Before she had gone to meet Adam, almost inadvertently – for she was then still a stone with only hail beating on it – she had bound her neck with the chiffon, rather tightly, as if to staunch a flow of blood.)

It was easy to follow Adam's progress through the sea. He was gold, the water cobalt. The simplicity of it pleased her. Shortly she saw the gold flash as he turned and came back to her.

Wading up out of the waves, metallically naked, he resembled something archaic and fabulous.

He lay down beside her on the beach, shading his eyes with one hand.

'It must be wonderful to swim so strongly,' she said.

'It's great. Why don't I teach you?'

'Oh no. I should be dreadfully afraid.'

'That's OK. It's easy when you know how.'

'You learnt when you were a child, I expect.'

'It doesn't make any difference, Sovaz. I wouldn't let you drown.'

She smiled drowsily. Although envious of his ability in the water, she had basically no desire to emulate him.

'No. I enjoyed watching you.'

'You should have thrown me a stick,' he said, with an unexpectedly acid humour.

He drew her into his arm and her heart began at once to drum excitedly as her skin encountered the texture of his, for she was adoring him. Each new mannerism which she had not seen before, each new message of his thought, seemed wonderful to her. They made love in a languorous slow motion induced by the sun and the rhythm of the sea.

Looking down at her afterwards, he noticed the absence of that expression of bewilderment – of fright almost – that he had seen on her face the first time.

He touched her cheek gently with his mouth, and she smiled. Her eyes were closed against the sun, the hat fallen away, the ebony glissade of her hair spread like an enchanted net on the sand.

It was impossible to associate with this day the day which had preceded it. Even less than she did he understand what had broken the spell on her. Some old guilt and pain, this much he had guessed, had been expunged in tears. All dread of her had vanished with her alteration. Now he felt only her warmth, her actual youth, what seemed to him her profound and innocent sweetness, those things which, as she had vaguely known, sprang from her chameleonism, her ability to become a mirror. Kristian, when he thought of him, was even more a figure of sick disgust. Kristian was the sorcerer. He wanted to free her from Kristian. Adam was impulsive with this desire, yet the calmness of the day somehow restrained him. There seemed time for everything.

About two o'clock they walked down the baked road to the little town, and ate omelettes and wine at one of the cafés whose tables now sprawled in the open under eau-de-Nil umbrellas. When they had finished eating, they progressed carelessly and unhurriedly about the winding streets. On the highest level of the town they found a market with goats and sheep in pens and bright birds in cages. The heat of the day had come, and fell in white squares between the stalls.

Sovaz paused among tubs of hyacinths and other flowers, fingering their clusters lightly. Adam instinctively recognized the ingenuous almost naive signal of a woman who has no money of her own but for whom everything she requires is bought. So he bought her flowers, though not with Kristian's money.

Sovaz fastened the stems of the yellow and blue flowers into the band of the scarf so that the heads spilled along the brim of her black hat. She laughed as she did so, as a child laughs. She did indeed look very young, he thought, the same age as himself. He caught her hand and they walked on palm to palm, as any pair of lovers might have done.

They talked a good deal. At least, he talked and she responded, prompting him. She did not seem to want to talk about herself, only about him. He spoke of New York, the cryogenic winters, the dry-as-dust summer madnesses, the parties and the drawing office, his mother with her chain-smoking affairs, the unborn yet often conceived and aborted book. He was neither self-conscious nor flattered at being made to tell her all these things. It seemed natural that she should have the groundwork of his life upon which to stand when later she might wish to reveal her own.

He mentioned the incomplete notation he had written, attempting to describe her. She laughed again. Her face seemed all the beauty of the day held in crystal. He was, without understanding it, experiencing the joy of the artist who has made, even if inadvertently, something fine. For he had given her this life.

Abruptly the sun went down, dusk washed over the streets.

The sky was brilliant with enormous stars as they strolled back again, still hand in hand, towards the shore, and about the wild tamarisks at the roadside fireflies winked their tiny neons.

Nevertheless, with the resurrection of night, some indefinable unease stole over Adam.

They did not at once return to the villa, but moved slowly, following the pale contours of the beach. Suddenly she said: 'Today has been wonderful, Adam.'

'It isn't the last day,' he said. 'Sovaz,' he said, 'why do you stay with him, with Kristian? You can't live like that for ever.'

The moment he had given in to the irresistible demand to say this, he regretted it. He saw everything at once in total proportion. He felt ashamed of speaking to her in such a way. She was a woman used only to certain modes of existence. He could not maintain her financial standards, had nothing to offer her. The atmosphere of the hothouse might limit the scope of the orchid, but take it outside into the intemperate world and it would die. Truly, she *could* live like that for ever, and in no other fashion.

As for Sovaz, a strengthless exhaustion overcame her at the thought of leaving Kristian.

The exhalation of night pressed suddenly on her.

'Adam,' she said, 'why should Thettalos loan you a house?'

'What?' Startled by the unexpected question – he had been expecting almost any other reaction from her – Adam let go her hand.

'Thettalos would never do such a thing,' Sovaz said. Her voice was light and cool. She stared out at the sea. 'Why should he? He only aids and abets in order to win Kristian's approval and custom, and he would know there would be no need for you to ask anyone other than Kristian for money.'

Adam swallowed. He was at a loss. Seeing she had realized the truth, it seemed better to concede the facts. In any case, it was such a stupid, irrelevant lie.

'OK, Sovaz. Krsitian's renting the house. Does it matter now?'

'No, Adam. Of course it doesn't matter in the least.'

He took her hand again. This time her hand was cold.

'Look,' he said impractically, 'tomorrow we could go some-place else . . .'

'Where?' she said. Her voice said, *Kristian is here with us after all. He is, as I had always thought, omnipresent. Where could we go to escape him?*

But Adam, Adam her youth – there was no strength to be found in him, no individual impulse of action. He, too, was part of Kristian's plan to be tidily rid of her until she might be purged and refashioned and returned to him in the mood of dull bored serenity with which she left all her lovers. All. Adam only one with all the rest. Her dog on a leash. Whose wages were not even paid by herself, but by her husband.

Reaching the villa, they ate a little of the cold food laid out for them, drank the wine, and later went to bed and made love together. Yet it was all done in an oddly wooden and desultory manner. They were trying to continue, unchecked, the happiness of the day, but now their actions had become imitative.

The tide retreated from the shore, and Sovaz, who did not often recollect her dreams, dreamed vividly a dream which woke her.

In the dream she had already woken.

The room was a black box, the windows oblongs of paler black, casting no light inwards, and she was alone. Around the house she heard soft footfalls circling on the sand.

In the way of dreams, not meaning to, she found herself at a window, looking out. The scenery was altered. The beach house – if house it still was – was perched on the crest of a sweeping broken hill, a hill roped with vines and ivies. The sky above was no longer black, but black-red, a sky of funeral fires, and green smoke, like the smoke of a volcanic altar, was rising up into it in places from fissures in the ground. On this ground were also other things. Euripides' bacchantes had recently passed this way in their frenzy, leaving the earth littered with the ribs of cattle and flags of flesh caught on trees.

Directly below the window a panther was feeding. As she glanced down at it, it raised its head. Its stare was blindly seeing as the lenses of cameras, its mouth was full of blood; yet blood which had crystallized, full of rubies.

She felt no particular fear. Perhaps something other than the dream woke her, for she opened her eyes with none of that frantic struggle which accompanies the escape from nightmare. However, conscious now in the dark room, the dream still jewel bright in her brain, she was at once overwhelmed by a nameless instinct that drove her out of bed and towards the window.

She released the blind, and there lay the blue-grey beach, the blue-black sea, the sky of stars.

The surge of her body settled. She stood at the window with an inexplicable sense of unfulfilment. Then came a sound from the back of the house – a sound like an animal's large pad descending on the sand. It struck her nerves, a silver chord ran over her. She thought: *I am afraid*.

She ran back across the room, yet halted at the door. She did not even recognize her fear. She felt the bemused and fascinated horror of vertigo, the abyss at the bottom of the height drew her, and she caught involuntarily at the walls to save herself.

'Adam,' she cried, but she did not really remember him at all.

Her movements had already disturbed him. As she discerned that morning he was aware of her even asleep.

'What is it?' he murmured.

'He has followed me here,' she said, still holding to the walls, still gazing sightlessly down the dark stairway.

'Who? Who did, Sovaz?'

'He's outside now,' she whispered.

In her mind she was seeing the surrealist black panther. She imagined it prowling across the veranda, slipping from shade to shade, stealthy as the night itself. Nevertheless, despite the waves of confused hysteria now converging on her brain, she knew perfectly well and with a deadly logic that the demon was real enough, and very near.

Adam had risen and was tugging on clothes swiftly.

'Calm down, Sovaz. I'll go and see. You know, perhaps it's nothing.'

Deep inside her (lost, unattended) a small nerve throbbed at his gentleness to her with a returning remorseful gentleness that was almost pity for him. He brushed her cheek with his finger, and then went by her, going down the stairs noiselessly. Passing the table in the living area below, he took up, with an off-hand and surprisingly brutal resourcefulness, an empty wine bottle.

'Stay there,' he said. 'I won't be long.'

She saw abruptly that he must open the house door. This thought terrified her. Only the shadow of the night was so far in the villa, but open the door and night's black face would peer round it.

The vampire, assuming the form of mist, could slip in through the slightest crack and materialize. And yes, the demon had been a vampire, for he drank the blood of his victim as he lay on her as if in the act of love. She wanted to scream out to Adam, to stop him, but already he had done the thing she dreaded. The door stood wide a moment then folded shut.

She was alone in the black house with her terror.

Of course, it was so simple. He had been watching her, she had always known it. He had returned the rubies as proof. (How could she have put him from her thoughts?) She had witnessed his crime. He must kill her. And how easy for him to follow her here, and what better spot than this, the isolated villa lapped by the sea and the dunes, only a beautiful boy to protect her, one who picked up a bottle to defend himself, without cunning . . . Sovaz ran from one end of the room to the other and back once more, in a trap. Yes. Perhaps she was trapped.

She stood quite still. Her whole body was pulsing, electric. It was no longer fear she felt, but a more ancient and more complex emotion, the extreme abandon of something hunted.

If the murderer (yes, yes, call him that, though he was also the demon, the magician), if the murderer had waited outside in the shadow, why could he not similarly wait until Adam had moved off a little way, searching, then slip into the villa, come softly up the stairs to her.

She pressed herself against the wall, and began to slide herself down it and down the unseen steps. If she could reach the side door she could run out, she could cry for help across the desert of the sands to the waste of the sea, and perhaps be heard.

Adam Quentin walked quietly around the house, then along the beach a little way. He was not, in fact, particularly uneasy. His itinerant life about the vitriolic slums of this and other cities had partly revived in him those primitive senses geared to deal with danger, and these same senses relayed no warning. The night seemed to offer nothing except its perpetual air of menace.

At first he believed she had imagined the intruder. Then her words *He has followed me here* struck him with a certain symbolism. She had been reservedly distressed since his admission that Kristian had after all financed him. Possibly a phantom Kristian stalked round the villa for her. This idea gave birth to another. Standing on the empty beach, he recalled Kristian's agents, the Englishman Prescott, the other men who discreetly followed Sovaz wherever she went about the city, to observe and report on her movements. It was feasible that she had seen such a man patrolling on the sand, incautious under the unlit windows.

The thought gripped Adam with a sudden fury. He envisaged at once a traditional carbon-copy spy lying on the dunes, perhaps with binoculars. The untroubled tenderness of the morning, their love-making on the beach, the gentle afternoon, all reduced by the professional outlook of the watcher to the insipidity all sentiment assumes when divorced from motive.

Adam looked around him.

About two hundred yards away, on an upper level of the beach, he could suddenly make out the ill-defined shape of a car without headlights. Adam swore softly.

It was rough going here, the sand slid from under his feet like silk. A little track came meandering down from the road and the car was parked just off it, among the drily whispering tamarisks. The stillness as well as the darkness of the vehicle impressed Adam as he came nearer, so that he moved more cautiously. Eventually he had come close enough to see in.

Inside the car a man and woman were embracing frenziedly,

writhing and entwining in total silence and with a faintly ludicrous concentration, as if afraid that, should their attention be permitted to wander for a moment, they would lose the thread of this physical conversation.

So much for Kristian's agent. Crazy to suppose he would be in the first parked car . . . A sense of foolishness came over Adam, also of slight shyness. He did not like to see his own sexual passion translated by the antics of others. Turning, fortunately unseen, he quickly and quietly moved away.

He had abandoned the quest. Reaching the level sand, he began to run back towards the house. He realized now he must have been gone almost half an hour, leaving her alone and distraught, as once before.

There were, even now, no lights in the windows. The door was shut, as he had left it.

As once before. As once before, the room was deserted, and the stairs.

'Sovaz!' he called, as once before. She did not answer.

He ran up the stairway. This time she was not in the bedroom.

He went over the villa methodically, turning on all the electric lights. Presently he discovered the side door standing open. He searched and found an oil lamp in the stone kitchen, lit it and went outside.

The shadows fled back in groups like black animals which had crept up to the house but retreated from fire.

Where was she – where had she gone? Purely instinctively he recognized the fear which had driven her into the open – his eyes ran automatically over the track which led from the villa back to the road. From the head of the track was visible the dull haze of neon still lingering over the town. Had she fled that way for comfort?

Adam left the lamp and hurried up the track, for some reason ignoring the possibility of using the sports car, and, feeling the hard clay of the road finally under his feet, he began to run in the direction of the town.

He ran for nearly a mile, then stopped. Sweat dried his shirt to his body in patches. He had been looking out for her at every step. But he could never hope to find her like this, it was too slow. He must go back for the car after all. (Something about the idea of the car repelled him; he pushed this from his mind.)

Besides, maybe she had returned to the house.

He trudged towards the shore, weary with anxiety. He felt a child and was disgusted by the childish sick fear that threatened him.

It was about three o'clock when he reached the beach house. He went in and called her name, but perfunctorily, without much expectation. Unanswered he went for the car.

It would not immediately start. It too seemed reluctant to take the journey, and, fractious, obstructed him. At last the motor engaged.

Glancing over his shoulder as the car moved up the track, he noted incongruously that he had left every light in the beach house burning brightly.

When she reached the smaller door of the villa, opened it, and stood there, confronted by the night, Sovaz had ceased to exist.

The night was cool and black. It inspired ancient fears and joys. These feelings had always been present in her, though her method of living stifled even while it encouraged them. Now, through a process of dreaming terrors and events magnified to terror, the inner elemental genius which was not Sovaz, but Sovaz deprived of all human conditions and desires, pared to the psychological and spiritual quick, emerged suddenly in the cold water of darkness and took possession of her shell of a woman's body.

If she felt anything at all, it was a sensation of release. As for fear itself, she was no longer afraid. What had driven her to flight now seemed unremarkable, almost normal. As when she had first run away from the murderer on the beach, the whole night was imbued with him, so that he was quite inescapable. And like the gods, he only asked for her consent, her surrender.

Yet she did not really think anything, or know what she did as she stepped out on to the sand drifts.

The landscape was full of unexpected forms – black birds or animals of shadow, while smoking tinsel galleys floated in the sky or on the sea.

Reduced to an ultimate in symbols, she followed at first a natural depression in the dunes, then, coming on the track, she followed this up to the road and so went along that, towards the dim phosphorescent glow above the town. The glow represented

Destination, the trackways and the road a means of getting there, but these things were merely occupations. For she was offering herself, unprotected, vulnerable in her robe of white Chinese silk, to the night and the demon.

She could not have said what she anticipated – the knife, the Shadow – she did not know how death would divulge himself or how she would greet him. She was trembling, vibrating with a wild excitement. Every touch of the air on her skin, every breath of wind that lifted her hair, was in itself a kind of ecstasy.

Her bare feet (she had cut them on stones and not noticed) walked briskly. Shortly she passed through the little town where another woman had sat beneath the umbrellas with flowers in her hat. The streets were now mostly deserted. A few dreary neons stared from the exteriors of bars. From a dark archway a chewing man came out and stopped to gape at her. She had all the appearance of a sleep-walker, or even a devil, so much so that he did not even lurch across to her to seize her arm as he might ordinarily have done with a stray woman seen on the night road. (About an hour later, a young American in a fast white car would come by, and give him money for this information.)

Sovaz went through the town following the road, and, because nothing had happened, continued on the other side of it.

The sea sounded very close on her left, though she was not aware of it. It threw itself against the rocks below with titanic explosions, as if trying to attract her attention. Hereabouts the great slopes began which fell down sheer beyond the railing – to the sea at high tide, or else to this vast lashing cauldron of rock and spray.

The wind blew up from the sea.

Coming from the town, Adam drove slowly, with a painful discipline, knowing she was probably ahead of him on the road. Reaching the first of the horrific roadside drops, his guts seemed to rise up and slam him in the chest, thinking of her wandering by in the state the opium-eater had described. Of course the man was drugged, yet his hallucinatory representation of the dark-haired woman in her thin white robe seemed, rather than to exaggerate, to strike the very essentials of her condition.

His hands sticky with sweat, Adam drove on at the same agonizing snail's pace.

Then he saw her. She was quite unmistakable, picked out by the headlights, walking at the very centre of the road. He managed to overtake her smoothly, pulling up ahead of her, getting out of the car and going back without moving too fast. She looked as though she were dreadfully shocked. Something must indeed have happened at the beach house after he had left her, yet there had been no sign of intrusion or violence.

Although she did not look at him, she had stopped still. Going up to her so carefully, in a rigour of tension accentuated by finding her, he abruptly recalled any number of the cheap horror movies illicitly seen in his childhood, lovely zombies in fluttering grave-clothes, décolleté heroines lured from their beds by vampires.

'Sovaz,' he said, unsteadily.

Her eyes were totally unfocused, yet she gave a brief polite little smile. He wondered whom she might be seeing in her brain that she greeted with such civil uninterest. He could not believe himself so entirely demoted. With a gradualness that made his arms shake, he reached out and took hold of her.

'Come to the car, Sovaz.'

She allowed him to direct her, quite docilely. He caught sight of her feet, the blood on them, and set her like eggs inside the vehicle and shut the door before he got in beside her.

A wash of desperate confusion went over him. There was no room to turn the car, only the steep bank going up on the right, the roaring descent on the left, crashing adjacent to his window. He saw he must go on in this same direction until he came to a wider and less perilous stretch of road.

He started the engine and began to drive swiftly north.

The road hugged itself to the flank of the up-slope, as if afraid of the sea below. Sovaz seemed to be staring out at it. All at once she said, with a sharp insistence, 'No.'

'What, Sovaz? Don't be scared, it's all right.'

'No,' she said again, 'I won't go with you. Let me alone.'

She screamed, a prolonged and terrible scream, and, turning towards him, began to scratch at his face.

Insurmountable horror attacked him. He put up his right arm to defend himself. She was no longer human. Her mouth and eyes were enlarged and quite mindless. He had a leopard locked in with him. Then, slashing at him with her left hand, she clutched and scrabbled with her right at the door.

'Sovaz!' he shouted.

He was trying to thrust her away and hold her in at the same time, while with the other arm he attempted to steady the car.

At this moment the road, swirling around a bend, presented one of its practical jokes. A broken cart – perhaps even one they had passed earlier on their journey south – with a great sugaring of smashed glass about it. The sports car shot forward and ploughed through the cart, the glass . . . Sovaz' door gave as if at a signal. Adam wrenched about involuntarily, instinctively, to snatch her back. Simultaneously a glass dagger stabbed into the front nearside tyre, which blew with the sound of a gunshot.

The car spun left on the impetus of its three remaining tyres. It spun against the railing, which capitulated without protest. The car leaped forward and was for a moment apparently poised in stasis on the starlit sky. Below, the sea gnashed its jaws hungrily.

Adam Quentin, flung sideways across the seat, the sleeve of his denim jacket now uselessly caught on the wheel, thought in a blazing jumble of emotions for which no words were possible, thought, as primitive man or as babies did, in pictures – but only for an instant, or perhaps twenty instants.

The car fell, still spinning, towards the explosions of rocks and sea.

Sovaz, lying on the road just clear of the cart and the broken glass, raised her head at the enormous boom of thunder that burst below, louder even than the waves.

A glare kicked up against the night.

Sovaz pulled herself to the shattered railing to look down at it, a huge chrysanthemum of flame alight on the rocks, the petrol burning blue and green on the water.

SIX

The house, caught in the last resinous light of the afternoon, had taken on the inanimate and empty look it frequently acquired by day, its blindness of windows unlit, the vines resembling cuttings of dark paper. It had seemed to the doctor, as he struggled up the steps towards it, like some great sarcophagus, to enter which inevitably invited a curse.

Dr Florentine was afraid of the woman, or, more accurately, of the condition in which he would find her. Kristian's note had been concise but unrevealing. Although additionally the limousine had been sent for him.

Kristian's valet ushered him into the study. The room was burnished with the unearthly sheen that invaded the whole house during the late afternoon and sunset, through the polarized windows. It was hard to tell anything about Kristian in this mezzotint, and yet it seemed clear to the doctor that he was changed.

'Please sit down,' Kristian said to him, and the quality of voice and manner were certainly the same. Dr Florentine sat, his short penguin flippers folded neatly over his bag. 'I had better put you in the picture, hadn't I?' Kristian said. 'My wife has been involved in a car accident, last night to be exact. She was driving in company with a friend' (the word was spoken quite implicitly) 'on the shore road about twenty-five miles south of the city. There was a wreck of some sort. I gather the young man swerved to avoid it and lost control of the car. The passenger door seems to have given way; my wife was discovered lying at the side of the road, unhurt. Her driver, however, had no time to get clear of the car before it broke through the railing. There is nothing that side except the sea, and rocks when the tide is out.'

'Dear God, how terrible,' the doctor murmured. The permanently unhealed wound of his compassion received this fresh pain with dismal fortitude. Through it he was able to wonder briefly at Kristian's exactness in describing the accident, even to details which did not concern Sovaz, all reeled off in that impersonal, almost casual fashion.

'My wife, although uninjured, is deeply shocked as you will imagine,' Kristian said to him. 'Which is my reason for troubling you.'

Again the doctor strove, half unconsciously, to detect behind Kristian's voice the motives and intents that moved him. It was not love or concern for the woman he lived with in this house, merely he wished her, like an expensive piece of precision machinery, to function. *It is a watch-mender not a doctor you require*, Dr Florentine thought, yet with no anger. He got to his feet.

'Very well. I will do all I can. But, as I have said before –'

'And as I have said before,' Kristian interposed smoothly, 'I intend the matter to go no further than yourself.'

The doctor spread one flipper as if to balance himself on the ice of Kristian's indifference.

'But Madame Sovaz is –'

'Is in need of your attention. You underestimate yourself, my dear doctor. You should have more faith in your own skill.'

So the doctor arrived once more at the threshold of the black bedroom, and thought, *I've been putting this off. What shall I see now?*

The black girl opened the door to him. Her expression was enigmatic. He glanced hurriedly about, and discovered Sovaz beside a half open window. She was seated in her silk wrap, her face bowed, intent as a child's, over a drawing. The memory of the other drawing he had seen accosted him – the leopard and the deer, with its obscurely dreadful label μαινάς. The grey autumn leaves of her press-cuttings, he noticed, had been removed, tidied or destroyed.

'Well,' said Dr Florentine, 'well, well.' And he went towards her briskly, as if stepping quickly under a cold shower.

She suffered his examination – this time more thorough and thus more complex – in a dreaming silence, a rapt inattentive submission not unlike her demeanour during the previous visit. Yet, as with Kristian, there was something altered, something not as it had been. Despite her appearance, her pulse was quite rapid. She seemed, but no longer was, apathetic. He recalled the extraordinary reaction that had come over her before in his presence, the look of waiting and anticipation, of frightened desire and longing which had so unnerved him.

The maid was clearing the drawing out of his way before he could examine it, as if instructed. He was not certain of this, but it added to his sense of unease. He found too in Sovaz evidence of some drug, possibly nembutal, probably adminis-tered to her last night as a sedative. This also somehow hinted at a form of coercion, of a jail. Kristian had mentioned no sedative to him.

Physically, she was sound enough, by some miracle. Only the

hidden region inside her skull seemed full of abrasions and plagues.

The driver of the car – what was he to her? A lover, surely, no less. And she said nothing, did not, when he probed with his awkward questions, respond at all. Yet she was no longer shocked as far as he could ascertain. Not even mildly so.

'I'm sorry to hear that your companion was killed. At least it would have been mercifully quick,' he eventually wildly said, attempting to unlock whatever strictures held back her emotions. But quite calmly, and with surprising cruelty, she answered, 'How is it possible to know? It may have seemed longer to him. Poor boy,' she added, but remotely, indifferently.

Packing his bag, the doctor found himself abruptly transported backwards in time. He recalled the old scholar, Sovaz' father, discovered smiling in the public surgery among the human wreckage, a small leather case of manuscripts tucked between his knees, and the sadly inadequate sentence (a sentence indeed in every sense), 'I am having some bother with a cough.' At first, suspecting cancer, Dr Florentine had treated him with a painful kindliness which shortly became nearly jovial when tuberculosis was instead diagnosed. For this a complete cure would almost certainly be possible, at the worst the progress of the illness could be arrested. Presently the doctor became aware that the scholar would not accept the cure. This was madness. The scholar shook his head.

'No, no, it's not feasible. I cannot give up the time. My work – do you know, only yesterday I received by post, from America, a request for a fresh translation of certain portions of Plato's *Republic* –'

'Either you will spare the time from your work now, in order to get well,' the doctor said, 'or you will have no time left to spare for anything. You must understand this. Now –'

'No, no,' the scholar said again. 'You see, I have many debts, yes, this is true, I am not ashamed. They are, shall I say, honourable debts. My work is more expensive than people suppose. And like you, I suspect, my dear Florentine, I don't always collect my fee. And there is my daughter, my Sovaz – how can she support herself while I am in some clinic? She's still such a child. That is my fault, I admit as much. I have made her as unworldly a being as myself . . . No, no, I must go on with my work for her sake, do you see? And I shall soon be better. I have not rubbed shoulders with these philosophers for nothing – the cure is in my hands, and in the impartial hands of the gods. I must show them I am worthy to be spared.'

There had flashed then across the doctor's mind, as suddenly as it did now, the remembered vignette of Sovaz as he had briefly glimpsed her at fourteen. Passing below on his way to assist at a birth, he had glanced up and seen a face like a cameo, set in the high twilit window of the scholar's house like a picture in a dark frame. There drifted down from behind the picture the scratchy recorded notes of a Khatchaturian piano concerto, which mingled eerily with the sullen pipes of snake charmers in a neighbouring street. Having met her earlier in company with her father, Dr Florentine raised his hand in greeting, for she seemed to be watching him. Yet even then her eyes were fixed inwards, she had not noticed, and he, feeling all the unaccountable foolishness of one who makes such a gesture in error to a stranger, passed on. The child, a male, which he delivered that night, was still-born. Malignant superstition had inextricably connected the dead baby with the girl hailed in the window. The doctor hated the roots of superstition in himself which refused to wither, just as he hated the superstitions of his patients which caused them to lay filthy and tetanus-conveying relics on their sores, and to practise contraception by means of a small scrap of cloth pasted over the navels of their women during intercourse. Nevertheless, now as then, he fell prey to the evil djinn. The boy baby died because the doctor had looked up at the girl's window; the girl's father died because he must keep her safe from the world. And yesterday a young man drove through a railing and down on to the broken rocks, and she was left beside the road unharmed –

No, all this was stupidity. He snapped shut his bag. He must speak to Kristian again, it was essential that she receive help of some kind other than his own. Perhaps a psychiatrist could unravel those areas of shadow in her skull. Certainly little Dr Florentine could not.

As he was going towards the door, he noted the black maid standing before the mirrors, Sovaz' drawing held defensively close, yet at such an angle that it was reflected in the glass behind.

Dr Florentine checked. He turned aside and held out his hand.

'Please. You will let me see that.'

73

A ripple of unmistakable fear went over the black girl's face. Dr Florentine saw at last it was the drawing itself she feared and therefore attempted to hide. She gave it up, however, immediately.

After a moment the doctor looked back at Sovaz. She had risen and was standing at the open window, her eyes staring blindly outwards.

'And what's this?' he asked her.

'Oh, that,' she said. And unexpectedly her head turned and she was looking straight at him, holding him in a clear and perfect focus as if in the sights of a gun. 'I am working on a painting taken from the *Bacchae*. Dionysos revenged himself on the king of Thebes, Pentheus, by sending him to spy on the maenads. I expect you recollect the story.'

'No. I don't remember,' the doctor said slowly.

'Why, the women found him and tore him to pieces. Because he had come between them and the god, do you see.'

Dr Florentine discovered that his hands were shaking. Like the black girl, he was experiencing a completely instinctive revulsion, though the picture itself, which showed the king in the grip of the shrieking women, was horrible enough. Setting the paper carefully down, he went out and stumbled along the gallery, clutching his bag like an amulet.

He had recognized again in her logical voice the cunning of the insane. And at the last moment her eyes had fastened on him so sharply. He realized now what had been wrong when he had spoken to Kristian in the study. For that antarctic and pitiless gaze had been today vacant and blurred over as the eyes of the woman had always been in the past, and suddenly were no longer.

The sun stood on its own fiery tail just above the purple water. The magnificence of its display was not quite lost on the Englishman. As he crossed the terraces of the garden, he paused to regard it, his hands in his pockets, yet not bothering to remove the tinted glass from his eyes that distorted all the colours.

As he watched, Prescott heard a woman's voice call his name from the avenue of lemons. He turned at once, and saw Sovaz in a long, white frock, the girl Leah waiting about three yards behind her. He walked towards them.

74

'Good evening, madame.'

She seemed unusually alert. The sun flamed on her face like the glow of a great fire, but her eyes, though narrowed, were intent.

'There is something I have been meaning to ask you,' she said.

He waited. He thought she would refer to the previous night, the blazing car on the rocks below, his own treatment of her, her inertia. She said: 'The last dinner party my husband gave at this house – do you recall?'

'Yes, Madame Sovaz. I think so.'

'Perhaps you were on the terrace outside the ballroom – at about nine o'clock?'

'Yes, madame. I was there until about nine. Then I went round to check the lawns, as I usually do.'

'On the terrace,' she said, 'did you notice a man? A tall slender man, very pale, handsome, with dark hair and eyes?' Her own eyes as she said this narrowed to slits.

'No, madame, I don't recollect seeing anyone like that.'

She drew in a breath.

'Please think,' she said. 'I am certain you must have seen him there.'

'Perhaps, if you could tell me who the man is.'

'I don't know his name. A guest at the reception, but not for dinner.'

Prescott looked at her implacably. The only man he had seen on the terrace had been the American boy, the golden boy now ash and charred bone. He had thought at first she had been going to speak of Adam Quentin.

'Possibly,' she said, 'he may have been with a woman – a woman with diamond earrings and garnet rings and a long evening scarf – a French woman.'

At once there rose from Prescott's adhesive mind the briefest of images – the dark garden, and the white flash of diamonds in a woman's ears catching the light from the open terrace windows, a scatter of words . . . *A là plage . . . je veux aller à la plage* –

'On second thoughts, madame, I passed a man and a woman as I was coming away from the terrace. The woman, if I remember, was dressed as you describe.'

'And this was all you saw?'

'Yes, madame.'

She smiled, but not at him. The conflagration in the sky still dyed her pale face like a blush of shame or delight.

'You think that she was a French woman?'

'Yes, madame. At least she was speaking French.'

'Good,' Sovaz said clearly, as if congratulating him. 'Thank you,' she said. She turned and moved back towards the house, and the black maid turned also and followed her.

Prescott drew from a crumpled pocket a crumpled pack of cigarettes and lit one. The peculiar conversation had stuck in his throat. They had not often spoken together, he and Kristian's wife, yet they shared a curious intimacy – the night years before when he had found her in the tenement on the quay, last night when he had found her lying at the edge of the road watching wide-eyed the burning thing below, its light reflected on her face as the sun had reflected on it here in the garden – these dialogues of darkness had tangled their lives together in a violent wilderness of actions.

The sun now threw itself beneath the ocean, symbol of death, of bright young lives snuffed out, and whom the gods loved, no doubt, died young indeed. And somewhere out there the ashes of the young American were blown by the sea currents in and out the fabulous caves, the mouths of fishes, and the scorched human bones drifted with the scorched bones of the car to the bottom, to lie among the bones of galleys, Roman legions swept away by naval wars, Greek merchantmen, Egyptian pirates, all turning to coral, suffering their sea-change, full fathom five, in a company unhindered by racial discrimination or the divisions of time.

At four AM Prescott, as a matter of routine, had come cruising by the beach house, driving from the direction of the town. As soon as the road dipped he saw the lights, and shortly he made out also that the door which gave on to the veranda was standing wide open, while a single lamp burned like a marker on the sands. Coming closer, he noted the absence of the white sports car from beside the villa.

Prescott parked his own vehicle and went down the beach and into the building. The first examination was slight, for he merely wished to ascertain the presence either of the boy or of Kristian's wife. Both were gone. The house had taken on necessarily a slightly Marie-Celeste quality, the open doors and burning lights, the lamp outside on the beach, and upstairs, the bed pulled open. Judging the direction the white sports had taken from the scuff of its treads on the verge, Prescott reversed his car and drove back towards the town, and consequently through it, travelling north.

He was taking the road at an average speed with already several of the huge drops behind him, when he became aware of a dull fluctuating colour, now orange, now blue, to the left, slightly ahead, and below. Coming round a bend, the headlamps broke over an upended cart and the diamanté glitter of glass; next a stretch of mashed and mutilated railing. He stopped the car at once, got out and, going to the railing, looked down.

The returning tide had already partially smothered the flames, although at intervals, between the inrush of surf, small oases of fire reasserted themselves.

No sense of shock or horror came over Prescott. The nacre of experience had long since hardened on his inner skin. Only disgust rose in his belly.

He had assumed that both of them had gone with the car on to the raw teeth of the sea. For Sovaz he felt only a mocking ghost of pity. It was the boy he visualized, the boy's broken limbs barbecued down there in that gape of spume and night. It came to him that he had been a little in love with the boy, or the idea of the boy, his youth. Not in love to any sexual or even sensual degree, for these titillations of the flesh had long since become a superfluity to Prescott's inartistic and sufficient body. It was what he himself had outgrown, or never possessed, attributes he had perhaps cynically observed, attributes now obliterated by gravity, fire, and flood, which now assumed an almost unbearable poignancy.

Then, half turning, Prescott caught sight of what he took in a moment of furtive incomprehension to be some extra merchandise from the fallen cart, a white shape lying just across the gap in the shattered railing.

But the fire leapt again below. Prescott saw the shape emerge on the light, the black foliage of hair, the glowing face made predatory by the movements of the flames. Sovaz.

The disgust in Prescott changed to a sort of loathing. The sensation had no basis in any kind of logic. Therefore he found himself unable to reason it away. He crossed to her and asked matter-of-factly, 'Are you hurt?'

Like a fish in a net, she flopped on to her back and stared up at him. She said something.

'What?'

He leaned closer. He realized she was speaking in Greek, one word over and over: 'βάκχη, βάκχη, βάκχη.'

He knelt down beside her and felt her over for broken bones. He had become conscious of the lucky solitude of the road and accepted the need to hurry. She seemed sound so he pulled her up. She gave a laugh then, a mindless yet lilting laugh.

'Shut up, you bloody bitch,' Prescott told her, and dragged her to the car and pushed her into the back where she fell down as limply as a swathe of white silk. But he did not trust her, for as she was she might be capable of anything. He went round to the boot of the car and presently returned with a coffee flask. He offered her a capsule – she only turned her head away. He took hold of her and forced the capsule brutally into her mouth and followed it with the coffee. She responded to this treatment with total obedience. The swallowed capsule did its work rapidly. Soon she slept.

Prescott returned in the car to the beach house, and parked a little way down on the track. This time he laboured methodically, tidying the house, packing the clothes of Kristian's wife, and separately those things of the boy, even making the bed, rinsing and stacking away the cutlery and china they had used, removing all trace of their presence. There would, naturally, be other forms of tidying to be done, by means of telephone and chequebook, once he had contacted Kristian.

As a matter of course, Prescott checked that nothing had been stolen from the villa while it stood empty, glancing especially into the unlocked travelling jewel case. The most precious items, the rubies, emeralds, sapphires and diamonds, that marked, like inexorable sparkling milestones, the seven birthdays that Sovaz had experienced as Kristian's wife, these had been omitted by Leah, as always on similar occasions of Sovaz' absence with a man. Only a scatter of little silver and gold ornaments remained, and one long string of pearls, a gift of her scholar father. Beneath the pearls was lying a closely folded square of newsprint. Prescott took it up and opened it carefully, in the line of his inquiry. A fragment of white paper fell out into his hand. It bore some Latin scrawl to which he paid no attention. Neither did he spare more than a glance for the piece of newsprint. That she should keep among her jewels the description of a murder was unsurprising to him. The memory of her sick, half-mad, merciless face had hinted at all manner of extremes. He replaced the cutting and the scrap of Latin, and shut the case.

Shortly, the villa put to rights, Prescott turned off the electricity and closed the door. He carried the bags to his car and, getting in, drove north while the dawn swept unsparing light over the land.

Standing smoking, he became aware that the two women, one all white, one all black, were poised like a couple of gulls high above him on the upper terrace.

Prescott looked back. The maid, of course, had halted because Sovaz had done so. Sovaz herself was gazing out towards the far edge of the shore where the sand ran after the retreating tide. Prescott, turning again, followed the direction of her eyes.

The short half-light had begun, dissolving contours, the darkening water ebbing before it. What was the woman searching for down there in the dusk?

Suddenly Prescott made out the figure of a man standing quite still on the glistening abandoned ridges of the sand. Seen from this height in this uncertain afterglow, it was impossible to tell anything of much significance about the figure. Only its complete immobility was apparent, an immobility that somehow conveyed a sense of waiting.

A man waiting for his girl perhaps – the beach was mostly very private. (*Je veux aller à la plage.*) The French woman had wanted to go to the beach. Prescott glimpsed again the diamond flash of her earlobes, her arm linked with that of a masculine companion. He had not paid much attention to them, just two shadows, that brilliance of a jewel, the words –

A circuit in Prescott's brain engaged.

The diamonds, the beach, the garnets, the French woman, the oblong of newsprint between his fingers unintentionally photographed by his retentive brain: *Madame Gallier, the twenty-nine year old wife . . . French consulate for three months . . . sadistic and apparently motiveless killing . . . diamond earrings and three garnet rings were found intact on the ears and fingers of the dead woman . . . police discovered Madame Gallier's body on the beach at dawn . . .*

The woman Sovaz had described to him, the woman he had glimpsed in the garden, had been the Gallier woman, arm in arm with a man. *Je veux aller à la plage.* If it had been her murderer with whom she had been walking, then he had taken her to the beach as she wished, and there he had cut her throat.

And what did Sovaz know about him? Why did she question Prescott?

Prescott sifted facts automatically. If Madame Gallier had been invited to the reception, some police inquiry at the house would have been inevitable; those hours had been her last. There had been no police. Thus it was the man, the unknown murderer, who was the invited guest, bringing with him, as so many reception guests were apt to do, the one permitted companion. This time the precious cold adornments of Kristian's house had been bait to snare the killer's victim. He had shown her – pathetic little social climber, wife of a nobody at the consulate, sporting her tiny gems – the rich man's house. Then on the shore, the knife's edge.

Did Sovaz understand this? Her description of the man, unlike her prosaic description of Madame Gallier, was self-consciously romantic. And in her jewel case she carried the details of his crime, like love letters or pressed flowers. Once more he saw the drained hunger of her face, the brimming hunger of her eyes, lit by the fire (the sun, the burning car) beneath. Yes. She would understand everything.

The Englishman turned again sharply, but the white gull and the black had vanished into the house. Crushing his cigarette underfoot, he noticed that the occult figure had now also vanished from the darkening beach below.

Tonight, there were white roses on the long table, selected, as were all other flowers ever impaled on the cruel metal quills within the porphyry bowls, for their lack of odour. It had been a habit of his mother's, which Kristian had observed throughout his life, not to mingle the scents of a garden with those of a dining table. Yet the eternal smell of the jasmine still drifted in the room.

Kristian seated himself at the table's head. Directly opposite him but some twenty yards distant, a place had been laid, as always, for his wife. This was the place which, during Kristian's dinner parties, she would occupy in her elegant black or white frocks of guipure lace, handpainted silk, or gauffered Egyptian linen, with flashing lanterns of faceted carbon or corundum at her wrists or throat or ears. For six years, apart from the occasions of the dinners and although her place was invariably laid, Sovaz had eaten no meal in this room. She and Kristian had never discussed the matter, for, having long since exhausted the topic of the disease, its symptoms were of little interest to either of them.

It was half past nine. The servants were already busy with the wines, and hovering like silent wasps about the silver. The doors opened suddenly.

An instant of total pause overcame the room. Even the precise hovering of the wasps was momentarily checked. The cessation of the slight breeze created by their movements caused even the tulip-headed flames of the candles to straighten.

Sovaz came through the room. She walked easily yet decisively. A wasp hurried to her chair, drew it out for her. Kristian came slowly, belatedly, to his feet. She sat. He sat.

She wore a white dress, but not the rubies – somehow he had expected her to wear the rubies – only emerald ear pendants and a great cameo ring.

He was unnerved, agitated by her presence. She appeared calm, yet very certain. It seemed to him he had never before encountered her in this mood. He was confronted by a stranger. After what had happened to her, after the outpourings of the little slum doctor, he had expected everything of her but this. His aesthetic dread was replaced merely by a new and more specific one. He did not trust her. Only the refuge which the presence of his servants afforded him steadied his hand on the glass.

'Good evening, Sovaz,' he said presently. 'This is an unusual pleasure.'

'Isn't it?' she said. 'But I thought tomorrow it might be more interesting to dine in the city. What do you think?'

'Whatever you like, of course,' he found himself saying.

'I mean with you,' she said, 'or do you have a previous engagement?'

He set down his glass. She had grown rather thin, a curious El Greco elongation was apparent in the lines of her. It seemed wise to be careful of her mood, although he had never troubled before.

'No,' he said, 'I think that should be possible.'

Her eyes were brilliantly fixed on him.

'I shall look forward to it, Kristian. Will you mind if I buy a new frock?'

Aside from these few sentences, they ate in silence.

The Englishman had telephoned about an hour after dawn. His explanation had been succinct, everything became clear at once, yet not quite everything, for it had seemed at first, as it had seemed to Prescott himself, that both the American and Sovaz were dead.

Immediately the vision of the car had shot into Kristian's mind, the spinning tyres, the shattering burst of the railing, the vehicle poised above the brink, the descent, the vast explosion of sound and light and flame on the darkness. In those seconds he had seen Sovaz at the wheel of the car, her hands in her lap, smiling her arrogant greeting to death, shortly cremated like the warrior, her consort, willing or unwilling, consumed at her side. Next moment, Prescott's voice, travelling along the wires, was speaking of the unconscious drugged woman lying in his car. The American of course had been driving, Sovaz had somehow fallen to safety. Sovaz could not, in any case, drive. Her passage to oblivion had lain in the mouth of a little bottle.

Kristian had avoided seeing her on her return. He had left instructions with Prescott, Leah, and finally with Florentine. With everybody. And now, his first sight of her, this metamorphosis, suggesting to him what they should do together with their social hours, precisely as he had seen his mother do with his father over half his lifetime before. An unreal death. A resurrection.

As she toyed with her sorbet, Kristian rose and went out and up to the library, where soon after the Englishman came to find him, and was told, through the medium of Kristian's valet, that whatever his business was it must wait until the following evening. Impartial, Prescott went away.

The limousine passed, like a black leopard on wheels, with a soft predacious purring, through the terracotta afternoon of the city, pausing here and there to make its kill (the bloody corpse of a dress carried away to be devoured) or to lap gasoline into its vitals.

From the body of the leopard, like a dark intention, at intervals, issued the black girl. She moved with a stately and imperious rhythm. Wardress and maid, she betrayed nowhere her unease – except in her eyes, held wide open. The first errand was the most diabolic, the argument with the jeweller, settled when he came out to the car.

In a salon fanned by the electric zephyrs of the wind machines in the walls, Sovaz submitted her body to highly paid slaves. Each had a mask-face of white enamel with red lips and, as they bent over the gold or black or green-white flesh of the women in the cubicles, these masks cracked into charming smiles spiked with the teeth of lynxes. Sovaz said nothing to these maenads, but the symbol was not lost on her. She was at peace beneath the deft hands of the hairdresser, the manicurist, the cosmetician with her box of paints.

Sovaz emerged into the dusk, her face, between the black grape clusters of her curled hair, now also enamel, kohl and flame, the tips of her white hands hennaed. She herself went this time into the jeweller's shop.

'Is it ready?'

'Yes, madame. I've followed your instructions, though I was grieved to do such a thing.'

'Your grief is unimportant to me. Please let me see.'

The jeweller produced for her a damask tray.

She probed among the gems to be sure he had done, after all, as she had told him. The great rubies, each now severed from each, fell individually between her fingers.

'Excellent,' she said.

'I'm glad you think so, madame. To destroy such a necklace was –'

Sovaz took up in her white and scarlet hand the central pendant of the dismembered mesh, and held it out to him.

'Take this to console you.'

'Madame, how can I . . . ? You're joking with me.'

'Don't be foolish. If you like I will make out a statement to the effect that it is a gift.'

'No, madame.' The jeweller's eyes flicked rapidly about the shop as if seeking help from his cases.

'Very well. If you prefer.'

She slipped the jewels carelessly into her purse, but, going out, let fall the pendant on the road, where it lay like a highly coloured sweet dropped by some child.

In the black bedroom the dress was taken from its wrappings. Sovaz stepped into it. In the mirrors she watched as Leah drew the zipper like a thin silver snake up her spine then stood back, waiting with dilated eyes at the foot of the bed. Posed like this, the black girl reminded Sovaz for an instant of the painting by Gauguin entitled *The Spirit of the Dead Watches*, which, as a child, had exerted over her an influence of fascination and terror.

The clock spoke in its delicate castrato.

It was nine in the evening. Sovaz took up the new scent she had chosen at the salon, and applied it to her skin. She poured the contents of her purse into the little evening bag. The severed rubies collided like smashed glass. She stood before the mirrors and placed the long chain of pearls around her neck, touching their round white bodies with her fingers.

'There's no need for you to wait up for me,' she said to the black girl. 'Go to bed, or go out. Whichever you wish.'

She moved to the window, and here also, though dimly, was reflected a drowned and darkly glowing image of herself. Now she could hear the sea fall distantly against the shore below, and cheated, hissing, slide away. She could smell the faint drifts of the jasmine, rising like smoke. Tonight, all things had a curious, marvellous savour, all these ephemeral things, for this was the last night of the world. She pressed her hand against the inky glass. Yes – yes – tonight – A surge of almost intolerable excitement rose in her throat.

In the pane she saw her own elliptoid face, the black holes of eyes, the scarlet mouth.

Sovaz stood at the window, telling the chain of pearls like a rosary, listening to the sounds that her husband made, putting on his clothes in the dressing room. Such immaculate, precise sounds; now the rustle of the linen shirt, now the icy clink of the cuff-link lifted from its onyx box. Presently he came into the room.

'You're dressed already.'

'Yes. I've been listening to you next door. It was amusing.'

She glanced at him. He looked, she saw (saw clearly in the bright dissection which infused her vision), tired and strained. His face was pale. He had not used the sun-lamp today probably. As if she had been half blind for years and suddenly put on spectacles, she observed, with a kind of delirious surprise, the lines of age which had gathered in his face, the cobwebs at the corners of the eyes which themselves seemed sunken. She stared at the elegant lean line of him beneath the beautiful dinner clothes – she had not seen his body for five years: what had happened to it? An old man had come into her room. Exultantly she smiled at him.

'Do you know, Kristian, I find you, at this moment, perfectly ridiculous.'

She measured delightedly how he controlled any reaction he might have felt at her words. To seem ridiculous was perhaps the worst fate for such a man. Rather burn in fire. She laughed.

'You have changed your mind then,' he said.

'Changed my mind?'

'You prefer to remain here tonight.'

'No,' she said. 'Much as you would like to, no.' She went towards the door. 'Let's go down.'

He stood quite still a moment, his eyes fixed on her.

'Is that the dress you bought this afternoon?'

'Yes.'

'It's the first time I have ever seen you wear red.'

She wanted to dance along the gallery, every sedate step she took tried to contort her mouth into fresh excited laughter. *Slow steps now, slow careful steps, or you will leave the rich old man behind with his wallet.* She felt free as fire in her red frock, she felt like a whore who loved her work and flaunted herself at the night, neoned in diamonds: HERE I AM. This man, this old man with his finicky ways, had been her lord, her master for seven years. Well, now her master was exchanged for a god of night, a prince of darkness, a destiny. She could therefore no longer bow herself like grass before the man. These desires which had possessed her always, the ultimate need of submission, slavishness, which her nature carried, those aching, agonized and wondrous chains which had held her at Kristian's feet in misery, had now accepted the ultimate soil which occasionally finds out the ultimate seeds.

The Devourer would have her. To him she gave homage. Kristian had become necessarily superfluous, his dominance, beside the other, absurd. She took vengeance on the dethroned monarch.

Kristian also was witnessing the change. He could hardly avoid it. The blood-red colour of her dress, the ornate styling of her hair – these alone were unique. Even the perfume radiating from her flesh was different, as if her chemistry were altered. Her manner startled. She was liable to do some monstrous thing – he had been vaguely aware all day that he was dreading this dinner alone with her.

Having some business to attend to in the city, he had found himself, at its conclusion, within walking distance of the great library. A compunction drew him towards it. The scabrous bronze daevas that dwelt in the foyer glared from their protuberant eyes. The dusts, the shafts of dusty light were unaltered. He did not comprehend what had taken him there until, crossing between the brooding wooden stacks, he had come to a window seat dappled over by the jade and ruby glass of the pane behind. A girl was sitting here, about seventeen or eighteen years old, a slender girl bent to a book, her black hair down her back. The vision was so perfectly reproduced, so uncanny, that he froze before it. The girl, sensing his presence, glanced up and, liking the look of him, flushed slightly and smiled. A compulsion to run away gripped Kristian as he stood there. The smiling girl he barely noticed, for it was the other, earlier girl he was seeing, who had looked up into his face coldly, vacantly at first, a welling of concentration gradually gathering in her eyes. He had made a journey through time.

Presently, outside in the caustic heat of the afternoon, he sat on a marble bench where sometimes the octogenarian intellectuals of the library came to sit. Perhaps the old man, the librarian and scholar, her father, had sat here too, hugging to him his case of translations and his deadly little cough.

SEVEN

The restaurant, though impeccable, was one Kristian had never before visited. Somehow it had seemed essential to take her to

86

some place where, even should he be recognized, which was quite probable, he would not be known as a regular patron, so that no dossier of evidence would wait on him, no knowledge of his likes and dislikes, of previous solitary dinners or dinners with certain women not Sovaz. More important, that there should be no expectation that he would return thereafter. He had robed himself in an aura of incognito, actually mostly ineffectual, so that whatever might occur, he could absent himself from the scene of the crime.

Their table was discreet, another precaution. But Sovaz was faultlessly decorous in her scarlet dress, yet somehow always smiling, almost laughing.

The meal progressed. She ordered dishes different from his own, as if on purpose. Also, pointedly, the most expensive dishes, which she then played with as a well fed domestic cat will play with a mouse it has caught.

Once, about eighteen years before, he had begun a liaison with an impoverished actress, because she was beautiful and seemed to possess that quality of soullessness which, for some reason he had never troubled to question, attracted him. She, on a visit such as this to some expensive eating house, had done exactly as Sovaz did now, asking for gold bars to be put on her plate, to show her independence, that she was *using* the rich man. A pathetic charade; she was already in love with him and shortly lost his interest. In the case of Sovaz, however, Kristian was aware of a difference.

Presently she asked for champagne.

This seemed to him, more than all the rest, offensive, bourgeois, indiscriminate. He told her, dispassionately, what she should drink instead. She had always obeyed him. This time she laughed exuberantly, as if at some delicious joke, and, calling back the waiter, ordered for herself.

As the man went away, Sovaz opened her evening bag and took something out which she laid on the table.

'Look,' she said, smiling.

Kristian sensed unerringly that the moment had come. It was an effort to control his alarm.

'What is that?'

'A ruby. Part of a necklace you gave me.' She opened the mouth of her bag farther and let him see the contents. 'I took it to a jeweller today to have it broken up into individual stones. At first he wouldn't. Then he couldn't. But I persuaded him. I expect you will get the bill tomorrow. Tomorrow,' she added, and her eyes clouded over sightlessly, but not for long. 'What do you say?'

'Am I supposed to say something?'

'You are supposed to say: "I am gravely disappointed in you for making so infantile and melodramatic a gesture." '

He wondered if she could see the sudden tremor in his hands.

The waiter returned. For a few moments they discussed the wine. When this was settled, Sovaz took up the jewel and placed it within the waiter's reach.

'For you,' she said, 'a ruby. For bringing me my champagne.'

The man was uncertain. He glanced at Kristian.

'Yes. Take it,' Kristian said, feeling it imperative that he speak.

'But, monsieur, if it is a –'

'Thank you,' Kristian said. 'We require nothing further for now.'

The waiter, nervous, suspicious, picked up the red drop from the cloth, turned and made off. Meeting another of his tribe, he stopped him. Soon heads swivelled like clockwork.

Sovaz smiled again, and drank from her fizzing glass.

'Do you want to leave, Kristian?' she murmured. 'I'm not ready to leave. I shall scream at you at the top of my voice if you suggest it. Or do you believe I wouldn't? Try me.'

He found himself confronted suddenly by his mother, his terrible mother who so far he had always managed to escape by the original means of demanding that her attributes be expressed by those unable to do so. Her smooth steel, her frigid fire, her elegant destructiveness, her cruel, charming, remote dominance which had held his father impaled on a female phallus of self-sufficiency. The woman who had actually driven her husband down to his death with her, not from a sense of need or histrionics, but simply because she found him so unimportant that she could not be bothered to thrust him out of the car.

'We will leave when you are ready,' Kristian therefore said to Sovaz. He felt dizzy, almost unwell. He knew the horror of a man in a gas-filled room who fears he will faint before he can break down the door.

But, meeting no opposition, she was prepared to leave after all.

She abandoned a further ruby on the table, dropped one with the skill of a perverse pick-pocket into the dinner jacket of a man going by in the foyer, let one fall on the pavement outside. Kristian was paralysed. He did not dare to remonstrate. This was what she had reduced him to – he did not *dare*.

Paul handed them into the limousine.

They drove slowly across the city. It was almost midnight, but traffic was still heavy. The icon face of Sovaz flashed on and off like a neon in the headlamps of passing cars.

Sovaz opened the window and cast out at the sides of the road a trail of rubies. She did it in a neat calculated manner. The exercise finished, she turned to him.

'Poor Kristian,' she said, with practically genuine sympathy. 'After tonight I shall be very docile. You will have no further worries about me.'

He had no notion what to say. The rest of the journey was made in silence.

As they went up through the gardens towards the house, she paused at each landing to touch, almost experimentally, the chess piece marbles. They reached the wide doors and went in. Her face had taken on, most unexpectedly, a gentle yielding look.

'I am going up now,' she said quietly. 'I may take a walk in the garden later, then I shall go to bed. Good night.'

She started to mount the stairs, then halted and looked back at him. Her eyes went over him, head to foot, next over the things surrounding him, the inanimates of the hall. A puzzled frown appeared between her eyes, then smoothed itself away. She turned and walked on up the stairway, the red dress pulsing on the shadow above long after the gleam of her hair and flesh had been extinguished.

Kristian moved heavily towards his study. He felt the need to be among his own things, the mementos of the great estate. Yet, as he crossed the tessellated floor, he saw Prescott politely awaiting him before the double doors.

At each step she thought, *I shall never do this again or I shall only do it one time more.*

And in the gallery she thought, *How insignificant all this is, the house, the ornaments of the house.* And yet they were beautiful too, ephemeral, bathed in the fascinated glare of terminus.

Reaching her room, having shut both doors which led into it, she unzipped the red dress and took the string of pearls from her neck, and put them both away. The girl, as she had instructed her, was gone, yet everything lay to hand. Sovaz bathed once again, scented herself, and sat before her mirrors, her combs and paints laid out before her.

She was now completely calm, yet there was so much time to waste: three hours at least before the house was safe and Kristian either absent or shut in the library.

A sort of nostalgia was coming over her, as if she were about to go travelling far away.

She did not anticipate death. As on the shore road she visualized neither the stroke nor its consequences. Certainly she did not see as far as extinction, the end of life. She foresaw – and this only with her body – the ecstasy of utter submission. And since it was to a god that she was offering herself – will-less, welcoming – she herself seemed strangely deified. As the sacrifices of pagan festivals walked with dignity and joy towards their destiny, so she walked now in her instinct, and the people showered her with flowers and begged for her holy blessing as she passed.

The rubies, scattered about the city, were a sort of symbol of this blessing. But also they were a message, a signal to the god. It did not really matter where she laid them; being ubiquitous, he could look down from the stars, out of the eyes of a cripple, or a banker, or a maître d'hôtel, and see at once what she had done, what she was saying to him. Since the first, she had vaguely understood he had been holding back only for this, her free surrender. *Nos cedamus Amori.*

As she stared pensively into the glass, picturing the mask of her own face which represented the Dionysos mask of the god, she recognized the great power the god had vested in her. Had she not destroyed the young boy, the American, in her fury at his intrusion, the coitus interruptus of her vision on the road? Yes. *She* had caused the car to swerve, to plunge. Like Agave, she had torn her Pentheus to shreds when he threatened the rite of love. Never had she felt such power in herself, such assurance, coupled so strongly with the knowledge of yielding and abnegation.

The little clock struck one, then two. The sea also struck its hours on the beach below. She retouched her lips and eyes meticulously, and examined her hands to which the effects of the manicure still adhered. At last she took from the closet the black lace frock, now faultlessly cleaned and repaired, and put it on. A communion, uncommon to her, had sprung up between her fingers and her flesh.

She was like a very young girl discovering her body for the first time, adoring it, striving to please it, this temple of her emotion, which because it was lovely, desirable, was also magic.

Presently she opened the windows wide.

He would see the light, the one who waited for her, as she for him, on the shore.

Warm night winds like the wings of birds filled the room, lifting her hair, disturbing the sheaf of drawings stacked neatly by the gramophone. She crossed to the bronze bowl in which she had burned joss sticks, an activity she recalled with wistful tolerance, the amusements of a child, and took up a box of matches. She struck a match and, selecting a drawing, she crumpled it and fed it to the flame, letting the paper fall into the bowl to burn and adding fresh ones instantly. Soon, gorged with its meal and made adventurous by the wind, the little fire shot up like the watchlight of an altar.

Perhaps he could see that too.

Fantastically aware of all her movements and her acts, Sovaz became for herself a sorceress who had created fire.

Not once did she look at the drawings to see what they might represent. It no longer mattered, for the internal theatre, like Kristian, was now superfluous. She had become at last her own canvas.

Prescott observed Kristian as he stood beside the case of guns, with the impartial evaluating composure so easily construed by others as good-mannered obedience. It was, after all, a part of Prescott's job to present himself in the guise of an intelligent dog, the kind that will carry things in its mouth and shake hands. Nevertheless, left to harden now for so long in this mould, he had actually lost interest in the ruthless vivisections of humanity which he still automatically carried out. The sort of scorn that Kristian and men of his class and type inspired in him in no way influenced Prescott's attitude or work. He waited patiently therefore for Kristian to digest what he had told him of Sovaz, as he had once waited seven years before.

Finally Kristian spoke to him.

'You say the man has been to this house?'

'Yes. I have the guest list with me, the list from the last reception and dinner. I've been making inquiries, and I think I have located him.' He held out the list, and indicated the spot so Kristian could see it.

'I don't recollect the name,' Kristian said.

'An invitation at the request of someone more important, perhaps,' Prescott suggested.

'Perhaps.' Kristian seemed preoccupied. 'You assume my wife is in danger.'

'Inevitably, if this man is the murderer, and I have good reason to think he is. Madame Sovaz has extended her friendship to him, clearly without realizing what he will be bound to do to her. He is a compulsive killer. Given the opportunity, he will not be able to resist cutting your wife's throat. Precisely as he did the throat of Madame Gallier, and possibly the throats of other women in the city.'

Kristian took from a jade box a cigarette, and lit it with the concentration of a man unaware of his surroundings. 'Why do you imagine he will come here tonight?'

'I've been talking to Leah. Madame Sovaz has been making certain preparations. As far as I can see, she will go down sometime tonight and open the small gate that gives on to the beach. That is the way he will gain admission, then up through the gardens, into the house about three o'clock or half past. The servants are either in bed or out at that time. She will reckon on your being in the library.'

Kristian sat slowly down. His eyes were blank. Surely, Prescott surmised, he also guessed the nature of Sovaz' interest. Prescott had spoken at some length with the black girl and with the chauffeur, Paul. He had built up a bizarre picture of Sovaz' behaviour over the period of time following the night of the murder. The press cutting, the drawings, the rubies, her apathy, her sudden decisiveness, her conversations with the doctor . . . all the paraphernalia of some unbalanced infatuation. This was what the American boy had become part of, her madness. Almost certainly what had killed him. Prescott felt no compunction to save the woman – it was merely part of his job to do so. As with Kristian, his personal feelings would not intrude.

'You have not contacted the police,' Kristian said.

'Naturally I informed you of the matter first.'

'Good.' Kristian rose and crossed to the case of guns. 'These pistols are in perfect working order. I shot with them only a few days ago.'

A glimmer of amusement lit deep down in Prescott's brain. The feudal aristocrat, absolute law on his own land. Kristian, bemused by his wife's madness, took refuge in his own past. Quite clearly, with these exquisite and perfectly kept weapons, they were about to gun the murderer down, the police business to be delicately settled afterwards, for those legendary strings-which-might-be-pulled were always available to the city rich. In some alley tomorrow night, a whore would perhaps stumble over the corpse of a man, or in a week some fishing boat would bring up a green and bloated fish from the bay.

Kristian, as he took out the pistols, examined and presently loaded them, felt a soothing sense of purpose come over him. He had handled these guns, or their fellows, so often. The reassuring psychometry of well known possessions. There was no need after all to analyse, to enter the cloud of confusion that had swept through his brain. He had become aware, though only in the farthest pit of his consciousness, behind all the thousand veils with which human beings conceal their own impulses from themselves, of the true possibility of Sovaz' death. He feared her, he hated her, he despised and shuddered at her monstrous attachment to his life, yet he was magnetized, he had known as much from the first moment of seeing her. She was *his* devil. The eternal presence which he must dominate and have no interest in, in order to achieve his sense of self, which in turn burdened him with its indispensability. And, like all addicts, he scented destruction with hungry terror. She must not die. Yet if she should . . . Not the independence of suicide. The helpless victim of a murder which he himself could permit.

It was half past two. He went with Prescott silently and in darkness down the stairs, across the ghostly ballroom, through the windows (open), and so on to the terrace of the house. Turning aside into the shadow of the jasmine, they saw her coming up the avenue of lemons towards them in her black lace frock.

She was touching the flowers as she came, lightly. She looked very young, very knowing, wary as an animal picking its way towards the house. She had a rose in her hair, a red rose. There was something horrible, obscene about her, like the stench on the breath of the beautiful vampire, unlooked-for poison. Both men felt it yet would not feel it; for their different reasons rejection of the gothic and the primeval was instantaneous. She slid in through the double windows.

'She's been to the gate,' Prescott said softly after a minute had gone by. 'This is the way he'll come.'

So they waited, ready to ambush death with their silver pistols.

The wind was not blowing from the city tonight with its freight of car horns, trains, music. There was only the flash and murmur of the tide. Prescott noticed that Kristian had put on gloves, as he had done on entering the slums seven years ago.

Then a step fell, like the drip of a tap – huge in the silence between the phrases of the sea.

Prescott glanced at the luminous dial of his watch. Five minutes to three. A shadow appeared through the lemon trees, following the path she had taken. What signal had been given him? Perhaps her lighted windows – lights now out – or some signal to him as he stood on the beach. Or probably he had come before and tried the ornamental gate, finding it always locked, tonight ajar.

The shadow moved, not with particular stealth or grace, rather clumsily in fact. The shade of the garden made identification impossible. Prescott had earlier suggested activating one of the master switches of the ballroom which lay beside the windows, flooding the area outside with light, and so apprehending the intruder by means of surprise. Kristian had ignored the suggestion, determined, Prescott supposed, to shoot the man.

Now the visitor, skirting the oleanders, began to climb the steps. He was ungainly, the foliage rustled. Prescott was reminded of a rat scuttling over a wharf among old paper and rinds. He anticipated some cue from Kristian; nothing came. The man entered abruptly into the black of the house. Kristian also was invisible and unmoving. Prescott had neither premonition nor suspicion. He only saw the chance of the man's escape, the work botched – he moved from concealment, disengaging the safety catch of the pistol as he did so.

A voice, out of the shadow ahead, the murderer's, high-pitched, anguished. A crack like the snapping of a bone followed, the safety catch of Kristian's gun. Prescott saw the perfect tailor-made stance of the professional shot, outlined only by starlight, as Kristian fired directly into the unseen area ahead that was a man.

Sovaz lay across the bed in the black night-silence. Every line of her was quiescent, only the pulse in her throat, a drum under her skin. The Sleeping Beauty in the Dark Tower. Lying, as if spent, still the sum of her was gathered, she was immensely aware of the huge inky womb in which she floated, of the approach of waking, the savage kiss.

Now he was in the ebony garden among the skulls of flowers, now perhaps in the shimmering ballroom. A pale electric current ran in her veins. Each step she had taken, he now took, noiseless, drifting like unheard music towards her through the dumb pyramid of the house. Now on the marble stairway, between the icicles of the candelabra. He came to her so slowly. An unbearable excitement murmured in her which only the touch of him on her in the black unseen could satisfy. She did not need to see him, knew him, could superimpose his image on the blindness of the room, white, gold, black, scarlet. The god.

Suddenly there was a crack of enormous sound. It pierced her stillness, raped her silence. She started up on the bed, staring sightlessly about. Having dismissed civilization and its concepts she could no more remember how to draw the drapes from the windows, turn on the light, than she could recall such things existed in the elemental world to which she had given herself up. So she crouched on the bed in the attitude of a cat or an ape confronted by the inexplicable sorcery of mankind. Shaken from her dream she was not, even so, awakened.

Some time passed. She did not register time as such. All at once she heard a footfall in the gallery outside.

Now she felt fear, extreme fear, ecstatic. She flung herself down in an attitude of abandonment, trembling and writhing, her mouth parted, her teeth set, her eyes shut.

A hand fumbled at the door. She uttered a little whimpering plea and spread her arms wide. The door opened.

She felt his presence in the room with her. A great wave, a sea

wave gushed through her. She stretched herself, arching her
body. Suspense, stasis.

'Sovaz,' a voice said.

She could not answer. Only the anguished entreaty of her
straining flesh responded.

'Sovaz,' the voice said, more insistently, 'the man was very
dangerous. I don't think you can have realized. We discovered
who he was and waited for him downstairs.'

She twisted, struggled against some invisible restraint. Her
eyes opened. She knew the voice, the man. She gave a sort of
hoarse inarticulate grunting sound.

The gallery outside was pitch dark, no light had come into the
room. She could not see. As he came nearer she could only smell
the odour of smoke from the pistol.

'I am afraid I had no choice but to shoot him,' Kristian said.

Neither could Kristian see her very well. He stood in the room
tiredly. The hidden urge in him had never reached fruition, he did
not know it. He had not switched on the lights.

Sovaz sprang from the bed across the floor to her husband. She
gave a series of screams that were heard throughout the house, as
not even the pistol shot had been. She hurled herself against him,
gripping him with legs, feet, teeth and one arm, in an embrace
like love, and, snatching with her right hand at the pistol he had
retained in his gloved fingers, she thrust the muzzle against his
chest and pulled the trigger.

The second bullet was ejected in a shattering spasm and
muffled roar of noise. He made no sound, but jerked like a
marionette between her limbs. A convulsion went over her that
seemed to uproot her heart, her lungs and her brain from her
flesh.

She slid down him, and as she let him go, he also fell.

She was kneeling on the floor above Kristian's dead body, her
hands and the front of her dress sticky with blood, the pistol in
her lap, when the Englishman ran up the stairs, along the gallery
and into the room.

Hearing the cries, the unexpected second shot, Prescott ran
upstairs and, reaching the bedroom, immediately depressed the
master switch of the electric light.

He saw at once that Kristian was dead. Sovaz seemed to be

dying, rocking limply in her bleeding gown. Then she raised her head and looked at him.

Her face was white, but her wide eyes were completely intelligent, rational. Despite the unnerving scene, she was in full possession of herself. It seemed to him he had never seen her so before.

'I thought,' she said quietly, 'that Kristian was the killer, coming for me. It was dark, I couldn't see. I was terrified. I somehow got hold of the gun and fired it into him.'

'The man used a knife, always,' Prescott said.

The murderer, impregnated by Kristian's bullet, huddled on the floor of the ballroom. A small body, its spine curved like a clerk's, and with receding hair, totally nondescript save for the stiletto in the pocket, so unlikely, yet highly polished for his victim, as a man might polish his shoes before visiting his mistress. He was not as Sovaz had described him. Even in the dark, it would be hard to mistake Kristian for such a creature.

'Prescott,' Sovaz said casually, 'I suggest that I confided in you a fear that the murderer might have armed himself with a gun in addition to the knife, and that this is why my husband fired on him so arbitrarily in the garden. I suggest that, hearing Kristian's shot, I was in terror that my husband and not the killer had been harmed. I suggest that, hysterical with panic and seeing a shadowy figure enter my room, I attacked it wildly, with such tragic consequence. Your supporting statement will be useful but is merely a formality. As you know, the police can be perfectly accommodating, particularly since my husband's money will devolve on me. I can pay to retain my good name. I shall also, in future, be paying your wages, your deservedly high wages. Unless, of course, there is some mistake about this dreadful business in which case no one will be able to pay you.'

She stood up now, imposing, in her dress of lace and blood. Prescott, seeing only the transformation, the result, could have no inkling of the vast cataclysm which had brought it about. She had been Agave, she had torn Pentheus and, in a metaphysical completion of the Dionysiac rite, she had devoured him. Prescott felt all the ancient erosion of his cowardice. It disguised itself as flights of fancy that women, particularly Sovaz, had always sparked off in him. And cowardice nodded his head to her, puppet-fashion. In fact he bowed it.

'Yes, madame. That makes sense.'

'Very good,' she said.

Downstairs he could hear the muted hubbub of the emergent servants, the flat voice of Paul taking charge, while somewhere out to sea, the requiem of a lost ship added its note to the night.

Sovaz glanced aside at the curtained window, as if the noise of the ship held some significance for her. Her face was arrogant, remote to a point almost of unworldliness, yet entirely sane. Her eyes seemed extraordinarily intent by contrast with the eyes of Kristian, glazed and unfocused bits of lapis lazuli in his death-mask on the floor.

As he looked at her in that split second, it seemed to Prescott that she, like the rakshas of Indian mythology, had acquired the ability to take on another form.

Kristian's.

THE STORIES

The Mermaid
After the Guillotine
Meow
Il Bacio (Il Chiave)
A Room with a Vie
Paper Boat
Blue Vase of Ghosts
Pinewood
The Janfia Tree
The Devil's Rose
Huzdra
Three Days

The Mermaid

A young woman named Anne Page generously gave me the idea for this story, in two or three succinct sentences.
Although I had always been drawn to the notion of the mermaid, such a possibility had never occurred to me. It is logical – therefore appalling.

Michael was a quiet man with never much to say for himself. He worked at his father's ironmongery business, which the old dad was now too frail to see to, and had taken on some new lines in hammer and nails and paint, which pleased the weekenders, who want their cottages all colours, and to hang up their trophy knick-knacks, their shells and dried weeds, and other dead hard things from out of the sea. It was the sea was the thing with Michael too, for though he would never tell you of it, she had bewitched him. As a child he was always on the shores climbing among the steep caves, fishing off the Rock, or just sitting staring away out to where there is nothing, you mind, but what the inner eye and the heart imagine. And it was the sea that gave to Michael the one long speech I ever heard him make.

I had known him since we were children in the village. And when I came back from the city, soul-sore and drinking down a bottle a day, he was the first thing I saw that I knew, as I walked from the train along the street. 'Hallo, Michael,' I said, 'how are you doing?' And Michael nodded and said to me, 'I'm going along,' as if he had only met me that morning, when it had been three years and more.

I began my writing then, up in the room over the Widow's bakery, and for all I was told *Watch out for the Widow*, she did me no harm except in the pastry way, fattening me up. But it got me

101

off the drink, so maybe it was not so bad a bargain.

And as I sought my path back into the village, and they stopped their jibes about the city and the stranger, I saw Michael here and there, in his father's shop, and in the pub sometimes of an evening, where I drank my two halves slow as cream, or walking along the shore at dusk, by the snow-blue water and under the ashy rose-petal sky, not grey, not pink, clearer than a washed glass, that only the sea knows how to bring.

But Michael, as I say, was no talker. He would stand his round, he would play his game of cards, he would put on the odd bet, he would help you if you needed an item or two and had not the cash, and once, when one of the holiday couples lost a dog, it was Michael went down and found it under the Rock, and brought it in his arms. And when the woman held out a bright leaf of money, Michael turned it gently aside.

But he would neither converse nor confide, not Michael. Nor he never married. And he was a nice-looking man, dark and blue-eyed and not yet much above forty. He could have had three or four but they had given up on him and taken elsewhere. There was never any idea, mind, that Michael had other tastes. He had even courted a girl, when he was a boy, but nothing came of it.

And then, when I had been back a year, there came the storm.

It waked me at three in the morning. I had forgotten how it would sound, the sea, when she was angry.

I stood in the window and looked down the village to the shore, and there were the great waves like spiked combs and the sky tearing at them, and this sound of guns the water makes, and the tall thunder, and the lightning flash like a knife. It filled me with terror and joy, and I put on my clothes and my boots and went out, and in the street I came on others, drawn forth as I had been as if by a powerful cry. We spoke of what boats might be out and if they had got to safety, but there was a primeval thing upon us, that had nothing to do with human sympathy or care. And in the end I went on down the street, past the pub, which had opened itself up again, and through the lane to the Rock.

And when I reached the place, the wind was rending and it was like the edge of chaos, so I stood there drunk as I had not been now in eleven months, with my mouth open, half-blinded, until I saw Michael was there before me, down along the Rock where the spray was coming up and the water ran black as oil. He stood with his feet planted, looking out.

'Come back a way, Michael,' I called, 'She'll have you off, man, and into all that.'

He turned and looked at me, and I saw he had my face, my drunkard's face, and suddenly he grinned and he said, 'Had me she already has.'

But then a great bomb of water burst against the Rock. I saw him go to his knees and I dashed forward, afraid he would be lugged over and lost. But he was not and he and I pulled away from the edge together.

'You've the right of it,' he said, when we stood back drenched on the track. 'For she's greedy tonight.'

There are moments when you foretell suddenly a man will speak to you, that there is something lodged in his spirit, and now it will be shown. It may be a diamond or a severed head and there is no means to guess, but you must not gainsay him. Not for your own hope, you must not. And so it was with Michael now. For he waited by me, and he said, 'I could do with a drink if Alec has the bar open.' And then, making no move, he said, 'You're a writer, you could write it down maybe.'

'Write down what, Michael?'

'The mermaid.'

So too when he puts the diamond or the hacked head before you, you do not say to him, Bloody rot, man.

'A mermaid is it?' I said. 'I always dreamed there were such things.'

'I dreamed it,' he said, 'since I was a boy, and the dad told me stories.' His lashes were strung with water so I could not see his eyes to be sure of them. We huddled into a lee of the Rock. It was the pub our flesh wanted, the warmth and the lamplight and the company, if not the liquor. But our souls kept us there in the loud corner of the storm. We could not go away, not yet, till he was done.

'When I was sixteen it was,' he said at last, under the scream of the wind. The glass waves smashed upon his voice but could not drown him out. That is how it is when a man must speak to you. Though he whisper in the whirlwind, you will hear, like Job, or Moses on the mountain.

His brain, Michael said, was once full of fantasies, day-dreams, and there were night-dreams too, very rich and beautiful, often remembered, all to do with the sea. It had been that way with him since he was a child, and his father told him sea-yarns of his fishing days, and some wonderful lies besides which to the child were no more than a proper truth, as perhaps in a sort they are. There were cities under the ocean, of coral and crystal and nacre, and great beasts like dragons that could swallow up a ship whole, and there were peoples, whose young girls swung upon the waves, as if upon a garden swing, combing their green-yellow hair the colour of canaries, singing, and if you stared you caught a glimpse of their pearl-white breasts and of their silken tails, for they had no legs but were fish from the belly down.

'You know how it is,' said Michael, 'you're coming to think of girls by then, and you get the strange feelings – between sweetness and sin. And it was those glimmer breasts on the waves, maybe. I'd dream of them after.'

'Nor would you be the first,' I said. 'That dream began long ago.'

Michael smiled. 'With the first fisherman,' he said.

We paused in the storm's corner, and the sea cursed us and all mankind. She was the very devil tonight, we said. And then he went on.

It was near the end of the summer of his seventeenth year, and he had been fishing but caught nothing, though it did not greatly trouble him. He was walking back along the shores, with the tide behind him, but he had nothing to fear for he knew its times better than his own body, which was still a surprise to him. It happens now and then at that season, seals stray in and lie along the rocks like tabby cats to sun themselves, and in the afternoon water they play. He had seen them before and liked them, and when first he came around the headland with the old tower, and saw the shape out among the offshore rocks, he reckoned it was a seal, and went carefully.

The sun was westering, and the water gleamed and the objects upon it and in it were dark. But then a big mallow cloud passed over the sun and the light softened, and he saw that on the rocks there sat no seal but a woman, naked as a baby, and with a hank of long hair down her back.

He took her for a holiday-making girl, who else would be so brazen as to swim without covering, and this was strange, for he had eyed the holiday girls all summer, and they him indeed, and he thought he knew them all, but this one was different. Her hair was very pale for one, and then, although he was too far off to see anything of her well, her skin seemed pale in the same odd fashion, but perhaps this was a trick of the glare upon the ocean. Just at that moment, the sun came out again, and she turned to a silhouette.

Michael stayed, wondering to himself if he had the nerve to go near and take a fair look. He had never seen a woman bare, except in his fancy with the aid of a few pictures picked up round and about. His pulses were beating, and he tingled at the notion. But what if she saw him? Could it be she would not mind? He had heard stories too of the loose girls from the towns. Michael began to tremble at this, as a young man will, and many an older man if it comes to it. He did not know whether to go nearer or to take himself right away. And it was as he was arguing it out that the girl herself decided to be off. Her exit was a simple one. She merely dived from her rock into the sea. He beheld her pale body and hair spring and turn over, and then the upending of some-thing that curved up like a bow against the shining sky, flickering a fan of silvered paper upon its utmost end. Then everything was gone down into the blaze of the water.

Michael stood amazed. And told himself he was seeing things, then that he had seen nothing at all, then that it was a seal, and next a girl, and lastly that he had looked upon that creature of the myth, the innocent, sweet sin of his adolescent lust, the mermaid.

'I never slept that night,' said Michael.

'I never thought that you would,' said I, softly. 'But did you tell a soul?'

'Not one. What could I tell? The dad would have thought me cracked, for all he claimed to have seen them himself in his sea days. No, I was ashamed. I was afraid.'

'And then, how long did you hesitate, till back you went?'

'Only the one day,' he said.

He returned in the afternoon, to the same spot and better, finding himself a vantage where the cliff comes down to the water and there are the caves. He lay about along a ledge and watched for her and knew she never would come, but as the sun moved over into the west and the sea began to sheen, come she did, up out of the slick mirror of the water, pulling herself he said like a live rope. And she sat upon a green rock and he saw her clearly

now and near enough, if he had gently thrown a stone, he might
have hit her. That was not near enough that he saw her face
beyond the form of it that was a woman's, or the details of her
body, beyond that she had a narrow back, slim arms, two breasts
upon her like little white cups and spangled with wet, and her
long hair, and that she combed her hair with a spiny shell, and
that below her flat belly she had no legs but a fish's tail, which
coiled over into the sea-froth, glittering and tensing with muscle,
and *alive* and *part* of her.

'She didn't sing,' said Michael. 'That was all I missed. She
made no sound, though once a gull went by, crying, and she
raised her head in the way a cat does after a bird. But she was real
as my own skin.'

And then his lust, for he did lust after her, this made him do a
pragmatic, cool thing. It made him look at her in dismay, thinking
that if she had no legs, then how might it be possible . . . But
there were some markings on her tail, he saw, like the flowering
apertures of dolphin. In a boiling rush of embarrassment, he
knew what they were, and because of it, not even knowing what
he would do, he stood up and shouted at her.

She moved her head, quite slowly, as she had at the passing of
the gull. There was nothing shy or timid in the gesture, but
something feral there was. Although he could not see her eyes, he
saw she stared at and beheld him.

It was a long moment. Every second he expected her to fling
herself over back into the sea. But she did not do it until he had
taken five or six strides down from the ledge. And then the
curving body, the flaunt of the tail, were limpid, nearly flirting.

It was as if she said, *I know your kind, as you know mine. I say
no, now. But perhaps not, tomorrow.*

For if the holiday girls were amoral, what must she be, this fey
half-being out of ocean?

He had seen her hair was green, too. Pale, pale green like those
cream peppermints you can buy in chocolate. Her skin looked
only lily white and her tail like the grey-silver foil that wraps up
tobacco and coffee.

Well, he would woo her. He would court her. And he knew
how it must be done. For where he would take the mortal girl a
carton of talcum or a bunch of flowers, he would bring this one
the fish of his catch, raw, as of course she would want them.

He had some pains over it. Going out at dawn the next day, baiting his line for the lovely dainty fish they call along the coast *fairies*, and catching them – because he must; filling up a crock with them, and carrying it down to the offshore rocks where she would come back – because he would accept nothing other.

The water was mild as milk and the beauty of the full-blown summer lay like a kiss upon the sea, the cliffs, the sky. It was a magic time, and anything might happen in it. This he had always truly believed, and now it had been given him to know it for sure.

When he went off he did not go far, only to the shore's edge where the wet sand sank between the claws of the rocks and their emerald gardens, and everything of the land ran out into the water, which looked blue now as the sky was gold.

She came early. He saw her, lifting her effortless, spilling body from the sea. She scented the fish at once, and though she acknowledged Michael with one upraised, untremulous glance, she hurried instantly to the catch and began ravenously to devour it.

Even now he was not near enough to see her sharply, only the suggestion of her features. And that she ate like a wild beast did not alarm or disgust him. She was a creature of the sea, and she was hungry.

When she was finished, she did something exquisite, too, as if to make up for the ravening. She rinsed her face with her hand, in the cat-like motion that seemed most ready with her. And having done this, she turned and stared towards him. She seemed to be considering, Michael thought, if he was anything to her or not.

And then his heart jumped up like a hare. For she made a movement, not cat-like, not creatural or oceanic. Lifting her left arm, lightly and unmistakably she *beckoned* him to come to her.

Well, he froze. He stopped there like a damned stone and could not make himself try a step. And even as this happened, he swore at himself with the terrible foul words he had gained with his sixteen to seventeen years. But it did no good. And presently, without any sign of displeasure or amusement, the sea-girl flipped over and was gone down once more into the water.

At that, he ran. He pelted full tilt at the place she had been, sliding and almost falling, and he was yelling too, pleading that she would stay. But when he reached the spot, there were only the fish bones lying there, some of them cracked by her teeth.

Michael looked out across the empty sea. From this vantage the sun was down behind the headland. A shadow filmed the water, making it transparent and opaque together. Again, before he knew what he did, Michael began to wade out into it, silent now, and he said that tears spurted from his eyes, he could not have said why.

Then from the sea, like a white bird, she darted out. He caught the flash of her – like the lightning it was, so unlooked for, yet expected. And her arm was raised, and it still beckoned, and he knew that she wished him to follow her, and in that moment he had gone far enough that he could do it.

Unlike half of the village he could swim, could Michael, and he launched himself into the warm sea without another thought.

'There was never,' he said, 'another hour like that one. It was more, you see, like flying than to swim. And all the doubt left behind on the land.'

He had her in sight, for she allowed it, keeping herself above the sea, and he could make her out easily, the glint of her hair and skin, and, every so often, the flare of her fish tail catching the last sun. She went around the cliffs, under the old tower, and he decided she would be going to the bluff beyond, which at low tide is set back from the sea, and crumbling, full of galleries and carious chambers, unsafe and unvisited. It seemed to him she would know this cliff, maybe it had been a land-haunt of hers for centuries, for did not her kind live three hundred years at least?

Sure enough she turned towards the bluff, to which the tide was now coming up, and swam in under a deep blind shadow that was falling down into the water from the rocks. She vanished there into some hidden channel, and then reappeared two minutes later above him, before he had got himself frantic, on a high dim overhang. She had ascended so swiftly it was like a challenge. Unable to locate the underwater passage, he dragged himself out and pushed up the bluff-side, slipping and stumbling, on his two legs, to reach her.

Between finally was a sort of tunnel, thickly dark, fishy, and cold, smelling of the core of the ocean, which in its time had been there very much, and when he had thrust himself through this, he found her cave before him.

There could be no doubt it was hers. It was littered with her things, her possessions, what she had borne in to tinker with, for she too was a visitor. She had her trophies of seaweeds, and a hoard of shells, and some keepsakes from the beach, a broken glass in a plastic frame, a scent bottle, a crushed and empty can of beer. Also, scattered about, were the familiar bones of fish, the carapace of a crab.

There was no comfort in the cave. It was stone and rock and slime and impending night. It chilled him right enough, but not sufficiently to send him away. For she was there, somewhere, in the dusk.

'I believe that I spoke to her,' said Michael, 'some courting phrase.'

He trod over the bones and the crab, cautious not to spoil the shells and glass and can, which were her toys, and then he made her out, stretched on the stones before him in the darkness. She glowed, like the phosphorus on the water by night. He gazed down, and she was less than three feet from him, lying there, and he saw her as she was at last.

'If I had thought,' he said, 'I would always have reckoned it to be like dying. The drowning death. And the door opens, and you see the face of God. All your days you've known you will come to it, and longed for and feared it, but it will be. But then as the door flies wide, you see – it is the *truth* you see. And truth is terrible.'

The image that shone up for him on the darkness was the truth of the mermaid.

She was a mammalian female from her head and torso to her lower belly, where she became the fish. But though she was a female, she was not properly a woman. Her face was flat, with little fluttering nostrils set without a nose, and her mouth was wide and lipless and through it he could detect the thin fence of narrow teeth, each of which was pointed. Her eyes were a fish's eyes, round and yellowish, lidless, the soulless eyes that glare from the net. Her hair streamed back and was not hair but a tangle of strange rubbery filaments, and he saw she had no ears but there were the gills there, flaccid as withered pods.

'Even her skin,' he said, 'for skin she had, to her waist, it was not like skin at all but the hide of a whale, thick and shiny, and here and there algae growing on it and little mosses out of the deep water, feeding on her.'

She stank of the ocean floor, of the fish she ate and was. The tail of her was huge and sinuous, gleaming, twitching, and the dark flowers of her ultimate femaleness stared from it. His gorge rose. He choked, but could not move away. He felt the trap, he knew there was no escape for him. She was the sea, which is older than the land, and he had gone to her and was hers.

And then she beckoned again, aimlessly, cruelly. It was like the waving of the sea-wrack in the tide, some ancient gesture she had learned, but it drew him closer, near to her, so he leaned and then he kneeled above her, and he could no more have not done it than a man can keep from his last breath.

She put her hand on him then, like his lover. He saw her hand, thin, so he noticed its jelly bones, and the webs between the three fingers which were all she had, and the long greenish curving nails. And in this nightmare instrument, groaning and praying, partly out of his mind, he watched his manhood rise erect for her. But when she drew him in, he shut his eyes.

'She was cold,' he said. When he said this to me, the word, the word *cold*, became a new word. Its entire meaning I did not grasp, but in a book you would find it by those other words: Terror, Hell, Evil and Despair. 'My body worked as she made it do. I clung in my mind and prayed and I do not know for what but I think I never called on God. She was *cold*, she was *cold*. She was all the old fish-stinking filth-drowning of the sea. She was the mud and the nothingness. She was the years of the world dying. Ah God. I was fucking death.'

He does not remember the end, though he is sure, Michael, that he served her as she required. He came up out of her, as from the bottom of the ocean, and he crawled away and vomited, bringing out the poison, but he could never rid himself of all. And somewhere as he writhed and spewed, he heard a faint silken splash under the bluff, and knew that she was gone, dived down into the deep of the evening tide, vanished, where the night and the horizon touch.

The stars were out when Michael crawled free of the cave and began his long walk homeward.

All the while he walked, in the clean air of the cliffs, he told himself it was done now.

'But it never was done,' said Michael. 'And never will be done.'

We stood together in the lee of the Rock. The storm was quietening and the waves sloping lower and lower. Sometimes with an angry hiss they came up the granite for us, but her rage was turning away towards some other place.

'Hark there,' said Michael, 'Alec is doing good trade.'

And from the village we heard a shouting and banging of the piano in the pub.

As Michael moved out into the slow rain, I nearly put my hand on his arm, to ask him or to tell him something. But I did not know what that would be, for he had said it through and no wise sentence of mine could change it. He had lain with the sea and could lie with no other. He had coupled with death and lived with the memory of that. Each night that he lay down upon his own belly did he feel that under him, that icy twisting and smothering and drawing? And did he dream of them still, the hollow girls swinging on the waves with their round annihilated eyes, their taloned fingers, their silent songs?

'Michael . . .' I said.

'What would you have?' he said.

'I'll buy you a drink,' I said.

'Thanks now, but no. It's late. The dad will want me up for the shop bright and early. Good night to you.'

He did not say, *Do you not believe me?* or *Never speak of this*. He walked away up the lane as though we had exchanged a few words over the storm. I took note of his progress, and when he had disappeared from sight, I wondered too if he had said any of it to me, that untalking man. But the sea is the thing now, it is she tells you. You have only to listen, to hear.

After the Guillotine

*In the 1980s I wrote a huge novel on the French Revolution –
my only 'straight' historical novel to date.*

*Off shoots from that book gave me several ingredients for
fantasy stories, of which this is one.*

*The characters are based on four actual people sent to the
blade by Robespierre. In one case at least, the invented name
casts a very thin veil over the original – Danton.*

The men went to the scaffold singing the Marseillaise, or shouting, or in tears, or – all three. At any rate, they made a great deal
of noise about death. The girl went sweetly and quietly, dressed
like a bride. There was a reason for that. There were, of course,
reasons for all of it.

To die at any time when you are not prepared to die is
objectionable. To die when you are comparatively young, when
there are things of paramount importance still to be accomplished, when, in dying, you will lose spring and hope, and those
who love you, that also you love; these are fair causes for
commotion. The famous figure, D'Antoine the Lion, however,
did not roar en route to la Guillotine. He had done his roaring in
the courtroom and it had achieved very little good, and actually
some harm. He had presently been 'legally' silenced, and that had
shut up every one of them. D'Antoine's enemies were terrified of
him, his speeches, his voice, his presence. Just as his friends loved
him to distraction.

As the tumbrils jounced slowly along over the cobbles of Paris
(a form of traffic that had become quite banal) the Lion only
occasionally grunted, or flexed his big body with bitter laughter.
D'Antoine, bully, kingly master, charmer, conniver, atheist. 'I'm

leaving things in a muddle,' he had said after they condemned him. For himself, he reckoned on nothing, once the blade came down, hence his bitterness, and his lack of confusion. He was not afraid, or only very little. He had made his mark in the living world. 'Show my head to the crowd,' he would instruct the executioner. 'It's worth looking at twice.' Let us agree with that.

Héros, in the same cart, was one of those who sang, but rather negligently. The others who did so were mostly trying to keep their courage up, for while they sang, some of their terror and despair was held at bay. But Héros did not seem to be either depressed or afraid. His name, in this instance, is perfect for him, combination that it is of Hero and Eros. Lover and gallant, the image that comes to mind is appealing. One of the handsomest men of the era, he is everything one would wish to be at the hour of one's public death: beautiful, couth, composed. In his not-long career, he had enjoyed most of the sins and pleasures of his day. He had been in the beds of princesses, perhaps even of a prince or two. Aristocrat to his fingertips, he knew how to face this final couching. He sang melodiously. To the screaming rabble he was aloof, to his friends remotely kind. He kissed them farewell at the foot of the scaffold, and went up first to demonstrate how quick and easy it all was, not worth any show. Thereby offering a faultless one.

But in his heart, handsome peerless Héros had kept a seed of the Catholic faith, which refused to wither. He believed, in some subdued, shallow bottom of his brain, that he was bound for Hell hereafter. As he disdained to fuss over the loss of his elegant head, just so he would not throw a tantrum at a prospect of centuries of torment in the inferno. His coolness was therefore even more admirable. Let us pause a moment to admire him.

The third man we examine in the forward tumbril, Lucien, rather than being what one would wish to, on the day of one's public death, is more what one fears one would be. As some of his biographers politely put it, there had been some 'difficulty' in persuading him from the prison to the cart. Once installed, raw-eyed from weeping, only the neighbouring strength of the Lion kept him upright. Then, as the reeking, railing crowd pressed in, anger and terror mingled, and rather than sing, Lucien began to shout. As the rabble screamed insults at him, so he screamed back. Ugly, where Héros was handsome and D'Antoine was grand, thin from prison, white and insane, and tearing his shirt in his struggles to escape the inescapable, or to be heard by the voluntarily deaf, he hurled charges and pleas until his voice, never strong, gave out. He had some justification. His was the spark that had initially fired the powder-keg of the Revolution. But no one listened now. The gist of all his words: *Remember what I did for you and set us free* – or, in short, *Let me LIVE!* – was entertaining, but no rallying point for the starving unanswered masses who, like vampires, had taken to existing on blood. There was, too, the matter of Lucien's wife, whom he adored, and who he feared, rightly, was on the same road to the guillotine as himself. To no avail, naturally, he was also trying to shout for her life.

We may be unpleasant here and say Lucien shouted his head off. Or we could say, journalist and pamphleteer that he was, that he wrote it off, by going into print with unwise assertions and demands.

As for an afterlife, he wrote, too, that he believed in the 'immortality of the soul'. So he did, but in a somewhat scattered, indefinite way. He had been anxious to impress, through his prison reading, the notion of continuance upon himself, as if he would need it where he would be going.

Let us, for the moment, stop talking about Lucien. And go on to that far more visual creature, his wife, the lovely Lucette.

There must have been something about Lucien. There he was, ugly, and there Lucette was – exquisite – and they were blissfully in love through several years of marriage. Maybe she preferred older men – he was ten years her senior. Or *younger* men – ten years her senior in age, he was in many other ways younger than everyone. The crime which sent Lucette to the scaffold was love. Because of love she had attempted to save her husband's neck, and thus proved troublesome to his powerful enemies. Thereafter it seemed to them she might become, through love, a focus for strife.

She made the journey to the guillotine some days after Lucien, Héros and D'Antoine. She travelled with an air of calm pleasure. She said, 'Lucien is dead and there is nothing further I want from life. If these monsters hadn't murdered him, I would now thank them with tears of joy for sending me to join him in eternity.' Lucette's inner secret was that she was by nature a priestess who

115

had made Lucien her High Altar. She expected, after her sacrifice, to fall straight from the blade of the guillotine into her husband's arms. Despite, or because of, his rather Dionysian leanings – religions of music, drama, lilies in fields – Lucette believed in Heaven. That Lucien, regardless of his faults, was already there, she did not doubt.

So, in her white dress, her fleecy golden hair cut short, she went blithely up to the platform and lay down for the stroke, barely seeming to notice, they said, what the executioner was doing.

The guillotine is very swift and supposedly humane, but who knows? Stories are told of severed heads which winked malignly from the basket, and even of one that brokenly whispered a request for water. Doubtless the climate has an effect on an outdoor apparatus of this type – shrinking or swelling the metal parts; on some days it might do its work an iota more slowly, or more quickly, or more neatly, than on others. Nothing the crowd would notice, of course. And then the physique of the victim must be taken into account. A large neck makes its own demands, and the fact that long hair, collars and neck-cloths were removed indicates even such as these could throw the blade. Louis Capet required more than one stroke; an unreassuring if unusual occurrence. Nor should one forget the condition of the subject's nerves – as opposed merely to his nervousness. No two human things are quite alike. One ventures to suggest that there have been as many different sorts of death under the guillotine as there have been heads lopped by it.

D'Antoine, for example. Who could judge splendid powerful D'Antoine would experience that partitioning in the same way as anyone else?

It seemed, when it came, like a blow, the blow of a sledgehammer, but not quite hard enough – so there was an instant's appalled thought: *Those bloody fools have botched it!* Then the perspective altered. The eyes glimpsed the basket as the head fell into it, and other faces, already forgotten, looked up at it with anxiety as it came to meet them. After this the light went and there was only one odd final sensation, the head lying where it was, but the last reflexive relaxing spasms of the body eerily somehow communicated to it. *Is this what a chicken feels?* And a moment of horror, wondering how long one must endure this *this*. Followed by oblivion.

Oblivion of course, for D'Antoine the atheist had reckoned on nothing. And here nothing was. All senses gone. The void. Blackness not even black, silence not even silence. Sans all.

There is a certain smugness attached to finding oneself perfectly right, even if one can no longer experience it.

Héros, who had been dispatched a short while before, *was* experiencing something similar.

In his case, the passage of the blade had been sheer. To use the analogy of hot knives through butter is in bad taste, but there. It is the best one. Stunned, Héros lost consciousness instantly. He may have expected to. When he opened his eyes again, everything was altered but still he saw only what he expected.

The way to Hell was gaudy, festive almost; the lighting, to say the least, theatrical. Flames leaped crimson on the subterranean cliffs that lined the path, and a grotesquerie of shadows danced with them. Héros was, on some unrecognized level, gratified to see that it had all the artistry of a good painting of the subject. Indeed, some of it was so familiar that it filled him with a slight sense of déjà vu. Presently a masked devil swooped down at him on bat-wings, with a shriek. Héros, unprotesting, elegant, moved towards his punishment.

The bright entrance and the gradients beyond were littered by howling, pleading, rioting or bravely joking damned. Among them he caught sight of certain prior acquaintance, just those he would, in fact, have anticipated. He also partly expected to see D'Antoine arrive at any moment, ushered in behind him. D'Antoine, who had led a magnificently licentious life, had believed that only oblivion followed death. His friend would have been interested to see D'Antoine's face when he discovered he was wrong. On the whole. Héros did not think Lucien would make up the party. Although Lucien had done a thing or two that would doubtless disqualify him from eternal bliss, he had a sort of faun-like innocence that would probably keep him out of the ultimate basement area.

Occasionally goaded, though never prodded, by appalling devils, Héros walked on and found himself at length in a sort of waiting-room with broad open windows. These gazed out across incendiary lakes and lagoons, and mountains of anguished structure. Actual torments were visible from here, but, being in the distance, not very coherently. It was a subtle arrangement, threatening, but restrained. If questioned, Héros would have confessed that he approved of it. At a stone table in the waiting-room, a veiled figure sat dealing cards. Héros, who had been inclined to cards in life, sat down opposite and, without a word, they began to play a hand.

The game seemed to last a very long time. An extraordinarily long time. Abruptly, Héros came to from a kind of daze, and with a strange feeling to which he could assign no name – for he felt, absurdly, almost guilty. It appeared to him at that moment as if, rather than being kept waiting here, most cruelly, to learn his exact awful fate, he *himself* – but no, that was plainly ridiculous. Just precisely then, a tall flame burst through one of the windows, and out of the flame a demon stared at him with a cat's wild eyes. Beckoned, somewhat relieved, Héros abandoned the cards, and went towards the demon, which suddenly grasped him and bore him out into the savage landscape beyond the room. A backward glance showed the veiled figure had disappeared entirely.

They did not exchange small-talk, the demon and Héros. Hell spoke for itself. They passed over laval cauldrons in which figures swam and wailed, and emaciated moaning forms chained to the sides of mountains and tormented by various . . . *things*. Others of the condemned crawled about at the edges of retreating pools, croaking of thirst. Some toiled like ants, great boulders on their backs. Still others were being flayed or devoured by fiends, from the feet up. Allusions both historic and classical were nicely mingled. There was something in a dreadful way reassuring about it all.

At length, the demon chose to hover in mid-air close to a weird contraption, a kind of swing. Back and back it flung itself, then forth and forth, with a tireless pendulum motion, until about a mile away it plunged into a torrent of fire, and far off screaming was detectable. But now it was swinging back again. Seated in a froth of summery dresses – the height of Revolutionary French fashion – two young women, quite unscathed, toasted each other in white sparkling wine.

As they drew nearer, Héros noticed that there was room on the swing for one more person. Just then, the blonder of the two ladies glanced up and beheld him.

'Why, it's Héros – Héros!' she cried; the darker girl joined in with: 'We saved a place for you, Héros darling.'

Héros smiled and greeted them. Both looked familiar, although he was not sure from where. Instead, each of them seemed like an amalgam of certain aspects of all the women he had known, the dark and the blonde, the coarse and the refined, aristo and plebeian – delightful. And no sooner had he concluded this, than his demon escort dropped him. There was no sensation of falling. One moment he was in the air, next moment in mid-flight on the swing, a girl either side, soft arms, warm lips, curly hair, and very good champagne being held for him to drink. 'Knock it back quickly, lovely Héros. In a minute, we'll be into *that* again.'

'The fire?' queried Héros. The swing had reached its furthest backward extent, paused, and now began once more to fly forward.

'Oh, the fire. The pain! The terror!'

'But it only lasts a moment,' said her friend and, indeed, his.

'You get used to it.'

They toasted the monarchy, something it had long since ceased to be sensible to do upstairs. Then they embraced.

The swing was broad and comfortable enough for almost . . . anything.

After a few extremely pleasant minutes, his two companions clutched at him with exclamations of fright and boiling red flames enveloped them. They all screamed with pain. Then the swing rushed out again and the pain vanished. They had not been burned, not even blistered. The champagne too retained its refreshing coolness, nor had any of it evaporated.

Héros relaxed amid the willing human cushions. Three seconds of agony against several minutes that were not agonizing at all seemed an excellent arrangement. Of course one suffered. One was supposed to. But the ratio could only be described as – civilized.

The next time they went into the fire they were all singing a very lewd song of the proposed Republic. They screamed briefly, though in perfect tempo, and came out again on the succeeding verse.

In perfect tempo too, Lucien felt the pain of the guillotine's blade. It was swift and stinging, not unendurable, leaving an after-image of itself that grew in intensity, not to greater pain but to a terrible struggle. Physically the guillotine had deprived him of sight, hearing and speech – but not totally of feeling. He hung there, formless, and for a long ghastly eternity fought to breathe, tried to swallow, and most of all to cry out.

When he broke from this, he did not know where he was, but that he was somewhere seemed self-evident. Still blind and deaf and dumb, he had convinced himself that he was now breathing, and because of this thought that he had somehow been rescued by the crowd, who must have pulled him clear of the crashing blade – by unimaginable means – at the last moment. But of course, there was no one near him, nothing. When he attempted to reach out, his hands found only emptiness, and besides, they were not hands. All *that* was done with. His body had been lost. Only he remained. And for a horrible second he was not even sure of that – But he held to himself grimly, to everything he could remember. This was the second struggle, and in the middle of it he managed to open his eyes, or at least, he began to see.

What he saw was not encouraging. It was truly a scene of total emptiness, a skyless desert made solely of the absence of things, and yet there seemed to be matter in it. For example, to stare at something was to produce a sort of illusory smoky shape. And then again, there was nothing to be stared at in the first place. His feeling now was of depression, a fear and misery he had never known to such a degree even on the volatile emotional seesaw of his life. And of loneliness, which was the worst of all.

Somehow he had survived death. Or had he? This seemed the most tenuous and precarious of survivals. *Limbo* was the notion that came to mind. If he still possessed a mind.

He found that he looked ceaselessly in all directions, but all directions were the same. He was searching for a method of escape, or a mode of return. His life was precious to him. He longed for it. He wanted to go back! There must be some way – And when this passionate yearning grew very strong, out of his confusion the desert seemed to fill with crowds and colour and noise. He was in a procession on horseback, or else watching one from the roadside. He heard the cannon booming over Paris on the day the Bastille fell; he heard – but these were only waking dreams. With an effort, each time he shook them off. The door to release was not to be found in this way.

It seemed then he rummaged about in the emptiness, or maybe hurried over it, or dug through it, all to no avail. And then, when he stopped, his thoughts grew very still and began gently to flow out from him. He was afraid to lose them, and himself. This fear was more dreadful than any of the others, more dreadful even than the fear of death had been.

There was anger too. None of this was what Lucien had believed would greet the 'immortal' soul. It was demonstrably useless to call on God. (He had done so.) Either God did not exist, or did not attend. There were also curious moments when it seemed to him that he, not God, had the key to all of this. But how could that be so?

Perched there in the depths of the waste, he huddled memories about him, warming himself at the recollections of beautiful Lucette, and crying over his child, or thinking that he cried. But the loneliness pressed down on him like an inexorable coffin-lid. Though he supposed he could people the colourless greyness, which was not even grey, with the figures of wife and friends, or with anything, he knew such toys were false, and useless.

Was everything he now experienced a punishment? Not the ridiculous Catholic Hell, but some more deadly state where he must wander for ever, weighted by depression, alone, until his own self was worn away as time washes smooth a stone? Lucette – Lucette –

Lucette, desiring her freedom so much, was already partly out of her body as the blade fell. She heard, and felt the stroke, but from some way off. Then the multitude, the blood-soaked guillotine, all Paris, the very world, dashed away beneath her. She rose into a sky almost cloudless and utterly blue. Whole and laughing and lovely, she entered Heaven with the lightest step, in her white dress, her hair already long again.

It was all so beautiful. It was as she had dreamed of it when a child. Balanced on their clouds of cirrus the streets of gold, the pearly dazzling palaces, the handsome people smiling and brave, the little animals that made free of every step and cornice, the birds and the kind angels that flew overhead, about the level of the fourth floor windows . . . She ran along, crying with pleasure, at every crossroads expecting to meet Lucien – probably sitting writing something, and so engrossed, he had momentarily forgotten the time of her arrival. But she did not find him. And at last, there in the golden sunlight of endless day, Lucette paused.

A stately woman in white robes came down the boulevard, and Lucette approached her.

'Madame, excuse me, but I should like to ask your advice.' The woman looked at her, gently smiling. 'I'm searching for my husband. He died some days ago, and I expected he would be here before me – The woman went on smiling. 'Madame – I can't find him.'

'Then perhaps he is not here.'

'There is nowhere else he could be,' said Lucette firmly.

'Ah, my dear, there are numerous other places. He could be in any one of them.'

Lucette frowned and her fine eyes flashed. Was this woman daring to suggest –

'Where?' said Lucette. It was a challenge. One did not live next to a fighter such as Lucien without some of the trademarks rubbing off.

But enigmatically, the woman only said, 'Seek and ye shall find.' And so passed on down the street.

Lucette sat under a portico to pet a pair of white rabbits. She told them about Lucien, and once about the child they had had to leave behind them, and then she wept. The rabbits were patient, and dried her tears on their fur.

Eventually Lucette rose and went on alone, determined to search every street and park, every room and cupboard of Heaven. She did so. Up stairs she hurried, over bridges under which ran the sapphire streams of Paradise, scattered with flowers and ducks. Into high bell-towers she went, and from the tallest roofs of all she gazed into rosy distances, between the flight paths of the angels. She did not grow tired. There could be no tiredness. But she grew unsure, she grew uneasy. Now and then she asked someone, once she even asked an angel, who stood calmly on a pillar some feet over her head. But no one could aid her. Lucien? Who was Lucien? She was accustomed, was Lucette, to being married to a famous man. It added to her sense of outrage and sadness that they did not know him.

Though there was no time, yet her search of Heaven took a lot of it. In the end, it seemed to her she had visited every inch.

Finally she sought a gate, and walked out of it into the clouds.
She turned her back on Bliss. It was not bliss, if her love was not
to be there with her.

An infinity of sky stretched away and away. Lucette moved
across it, still searching, and the glow of the ethereal city faded
behind her. Like an . . . illusion.

On the astral plain, though illusions may be frequent, one does
not sleep, let alone turn in one's sleep; neither does one do so in
annihilation. Nevertheless, in a manner of speaking, D'Antoine
did 'turn' in his 'sleep'.

It was as if, determined to wake up at a particular hour, he now
partly surfaced from deep slumber to ask himself, drowsily,
unwillingly, 'Is it time, yet?' But apparently it was not yet time.
With a – metaphorical – grunt, the Lion who no longer remembered he had been the Lion sank down once more into the cosy
arms of oblivion, burrowed, nestled, and was gone again.

The demon whose turn it was on the spit with Héros stared at him
quizzically.

'Don't you find all this,' said the demon, 'a bit samey?'

'Being tortured, do you mean? I suppose, as torturer, *you*
might find it so. We can swap places if you like.'

'You miss the point,' said the demon.

Héros eyed the demon's pitchfork. 'Not always.'

As it had turned out, the lascivious fiery swing was not the only
appliance to which Héros had been subjected. He had suffered
many more stringent punishments. Although strangely enough,
only when he himself began to consider the lack of them. But
doubtless that was merely the prescience of guilt. Strangely too,
more strangely in fact, even the worst of the tortures seemed
rather hollow. This one, for example, of being slowly roasted
alive, stabbed the while at suitable junctures by the pitchfork –
somehow it was difficult to retain the sense of agony. One's mind
unaccountably wandered. One had to *remember* to writhe. It was
not that it did not hurt. It hurt abominably. And yet –

'I apologize,' said Héros, 'if I don't seem properly attentive.
No fault of yours, I assure you.'

'Perhaps,' said the demon, 'yours?'

'Oh, undoubtedly mine.'

'Perhaps,' said the demon, 'you shouldn't be here.'

The spit had stopped revolving. The roasting flames grew pale.

'I can't think where else.'

'Try,' said the demon.

Héros frowned. Now one thought of it, this was the first occasion one of the minions of Hell had held a conversation with one. Since his bonds had disappeared, Héros sat up and looked about him. Hell seemed oddly inactive, and dull, as if it were cooling down, a truly appalling idea. Weary spirals of old smoke, as if from something as mundane as burnt pastry, crawled upwards from the cold grey obsidian rocks. Nothing else moved. When Héros turned to the communicative demon, it too was gone.

The fires of Hell went out, and Héros sat alone there. No friend, no enemy, for whom to exhibit courage, no audience for whom to shine.

After a long time, a feeling of discomfort, *spiritual* malaise, drove him to his feet. He walked along the shelving greynesses, searching for something, unable to realize what. And as he did so he ceased to walk, began simply to progress.

Calm arrived suddenly. It was like letting drop a ton weight you had been holding on to for years; it was wonderful. And almost immediately on the lightening and the calm began a quickening of interest, a dramatic, pervasive excitement –

Lucien started up – and in that instant was aware he was no longer Lucien, was no longer even *he* – and that it did not matter. That it was, actually, a great relief.

Simultaneously all the greyness went away. The desert went. Instead . . . Here one is presented with the problem of describing a rainbow to those blind from birth, when one is, additionally, oneself as blind. But there is that marvellous beast again, the analogy. Analogously, then. The small bit of psychic fibre which had been, a few seconds or years ago, the young man Lucien, passionate revolutionary, first-class writer, fairly consistent hysteric, and post-guillotinee, was all at once catapulted out of its self-constructed prison of terrors and miseries, into a garden of sun and flowers and birdsong. No, not Heaven. But so glorious the garden was, and limitless, it would have put Heaven to shame. And over there were mountains to be climbed, and over there seas to be swum, and up there, a library of wisdom with

124

wide-open doors. And most charming of all, drifting here and there in earnest discussion with each other, or merely quietly reposing together, or quite alone yet *still* together – others, who were family and friends, thousands of them, the closest and the best; old rivals to be tussled with, familiar loves to be embraced. And imbuing it all a spirit of gladsome and determined, ferocious curiosity. Of course, it was not like this. Not at all. Yet, it was. Suffice it to say that the soul which had last been Lucien dashed into it with the psychic equivalent to a howl of joy, and was welcomed. And here is one more analogy. Imagine you were rendered voluntarily amnesiac (absurd, but imagine it), and came to believe you were a small wooden post located in a cellar. And as the time went by, you saw the advantages of being a small wooden post, began, adaptable creature that you were, to like it, and so to *dislike* the idea of being anything else. And then the cellar door opened. And then the amnesia lifted.

Somewhere on the edges of the analogous garden, the soul that had been Lucien met the soul that had been peerless, assured Héros, entering in a bemused, nervous sort of way. And the two souls greeted each other and reassured each other that everything was all right, before dashing off to discover all the things they were now so eager to find out about.

While somewhere close by, close as the bark to the inside of a tree, yet totally distanced, D'Antoine 'turned' again in his 'sleep', muttered something, metaphorically, and nodded off into oblivion once more.

That oblivion of his was turning out rather easy. Had she known, Lucette might have envied it. But as it was, her own sleepless journey reminded her of the tasks of Psyche in the Greek myth, a story Lucien had once told her, at the Luxembourg Gardens, and which had retained for her ever after the shattering poignancy of that time. In this way, it sometimes seemed a malign fate, even a malign goddess, hindered her.

Sometimes, the perimeter of her vision conveyed the image of a flock of fierce golden sheep with terrible teeth, or else she seemed to be kneeling, sorting grains on the ground. Eventually, she toiled with a pitcher up a steep, featureless hill. The sky was misty now, no longer blue but a colourless almost-grey. She too had entered the region of *limbo*, though she did not know it. She did know she must fill the pitcher at the black stream of Lethe, which brought forgetfulness, which, in effect, took all awareness of self away. Only by filling the pitcher, fulfilling the task, could she ever hope to find Lucien.

Unlike the myth, there was no opposition at the stream. As she bent towards the water, Lucette saw her reflection, just as she had seen it, living, in so many mirrors, even in a mirror that had also, once, reflected the face of Marie Antoinette. And in that moment, Lucette felt a pang of compassion for all lovely young discarded bodies, the white skin, the sunlit hair – for they were of no more use, nor hers to her, and now she understood as much.

Next time, she thought. But, *next time*, what? Then, letting fall the pitcher, and letting it vanish, too, she lifted a handful of the black water of forgetfulness, and with a last wistful thought of love, she drank it.

The incorporeal state did not seem quite right to the one who had been Lucette. She – it – was young, yet old enough that intimations reached through of one day when incorporeality would seem pleasant and informative, and another day, centuries in the future, when incorporeality would be yearned for. Meanwhile, these conditions were imperfect, yet they were not, after all, alien. Then, the young soul advanced or circled or perhaps did not move at all, and in doing so found the soul which had been Lucien.

Though neither was as they had been, no longer Lucien, no longer Lucette, no longer male or female, even so, the aura of love and kindness they had shared still bonded them, attracted them both to the other's vicinity. But there were many such bonds now open to each of them. They came together now, and would come together often, and touch in the way souls do touch, which is naturally the rainbow and the blind again. But since there was no loneliness and no rejection and no anguish where now they were, they did not need to cling together, a single unit of two, against a hostile environment. For this environment was benign, and it and they were one.

In this story, you see, the lovers do not join for ever to violin accompaniment on a cloud of mortal love. The lovers are no longer mortal, and there are no violins, no clouds. It is difficult not to experience annoyance or mournfulness, or even fear, that individual liaisons do not need to persist, in frantic intensity, *there* where the love is all-pervasive, calm and unconditional. We must try not to lament or to be irritated by them. Only note how happy they are, even if 'happy' is an analogous word.

While, somewhere close as a hand to a glove, D'Antoine 'turns' over and finally wakes, and is no longer D'Antoine. The lengthy sleep of nothingness has acted like a sponge, and wiped away physical identity. Though the emerging soul remembers it, of course, as all of them remember who they have been, plan who they *will* be (no unfinished business is ever left unfinished; there will be other work, other loves, other springs), it is now a garment held in the hands, not the substance of the self. The true self is quite free. It leaps forward into liberty with an analogous roar of delight and resolution.

The resonance of such roars is a commonplace of the astral. Just as the sound of tears, the cry of pain, and the falling crash of the guillotine are a commonplace, here.

Meow

I first wrote this story when I was about eighteen. In later years, actual experience led me to rewrite, awarding more Americanism, more light – and inevitably more darkness.

The denouement, however, and the last line, remain the same.

I was young, last year. I was twenty-six. That was the year I met Cathy.

I was writing a novel that year, too. Maybe you never read it. Midnight and four AM, five or six nights a week, I used to do my magician act at the King of Cups, on Aster. It paid some bills, and it was fun, that act. Even more fun when you suddenly look out over the room, and there's a girl with hair like white wine, and the flexible fluid shape of a ballet dancer, looking back at you, hanging on every breath you take.

Later, around four thirty, when we were sitting in a corner together, I saw there was a little gold cat pendant in the hollow of her throat. Later still, when we'd walked back, all across the murmuring frosty pre-dawn city, with the candy-wrapper leaves blowing and crackling underfoot, I brushed the cat aside so I could kiss her neck.

I didn't realize then, I was going to have trouble with cats.

I might have thought the trouble could have been over money. You know the sort of thing – well-off girl meets male parasite. Somehow we worked it out, keeping our distance where we had to, not keeping it where we didn't. We were still finding the way, and she was shy enough, it was kind of nice to go slowly.

But, she did own this graystone house, which her parents had left her when they went blazing off in a great big car and killed themselves. She'd been sixteen then. She'd just made it into adulthood before they ditched life and her. Somehow, I'd always resented them. They'd done a pretty good job of tying her up in their own hang-ups, before they split and gave her another one.

The house was still their house, too. It was jammed full of their trendy knick-knacks and put-ons, and their innovative furniture you couldn't sit on or eat off. And it was also full of five cats.

Cathy had acquired the cats, one by one, after her parents died. Or the cats had acquired her. After that, the house was also theirs. They personally engraved the woodwork, and put expert fringes on the drapes. And on anything else handy, like me. You're right. I had a slight phobia. Maybe something about the fanged snake effect of a cat's head, if you forget the ears. Cathy was always telling me how beautiful the cats were, and I was always trying to duck the issue. And the cats. They knew, of course, about my unadmiration, I'd have sworn that right from the start. They'd leap out on me and biff me with their handfuls of nails. They'd jump on the couch behind my shoulders and bite. When Cathy and I made love, I'd shut the bedroom door, and the cats would crouch outside, ripping the rug. I'd never dared make it with her where they could see and get at me.

I'd spot their eyes in the early morning darkness when I brought her home, ten disembodied dots of crème de menthe neon spilled over the air. Demons would manifest like that. Ever seen a cat with a mouse or a bird? I used to have a dumb dove in my act, called Bernie, and one day Bernie got out on the sidewalk. He was such a klutz, he thought everyone was his damn friend, even the cat that came up and put its teeth through his back. No. I didn't like cats much.

One night it was Cathy's birthday, and we had to be in at the house. Cathy was rather strange about her birthdays, as if the ghosts of Mom and Pop walked that night, and maybe they did. I'd tried to get her to come out, but she wouldn't, so we sat in the white-and-sepia sitting room, under the abstract that looked like three melting strawberries, and ate tuna fish and drank wine. I'd managed to get the cash and buy her the jade bracelet that had sat in a store window the past five weeks, crying to encircle her wrist. When I'd given it to her, she too cried for half a second. It was often harder to get closer to her when she was emotional than at any other time. By now the jade was warm as her own smooth skin, and the wine not much colder. The cats sat round us in a ring, except when Cathy went out to the kitchen; then they followed her with weird screechings. The cats always responded to activity in the kitchen in the same way, even to something so small as the dim, far-off clink of a plate. When the house was empty of humans, I could imagine every pan and pot holding its breath for fear of attracting attention.

Finally, Cathy stopped playing with her tuna, and gave it to the cats.

'Oh, look, Stil,' she said, gazing at them Madonna-like as they fell in the dish. 'Just look.'

'I'm looking.'

'No you're not,' she said. 'You're glaring.'

I lifted the guitar from the couch and started to play some music for us, and the cats sucked and chewed louder, to show me what they thought of it.

We sang Happy Birthday to the tune of an old Stones number, and some other stuff. Then we went up to the bedroom and I shut the door. She cried again, afterwards, but she held on to me as if afraid of being swept away out to sea. I was the first human thing she'd really come across since her parents left her. That night at the King had been going to be her experiment in failure. She thought she'd fail at communicating, at being gregarious, and she'd meant to fail, I guess. That would give her the excuse for never trying again. But somehow she'd found me. I didn't really think about the responsibility on my side of all this. It was all too dreamy, too easy.

A couple of the cats noisily puked back the tuna on the Picasso rug outside.

'Why don't you,' I said, 'leave this godawful house. Let's take an apartment together.'

'You have an apartment.'

'I have a room. I mean space.'

'You can't afford it.'

'I might.'

'You want to live off me,' she said. The first time she ever said it.

'Oh look,' I said, 'if that's what you think.'

'I didn't mean it.'

'Sure you did. Just don't mean it again. Next year MGM'll be making a movie of my book.'

'It isn't even published yet.'

'So, it will be.'

'I'd better go and clean up after the cats,' she said.

'Why don't you train them to clean up after themselves?'

We lay awhile, and pictured the cats manipulating mop, pail and disinfectant. But somewhere in me, I was saying to them: If there are any parasites round here, I know just who. Make the most of it, you gigolos. Your days are numbered.

I really did have it all worked out. Cathy was going to sell the house and I was going to sell the book. We were going to take an apartment, and I was going to keep us in a style to which I was unaccustomed. Cats aren't so hot ten floors up in the air. And five of them, in those conditions, are just not on. Of course, I knew she wouldn't leave them without a roof, and I'd already become a used cat salesman. But suddenly it seemed everyone I knew had one cat, two cats or three. Except Genevieve, who had a singularly xenophobic dog. Everybody, even Genevieve, told me cats are bee-ootiful, and I should let Cathy educate me over my phobia.

Then someone got interested in the book. Things seemed to be coming along, so I sat up from five in the morning until eleven the next night a few times, and finished the beast with heavy hatchet blows from the typer.

I got ready to broach the apartment idea again to Cathy. I began to dream crazy schemes. Like renting out Cathy's parents' house, and whoever took it on got the cats as a bonus, while we had the cats to visit us twice a week. Or buying the cats a ranch in Texas. Or slipping them cyanide in their Tiger-Cookies.

I was fantasizing because I basically understood Cathy wouldn't agree. And she didn't agree.

'No, Stil, I can't,' she said. 'Can't and won't. You're not making me leave my cats.'

'I need you,' I said, striking a pose like Errol Flynn. It wasn't only the pose that wasn't one hundred percent true. I was wondering how exactly I did analyze my feelings for her, the first time I'd had to do that, when, brittle and hard as dry cement, she said: 'You just need my money.'

'Oh Jesus.'

'You want to use me.'

'Yeah, yeah. Of course I do.'

I stood and wondered now if I was only demanding we live together because I wanted her to choose between me and the zoo. Did I really want to be with her that much, this white-faced maniac with green electric eyes?

'You bastard,' she whispered. 'Dad always told me I'd meet men like you.'

And she pulled off the jade bracelet and flung it at me, the way girls fling their engagement rings in old B movies. Like a dope, I neatly caught it. Then she turned and ran.

I stood and looked at the sidewalk where the colored lights of the King of Cups were going like a migraine attack. I now had the third wonder, wondering what I felt. But I felt too numb to feel anything. Then I went into the club and perpetrated the worst goddam magician act I hope never to live through again.

Two weeks later Carthage Press bought my book, with an option on two more. I got a standing ovation at the King, got drunk, slept with a girl I can't remember. Three weeks later, Genevieve, who reads Tarot at the King, came over and stood looking at me as I was feeding the dental-floss-white rabbit I'd just accumulated to put in the act as a cliché.

'You know, Stil,' said Genevieve, gazing up at me from her clever, paintable, lookable-at face, and all of her five foot one inch, 'you are going all to hell.'

'I'd better pack a bag, then.'

'I mean it, Stil,' said Genevieve, helping me post the rabbit full of lettuce. 'The act is lousy.'

'Gee thanks, Genevieve,' I gushed.

'It's technically perfect, and it's getting better, and it's about dead as Julius Caesar.'

'Gosh, is he *dead*? How'd it happen, hit and run?'

'No, I'm not laughing,' said Genevieve, not laughing. 'I want to know where that girl is, the blond girl.' She waited a while, and when I didn't say anything, Genevieve said: 'Let's get this straight. I'm worried about *her*. She was on a knife-edge, and you were easing her off it. Now I guess she's back on the knife-edge. You're not usually so obtuse.'

'Not that it's any of your business, but we had nothing left to say to each other.'

'To coin a phrase. That's why the act stinks. That's why the next novel will stink.'

'Genevieve, I honestly don't know if I want to see her again or I don't.'

'I know,' said Genevieve. She smiled, riffled the cards, and picked the Lovers straight out of the pack. 'Just,' said Genevieve, 'go knock on her door, and see what happens to you when she opens it.'

I went out, to the pay-phone in the Piper Building down the block. I didn't realize till I came to put in the dime I still had a leaf of lettuce in my hand.

I didn't think anyone would answer. Or maybe one of the cats would take the call, and spit. Then there was her voice.

'Hi, Cathy,' I said.

I heard her drag in a deep breath, and then she said, 'I'm glad you called. It doesn't make any difference, but I want to apologize for what I said to you.'

'It does make a difference,' I said.

'Thank you for mailing me back the bracelet,' she said. 'I'm going to hang up now.'

'Carthage are doing my book,' I said.

'I'm so glad. You'd never read me any. I'll be sure and buy it. I'm going to hang up right now.'

'OK. I'll be with you in twenty minutes.'

'No –'

'Yes. Give the cats a dust.'

It was a quarter to five when I reached the house, and a premature white snow was coming down like blossom on the lawns along the street.

Here goes, Genevieve, I thought, as I pressed the doorbell. Now let's see what *does* happen to me when Cathy opens the door.

What happened was a strange, strange thing, because I looked at Cathy, and I just didn't know her. For one thing, I'd never properly seen how beautiful she was, because she'd looked somehow familiar from the first time I saw her. But now, she was brand new, unidentifiable. And looking in her clandestine face, I wondered (always wondering) if I was ready to break the cellophane wrapper.

'There's snow in your hair,' she said quietly, and with awe. And I comprehended she, too, was seeing something new and uncannily special in me. 'Are you sure you want to come in?'

'You're damn right I do. I'm getting cold out here.'

'If you come in,' she said, 'please don't try and make me agree to anything I don't want. Please, Stil.'

'Cross my heart.'

She let me in then, solemnly. We went into the living room. The once-conversation-piece electric fire, which didn't look like a fire at all but some sort of space-rocket about to take off and blast its way through the ceiling to Venus, exuded a rich red glow. It enveloped five squatting forms, and their fur was limned as if in blood.

'Hi, cats,' I said. I knew by now I was probably going to have to concede, perhaps even share my life with them. Maybe I could get to love them. I reached down slowly, and a fistful of scythes sloughed off some topskin. So. I could tie their paws up in dinky little velvet bags, I could cover the floors with washable polythene, I could always carry a gun. Cats don't live so long as humans. Unless they got you first.

We sat by the fire, the seven of us. Cathy and I drank China tea. The cats drank single cream from five dishes.

There were some enormous fresh claw-marks along the fire's wood surround, bigger and higher than any of their previous original etchings. Cathy must have gone out at some point and missed one of their ten or eleven mealtimes, and they'd got fed up waiting. I surreptitiously licked my bleeding hand.

'Genevieve told me,' I said, 'about a ground-floor apartment just off Aster. There's a back yard with lilac trees. They'd enjoy scratching those.'

'You still want me to sell this house,' said Cathy. 'My parents' house, they wanted me to have.'

'Not sell. You could rent it.'

She looked at the fire, which also limned her now, her bone-china profile, the strands of her hair, with blood.

'I thought I'd never see you again,' she said.

'The Invisible Man. It's OK. I took the antidote.'

'I thought I'd just go back to where I was, the years before I met you. That I'd always be alone. Me, and the cats. I thought that was how it would be.'

I took her hand. It was cold and stiff, and her nails were long and ragged. Down below, the cats were poised over their empty plates, staring up at her, their eyes like blank glass buttons.

'So I said to myself,' she said, 'I don't need anyone. I've got the cats. I don't need anyone human at all.'

She pulled her hand out of mine, and got up.

'I'm not,' she said, 'leaving this house.'

'All right. Good. Sit down.'

'In a minute,' she said. 'I have to feed the cats.'

'Oh, sure. The cream was an apéritif. Which is the starter? Salmon or caviar?'

She considered me, her eyes just like theirs. She wasn't laughing either. She went out to the kitchen, and the cats trotted after her. They didn't screech this time, but I could imagine all that cream slopping loudly about in their multiplicity of guts.

Alone, I sat and contemplated the Venus rocket, and the huge new claw-marks up the wood. It looked, on reflection, really too high for the cats to have reached, even balanced on tip-claw. Maybe one had teetered on another one's head.

After a while, none of the cats, or Cathy, had come back.

The tea was stone cold, and I could hear the snow tapping on the windows, the house was so quiet, as if no one else but me was in it. Finally I got up, and walked softly, the way you tread in a museum, along to the kitchen door. There was no light anywhere, not in the passage, not in the dining area, or the kitchen itself. And scarcely a sound. Then I heard a sound, a regular crunching, mumbling sound. It was the cats eating, there in the dark. I must have heard it a thousand times, but suddenly it had a unique syncopation all its own. It was the noise of the jungle, and I was right in the midst of it. And the hair crawled over my scalp.

I hit the light switch on a reflex, and then I saw.

There on the floor, in a row, were the five cats. And Cathy.

The cats were leaning forward over their paws, chomping steadily. Cathy lay on her stomach, the soles of her feet pressed hard against the freezer, supporting her upper torso on her elbows. Her hair had been draped back over one shoulder so it

136

wouldn't get in the way as she licked up the single cream from the saucer.

She continued this about a couple of seconds after the light came on, long enough for me to be sure I wasn't hallucinating. Then she raised her head like a snake, and licked her lips, and watched me with her glass-button eyes.

I backed out the kitchen. I went on backing until I was half along the passage. Then I turned like a zombie and walked into the living room.

Nothing was altered. Not even the big new runnels in the wood surround of the fire.

I was sweating a dank cold sweat and breathing as fast as if I'd just got out from a lion's cage, which I hadn't, yet. It was some kind of primitive reaction, because what I'd seen was really very funny, a joke. But I don't think I could have been more shaken if she'd come at me with a steak knife.

I pondered my alternatives. I could make it out the door, and run. I needn't come back. She'd know why not. Or I could stay and try to figure her out, try to persuade her to tell me what the game was and why she was playing it, and how I could help stop her going insane.

I was deliberating, when she came into the room. She looked straight at me, and she said, 'I'm sorry you saw that.'

'Are you? Somehow I had the feeling I was meant to see. What's the idea?'

'No idea. I like it. I like scratching the wood, too. Over the fire. See? You look nervous.'

'Must be because I am.'

She glided across the room, and slid her arms round my ribs. 'You're nervous of me.'

'I'm terrified of you.'

She kissed my jaw, and each time she kissed, I felt the edges of her teeth. I could imagine what she'd be like if I made love to her now. Not that I wanted to make love to her.

I wanted to leave her and run. That was all I wanted, but concern gets to be a habit, and I guess we all know about habits. Besides, you find a girl sitting with a bottle of pills and a razor blade, and you go out and shut the door? And then, in any case, I realized she was trembling. I'd thought it was just me.

'Get your coat and your boots,' I said.

'It's snowing.'

'Excuses, excuses. Get your coat.'

'All right.'

Ten minutes later, we were on the street. The cold silvery air seemed to blow through my head, and I started to ask myself where I was taking her. But Cathy didn't speak, just walked beside me, like a good little girl doing what the adults tell her though she doesn't understand.

We rode the subway, and came back up out of the ground and walked to my place, to which I never take anyone unless I must, not even a rabbit. The King of Cups is where I live; 23 Mason is where I occasionally eat, and less occasionally sleep, thrash a typewriter, and worry. And that's the way it looks. It's a couple of flights up, or chiropractical jerks if you use the elevator. In the snow-light, it was gray and chill and scattered with reams of paper, magazines and dust. My world and no one else's, and I didn't want her here, and this was where I'd brought her. Why? Because part of me had subconsciously worked out that this place had been built from my own individual ectoplasm, and I was going to use it to bawl her out and back to sanity, louder than any shout I could make with my throat.

We got inside the door, and she glanced drearily around. We hadn't offered a word to each other since leaving the house.

'Every luxury fitment,' I now said. 'Most of them not working.'

Cathy crossed to the window, and stood there in her coat with the snow dissolving on its shoulders. She looked at the yard two floors down, and the trash-cans and broken bottles in their own cake-frosting of snow. When she turned round, her face was gleaming, waves of tears running over it. She sprang to me suddenly and held on to me. I knew the grip. I knew I'd gotten her back. If I wanted her. Her hair seemed the only thing in the room which had color, and which shone.

'I'm sorry,' she muttered, 'sorry, sorry.'

I felt tired and it all seemed faintly absurd. I stroked her hair, and knew in the morning I was going to call Genevieve, and ask her what the hell to do next.

In the morning, about seven, I slunk out of bed, put some clothes on, and went out, leaving Cathy asleep. The pay-phone in the entry, as usual, was bust, so I walked down to the booth on the corner of Mason and Quale. The snow lay thin and moistly crisp as water-ice, and the sky was painting itself in blue as high summer. It was an optimistic morning, full of promises of something. I got through to Genevieve, who hardly ever sleeps, and told her all of it, feeling a fool.

'Oh boy,' said Genevieve. And then: 'Bring her over here to breakfast, why don't you. Maybe the dog'll chase her up a tree.'

'You think I'm on something and I imagined it.'

'No.'

'You think I should laugh it off, it doesn't matter.'

'It matters.'

'Well?'

'Well. I think you're going as bats as she is. I don't know what I can do except feed you pancakes – little children like those, don't they? But I know a guy might help.'

Genevieve genuinely knows a remarkable number of guys who can help. Help you get to sing with the opera, help you find out who you were six hundred years ago in medieval Europe, or help you find a cop who cares somebody mugged you and stole the fillings from your teeth.

'A shrink.'

'Sort of. Wait and see.'

'It has to be gentle, Genevieve. Very, very gentle.'

'It will be. Bring her. I'll expect you by eight.'

Once you've passed the buck, you feel better. I felt better. I walked back through the snow, identifying the footprints in it like a kid: human, bird, dog. I knew I could leave all the delicate maneuvering to Genevieve, who is one of the best social surgeons there are. Sometime later, I'd have to decide where I wanted to be in all of this, but I didn't have to do it right now.

I got up to the second floor, and let myself in the apartment, and Cathy was gone.

The bed was empty, the bathroom, even the closet. I was working myself into a panicky rage when I saw her purse lying under the window. The window was just open, and the dust-drape of snow on the fire-escape had neat dark cuts in it the shape of shoe-soles. I climbed through on to it, and looked down and saw Cathy standing in the yard, with her back to me.

I didn't react properly. I was just so relieved to find her. I leaned on the rail and shouted.

'Hey Cathy. We're going to Genevieve's for breakfast.'

She turned round, then, and her eyes came up to mine, but without a trace of recognition. And then I saw what it was she had in her mouth. It was a bleeding, fluttering, almost-but-not-quite-dead pigeon.

Cathy had found her breakfast already.

Il Bacio (Il Chiave) –
'The Kiss (The Key)'

This too was firstly begun – though not finished – in my teens. It developed from my craving after Renaissance Italy, the realms of the Borgias.

In the first version, the key related to a bedchamber. But then, of course, it still does . . .

Roma, late in her fifteenth century After the Lord, packed on the banks of her yellow river, had entered that phase of summer known by some as the *Interiore*. This being a kind of pun – an interior place, or – frankly – entrails. It was a fact: Roma, brown and pink and grey and white and beautiful, ripely stank. Before the month was over, there might very possibly be plague.

Once the red cannon-blast of the sunset, however, left the cool garden on the high hill, the dusk began to come with all its tessellated stars, and the only scent was from the grape-vines and the dusty flowers, and the last aromas of the cooked chickens now merely bones on a table. Four men had dined. From their garments and their demeanour it was easy to locate their portion, the noble rich, indolent and at play. They had no thought of plague, even though they had disparagingly discussed it an hour before. They were young, the youth of their era – the oldest not more than twenty years – and in the way of the young knew they would live forever, and in the way of their time, as in the way of all times, understood they might die horribly in a month, or a day. And naturally also, since such profound and simple insight is essentially destructive where too often recognized, they knew nothing of the sort.

There had, very properly, been talk of horses, too, and clothing and politics. Now, with the fruit and the fourth or fifth

141

cups of wine, there came talk of women, and so, consecutively, of gambling.

'But have no fear, Valore, you shall be excluded.'

'Shall I? A pity.'

'Yes, no doubt. And worse pity to have you more in debt to us than already you are.'

'You owe me two hundred ducats, Valore, since the horse-race. Did you forget?'

'No, dearest Stephano. I very much regret it.' Valore della Scorpioni leaned back in his chair and smiled upon them with the utmost confidence. Each at the table was fine-looking in his way, but Valore, a torch among candles, far out-shone them and blinded, for good measure, with his light.

His was that unusual and much-admired combination of dark red hair and pale amber skin sometimes retained in the frescoes and on the canvases of masters, a combination later disbelieved as only capable of artificial reproduction. Added to this, a pair of large hazel eyes brought gorgeousness to the patrician face, white teeth blessed it; while all below and beyond the neck showed the excellent results of healthful exercise, good food not consumed in excess, and the arrogant grace evolving upon the rest. In short, a beauty, interesting to either sex, and not less so to himself.

Added to his appearance and aura, however, Valore della Scorpioni had the virtue of an ill-name. His family drew its current rank by bastardy out of an infamous house not unacquainted with the Vatican. As will happen, bad things were said of it, as of its initiator. Untrue as the friends and adorers of Valore knew all such things to be, yet they were not immune to the insidious attraction of all such things. No trace of witchcraft or treachery might be seen to mar the young man, scarcely eighteen, who sat godlike in their midst. That he, rich as they, owed money everywhere, was nothing new. It pleased them, perhaps excited them, Stephano, Cesco, Andrea, that this creature was in their debt.

'Well,' said Andrea now. 'I, for one, have nothing left to put forward on the dice, save my jewels.'

'And I,' said Valore della Scorpioni, with a flame-quick lightness that alerted them all, 'have only *this*.'

On the table, then, among the bones, fruit, and wine cups, was set an item of black iron at odds with all. A key. Complex and encrusted, its size alone marked it as the means to some portentous entry.

'Jesu, what's this,' Stephano cried, 'the way into your lord father's treasury?'

Valore beamed still, lowering his eyes somewhat, giving them ground.

'It's old,' said Andrea. 'It could unlock a secret route into the catacombs –'

And Cesco, not to be outdone: 'No, it is the door to the Pope's wine-cellar, no less. Is it not, Valore?'

The hazel eyes arose. Valore looked at them.

'It is,' he said, 'the key to a lady's bedchamber.'

They exclaimed, between jeering mirth and credulity. They themselves were unsure of which they favoured. The dark was now complete, and the candles on the table gave the only illumination. Caught by these, Valore's beautiful face had acquired a sinister cast, impenetrable and daunting. So they had seen it before, and at such moments the glamour of evil repute, though unbelieved, seemed not far off.

'Come, now,' Andrea said at length, when the jibes had gone unanswered. 'Whose chamber is it? Some harlot –'

'Not at all,' said Valore. He paused again, and allowed them to hang upon his words. 'Would I offer you such dross in lieu of honest recompense for my debts?'

'Oh, yes,' said Cesco. 'Just so you would.'

'Then,' said Valore, all velvet, 'for shame to sit here with such a wretch. Go home, Cesco, I entreat you. I'd not dishonour you further.' And when Cesco had finished uneasily protesting, Valore picked up the great black key and turned it in his flexible fingers. 'This, sweet friends, fits the lock of one, a lady of high birth. A lady most delectable, who is kindred to me.'

They exhibited mirth again, sobered, and stared at him.

Andrea said, 'Then truly you make sport here. If she is your kin, you would hardly disgrace her so.'

'She's not disgraced. She will not be angry.' In utter silence now they gazed on their god. Valore nodded. 'I see you doubt her charms. But I will show you. This attends the key.' And now there was put on the table a little portrait, ringed by pearls, the whole no bigger than a plum.

One by one, in the yellow candlelight, they took it up and

peered at it. And one by one they set it down; and their faces, also oddly lit, their eyes en-embered, turned strange, unearthly, and lawless.

There was no likelihood the woman in the painting was not kindred of the Scorpion house. Evident in her, as in the young man at the table, was that same unequivocal hair falling about and upon that same succulent skin. The contour of the eyes and of all the features were so similar to Valore's own that it could have been modelled on himself, save for some almost indefinable yet general difference, and a female delicacy absent from the masculine lines of the one who – in the flesh and to the life – sat before them, indisputably a man.

'But,' Stephano murmured eventually, 'she might be your sister.'

'My sisters, as you are aware, Stephano, do not so much resemble me. They are besides raven-haired. Therefore, the lady's not my sister. Nor, to forestall you, my cousin, my mother, any sister of my mother's or my sire's, or even, *per Dio*, any forward daughter of my own. Yet she is kin to me. Yet this key is the key to her chamber. Yet she will not turn away whoever of you may win it at the dice. If any win, save I. If not it is mine, as now mine. I have done.'

The fox-lit faces angled to each other.

'An enigma.'

'If you wish.'

At that moment, one of Andrea Trarra's servants came out into the garden like a ghost. Bending to the master of the feast, the man whispered. Andrea's face underwent a subtle fortuitous alteration. He spoke in assent to the servant, who moved away. Then turning to the company, he dazzled them with the words: 'A fourth guest has just now arrived.'

There followed a popular demand as to who this guest might be, formerly unexpected, conceivably unwelcome. Valore did not join in the outcry. He sat, toying with the key, and only stilled his fingers when Andrea announced: 'It is one you know of. Di Giudea.'

'What do you say?' protested Cesco, flushing. 'We must sit at table with a Jew?'

'Not at all,' said Andrea placidly, and with a little soft sneer. 'Being a Jew, as you note, Olivio di Giudea will not eat with anyone, since the way we prepare our meat and wine is contrary to his religion.'

'And even so,' said Stephano, 'it's not at all certain he's a Jew by blood. He has travelled widely in the East, and is perhaps titled for that. No one, it seems, credits this his real name – I cite "Olivio" – that does not strike the Judean note.'

'I, for one,' said Cesco, 'resent your act, Andrea, bringing the man upon us in this way. Did you invite him?'

'My house was open to him on his return to Roma. He is an alchemist and a painter of some worth, who has been recognized by the Holy Father himself. Am I to put myself above such social judgements? Besides, I have business with him.'

'To cheat money from your countrymen – ever a Jew's business.'

'Actually to debate the repair of some frescoes in my villa at Ostia. There is no craftsman like Olivio for such things. The man's a genius.'

'He is a *Jew*,' said Cesco, and he rose magnificently to his feet, bowing in anger to the table. 'Thanks for the pleasant supper, Andrea. I hope to see you again at a more amenable hour.'

With a flurry of snatched mantle he strode from the garden and passed in the very doorway a tall straight darkness, to which he paid no heed at all.

'I trust,' Andrea said, 'no other will take flight.'

'Why,' said Stephano, 'my nicest whore is a Hebrew. It's nothing to me.'

'And we should recall, perhaps,' added Valore della Scorpioni gently, 'that the Christ Himself –'

'No, no, an Egyptian, I do assure you –'

Someone laughed, a quiet and peculiarly sombre laugh, from the shadow beyond the vines. A man stepped out of the shadow a moment later, and stood before them in the candlelight for their inspection. He was yet smiling faintly, without a trace of bitterness, rage, or shame. It might be true he was of the Judean line, for though he had no mark of what a Roman would deem Semitic, yet he had all the arrogance of the Jew. He carried himself like a prince and looked back at them across a vast distance through the black centres of his eyes. His hair, long and sable, fell below his wide shoulders; he was in all respects of apparel and appurtenance a man of fashion, the swarthy red cloth

145

and snow-white linen hung and moulded on an excellent frame. Nor was there anything vulgar, or even anything simply challenging in his dress. He had not sought to rival the splendours of the aristocracy, rather he seemed uninterested, beyond all such concerns, having perhaps precociously outgrown them, for he appeared not much older than Andrea's twenty years. But there was in Olivio called di Giudea that unforgivable air of superiority, whether religious or secular, genuine, or false, which had from the time of the Herods – and indeed long before – been the root cause of the hatred towards and the endlessly attempted ruin of the Jewish race.

It was Andrea who was momentarily ill at ease, Stephano who donned an almost servile smirk of condescension. Valore della Scorpioni merely watched.

'Good evening to you, 'ser Olivio,' said Andrea. 'Be seated. Is there anything I may offer you?'

'I think not, as you will have explained to your guests.' The voice of the Judean, if so he was, was firm and clear, and of the same dark flavour as his looks. 'Had I known you entertained these gentlemen, my lord, I should not have intruded.'

'It's nothing, 'ser Olivio. We had just foundered on the serious matter of a dice-game, and you have saved me from it.'

'Not at all.' It was Valore who spoke. 'Escape is impossible.' Valore himself smiled then, into the face of the newcomer, a smile of the most dangerous and luminous seduction imaginable. 'And perhaps your friend will join the game, since Cesco was so suddenly called away. Or do you also, sir, omit to gamble, along with all these other omissions?'

Di Giudea moved around the table and sat calmly down in Cesco's emptied place. Another servant had come during the interchange, with more wine. As the jar approached, not glancing at it, the man placed one hand over the vacant cup.

'I gamble,' he said quietly, returning the golden regard, seemingly quite resistant to it. 'Who can say he lives, and does not?'

Stephano grunted. 'But your laws do not bar you from the dice?'

'Which laws are these?'

'The laws of your god.'

The Jew seemed partly amused, but with great courtesy he

replied, 'The god to whom you refer, my lord, is I believe the father of your own.'

There was a small clatter. Valore had tossed the dice on to the table, and now held up the iron key before them all.

'We are playing for this,' he said, 'and this.' And he reached for the portrait of the girl, shifting it till it lay directly in front of di Giudea. 'The first gives access to the second.'

Stephano swore by the Antichrist. Even Andrea Trarra was provoked and protested.

'The play is open to all your guests,' said Valore. 'This gentleman is rich; I will accept his bond. And you, sir, do you understand what is offered?'

'Such games were current in this city in the time of the Caesars,' di Giudea said, without a hint of excitement or alarm.

'And even then,' Valore softly remarked, 'my forebears had their booted feet upon the necks of yours.'

Di Giudea looked from the portrait back to its owner. The foreigner's face was grave. 'There,' he said, 'is your booted foot. And here, my neck. Should you try to bring them closer, you might find some inconvenience.'

Valore said smoothly, 'Am I threatened? Do you know me, sir, or my family?'

'The banner of the Scorpion,' said the Jew, with a most insulting politeness, 'is widely recognized.'

'Scorpions,' said Valore, 'sting.'

'And when surrounded by fire,' the Jew appended mercilessly, 'sting also themselves to death.'

Valore gazed under long lids.

'Where is the fire?'

'It's well known, though all its other faculties are acute, the power of observation is, in the scorpion, very poor.'

Valore widened his eyes, and now offered no riposte. Andrea and Stephano, who had sat transfixed, broke into a surge of motion. They had been stones a second before, and all the life of the table concentrated at its further end.

'Come,' Stephano almost shouted, 'if we are to play, let's do it.'

'No, no,' said Andrea. 'I shall abstain. 'Ser Olivio –'

'He plays,' said Valore. 'Do you not?'

Andrea wriggled like a boy. Olivio di Giudea was immobile,

147

save for the hand that took up the pair of dice.

'I have,' he said, 'examined your frescoes, my lord Andrea. I regret they are beyond my help, or anyone's.'

Andrea's face fell heavily.

Presently, the dice also fell.

The game, now common, next subject to certain innovations of a pattern more complex and more irritant, grew dependently more heated. The dice rang, chattered, scattered, and gave up their fortunes. The wine ran as the dice ran, in every cup save that adjacent to the chair of the Judean. Stephano waxed drunken and argumentative, Andrea Trarra, as was his way, became withdrawn. On Valore, the wine and the game made no decided impression, though he lost consistently; and it came upon them all, perhaps even upon the sombre and dispassionate intellect of the Jew, that Valore meant this night to lose and to do nothing else. Only the frenzy of the dice went on and on, and then finally and suddenly stopped, as if tired out.

It was almost midnight. The city lay below and about the garden, nearly black as nothingness, touched only here and there by lights of watch or revelry. There was no breeze at all; and far away a bell was ringing, sonorous and dreadful in the silence.

Valore offered the key. Andrea turned from it with a grimace, and Stephano with a curse.

'Well, sir. My noble familiars reject their prize. I must spew ducats for them, it seems. But you, I owe you more now than all the rest. Do you accept the key, and allow its promise to cancel my debt? Or will you be my usurer?'

Olivio di Giudea extended that same strong graceful hand which had sealed off the wine cup and plucked up the dice.

'I will accept the key.'

Stephano rounded on him, striking at his arm.

'You forget yourself. *Per Dio*! If he speaks the truth, a lady's honour is at stake – and to be yours, you damned infidel dog!'

The Jew laughed, as once before in the shadow beyond the candlelight, mild and cruel, unhuman as the bell.

It was Valore who leaned across the table, caught Stephano's shirt in his grip and shook the assemblage, linen and man. And Valore's eyes which spat fire, and Valore's lips which said: 'You would not take it. If he will, he shall.'

And Stephano fell back, grudging and shivering.

Valore got to his feet and gestured to the alien who, rising up, was noticed as some inches the taller.

'I am your guide,' Valore said. 'Think me the gods' messenger and follow.' He put away the portrait in his doublet, and – catching up his mantle – turned without another word to leave Andrea's garden. It was di Giudea who bowed and murmured a farewell. Neither of the remaining men answered him. Only their eyes went after, and lost their quarry as the low-burning candles guttered on their spikes. While in the heart of the city the bell died, and the melancholy of the ebbing night sank down upon the earth.

It appeared the lordly Valore had not brought with him any attendant, and that di Giudea had been of like mind. No torch walked before them; therefore, they traversed the scrambling streets like shadows in that black hour of new-born morning. A leaden moisture seemed to have fallen from the sky, dank but hardly cold; and the stench of the narrower thoroughfares might have disgusted even men well used to it. Both, however, in the customary manner, were armed, and went unmolested by any mortal thing. So they turned at length on to broader streets, and thus towards a pile of masonry, unlit, its sentinel flambeaux out, that nevertheless proclaimed itself by the escutcheon over its gate as the palace now in the possession of the Scorpioni.

Having gone by the gate, they sought a subsidiary entrance and there passed through into an aisle of fragrant bushes. Another garden, spread under the walls of the palace, lacking form in the moonlessness.

'Keep close, or you may stumble,' Valore said with the solicitousness of a perfect host: the first words he had uttered since their setting out. Di Giudea did not, even now, reply. Yet, moving a few steps behind Valore across the unfamiliar land, it seemed his own sense of sight was more acute than that of the scorpion he had mentioned.

Suddenly, under a lingering, extending tree, Valore paused. The second shadow paused also, saying nothing.

'You do not anxiously question me,' Valore said, 'on where we are going, how soon we shall arrive, if I mean to dupe you, if you are to be set on by my kinsmen – are such things inconsequent to you, Olivio of Judea? Or can it be you trust me?'

After a moment, the other answered him succinctly.

'Your family have left Roma to avoid the heat. A few servants only remain. As to our destination, already I behold it.'

'*Sanguigno,*' swore Valore softly. 'Do you so?'

Some hundred paces away, amid a tangle of myrtles, a paler darkness rose from black foliage to black sky. To one who knew, its shape was evident, for memory filled in what the eyes mislaid. Yet it transpired the foreigner, too, had some knowledge, not only of the departure of the household, but of its environs and architecture left behind.

What stood in the myrtle grove of the Scorpioni garden, long untended, a haunted, eerie place even by day, was an old mausoleum. Such an edifice was not bizarre. In the tradition of the city, many a powerful house retained its dead. The age of the tomb, however, implied it had preceded the advent of the noble bastardy which lifted the Scorpioni to possession of this ground – or, more strange, that the sepulchre had been brought with them from some other spot, a brooding heirloom.

'Come on, then, good follower,' said Valore, and led the way over the steep roots of trees, among the sweet-scented myrtles, and so right up to a door bound with black ironwork. A great lock hung there like a spider. It was but too obvious that the mysterious key belonged to this, and to this alone.

The foreigner did not baulk. He came on, as requested, and stood with Valore, whose fire and gold were gone to soot and silver in the dark.

'A lady's bedchamber,' said di Giudea, from which it appeared he divined rather more of the conversation at Andrea's table than supposed.

Valore was not inclined to debate on this.

'So it is. A woman lies sleeping within, as you shall witness, have you but the courage to employ the key. A being as beautiful as her picture, and my kin, as I have said. Nor will she deny you entry to the room, or think herself dishonoured. You will be fascinated, I assure you. It is a marvel of my family, not frequently revealed to strangers.'

'Which you yourself,' said Olivio di Giudea, 'have never ventured to inspect.'

'Ah! You have me, messer Jew. But then, I happened upon the key only yesterday. Why deny some friend, also, a chance to see the wonder, which is surely most wonderful if as the parchment describes it.'

Di Giudea raised the key and pierced the heavy lock. The awful spider did not resist him, its mechanism grated and surrendered at the insistence of that strong hand. His composure hung about him yet; it was Valore's breath which quickened.

The door swung wide, its iron thorns outstretched to tear the leaves from the myrtles. Beyond, a fearful opening gaped, black past blackness, repellent to any who had ever dreamed of death.

Valore leaned to the earth, arose, and there came the scrape of kindled flame. Candles had been left lying in readiness, and now burst into flower. Colour struck against the void of the mausoleum's mouth, and did it no great harm.

'Take this light. You may hereafter lead the way, *caro*. It is not far.'

Di Giudea's eyes, polished by the candle as he received it, seemed without depth or soul; he in his turn had now absorbed a wicked semblance from the slanted glow. It was a season for such things. He did not move.

'Afraid to enter?' Valore mocked, himself brightly gilded again on the night. 'Follow me still, then.' And with this, walked directly into the slot of the tomb.

It was quite true, he had not previously entered this place. Nor was it fear that had kept him out, though a kind of fear was mingled in his thoughts with other swirlings of diverse sort. Neither pure nor simple were the desires of Valore della Scorpioni, and to some extent, even as he revelled in himself, he remained to himself a mystery. What he asked of this adventure he could not precisely have confessed, but that the advent of the infamous magnetic Jew had quickened everything, of that he was in no doubt.

So, he came into the tomb of which the brown parchment had, in its concise Latin, informed him.

It was a spot immediately conjurable, dressed stone of the antique mode, the light barely dispelling the gloom, yet falling out from his hand upon a slab, and so impelling the young man to advance, to search, to find the curious miracle which the paper had foretold.

'Ah, by the Mass. *Ipsissima verba*.'

And thus Olivio di Giudea came on him an instant later, his

words still whispering in the breathless air and the candlelight richening as it was doubled on the stone and the face of what lay on that stone.

She was as the portrait had given her, the hair like rose mahogany shining its rays on the unloving pillow, the creamy skin defiled only by the gauzy webs that had clustered too upon her gown of topaz silk, now fragile as a web itself, and all its golden sequins tarnished into green. Her face, her throat, her breast, the long stemmed fingers sheared of rings – these marked her as a girl not more than nineteen years of age, a woman at the fullness and bloom of her nubility. There was about her, too, that indefinable ghastliness associated with recent death. It would have seemed, but for the decay of her garments, that she had been brought here only yesterday. Yet, from her dress, the gathering cobwebs, it had been considerably longer.

'You see,' Valore said, very low, 'she is as I promised you. Beautiful and rare. Laid out upon her couch. Not chiding, but quiescent. To be enjoyed.'

'And you would wake her with a kiss?'

Valore shuddered. 'Perhaps. My reverie is not lawful as I look at her. No holy musings come to me. Her flesh is wholesome, lovely. I would ask her if she went to her bed a virgin. Alas, unpardonable sin.'

'You have lain with your sisters. What's one sin more?'

Valore turned to study his companion, but that face had become a shadow upon shadows.

'*Caro*, she is too old to tempt me, after all. Let me tell you what the parchment said of her. Aurena della Scorpioni, for that was her name, unknown in the days of our modesty, lived unwed in her father's house until that year the Eastern Plague fell upon Roma as upon all the world. And before the merciful, if dilatory, angel stood upon the Castel San Angelo to sheathe his dripping sword, shut up in that house, Aurena took the fever of the *peste* and life passed from her. Having no mark upon her, it was said she had died the needle-death – for they believed, *caro*, that certain Jews had gone about scratching the citizens with poisoned needles . . . And the year of her death is graven there, beneath her feet. You see the candle shine upon it?'

Di Giudea did not speak, but that he had noted the carving was quite likely. It revealed clearly enough that the pestilence to which the younger man referred was that which would come to be known uniquely as The Death, or the Black Death, and that Aurena della Scorpioni, lying like a fresh-cut rose, had died and been interred almost a century and a half before.

Valore leaned now to the dead girl, close enough for sure to have embraced her. And to her very lips he said, 'And are we to believe it?'

The Jew had set his candle in a little niche in the wall, where once maybe a sacred image had been placed, now vanished. As the young man flirted with the corpse, bending close, his long hair mingling with hers and of the self-same shade as hers, di Giudea stood in silence, his tall straight figure partly shrouded in the dark, his arms folded. There was about him a curious air of patience, that and some inexorable and powerful quality having no name. The tomb, with its pledge of death, the miracle that lay there, if miracle it was and not some alchemical trick, each seemed to have left him undisturbed. The younger man sparkled on the dark like a jewel; the Judean was, in some extraordinary way, an emissary and partner of that dark. So that, looking up once more, Valore very nearly started, and might be forgiven for it, as if he had glimpsed the figure of Death himself.

But, 'Well,' said Valore then, regaining himself in a moment, 'what shall we do? Shall we withdraw? I for one am loath to desert her. How long she has endured alone here, unvisited save by beetles, unwooed save by worms. If I could wake her, as you postulate, with a loving kiss – shall I try it, noble pagan? Will you act my brother at this wedding, stay and kiss her, too . . . ?' Olivio di Giudea did not respond, standing on, the shadows like black wings against his back. And Valore offered him again that glorious smile, and put down his beautiful face towards the beautiful face of the dead. The lips met, one pair eager with heat, one passive and cool. Valore della Scorpioni kissed his kindred with great insistence, his mouth fastened on hers as if never to be lifted, his fingers straying, clasping, the smooth flesh of her throat, the loose knot of her fingers on her breast.

The Jew watched him.

Valore raised his head, staring now only at the woman. 'Divine madonna,' he exclaimed, 'beloved, can I not warm you? I must court you further, then –' And now he half lay against the body, taking it in his arms, his eyes blazing like gold coins –

And for the third occasion of that darkness, the Jew laughed.

Valore acknowledged this only by the merest sound, his lips active, his hands at work, his pulses louder in his ears than any laughter.

But in another instant, di Giudea left his post by the wall, breaking the shadows in pieces, and striding to the slab. Here he set a grip like iron on the young man's shoulder and prized him from his employment. With a slitted gaze, now, breathing as if in a race, Valore looked at him perforce, and found him laughing still, mainly the two eyes glittering like black stones with laughter.

'Your kisses after all, I fear, leave her but too cold,' said the Judean.

'Oh, you will do better? Do it. I shall observe you closely and take instruction.'

'Firstly,' said di Giudea, holding him yet in that awesome iron grip, 'I will tell you this much. You rightly suppose she is not dead. She only sleeps. Should she rouse, will you run away?'

'I? I have seen many things done, and stayed to see others. Things even you may never have looked on.'

'That I doubt. I am older than you, and much-travelled.'

Valore attempted to dislodge the iron vice, and failed. He relaxed, trembling with excitement, anger, a whole host of emotions that charged him with some delicious sense of imminence. Even the punishing hand that held him was, in that moment, not displeasing.

'Do as you wish, and all you wish,' said Valore hoarsely. 'And you will find me here, obedient.'

The Jew showed his white teeth and with a casual violence quite unlooked-for, flung the young man from him and simultaneously from the couch. Valore rolled on the floor and came to rest against the worn stones of one wall. Dazed, he lay there, and from this vantage saw the tall figure of the Judean stoop as he himself had done towards the slab. 'You will learn now,' the voice said above him, 'which kiss it is that wakens.' But there was no meeting of the lips. Instead the dark head bent, black hair fell upon white skin, yellow silk. It was the throat di Giudea kissed, and that only for a space of seconds. Then the dark head was lifted, strong and slowly as some preying beast's from a kill, and there, a mark, a blush left behind on the skin, the silk.

Valore ordered himself. He came to his feet and stole back across the tomb, and so beheld, with an elated astonishment, how his shadowy companion milked the broken vessel of the throat with his fingers, smearing them, then pressed these fingers to the lips of the dead. Which quietly, and apparently of their own accord, parted to receive them.

'Take,' said di Giudea, the one word a sound like smoke. And the parted lips widened and there came a savage glint of teeth. So Valore had seen a dog maul the hand of its master! Yet the Judean was impassive as this terrible thing occurred, still as the night, until he spoke again, a second word: 'Enough.' And the mouth slackened, and he drew his fingers away, bloody and appalling, seeming bitten through – The sight of all this sent Valore reeling. He fell against the couch again, full finally of a sensation that prompted him to hilarity or screaming, he was not sure which.

'What now?' he cried. 'What now?' Swaying over her, his Aurena, supported by one hand against the slab, the other fixed on the Jew's wrist. But the question required no answer. Fed by that elixir of blood the Jew had given her, her own, and his, the being that lay before them both began, unconscionably, to awaken. The signs of it were swift, and lacking all complexity. The parted lips drew a breath, the eyelids tensed and unfurled. Two eyes looked out into the world, upon the vault, upon the form of Valore. She had seemed in all else very like him, but those eyes of hers were not his eyes. They were like burnished jets; the eyes, in fact, of Olivio di Giudea.

'She is more beautiful than truth,' Valore remarked, staring down at her. 'Is it a part of your spell, o Mago, to set your own demoniac optics in her head?' But then he began to murmur to her, caressing her face, smiling on her; and she, as if lessoned in such gestures by him, smiled in return.

It was a joy to Valore, a joy founded upon exquisite fear, to feel her hands steal to his waist and seek to pull him to her. His hold on the other man he relinquished, and taking hold instead once more of her, sank down.

The Jew spoke quietly at his back.

'It would seem, locked in her father's house against the coming of the plague, she could not find escape, nor would she prey on her kindred. But she has been hungry a great while and forgotten all such nepotism.'

His face buried in Aurena's breast, Valore muttered. It was a name, the name of one who, a legend and a sorcerer, cursed by the Christ to an eternal wandering until Doomsday, when and if it should ever come, was also a Jew; and this persona he awarded Olivio di Giudea now. '*Ahasuere.*'

Di Giudea stood at the door of the tomb, looking upon blackness and a faint threat of greyness in the east, where all the stars went out, and from which all the plagues of the world had come – sickness, sorcery, and religion.

'Ahasuerus? But if I am he, and immortal,' the Judean replied, 'there must be some reason for it, and some means. Say then, perhaps, my presence at your side tonight also had some reason and some means. You will come to understand, there are other kindred than those of the flesh. And only one race which may safely spurn all the rest.'

Valore did not hear this. There was a roaring like a river in his ears, a burning that ran from his neck into his heart. As he lay in her arms Valore knew it was his blood now she drank. And first it was an intolerable ecstasy, so he clung to her, but soon it passed into a wonderful and spiritual state wherein he floated, free of all heaviness. But at length this too was changed, and he was invaded by a dreadful languor and an iciness and a raging thirst and a searing agony of the limbs and nerves, so that he would have pulled himself away from her. However, by then it was too late, and helplessly he sprawled upon her till she had drained him.

An emptied wine-skin he lay then, void and dry. The doorway was long-empty also of any other companion, and the door rightly shut against the impending dawn.

Aurena della Scorpioni reclined beneath the coverlet of her victim, her head flung back, her eyes enlarged, her lips curved, smiling still.

Beyond the tomb, the garden and the wall, the city was wakening also, throwing off its stygian sleep.

By noon, some would have asked aloud for Valore, the Scorpion's child, and found him not. It was the same with the clever Judean, he and all his arts and skills and sciences, vanished with and in like manner to the darkness. From those who had supped at Andrea's table and remained, uneasy fancies sprang. As days went by thereafter without clue, there began to be a certain hideous curiosity concerning corpses dredged from the yellow river. But twenty days later the veiled person of plague entered the *Interiore*, and thence the forums, and the markets, and the churches, and the proliferation of the dead ended such speculation.

It was not until the winter came to cleanse the ancient thoroughfares with blades that Andrea Trarra, going one evening into his garden to inspect the frost-crippled vines, was shocked to find a figure there before him.

After a moment, recovering somewhat, Andrea stepped briskly forward.

'Valore – where in God's name –'

'Ah,' said Valore, his face deadly white in the dusk, but beautiful and charming as ever, 'I have countless secrets. Do you, for example, remember when we diced for this?' And held up before the other a great key of iron, now no blacker than the centres of his eyes.

A Room With A Vie

*I have myself, and have met others who have, heard particular
rooms breathing. Whether this is some freak temporary noise
in the ears, or due to another more mysterious, more funda-
mental cause – electric wiring, some murmur of the Earth
itself – I can't say. It provided the germ of the idea, and the
rest of the story developed from it with a horrible inevitability.*

'This is it, then.'

'Oh, yes.'

'As you can see, it's in quite nice condition.'

'Yes it is.'

'Clothes there, on the bed. Cutlery in the box. Basin. Cooker.
The meter's the same as the one you had last year. And you saw
the bathroom across the corridor.'

'Yes. Thank you. It's all fine.'

'Well, as I said. I was sorry we couldn't let you have your other
room. But you didn't give us much notice. And right now,
August, and such good weather, we're booked right up.'

'I understand. It was kind of you to find me this room. I was
lucky, wasn't I? The very last one.'

'It's usually the last to go, this one.'

'How odd. It's got such a lovely view of the sea and the bay.'

'Well, I didn't mean there was anything wrong with the room.'

'Of course not.'

'Mr Tinker always used to have this room. Every year, four
months, June to September.'

'Oh, yes.'

'It was quite a shock last year, when his daughter rang to
cancel. He died, just the night before he meant to take the train

to come down. Heart attack. What a shame.'

'Yes, it was.'

'Well, I'll leave you to get settled in. You know where we are if you want anything.'

'Thank you very much, Mrs Rice.'

Mr Tinker, she thought, leaning on the closed door. *Tinker*. Like a dog, with one black ear. Here, Tinker! Don't be silly, she thought. It's just nerves. Arrival nerves. By the sea nerves. By yourself nerves.

Caroline crossed to the window. She stared out at the esplanade where the brightly coloured summer people were walking about in the late afternoon sun. Beyond, the bay opened its arms to the sea. The little boats in the harbour lay stranded by an outgoing tide. The water was cornflower blue.

If David had been here, she would have told him that his eyes were exactly as blue as that sea, which wasn't at all the case. How many lies there had been between them. Even lies about eye colour. But she wasn't going to think of David. She had come here alone, as she had come here last season, to sketch, to paint, to meditate.

It was a pity, about not being able to have the other room. It had been larger, and the bathroom had been 'contained' rather than shared and across the hall. But then she hadn't been going to take the holiday flat this year. She had been trying to patch things up with David. Until finally, all the patching had come undone, and she'd grasped at this remembered place in a panic – I must get *away*.

Caroline turned her back to the window. She glanced about. Yes. Of course it was quite all right. If anything, the view was better because the flat was higher up. As for the actual room, it was like all the rooms. Chintz curtains, cream walls, brown rugs and jolly cushions. And Mr Tinker had taken good care of it. There was only one cigarette burn in the table. And probably that wasn't Mr Tinker at all. Somehow, she couldn't imagine Mr Tinker doing a thing like that. It must be the result of the other tenants, those people who had accepted the room as their last choice.

Well now. Make up the bed, and then go out for a meal. No, she was too tired for that. She'd get sandwiches from the little café downstairs, perhaps some wine from the off-licence. It would be a chance to swallow some sea air. Those first breaths that always made her giddy and unsure, like too much oxygen.

She made the bed up carefully, as if for two. When she moved it away from the wall to negotiate the sheets, she saw something scratched in the cream plaster.

'Oh, Mr Tinker, you naughty dog,' she said aloud, and then felt foolish.

Anyway, Mr Tinker wouldn't do such a thing. Scratch with a penknife, or even some of Mrs Rice's loaned cutlery. Black ink had been smeared into the scratches. Caroline peered down into the gloom behind the bed. *A room with a view*, the scratching said. Well, almost. Whoever it was had forgotten to put in the ultimate double-u: *A room with a vie*. Either illiterate or careless. Or smitten with guilt nine-tenths through.

She pushed the bed back again. She'd better tell the Rices sometime. God forbid they should suppose she was the vandal.

She was asleep, when she heard the room breathing. She woke gradually, as if to a familiar and reassuring sound. Then, as gradually, a confused fear stole upon her. Presently she located the breathing sound as the noise of her own blood-rhythm in her ears. Then, with another shock of relief, as the sea. But, in the end, it was not the sea either. It was the room, breathing.

A kind of itching void of pure terror sent her plunging upward from the bed. She scrabbled at the switch and the bedside light flared on. Blinded and gasping, she heard the sound seep away.

Out at sea, a ship mooed plaintively. She looked at the window and began to detect stars over the water, and the pink lamps glowing along the esplanade. The world was normal.

Too much wine after too much train travel. Nightmare.

She lay down. Though her eyes watered, she left the light on.

'I'm afraid so, Mrs Rice. Someone's scratched and inked it on the wall. A nostalgia freak: "A room with a view." '

'Funny,' said Mrs Rice. She was a homely woman with jet black gypsy hair that didn't seem to fit. 'Of course, there's been two or three had that room. No one for very long. Disgusting. Still, the damage is done.'

Caroline walked along the bay. The beach that spread from the south side was packed by holiday makers. Everyone was paired, as if they meant to be ready for the ark. Some had a great luggage of children as well. The gulls and the children screamed.

Caroline sat drawing and the children raced screaming by. People stopped to ask her questions about her drawing. Some stared a long while over her shoulder. Some gave advice on perspective and subject matter. The glare of sun on the blue water hurt her eyes.

She put the sketchbook away. After lunch she'd go farther along, to Jaynes Bay, which she recollected had been very quiet last year. This year, it wasn't.

After about four o'clock, gangs of local youth began to gather on the esplanade and the beach. Their hair was greased and their legs were like storks' legs in tight trousers. They whistled. They spoke in an impenetrable mumble which often flowered into four-letter words uttered in contrastingly clear diction.

There had been no gangs last year. The sun sank.

Caroline was still tired. She went along the esplanade to her block, up the steps to her room.

When she unlocked the door and stood on the threshold, for a moment –

What?

It was as if the pre-twilight amber that came into the room was slowly pulsing, throbbing. As if the walls, the floor, the ceiling, were –

She switched on the overhead lamp.

'Mr Tinker,' she said firmly, 'I'm not putting up with this.'

'Pardon?' said a voice behind her.

Caroline's heart expanded with a sharp thud like a grenade exploding in her side. She spun around, and there stood a girl in jeans and a smock. Her hand was on the door of the shared bathroom. It was the previously unseen neighbour from down the hall.

'I'm sorry,' said Caroline. 'I must have been talking to myself.'

The girl looked blank and unhelpful. 'I'm Mrs Lacey,' she said. She did not look lacy. Nor married. She looked about fourteen.

'You've got number eight, then. How is it?'

Bloody nerve, Caroline thought. 'It's fine.'

'They've had three in before you,' said fourteen year old Mrs Lacey.

'All together?'

'Pardon? No. I meant three separate tenants. Nobody would stay. All kinds of trouble with that Mrs Rice. Nobody would, though.'

'Why ever not?' Caroline snapped.

'Too noisy or something. Or a smell. I can't remember.'

Caroline stood in her doorway, her back to the room.

Fourteen year old Mrs Lacey opened the bathroom door.

'At least we haven't clashed in the mornings,' Caroline said.

'Oh, *we're* always up early on holiday,' said young Mrs Lacey pointedly. Somewhere down the hall, a child began to bang and quack like an insane automatic duck. A man's voice bawled: 'Hurry up that piss, Brenda, will you?'

Brenda Lacey darted into the bathroom and the bolt was shot.

Caroline entered her room. She slammed the door. She turned on the room, watching it.

There *was* a smell. It was very slight. A strange, faintly buttery smell. Not really unpleasant. Probably from the café below. She pushed up the window and breathed the sea.

As she leaned on the sill, breathing, she felt the room start breathing too.

She was six years old, and Auntie Sara was taking her to the park. Auntie Sara was very loving. Her fat warm arms were always reaching out to hold, to compress, to pinion against her fat warm bosom. Being hugged by Auntie Sara induced in six year old Caroline a sense of claustrophobia and primitive fright. Yet somehow she was aware that she had to be gentle with Auntie Sara and not wound her feelings. Auntie Sara couldn't have a little girl. So she had to share Caroline with Mummy.

And now they were in the park.

'There's Jenny,' said Caroline. But of course Auntie Sara wouldn't want to let Caroline go to play with Jennifer. So Caroline pretended that Auntie Sara *would* let her go, and she ran very fast over the green grass towards Jenny. Then her foot caught in something. When she began to fall, for a moment it was exhilarating, like flying. But she hit the ground, stunning, bruising. She knew better than to cry, for in another moment Auntie Sara had reached her. 'It doesn't hurt,' said Caroline. But Auntie Sara took no notice. She crushed Caroline to her. Caroline was smothered on her breast, and the great round arms bound her like hot, faintly dairy-scented bolsters.

Caroline started to struggle. She pummelled, kicked and shrieked.

It was dark, and she had not fallen in the grass after all. She was in bed in the room, and it was the room she was fighting. It was the room which was holding her close, squeezing her, hugging her. It was the room which had that faint cholesterol smell of fresh milk and butter. It was the room which was stroking and whispering.

But of course it couldn't be the damn room.

Caroline lay back exhausted, and the toils of her dream receded. Another nightmare. Switch on the light. Yes, that was it. Switch on the light and have a drink from the small traveller's bottle of gin she'd put ready in case she couldn't sleep.

'Christ.' She shielded her eyes from the light.

Distantly, she heard a child crying – the offspring probably of young Mrs unlacy Lacey along the hall. 'God, I must have yelled,' Caroline said aloud. Yelled and been heard. The unlacy Laceys were no doubt discussing her this very minute. The mad lazy slut in number eight.

The gin burned sweetly, going down.

This was stupid. The light – no, she'd have to leave the light on again.

Caroline looked at the walls. She could see them, very, very softly lifting, softly sinking. Don't be a fool. The smell was just discernible. It made her queasy. Too rich – yet, a human smell, a certain sort of human smell. Bovine, she concluded, exactly like poor childless Sara.

It was hot, even with the window open.

She drank halfway down the bottle and didn't care any more.

'Mr Tinker? Why ever are you interested in him?'

Mrs Rice looked disapproving.

'I'm sorry. I'm not being ghoulish. It's just – well, it seemed such a shame, his dying like that. I suppose I've been brooding.'

'Don't want to do that. You need company. Is your husband coming down at all, this year?'

'David? No, he can't get away right now.'

'Pity.'

'Yes. But about Mr Tinker –'

'All right,' said Mrs Rice. 'I don't see why I shouldn't tell you. He was a retired man. Don't know what line of work he'd been in, but not very well paid, I imagine. His wife was dead. He lived with his married daughter, and really I don't think it suited him, but there was no alternative. Then, four months of the year, he'd come here and take number eight. Done it for years. Used to get his meals out. Must have been quite expensive. But I think the daughter and her husband paid for everything, you know, to get a bit of time on their own. But he loved this place, Mr Tinker did. He used to say to me: "Here I am home again, Mrs Rice." The room with his daughter, I had the impression he didn't think of that as home at all. But number eight. Well, he'd put his ornaments and books and pieces round. My George even put a couple of nails in for him to hang a picture or two. Why not? And number eight got quite cosy. It really *was* Mr Tinker's room in the end. My George said that's why other tenants'd fight shy. They could feel it waiting for Mr Tinker to come back. But that's a lot of nonsense, and I can see I shouldn't have said it.'

'No. I think your husband was absolutely right. Poor old room. It's going to be disappointed.'

'Well, my George, you know, he's a bit of an idiot. The night – the night we heard, he got properly upset, my George. He went up to number eight, and opened the door and told it. I said to him, you'll want me to hang black curtains in there next.'

Beyond the fence, the headland dropped away in dry grass and the feverish flowers of late summer to a blue sea ribbed with white. North spread the curved claw of Jaynes Bay and the grey vertical of the lighthouse. But the sketchpad and pencil case sat on the seat beside Caroline.

She had attempted nothing. Even the novel lay closed. The first page hadn't seemed to make sense. She kept reading the words 'home' and 'Tinker' between the lines.

She understood she was afraid to return to the room. She had walked along the headlands, telling herself that all the room had wrong with it was sadness, a bereavement. That it wasn't waiting. That it wasn't alive. And anyway, even sadness didn't happen to rooms. If it did, it would have to get over that. Get used to being just a holiday flat again, a space which people filled for a few weeks, observed indifferently, cared nothing about, and then went away from.

Which was all absurd because none of it was true.

Except, that she wasn't the only one to believe –

She wondered if David would have registered anything in the room. Should she ring him and confide in him? Ask advice? No. For God's sake, that was why she was imagining herself into this state, wasn't it? So she could create a contact with him again. No. David was out and out David would stay.

It was five o'clock. She packed her block and pencils into her bag and walked quickly along the grass verge above the fence.

She could walk into Kingscliff at this rate, and get a meal.

She wondered who the scared punster had been, the one who knew French. She'd got the joke by now. A room with a vie: a room with a *life*.

She reached Kingscliff and had a pleasantly unhealthy meal, with a pagoda of white ice-cream and glacé cherries to follow. In the dusk the town was raucous and cheerful. Raspberry and yellow neons splashed and spat and the motor-bike gangs seemed suitable, almost friendly in situ. Caroline strolled by the whelk stalls and across the carpark, through an odour of frying doughnuts, chips and fierce fish. She went to a cinema and watched a very bad and very pointless film with a sense of superiority and tolerance. When the film was over, she sat alone in a pub and drank vodka. Nobody accosted her or tried to pick her up. She was glad at first, but after the fourth vodka, rather sorry. She had to run to catch the last bus back. It was not until she stood on the esplanade, the bus vanishing, the pink lamps droning solemnly and the black water far below, that a real and undeniable terror came and twisted her stomach.

The café was still open, and she might have gone in there, but some of the greasy stork-legs she had seen previously were clustered about the counter. She was tight, and visualized sweeping amongst them, conquering their adolescent nastiness. But presently she turned aside and into the block of holiday flats.

She dragged up the steps sluggishly. By the time she reached her door, her hands were trembling. She dropped her key and stifled a squeal as the short-time automatic hall light went out.

Pressing the light button, she thought: Supposing it doesn't come on?

But the light did come on. She picked up her key, unlocked the door and went determinedly inside the room, shutting the door behind her.

She experienced it instantly. It was like a vast, indrawn, sucking gasp.

'No,' Caroline said to the room. Her hand fumbled the switch and the room was lit.

Her heart was beating so very fast. That was, of course, what made the room also seem to pulse, as if its heart were also swiftly and greedily beating.

'Listen,' Caroline said. 'Oh God, talking to a *room*. But I have to, don't I? Listen, you've got to stop this. Leave me alone!' she shouted at the room.

The room seemed to grow still.

She thought of the Laceys, and giggled.

She crossed to the window and opened it. The air was cool. Stars gleamed above the bay. She pulled the curtains to, and undressed. She washed, and brushed her teeth at the basin. She poured herself a gin.

She felt the room, all about her. Like an inheld breath, impossibly prolonged. She ignored that. She spoke to the room quietly.

'Naughty Mr Tinker, to tinker with you, like this. Have to call you Sara now, shan't I? Like a great big womb. That's what she really wanted, you see. To squeeze me right through herself, pop me into her womb. I'd offer you a gin, but where the hell would you put it?'

Caroline shivered.

'No. This is truly silly.'

She walked over to the cutlery box beside the baby cooker. She put in her hand and pulled out the vegetable knife. It had quite a vicious edge. George Rice had them frequently sharpened.

'See this,' Caroline said to the room. 'Just watch yourself.'

When she lay down, the darkness whirled, carouselling her asleep.

In the womb, it was warm and dark, a warm blood dark. Rhythms came and went, came and went, placid and unending as the tides of the sea. The heart organ pumped with a soft deep noise like a muffled drum.

How comfortable and safe it was. But when am I to be born? Caroline wondered. Never, the womb told her, lapping her, cushioning her.

Caroline kicked out. She floated. She tried to seize hold of something, but the blood-warm cocoon was not to be seized.

'Let me go,' said Caroline. 'Auntie Sara, I'm all right. Let me go. I want to – please –'

Her eyes were wide and she was sitting up in her holiday bed. She put out her hand spontaneously towards the light and touched the knife she had left beside it. The room breathed, regularly, deeply. Caroline moved her hand away from the light switch, and saw in the darkness.

'This is ridiculous,' she said aloud.

The room breathed. She glanced at the window – she had left the curtains drawn over, and so could not focus on the esplanade beyond, or the bay: the outer world. The walls throbbed. She could *see* them. She was being calm now, and analytical, letting her eyes adjust, concentrating. The mammalian milky smell was heavy. Not precisely offensive, but naturally rather horrible, in these circumstances.

Very carefully, Caroline, still in darkness, slipped her feet out of the covers and stood up.

'All right,' she said. 'All right then.'

She turned to the wall behind the bed. She reached across and laid her hand on it –

The *wall*. The wall was – *skin*. It was flesh. Live, pulsing, hot, moist –

It was –

The wall swelled under her touch. It adhered to her hand eagerly. The whole room writhed a little, surging towards her. It wanted – she knew it wanted – to clutch her to its breast.

Caroline ripped her hand from the flesh wall. Its rhythms were faster, and the cowlike smell much stronger. Caroline whimpered. She flung backward and her fingers closed on the vegetable knife and she raised it.

Even as the knife plunged forward, she knew it would skid or rebound from the plaster, probably slicing her. She knew all that, but could not help it. And then the knife thumped in, up to the handle. It was like stabbing into – into meat.

She jerked the knife away and free, and scalding fluid ran down her arm. I've cut myself after all. That's blood. But she felt nothing. And the room –

The room was screaming. She couldn't hear it, but the scream was all around her, hurting her ears. She had to stop the screaming. She thrust again with the knife. The blade was slippery. The impact was the same. Boneless meat. And the heated fluid, this time, splashed all over her. In the thick un-light, it looked black. She dabbed frantically at her arm, which had no wound. But in the wall –

She stabbed again. She ran to another wall and stabbed and hacked at it.

I'm dreaming, she thought. Christ, why can't I wake up?

The screaming was growing dim, losing power.

'Stop it!' she cried. The blade was so sticky now she had to use both hands to drive it home. There was something on the floor, spreading, that she slid on in her bare feet. She struck the wall with her fist, then with the knife. 'Oh, Christ, please die,' she said.

Like a butchered animal, the room shuddered, collapsed back upon itself, became silent and immobile.

Caroline sat in a chair. She was going to be sick, but then the sickness faded. I'm sitting here in a pool of blood.

She laughed and tears started to run from her eyes, which was the last thing she remembered.

When she woke it was very quiet. The tide must be far out, for even the sea did not sound. A crack of light came between the curtains.

What am I doing in this chair?

Caroline shifted, her mind blank and at peace.

Then she felt the utter emptiness that was in the room with her. The dreadful emptiness, occasioned only by the presence of the dead.

She froze. She stared at the crack of light. Then down.

'Oh no,' said Caroline. She raised her hands.

She wore black mittens. Her fingers were stuck together.

Now her gaze was racing over the room, not meaning to, trying to escape, but instead alighting on the black punctures, the

169

streaks, the stripes along the wall, now on the black stains, the black splotches. Her own body was dappled, grotesquely mottled with black. She had one white toe left to her, on her right foot.

Woodenly, she managed to get up. She staggered to the curtains and hauled them open and turned back in the full flood of early sunlight, and saw everything over again. The gashes in the wall looked as if they had been accomplished with a drill or a pick. Flaked plaster was mingled with the – with the – blood. Except that it wasn't blood. Blood wasn't black.

Caroline turned away suddenly. She looked through the window, along the esplanade, pale and laved with morning. She looked at the bright sea, with the two or three fishing boats scattered on it, and the blueness beginning to flush sky and water. When she looked at these things, it was hard to believe in the room.

Perhaps most murderers were methodical in the aftermath. Perhaps they had to be.

She filled the basin again and again, washing herself, arms, body, feet. Even her hair had to be washed. The black had no particular texture. In the basin it diluted. It appeared like a superior kind of Parker fountain pen ink.

She dressed herself in jeans and shirt, filled the largest saucepan with hot water and washing-up liquid. She began to scour the walls.

Soon her arms ached, and she was sweating the cold sweat of nervous debility. The black came off easily, but strange tangles of discolouration remained behind in the paint. Above, the holes did not ooze, they merely gaped. Inside each of them was chipped plaster and brick – not bone, muscle or tissue. There was no feel of flesh anywhere.

Caroline murmured to herself. 'When I've finished.' It was quite matter-of-fact to say that, as if she were engaged in a normalcy. 'When I've finished, I'll go and get some coffee downstairs. I won't tell Mrs Rice about the holes. No, not yet. How can I explain them? I couldn't have caused that sort of hole with a knife. There's the floor to do yet. And I'd better wash the rugs. I'll do them in the bath when the ghastly Laceys go out at nine o'clock. When I've finished, I'll get some coffee. And I think I'll ring David. I really think I'll have to. When I finish.'

She thought about ringing David. She couldn't guess what he'd say. What could *she* say, come to that? Her back ached now, and she felt sick, but she kept on with her work. Presently she heard energetic intimations of the Laceys visiting the bathroom, and the duck-child quacking happily.

She caught herself wondering why blood hadn't run when the nails were hammered in the walls for Mr Tinker's pictures. But that was before the room really came to life, maybe. Or maybe the room had taken it in the spirit of beautification, like having one's ears pierced for gold earrings. Certainly the knife scratches had bled.

Caroline put down the cloth and went over to the basin and was sick.

Perhaps I'm pregnant, she thought, and all this is a hallucination of my fecundity.

David, I am pregnant, and I stabbed a room to death.

David.

David?

It was a boiling hot day, one of the last fling days of the summer. Everything was blanched by the heat, apart from the apex of the blue sky and the core of the green-blue sea. Caroline wore a white dress. A quarter before each hour, she told herself she would ring David on the hour: ten o'clock, eleven, twelve. Then she would 'forget'. At one o'clock she rang him, and he was at lunch as she had known he would be, really.

Caroline went on the pier. She put money into little machines which whizzed and clattered. She ate a sandwich in a café. She walked along the sands, holding her shoes by the straps.

At half past four she felt compelled to return.

She had to speak to Mrs Rice, about the holes in the walls.

And then again, perhaps she should go up to number eight first. It seemed possible that the dead room would somehow have righted itself. And then, too, there were the washed rugs drying over the bath that the Unlaceys might come in and see. Caroline examined why she was so flippant and so cheerful. It was, of course, because she was afraid.

She went into the block, and abruptly she was trembling. As she climbed the steps, her legs melted horridly, and she wished she could crawl, pulling herself by her fingers.

As she came up to the landing, she beheld Mr Lacey in the corridor. At least, she assumed it was Mr Lacey. He was overweight and tanned a peachy gold by the sun. He stood, glowering at her, blocking the way to her door. He's going to complain about the noise, she thought. She tried to smile, but no smile would oblige.

'I'm Mr Lacey,' he announced. 'You met my wife the other day.'

He sounded nervous rather than belligerent. When Caroline didn't speak, he went on, 'My Brenda, you see. She noticed this funny smell from number eight. When you come along to the bathroom, you catch it. She was wondering if you'd left some meat out, forgotten it.'

'No,' said Caroline.

'Well, I reckoned you ought to be told,' said Mr Lacey.

'Yes, thank you.'

'I mean, don't take this the wrong way, but we've got a kid. You can't be too careful.'

'No. You can't.'

'Well, then.' He swung himself aside and moved a short way down the corridor towards the Lacey flat. Caroline went to her door. She knew he was watching her with his two shining Lacey piggy eyes. She turned and stared at him, her heart striking her side in huge bruising blows, until he grunted and went off.

Caroline stood before the door. She couldn't smell anything. No, there was nothing, nothing at all.

The stink came in a wave, out of nowhere. It smote her and she nearly reeled. It was foul, indescribably foul. And then it was gone.

Delicately, treading soft, Caroline stepped away from the door. She tiptoed to the head of the stairs. Then she ran.

But like someone drawn to the scene of an accident, she couldn't entirely vacate the area. She sat on the esplanade, watching.

The day went out over the town, and the dusk seeped from the sea. In the dusk, a police car came and drew up outside the block. Later, another.

It got dark. The lamps, the neons and the stars glittered, and Caroline shuddered in her thin frock.

The stork-legs had gathered at the café. They pointed and

172

jeered at the police cars. At the garden pavilion, a band was playing. Far out on the ocean, a great tanker passed, garlanded with lights.

At nine o'clock, Caroline found she had risen and was walking across the esplanade to the holiday block. She walked right through the crowd of stork-legs. 'Got the time?' one of them yelled, but she paid no heed, didn't even flinch.

She went up the steps, and on the first flight she met two very young policemen.

'You can't come up here, miss.'

'But I'm staying here,' she said. Her mild voice, so reasonable, interested her. She missed what he asked next.

'I said, what number, miss.'

'Number eight.'

'Oh. Right. You'd better come up with me, then. You hang on here, Brian.'

They climbed together, like old friends.

'What's the matter?' she questioned him, perversely.

'I'm not quite sure, miss.'

They reached the landing.

All the way up from the landing below, the stench had been intensifying, solidifying. It was unique. Without ever having smelled such an odour before, instinctively and at once you knew it was the perfume of rottenness. Of decay and death.

Mrs Rice stood in the corridor, her black hair in curlers, and she was absentmindedly crying. Another woman with a handkerchief to her nose patted Mrs Rice's shoulder. Behind a shut door, a child also cried, vehemently. Another noise came from the bathroom: someone vomiting.

Caroline's door was open wide. A further two policemen were on the threshold. They seemed to have no idea of how to proceed. One was wiping his hands with a cloth, over and over.

Caroline gazed past them, into the room.

Putrescent lumps were coming away from the walls. The ceiling dribbled and dripped. Yet one moment only was it like the flesh of a corpse. Next moment, it was plaster, paint and crumbling brick. And then again, like flesh. And then again –

'Christ,' one of the policemen said. He faced about at his audience. He too was young. He stared at Caroline randomly. 'What are we supposed to do?'

Caroline breathed in the noxious air. She managed to smile at last, kindly, inquiringly, trying to help.

'Bury it?'

Paper Boat

The strange death of the poet Shelley inspired this. Circum-
stances surrounding the event are themselves so bizarre, so
fate-laden, that they seemed crying out for rehearsal, and for
the opium prose that formed upon the story's bones.

The summer heat had come. It burned the hills to blocks of
standing smoke. It filled the bowl of the shore and the spoon of
the bay with its opium, it painted the terracotta of the house in
progressively darkening washes of red and umber. The sea, a
throbbing indigo, pulled itself to the beach and tumbled there as
if drugged. The island lay dumb, half conscious, scarcely breathing, vanquished.

It seemed to the poet he was made of some form of clockwork
and the clock had stopped. He stood by the narrow window,
looking at the blue-black sea, the distant shadow of a dreamlike
mainland chalked in haze. Perhaps this was how the island itself
felt, the sea, the rock . . . this lifeless numb internal silence,
devoid of anything, even questioning or fear.

This was where they had planned to spend the summer. This
island and this house. This house, like a doll's house. If you
opened the side of it you would see all the pretty dolls in their
doll-like attitudes of occupation. Laura scribbling bitter witty
prose with the yellow blind shielding her window from the sun,
turning her to amber, a fierce amber hand, the scorched ember-
coloured pages. Farther down, Sibbi bending like an Egyptian
over a bowl of osiers and sun-mummified flowers, Sibbi with her
magical face and her bright shallow brain, and her husband
Arthur, a bear, at the eternal business of his pipe, knocking out
dottle, refilling it, that rank black tobacco odour woven by now

175

into the scalding incense of every room. And somewhere Albertine, like a tall white goddess from a frieze moving silently and gently about, being careful to tread on the paws of none of them, this moody tribe of cats who inhabited her domestic landscape.

And he, the black cat at the top of the house, the black cat in the symbolical tower with a door up to the roof where, under the golden awning, the metallic telescope was pointing like a tongue at the sea. The black cat was a poet and scholar. So, if you had opened the doll's house you should see him seated in the brown shadow at the desk, lost in some elegy or epic, among the open paper mouths of Plato, Virgil and Homer. And instead you saw him at the narrow window, the doll poet with the clockwork stopped inside him.

Below, the silver hammers of the piano began to strike each other, and a girl's lovely singing winged up, yet the sounds had an undersea quality, stifled by the leaden air. Sibbi, her flowers meticulously imprisoned in their bowl, singing her siren's song to the poet in the tower. She sang to disturb him as he worked, to get her image between the pen and the paper. If he should say to her as they ate dinner: 'I heard you sing,' she would answer: 'Oh, I am sorry. Did I disturb you? I never thought you could hear me.' Her eyes were the colour of blue irises; they gave an impression of great depth simply because a world of vacuity opened behind them. She was a claw delicately scratching at him. All three women, the priestesses presumably of his shrine, were claws in his body – Sibbi clawed at his loins, very softly and with her own curious art, promising and never quite giving, giving, and promising more, like all empty vessels offering an illusion of hidden things. Laura clawed at his conscience; sharp-tongued and clever Laura, reminding him of her rights to him by means of a past neither wished to recapture.

Only Albertine clawed at his heart. Albertine who was sad and travailed not to show it, who was brave and good and adored him, Albertine the best of women, whom he no longer loved. They had metamorphosed into different people from the two impassioned children who met in a graveyard in order to be secret, embraced on graves, and finally, hero and heroine of their own romance, had fled security with a wild hymn of abandon. Now they had grown up, security had gathered on them after all, like barnacles. The dismal shadow of reality overlay them both. They had found out they were not gods and they were not suited.

The light from the sea, so darkly bright, made him shut his eyes. Sibbi sang below. No one else responded to the heat as he had done with this anaesthetic languor. There was a timelessness around him now. No past, no present, nothing to come. He could sense the mechanism stilled, the unheard drone of the sun. A perpetual, well known knowledge of loneliness gnawed somewhere inside him, yet he scarcely felt it. Only the sullen noises of the sea ran up the beaches of his mind and swooned like an indigo woman against him, and slipped away through his fingers sighing when he tried to hold her, while down below Arthur Merton knocked the dottle from his pipe, refilled it, lit it, and leaned back in his chair, and considered it was very hot.

'Damned hot,' he said.

Through the smoke of the pipe, and through the embalmed-looking stalks and scarlet rose-heads in the Indian bowl, he could see Sibbi at the piano in the next room, playing and singing prettily, sometimes glancing towards the open veranda doors with the sly, half-excited, half-evaluating look she reserved for Ashburn. Inadvertently Merton's eyes slid up towards the weary stucco of the ceiling. Above them all, Robert Ashburn would be writing in the tower room, working in this infernal heat. If he was. Too hot to do much now. Even the boat, Ashburn's love, lay neglected by the quay. The sailing days had been good. When it was cooler –

Merton sensed, as if through the steam or fog of his thoughts, the glamour of the girl at the piano, the witchery of that curious straying glance, once turned to advantage on himself. He felt no resentment. He also, in an improbable, asexual way, stirred at the thought of the dark young man above, the anguished poet – anguished by everything or nothing. The moods of the poet lit up dim glares of unrealized fire in Merton himself. Sonnets he did not properly understand, written perfectly obviously to his wife Sibbi, nevertheless pierced Merton's wooden soul like splinters of glass with a painful, inexplicable delight.

Sibbi finished her song. Notes and voice ebbed from the room, and the heat seemed to flood into the empty spaces. Presently she came to the doorway and stood looking at him, like a cat with a canary dead in its mouth, contemptuous, cruel and affectionate, knowing it will be forgiven simply because it is as it is.

'That was very nice,' Merton observed.

Sibbi smiled. 'How would you know? You don't care for music.'

'Well, I care for yours, you know.'

'Actually, I was playing for Robert, but I'm glad you enjoyed it, Arthur dear.' She leaned her hand with its wedding ring on the upright of the door, admiring it, her eyes a little glazed with heat and excitement. 'How bad of him to be in the garden at this hour, when he should be working. Laura will scold him, I expect. He hasn't completed anything this summer.'

Merton laughed.

'We shall have to visit the eye specialist after all,' he remarked. A year ago she had been threatened with the nemesis of spectacles; now some little spark of intransigent animosity made him refer to the terror whenever possible, in the form of a joke. 'Robert was never in the garden.'

'Don't be absurd. I saw him quite clearly. I see better than you do.'

'But you don't hear better, Sibbi. I heard him upstairs, walking about while you were at the piano. You know how he walks, like an animal in a cage, up and down.'

'I think you must have sunstroke. You had better lie down. I saw Robert absolutely distinctly, by the stone urn at the end of the walk, listening while I played.'

Merton got up with a reluctant irritating air of investigation and went slowly across the room, past Sibbi, to the veranda doors. The garden, stripped of shadow by the two o'clock sun, offered a vista of lank and blistered green with clumps of statuary, like unhealthy fungus or sores, pushed up at intervals. The local gardener was trudging complainingly beside Albertine along the walk. The old sunburned islander and the tall fair girl advanced in a desultory slow motion; nothing else stirred except for an inflammatory scatter of crickets, crackling as if trying to set the grass on fire.

'I spy with my short-sighted eye Albertine and that old devil from the village.'

Sibbi came to his side. 'Well, no doubt Robert's come indoors. He was just there a moment ago.'

'Then he'd come through these doors here, wouldn't he? The only other way is to jump off the wall and, since the tide's in,

178

swim round to the front, which seems,' he knocked dottle from his pipe to stress the point, 'unnecessary.'

'Then he's still in the garden. What a fuss you're making.'

'You, my dear, are the one making the fuss.'

Merton went out on to the terrace and waved to Albertine. The girl lifted her head; the gardener picked his fangs, disdaining the mad people of the house, recounting whose debaucheries and insanities kept him in free liquor at the village.

'Did you pass Robert on the walk?'

'Why no, he's upstairs in the tower room.'

'You see,' Merton exulted.

Sibbi shook her head. Her teeth snapped on canary bones. 'I distinctly saw him, I tell you.'

Albertine crossed the lawn, glancing up anxiously at the shuttered landward window of the little tower and at the yellow awning above.

'Now you've made Albertine uneasy,' Sibbi said crossly. She glanced at the girl with the same mixture of contempt and liking she had displayed for her husband. She had enchanted the poet, and could afford to be generous to his dull, pleasant handmaiden. Laura, the serpent-tongued, was the one she feared.

Albertine called in a high light voice: 'Robert,' and then again: 'Robert!'

They all stared up as if mesmerized at the closed shutters; even the mahogany gardener, his thumbnail worrying at his canines, added an oil-black stare to theirs.

'Robert,' Sibbi suddenly sang out, as if certain her magic would conjure him where Albertine's could not. The heat swirled sulkily and reformed.

The gardener muttered ominously: 'He write. He deaf to you.'

Abruptly, for no particular reason, each one of them shouted at the masked window.

'Here I am,' Ashburn said.

They looked down and saw him coming between the veranda doors.

Albertine and Sibbi exclaimed; the gardener turned and spat disgustedly. Merton said: 'Well, well. Just down from the tower.'

'That's right.'

'But you were in the garden,' Sibbi asserted almost angrily. 'I saw you standing on the walk while I played.'

The poet looked at her and seemed not quite to see her. His eyes, also glazed by the heat, and very dark, appeared to gaze inwards, backwards into the shadows of his brain. He gave one of his absent, charming, half-apologetic smiles.

'Yes, I heard you singing upstairs.'

Sibbi failed to take up her cue. She looked feverish, annoyed; she went to him and touched his hand and gave a little hard silver laugh like piano notes.

They went in arm in arm to dinner. Merton trailed after.

'Perhaps, you know, we have a ghost.'

The food was served and partly eaten. It was too hot for food. Merton, watching Albertine's gentle cameo face, the barley-coloured hair, visualized all the paraphernalia of a saint, fashioned for crucifixion. She ate little. If Ashburn looked at her she might eat something, pathetically attempting to deceive him. Merton passed her rolls reverently and helped her to wine. She was a fine woman, a sweet girl. Her devotion to the poet moved Merton, for perhaps, in some obscure way, it justified his own devotion to his blue-eyed cat wife.

Now, striving to cheer everyone up after the labour of eating, he revived his little piece, and filled his pipe.

'Do you think we might have a ghost?'

'*Such* fun,' Laura observed acidly.

Albertine lowered her eyes and played with a piece of bread. 'I'd far rather we hadn't.'

Sibbi, quickened, seated next to Ashburn, caught his eye.

'But how romantic – to think I supposed it was you, and all the time it was a spirit. How edifying!' The wine had gone to her head, and her appetite was unimpaired.

'These old houses, you know,' Merton went on, 'though I don't really believe in such stuff myself. Rather wish I did, you know.'

'Of course,' Sibbi said, 'you'd frighten any ghost to death.'

Laura said: 'Does it also write poetry, I wonder? Though, of course, Robert doesn't write anything at present.'

'Don't chide me, dear Laura,' he said.

'I shall always chide you,' Laura said. 'No one else dares to do it, and without chiding you would perish.'

Albertine rose.

'I wish it weren't so hot,' she said.

She drifted towards the windows. Merton stared at his plate.

180

Albertine's eyes were full of tears, a nakedness which thrilled and embarrassed him.

'Just think,' Laura said, also rising, 'if there were a ghost we should have to call one of those village priests to exorcise it.' She crossed to stand behind Ashburn's chair, and set one hand very lightly on his shoulder. 'Do you know,' she said, 'they are praying for rain – actually *praying*. And never in my life did I hear such pagan screaming as emanates from the Catholic church. Come now, Robert, we will take a walk in the garden, you and I, and you shall tell me what you are writing.'

Sibbi said: 'Yes, the garden, I think I shall come with you –'

Laura smiled at her. 'I have a much better idea. I heard you playing earlier. You have such a delicate touch and yet, I believe, that latest piece would benefit from practice – why not practise now, Sibbi? It's a little cooler, I think.'

Sibbi narrowed her cat's eyes as Laura and Ashburn strolled into the garden. She stalked to the piano and began to play very loudly and brilliantly.

'How do you stand that woman, Albertine?' she demanded. 'Does she suppose she owns everything?'

Albertine sat in the wicker chair by the veranda doors. Her dress spilled about her feet like a pool of milk.

'Never mind,' she said soothingly, as if to a child.

She watched Ashburn and Laura go up and down the walks among the burning green with its little filigree flickers of shade. The brazen clangour of heat was mulling, darkening, lying down like lions under the trees. Albertine could imagine Laura saying to Ashburn: 'Yes, I know what I am to you. Albertine is your heart, and this silly little Sibbi your appetite. And I am your brain. Do you think you can relinquish me?'

Albertine imagined she saw how the poet became animated, speaking of what he wrote to Laura. She sat very still in the wicker chair, watching them. A whole procession with its banners travelled through her mind, the first meeting, the first dream, the first embrace, the green graves, the seascapes, the hot gypsy summers with, superimposed upon it all, Laura, with her sharp dark gown slashing at the grass.

Suddenly Sibbi jumped up.

'Why didn't I think of it before? We must hold a séance. There is an ideal little table, and I recall there is something one does with a wine-glass –' She ran to the veranda doors and called out. Ashburn turned at once. Sibbi stood, like a slender flower stalk, holding out her hand to him across the lawn.

And shortly they all sat round a table, like figures inscribed on a clock.

They held hands, the obdurate glass discarded. Nothing had happened, but it was too hot to move. Merton, seated between Sibbi and Laura, fell suddenly asleep and woke as suddenly with a wild grunt. As it had mummified the flowers, the earth, the island, the heat mummified the two men and three women at the table.

Only the eyes of the women sometimes darted, like needles stabbing between their lashes, observing the poet. Sibbi held one of his hands, Albertine the other. Ashburn, blinded by the heat, shut his eyes and experienced the sensation of two leeches, one on either palm, sucking his blood from him. He thought he had fallen asleep for a moment as Merton had done; he could not resist looking down at his hands. Albertine's hand was cold as ice, Sibbi's warm and dry. A peculiar stasis had fallen over them all. The poet glanced up and saw the clock had fittingly stopped on the mantelshelf. The eyes of the three women and of the man, as always, were on him.

'This is very irksome,' Laura said. 'Really, Sibbi, can't you use some blandishment to persuade your ghostie to appear? I have three letters to write –'

'I could sing,' Sibbi said, and her hand moved in his. 'If Robert thinks I should.'

'That should charm any ghost, I'm sure,' stung Laura.

They had drawn the blinds; the room was drowned in a bloody shadow. The poet stared at the silent clock.

'What would you like me to sing?' Sibbi murmured, offering the sting so that he could draw the poison from it.

'Anything,' he said. *What does it matter*, he thought, *what she sings?* Desire ran through her hand into his body, yet he scarcely felt it, sex, like an absent limb, lost in some war, castrated by some mental battle . . . His eyes unfocused on the face of the clock. He did not want to go back to the room in the tower, to the unfinished work, the spell which evaded him, urgent once, now meaningless. He had put it off. The girl began softly to sing; she sang as if far away over some hill of the mind, words he had written to an old tune of the island:

> Stream, from the black cold sun of night,
> Phantoms in robes of darkest light,
> To muddy the clear waters of our lives
> With dreams.

And after this dream, what? The room began to breathe about him, or else it was the sea. Nothing achieved or to come, and if achieved what did it signify? Ants crawling in ant cities . . . He felt the floor tilt a little beneath his chair, and thought distantly: *Now, an earthquake*.

But it was the sea, the sea cool and green, washing in across the floor.

'By George, we're flooded,' Merton observed jovially, without rancour or alarm. 'And the roof's come down.'

The house was gone. In a paper boat they rocked gently over an ocean glaucous and slippery as the backs of seals.

'Look at this,' Merton said, prodding the paper. 'Soon sink. Dear chap, I said the shipwright should look at her. Not seaworthy, you know.'

The ship was composed of manuscripts. The ink ran and darkened the water.

'You have had my wife, of course,' Merton said, 'but it's all for the best. Ballast, you know. Jettison extra cargo.'

The poet looked down and saw that Laura and Sibbi floated under the glass-green runnels of waves with wide eyes and fish swimming in their hair and in and out of their open mouths. With his right hand he was holding Albertine beneath the water, while her garments floated out like Ophelia's, and she smiled at him sadly, encouraging him to do whatever was necessary to save himself.

Ashburn leapt to his feet and the bottom gave way in the paper boat and, as the water closed over his head like salty fire, he saw Merton knock the dottle from his pipe –

Albertine still lay against his arm, he was trying to lift her above the sea and she was calling to him and struggling with him and suddenly he found himself in the blood-red room with fragments of glass on the table, Sibbi cowering in her chair, and no hands visible except Albertine's, both holding on to him as if he and she were drowning indeed.

But it was night which drowned everything, all confusion and outcry.

It swooped on the island. The sea turned red then black, the sky opened itself to an ochre moon. A serpent of lights wound out of the village at sunset and settled upon the beach below the house with the hoarse screeches of predatory bats.

'Our favourite pagan-Christians are restive again,' Laura said. 'Dear God, who would believe such ceremonies could still exist. Are they sacrificing maidens to the sea?'

'Praying for rain,' Merton said. 'Poor beggars. They get little enough from the land in a good year, but this drought – well, there's no telling.'

'Their hovels are empty of food, clothing and furniture,' Laura said, 'and in the church are three gold candlesticks. How can such fools hope to survive?'

Merton lit his pipe and relapsed in his shadowy chair. Sibbi sat slapping down cards before the lamp; Laura, her wormwood letters written, stood at the window gazing out at the firefly glare on the foreshore. And above? From time to time each of the three looked up at the ceiling. The poet and his pale woman were locked in some curious, stilted, yet private and unsharing communion.

My satisfaction lies only in observing my fellow exiles, Laura thought, and glanced at Sibbi with a dark little smile. 'Really, dear Sibbi, you did get such a scare, didn't you?'

Sibbi slapped down the coloured cards, commonly, as Laura had seen the market women do with fish.

'I don't know what you mean. Anyone might be taken ill in this weather.'

'Yes, of course,' Laura smiled, 'and scream at the top of his lungs, and frighten little Miss Muffet into a flawless fit. Did you imagine only women are permitted to have hysterics? You will have to get accustomed to such things in this house.'

'Some sort of – of nightmare,' Merton ventured. 'Dropped off myself.'

Laura showed her teeth, as sharp, predatory and feline as Sibbi's and with no pretence.

'What does Sibbi see in the cards? Good fortune, health and happiness? Or is it a soupçon of undying love?'

She leaned back against the window frame. The torches were guttering out, the howling voices blown to cindery shreds on the wind. A melancholy hollowness yawned inside her, a disembowelling ache. She suffered it, waiting, as if for a spasm of pain, until it passed. *Does nothing die?* she thought, her heart squeezing its bitterness like a lemon into her veins.

The shore was all darkness now. The foxy moon meanly described only the edges of the sand, the ribs of the water. Above on the tower, the awning gave a single despotic flap like the wing of a huge bird. Laura looked upward, then down, and made out a figure walking along beneath the garden wall, towards the beach and the sea. For a moment she did not question it, saw only some fragment of the night, a metaphysical shape without reference. Then, from the turn of the head, the manner of moving, she recognized Ashburn.

'Merton – look –' Merton came rumbling to the window. His pipe smoke enveloped Laura; she thrust it from her eyes. 'Do you see? What can he be doing?'

'Good lord,' Merton muttered, 'good lord.'

'For heaven's sake, go after him,' Laura cried. 'In this state, he'll walk into the sea and never realize it.'

They ran together towards the front of the house and burst out wildly on to the beach, Merton stumbling, Sibbi erupting in a frenzy of curiosity, demand and fright after them. The dreadful, enormous intimacy of the darkness swept over them, the hot dim essence of the night which still faintly carried the arcane noises of the islanders and the smell of torch smoke.

'Oh, where is he?' Laura cried. She could not reason why she was so afraid, yet all three had caught the fear, like sickness.

'There, I see him. You stay here –' Merton set off across the sand, a blundering, great, bear-like form, shouting now: 'Ashburn! Robert!'

'Oh, the unsubtle fool,' Laura moaned.

Sibbi half lay against the door, biting her wedding ring, hissing over and over: 'I can't bear it, I simply won't bear it.'

Merton plunged towards the sea, waving his arms, yelling; then abruptly stopped. Simultaneously the seaward window of the tower opened, and the wind snatched pale handfuls of hair out upon itself as if unravelling silver wool from the head of Albertine.

185

'What's wrong?' she called down, in a soft, panic-stricken voice.

'Don't you know?' Laura screamed at her.

'Oh, please be quiet,' Albertine implored. 'Don't wake him, for God's sake.'

Laura ran out on to the shore, stared up at the window, then towards the bone-yellow breakers of the sea smashing at Merton's feet.

'I saw Robert walking towards the water,' Laura said. 'So did Arthur.'

'But he's sleeping,' Albertine protested. She glanced over her shoulder into the tower room. Her normally calm face betrayed itself when she looked again downwards at Laura. It was convulsed in horrified accusation and loathing, and white as the face of a clock. She shrank back and closed the window after her with violent noiselessness.

Merton came up the beach, sweat ran down his cheeks. He looked at Laura silently and passed on. Sibbi giggled wildly in the doorway. 'I didn't see,' she cried. The breakers clashed on the shore and raked the sand with their black fingers.

They had expressions suitable for everything.

They breathed closely, at midnight, like a woman on the poet's pillow, her ocean voice sounding in the seashell of his ear. He woke and searched for her, a woman with any number of faces. But no woman lay on the narrow bed in the tower, only a girl sat asleep in a chair near the window.

He got up quietly and went to look at her, yet somehow had no fear that she would wake. Her profile, her defenceless hands and alabaster torrent of hair, all these touched him with a listless tenderness. He wanted to stroke the tired lines away from her mouth which, even in sleep, had a touch of the hungry recalcitrant childishness that generally moulds only the mouths of old women. He wanted to soothe her, go back with her to the green shades of the past. Yet he had no energy, no true impulse. He stood penitently before her, as if she were dead. He desired nothing from her, really desired nothing from any of them, and they clamoured to load him with their gifts, to fetter him with their kindness.

What do you want then? Undying fame, the glory of the king whose monument is made of steel and lasts for ever? Or does any

186

monument last, or any hope? And does any wish of a man matter?

He left her slumped there and went down the stair from the tower. In her wasp-cell Laura would be sleeping, curled like a foetus around her hate and pain. And pretty Sibbi, probably quite content in the arms of her bear. He crossed the room where the piano stood like a beast of black mirror. He opened the veranda doors yet the garden seemed more enclosed even than the house, full of heat and shadows like lace, and the huddled leper colony of statues. He went out on to the terrace nevertheless, and stood there, and the noise of the sea poured around him and on the beaches inside his brain.

He felt nothing.

He wanted nothing, expected nothing.

He did not quite expect the man who came from the side of the house, along the terrace.

A slight dark man, walking, looking out of dark eyes, carrying with him the primeval green odour of the sea. The poet turned and looked at the man. A little white hot shock passed through his heart, but he felt it only remotely. The man was himself.

Ashburn said quietly: 'Well?'

The man who was himself gazed back at him, without recognition, without dislike, without love. His clothes, Ashburn's clothes, were soaked, as if he had been swimming in the sea. Incredible black and purple weeds had attached themselves to his shoulders.

'How long,' the man said to him, 'will you make me wait for you?'

Ashburn leaned back against the wall of the house. All the strength had gone out of him; it seemed as if his body had fainted yet left his mind conscious and alert. He laughed and shut his eyes. 'I have called up my own ghost,' he said, and looked again, and the man had gone. The poet rubbed his head against the hot hard wall and discovered, with little interest, that he was weeping. The tears tasted of the sea, teaching him.

Yet, 'Don't go,' Albertine said in the morning, as she stood on the shallow step by the royal blue water. Her eyes were fixed, not on him, but on the little boat, the young brown islander arrogantly at work on her rigging, fixed on Merton standing on the beach, smoking his pipe, nodding at the waves.

'The sea's as calm as glass, look at it,' Ashburn said. He smiled at her, took her hand. 'Do you think Merton would risk the trip otherwise, or the island boy?'

Albertine reached out and took his face fiercely between her hands.

'Don't go, don't leave me –'

'There are things we need from the mainland, my love, beside Laura's vitriolic letters to be posted.'

'No,' she said. Her eyes were wide and desolate as grey marshes; her cold hands burned.

Merton came up, patted her arm.

'Come now, it's just what we all need.' He winked anxiously, indicating to her that Ashburn would benefit from an hour or so in the boat. 'Sea's like blue lead, and it's hot enough to fry fish in that water.'

Albertine suddenly relinquished her hold on the poet. Her eyes clouded over and went blank as if she had lost her sight.

'Goodbye,' she said. She turned and went back into the house. Merton, glancing up, saw her emerge presently on the flat roof of the tower, and wait by the black telescope beneath the awning.

The two men walked towards the boat together. The village boy nodded sneeringly and let them, as a particular favour, get in, packing his brown bony limbs in position as he took the tiller. They cast off. The silken arms of the water drew them in.

The ship clove the waves gracefully, with a gull-like motion, her sails opening like flowers to the wind. The island and the red house dwindled behind them, and the smoking hills.

'Cooler here,' Merton said. He knocked the dottle from his pipe as if relieved to be rid of it. 'Feel better now, I expect, old chap?'

The poet smiled as he lay against the side of the boat, ineffably relaxed. The sea and sky seemed all one colour, one ebony blue. He was aware of a lightness within himself, an inner silence. All the busy organs of the body had ceased, the ticking clocks, all unwound, all at peace, no heartbeat, no beat in the belly or loins, no chatter in the brain. The sky appeared to thread itself between sail and mast like sapphire cotton through a needle. The heat was almost comforting, a soporific laudanum summer breath sighed into the motionless bellows of his lungs. He smiled at Merton, he smiled compassionately. He felt himself regarding a man who is unaware that in his flesh the advanced symptoms of an incurable illness have manifested themselves. *Should I tell him? No, poor creature, let him be. Let him go on in impossible hope.*

'Do you swim?' Ashburn asked.

'Swim? Why yes, you know I do, unlike yourself.'

The poet turned to the brown boy with the same smiling compassion. 'And you?'

'I? I swim like dolphin.' He glared at them, however, with the kingly eyes of a shark.

'What's all this worry about swimming?' Merton said, lighting the pipe. 'Afraid we'll capsize or something?'

'Look,' Ashburn said, softly.

Merton looked. He saw a strange, mysterious phenomenon, a bank of nacreous fog, afloat like a great galleon and bearing down on them.

'Good God.'

'Yes,' Ashburn said, 'a good God, who sends his people rain.'

With an abrupt entirety as if a grey glove had seized the ship, the fog closed over them and they lost each other in it.

'Turn back for shore!' Merton shouted. No one apparently heard him. The boat swung drunkenly sideways. The drums of his ears seemed to stretch tight; there was a growling in the air. The sky and sea tilted to meet each other, and slammed together as thunder shattered the ocean into a broken plate. A lightning appeared to strike to the vitals of the boat itself: wood splintered, a terrifying unreasonable sound. Merton fell to his knees; he could hear the boy screaming about a rock in the sea.

'Ashburn, where are you?' he cried, groping with his hands through the greyness, but the wind rushed into his throat, and the world leaned sideways and flung him into its salty mouth, and gulped him down.

Albertine was still waiting at the telescope. She had watched the ship bob on the leaden sea, she had watched the fog rise like a hand from the floor of the ocean and gather the vessel into itself.

Soon the sky broke up. Explosions of thunder and dazzling lightnings divided the landscape between them. Viscous rain began to fall, at first like great gems, opals or diamonds, then in a boiling sheet of white fire that flamed across the house, the shore, the sea in impenetrable gusts. From the village the islanders came running, shouting, opening their arms to the storm. Albertine, her hair flattened to her skull and shoulders, the colour of the rain itself, stared through the one-eyed thing towards the abstracted ocean.

The storm was brief; it failed and fled away shrieking over the land trailing its torn plumes. The sky cleared, the sea, the shore, even the distant coast became visible. Nothing stood between the island and the coast. The ship had vanished.

The black tongue of the telescope licked to left and right, probing with its cold cyclopean glass, but not for long.

Soon, Albertine drew away from it. Her clothes and her hair ran water as if she had come from the sea. Yellow water dripped from the slag-bellied awning. As if across miles of desert, she could hear the voice of a frenzied woman in the house below her feet. 'Poor Sibbi,' she whispered, as if comforting herself. 'Poor Laura.' She did not cry, only frowned a little, striving to comprehend the perfection of her knowledge, the completeness of the event which had befallen her. She rocked her grief in her arms like a sleeping child.

When she turned down the stairway into the tower room, she saw the poet at his desk, the manuscripts, the open books, set out before him. He looked up at her, not with a lover's face or the face even of an enemy, but merely with the soulless look of something which is only spirit. She held her grief in her arms and watched the poet's ghost fade like water in the air of the room, until only the room, the shadows, remained, and the unfinished poem, spread like the white wings of a dead pigeon on the desk.

Blue Vase of Ghosts

*In my family we tend to be surprise-gift givers, and one
afternoon my father gave me a blue glass vase. I have always
been enamoured of coloured glass in all forms, but the instant
I saw the vase, the title opened in my mind. The story came at
once, with all its stained-glass colouring.*

1
Subyrus, the Magician

Above, the evening sky; dark blue, transparent and raining stars.
Below, the evening-coloured land, also blue to the depths of its
hills, its river-carven valley, blue to its horizon, where a dusting
of gold freckles revealed the lights of the city of Vaim.

Between, a bare hillside with two objects on it: a curious stone
pavilion and a frightened man.

The cause of the man's fear, evidently, was the pavilion, or
what it signified. Nevertheless, he had advanced to the open door
and was peering inside.

The entire landscape had assumed the romantic air of faint
menace that attends twilight, all outlines darkening and melting
in the mysterious smoke of dusk. The pavilion appeared no more
sinister than everything else. About eight feet in height with a flat
roof set on five walls of rough-hewn slabs, its only truly occult
area lay over the square step and through the square doormouth –
a matched square of black shadow.

Until: 'I seek the Magician-Lord Subyrus,' the frightened man
exclaimed aloud, and the black shadow vanished in an ominous
brazen glare.

The man gasped. Not so much in fear, as in uneasy recognition of something expected. Nor did he cry out, turn to run or fall on his knees when, in the middle of the glare, there evolved an unnatural figure. It was a great toad, large as a dog and made of brass, which parted its jaws with a creaking of metal hinges, and asked: '*Who* seeks Subyrus, Master of the Ten Mechanicae?'

'My name is not important,' quavered the man. 'My mission is. Lord Subyrus is interested in purchasing rarities of magic. I bring him one.'

Galaxies glinted and wheeled in bulbous amphibian eyes.

'Very well,' the toad said. 'My maker hears. You are invited in. Enter.'

At which the whole floor of the pavilion rushed upwards, with the monster squatting impassively atop it. Revealed beneath was a sort of metal cage, big enough to contain a man. Into this cage all visitors must step, and the frightened visitor knew as much. Just as he had known of the hill, the pavilion, the glare of unseen lamps and the horrendous brazen guardian. For down the trade roads and throughout the river ports of Vaim, word of these wonders had spread, along with the news that Subyrus, Master of the Ten Mechanicae, would buy with gold objects of sorcery – providing they were fabulous, bizarre and, preferably, unique.

The visitor entered the cage, which was the second of the Ten Mechanicae (the toad being the first). The cage instantly plunged into the hollow hill.

His entrails seemingly left plastered to the pavilion roof by the rapid descent, the visitor clutched to himself the leather satchel he had brought, and thought alternately of riches and death.

Subyrus sat in a chair of green quartz in a hall hung with drapes the colours of charred roses and black panthers. A clear pink fire burned on the wide hearth that gave off the slight persuasive scent of strawberries. Subyrus studied the fire quietly with deep-lidded dark eyes. He had the face of a beautiful skull, long hands and a long leopardine body to concur with that image. The robe of murky murderous crimson threw into exotic relief his luminous and unblemished pallor, and the strange dull bronze of his long hair that seemed carved rather than combed.

When the cage dashed down into the hall and bounced on its cushioned buffers, throwing the occupant all awry, Subyrus

looked up, unsmiling. He regarded the man who staggered from
the cage clutching a satchel with none of the cruel arid expressions or gestures the man had obviously anticipated.

Subyrus' regard was compounded of pity, a vague inquiry, an
intense drugged boredom.

It was, if anything, worse than sadism and savagery.

A melodramatic laugh and glimpse of wolf-fangs would have
been somehow preferable to those opaque and disenchanted
eyes.

'Well?' Subyrus said. Less a question than a plea – *Oh, for the
love of the gods, interest me in something.* The plea of a man (if he
were that alone) to whom other men were insects, and their deeds
pages of a book to be turned and turned in the vain hope of a
quickening.

The man with the satchel quailed.

'Magician-Lord – I had heard – you wished marvels to be
brought to you that you might . . . acquire them.'

Subyrus sighed. 'You heard correctly. What then have you
brought?'

'In this satchel, lordly one – something beyond –'

'Beyond what?' Subyrus' sombre eyes widened, but only with
disbelief at the tedium this salesman was causing him. 'Beyond
my wildest dreamings, perhaps you meant to say? I have no wild
dreamings. I should welcome them.'

In a panic, the man with the satchel blurted something. The
sort of overplay he might have used on an ordinary customer; it
had become a habit with him to attempt startlement in order to
gain the upper hand. But not here, where he should have left well
alone.

'What did you say?' Subyrus asked.

'I said – I said –'

'Yes?'

'That the Lady Lunaria of Vaim – was wild dream enough.'

Now the satchel-man stood transfixed at his own idiocy, his
very bones knocking together in wretched fright. Indeed, Subyrus
had lost his mask of boredom, but it had been replaced merely by
an appalling contempt.

'Have I become a laughing stock in Vaim?'

The query was idle, mild. Suddenly the man with the satchel
realized the contempt of the magician was self-directed. The man

slumped and answered, truthfully: 'No one would dare laugh, Magician-Lord, at anything of yours. The length of the river, men pale at your name. But the other thing – you can hardly blame them for envying you the Lady Lunaria.' He glanced up. Had he said the right words, at last? The magician did not respond. The frightened satchel-man had space to brood on the story then current in the city, that the Master of the Ten Mechanicae had taken for his mistress the most famous whore this side the northern ocean, and that Lunaria Vaimian ruled Subyrus as if he were a toothless lion, ordering him to this and that, demanding costly gifts, setting him errands, and even in the matter of the bedchamber, herself saying when. Some claimed the story an invention of Lunaria's, a dangerous game she played with Subyrus' reputation. Others said that Subyrus himself had sent the fancy abroad to see if any dared mock him, so he might cut them down with sorcery in some vicious and perverse fashion.

But the satchel-man had come over the mountain roads to Vaim. A stranger, he had never seen Lunaria for himself, nor, till tonight, the magician-lord.

'Well?' Subyrus said drowsily.

The satchel-man jumped in his skin.

'I suggest,' Subyrus said, 'you show me this rare treasure beyond wild dreamings. You may mention its origin and how you came by it. You may state its ability, if any, and demonstrate. You may then name your price. But, I beg you, no more sales patter.'

Shivering, the satchel-man undid the clasps and drew from the leather a padded bag. From the bag he produced a velvet box. In the box he revealed a sapphire glimmer wrapped in feathers. The feathers drifted to the floor as he lifted out a vase of blue crystal, about a foot in length, elongated of neck, with a broad base of oddly alternating swelling and tapering design. The castellated lip was sealed by a stopper that appeared to be a single rose-opal.

Prudently silent, and holding the vase before him like a talisman, the visitor approached Subyrus' chair.

'Charming,' said Subyrus. 'But what does it do?'

'My lord,' the satchel-man whispered, 'my lord – I can simply recount what it is *supposed* to have done – and to do. I myself have not the skill to test it.'

'Then you must tell me immediately how you came by it. Look

at me,' Subyrus added. His voice was all at once no longer indolent but cool and terrible. Unwilling, but without choice, the satchel-man raised his head. Subyrus was turning a great black ring, round and round, on his finger. At first it was like a black snake darting in and out, then like a black eye, opening and closing.

Subyrus sighed again, depressed at the ease with which most human resistance could be overcome.

'Speak now.'

The satchel-man dutifully began.

Mesmerized by the black ring, he spoke honestly, without either embroidery or omission.

2
The Satchel-Man's Tale

An itinerant scavenger by trade, the satchel-man had happened on a remote town of the far north, and learned of a freakish enterprise taking place in the vicinity. The tomb of an ancient king had been located in the heart of one of the tall iron-blue crags that towered above the town. Scholars of the town, fascinated by the tomb's antiquity, had hired gangs of workmen to break into the inner chamber and prize off the lid of the sarcophagus. At this event, the satchel-man was a lurking bystander. He had made up to several of the scholars in the hope of some arcane jewel dropping into his paws. But in the end, all that had been uncovered were dust, stench, decay and some brown grinning bones – clutched in the digits of which was a vase of blue crystal stoppered with rose-opal.

The find being solitary, the scholars were obliged to offer it to the town's Tyrant. He graciously accepted the vase, attempted to pull out the opal stopper; failed, attempted to smash the vase in order to release the stopper; failed, ordered various pounding devices to crush the vase – which also failed, called for one of the scholars and demanded he investigate the nature of the vase forthwith. This scholar, who had leanings in the sorcerous direction, had also become the host of the parasitic satchel-man. The satchel-man had spun some yarn of ill luck which the scholar, an unworldly intellectual, credited. So the satchel-man was informed as to the scholar's magic assaults on the vase. Not that the satchel-man actually attended the rituals first hand (as, but for the mesmerism, he would have assured Subyrus he had). Yet he was advised of them over supper, when the fraught scholar complained of his unsuccess. Then late one night, as the satchel-man sprawled on a couch with his host's brandy pitcher, a fearsome yell echoed through the house. A second or so later, pale as steamed fish, the scholar stumbled into the room, and collapsed whimpering on the ground.

The satchel-man gallantly revived the scholar with some of his own brandy. The scholar spoke.

'It is a sorcery of the Brink, of the Abyss. More lethal than the sword, and more dreadful. In the hands of a Power, what mischief could it not encompass? What mischief it *has* encompassed.'

'Have a little extra brandy,' said the satchel-man, torn between curiosity, avarice and nerves. 'Say more.'

The scholar drank deep, grew sozzled, and elaborated in such a way that the hairs bristled on the satchel-man's unclean neck.

Searching an antique book, the scholar had discovered an unusual spell of Opening. This he had performed, and the rose-opal had jumped free of the mouth of the vase. Such a whirling had then occurred inside it that the scholar had become alarmed. The crystal seemed full of milk on the boil and milky lather foamed in the opening of the castellated mouth. In consternation, the scholar had given vent to numerous rhetorical questions, such as: 'What shall I do?' and 'What in the world does this bubbling portend?' Finally he voiced a rhetorical question that utilized the name of the ancient king: 'What can King So-and-So have performed with such an artifact?'

Rhetorical questions do not expect answers. But to this question an answer came. No sooner was the king's name uttered than the frothing in the vase erupted outwards. A strand of this froth, proceeding higher than the rest from the vase's mouth, gradually solidified. Within the space of half a minute, there balanced in the atmosphere above the vase, deadly white but perfectly formed, the foot-high figure of a man, lavishly bearded and elaborately clad, a barbaric diadem on his head. With a minute sneer, this figure addressed the scholar.

'Normally, further ritual with greater accuracy is required. But since I was the last to enter, and since I have been within a mere four centuries, I respond to my name. Well, what do you wish, O absurd and gigantic fool?'

A dialogue then ensued which had to do with the scholar's astonishment and disbelief, and the white midget king's utter irritation at, and scorn of, the scholar.

In the course of this dialogue, however, the nature of the vase was specified.

A magician had made it, though when and how was unsure. Its purpose was original, providing the correct magic had been activated by rite and incantation. That done, whoever might die – or whoever might be slain – in the close neighbourhood of the vase, their soul would be sucked into the crystal and imprisoned there till the ending of time, or at least of time as mortal men know it. Since its creation, countless magicians, and others who had learned the relevant sorcery, had used the vase in this way, catching inside it the souls, or ghosts, of enemies, lovers and kindred for personal solace or entertainment. It might be reckoned (the king casually told the scholar) that seven thousand souls now inhabited the core of the vase. ('How is there room for so many?' the scholar cried. The king laughed. 'I am not bound to answer questions. Therefore, I will do no more than assure you that room there is, and to spare.') It appeared that whoever could name the vase-trapped ghosts by their exact appellations might call them forth. They might then reply to interrogation – but only if the fancy took them to do so.

The scholar, overwhelmed, dithered. At length the miniature being demanded leave to return into the vase, which the scholar had weakly granted. He had then flown downstairs to seek comfort from the satchel-man.

The satchel-man was not comforting. He was insistent. The scholar must summon the king's ghost up once again. Positively, the king would be able to tell them where the hoards of his treasure had been buried, for all kings left treasure hoards at death, if not in their tombs, then in some other spot. Was the scholar not a magus? He must recall the ghost and somehow coerce it into malleability, thereby unearthing incredible secrets of lore and (better) cash.

The scholar, convinced by the satchel-man's persistence and the dregs of the brandy, eventually resummoned the king's ghost.

Nothing happened. The scholar and the satchel-man strenuously reiterated the summons. Still nothing. It seemed the ghost had been right in hinting that the ritual was important. He had obeyed on the first occasion because his had been the last and newest soul in the vase, but he had no need to obey further without proper incentive.

Then the scholar fell to philosophizing and the satchel-man fell to cursing him. Presently the scholar turned the satchel-man out of his house. That night, while the scholar snored in brandy-pickled slumber, the satchel-man regained entry and stole the vase. It was not his first robbery, and his exit was swift from practice.

Thereafter he wandered, endeavouring to locate a mage who knew the correct magic to name, draw forth and browbeat the ghosts in the vase. Or even merely to draw out the rose-opal stopper with which the scholar had inconsiderately recorked it.

Months passed with the mission unaccomplished, and despair set in. Until the satchel-man caught word of the Magician-Lord Subyrus.

To begin with, the satchel-man may have indulged in a dream of enlisting Subyrus' aid, but rumour dissuaded him from this notion. In the long run, it seemed safer to sell the vase outright and be rid of the profitless item. If any mage alive could deal with the thing it was the Master of the Ten Mechanicae. And somehow the salesman did not think Subyrus would share his knowledge. To accept payment in gold seemed the wisest course.

The satchel-man came to himself and saw the fire on the wide hearth had changed. It was green now, and perfumed with apples. The fire must be the third of the Mechanicae.

Subyrus had not changed. Not at all.

'And your price?' he gently murmured. His eyes were nearly shut.

'Considering the treasure I forgo in giving up the vase to your lordship –' The satchel-man meant to sound bold, succeeded in a whining tone.

'And considering you will never reach that treasure, as you have no power over the vase yourself,' Subyrus amended, and shut his eyes totally from weariness.

'Seven thousand vaimii,' stated the satchel-man querulously.

'One for each of the seven thousand ghosts in the vase.'

Subyrus' lids lifted. He stared at the satchel-man and the satchel-man felt his joints loosen in horror. Then Subyrus smiled. It was the smile of an old, old man, dying of ennui, his mood lightened for a split second by the antics of a beetle on the wall.

'That seems,' said Subyrus, 'quite reasonable.'

One hand moved lazily and the fourth of the Mechanicae manifested itself. It was a brazen chest which sprang from between the charred-rose draperies. Subyrus spoke to the chest, a compartment shot out and deposited a paralysing quantity of gold coins on the rugs at the satchel-man's feet.

'Seven thousand vaimii,' Subyrus said. 'Count them.'

'My lord, I would not suppose –'

'Count them,' repeated the magician, without emphasis.

Anxious not to offend, the satchel-man did as he was bid.

He was not a particularly far-sighted man. He did not realize how long it would take him.

A little over an hour later, fingers numb, eyes watering and spine unpleasantly locked, he slunk into the mechanical cage and was borne back to the surface. This time, his guts were left plastered to the lowermost floor of the hollow hill.

Musically clinking, and in terror lest he himself be robbed, the satchel-man limped hurriedly away through the starry and beautiful night.

3

Proving the Vase

The fire burned warmly black, and smelled of musk and ambergris. This was the aspect of the fire which Subyrus used to recall Lunaria to him. The idea of her threaded his muscles, his very bones, with an elusive excitement, not quite sexual, not quite pleasing, not quite explicable. In this mood, he did not even visualize Lunarie Vaimian as a woman, or as any sort of object. Abstract, her memory possessed him and folded him round with an intoxicating, though distant and scarcely recognizable, agony.

It was quite true that she, of the entire city of Vaim, defied him. She asked him continually for gifts, but she would not accept money or jewels. She wanted the benefits of his status as a magician. So he gave her a rose which endlessly bloomed, a bracelet which, at her command, would transmute to a serpent, gloves that changed colour and material, a ring that could detect the lies of others and whistle thinly, to their discomfort. He collected sorcerous trinkets and bought them for gold, to give to her. In response to these gifts, Lunaria Vaimian admitted Subyrus to her couch. But she also dallied with other men. Twice she had shut her doors to the Master of the Ten Mechanicae. Once, when he had smitten the doors wide, she had said to him: 'Do I anger you, lord? Kill me then. But if you lie with me against my will, I warn you, mighty Subyrus, it will be poor sport.'

On various occasions, she had publicly mocked him, struck him in the face, reviled his aptitude both for magic and love. Witnesses had trembled. Subyrus' inaction surprised and misled them.

They reckoned him besotted with a lovely harlot, and wondered at it, that he found her so indispensable he must accept her whims and never rebuke her for them. In fact, Lunaria *was* indispensable to the Magician-Lord, but not after the general interpretation.

Her skin was like that dark brown spice called cinnamon, her eyes the darker shade of malt. On this sombreness was superimposed a blanching of blonde hair, streaked gold by sunlight and artifice in equal measure. Beautiful she was, but not much more beautiful than several women who had cast themselves at the feet of Subyrus, abject and yielding. Indeed, the entire metropolis and hinterland of Vaim knew and surrendered to him. All-powerful and all-feared and, with women who beheld his handsomeness and guessed at his intellect, all-worshipped. All that, save by Lunaria. Hence, her value. She was the challenge he might otherwise find in no person or sphere. The natural and the supernatural he could control, but not her. She was not abject or easy. She did not yield. The exacerbation of her defiance quickened him and gave him a purpose, an excuse for his life, in which everything else might be won at a word.

But this self-analysis he concealed from himself with considerable cunning. He experienced only the pangs of her rejection and scorn, and winced as he savoured them like sour wine. Obsessed, he gazed at the vase of blue crystal, and pondered the toys of magic he had given her formerly.

The vase.

The stopper of rose-opal had already been removed by one of the spells of the *Forax Foramen*, a copy of which ancient book (there were but three copies on earth) was the property of Subyrus. At this spell, written in gold leaf on sheets of black bull's hide, Subyrus had barely glanced. His knowledge was vast and his sorcerous vocabulary extensive. The stopper leapt from the neck of the vase – Subyrus caught it and set it by. Inside the crystal there commenced the foaming and lathering which the scholar had described to the satchel-man.

At Subyrus' other hand lay a second tome. No exact copies of this book existed, for it was the task of each individual mage to compile his own version. The general title of such a compendium being *Tabulas Mortem*, Lists of the Dead.

From these lists Subyrus had selected seventy names, a hundredth portion of the number of souls said to be trapped in the vase. They were accordingly names of those who had died in peculiar circumstances, and in an aura of shadows, such as might indicate the nearness at that time of the soul-snaring crystal and of someone who could operate its magic.

With each name there obtained attendant rituals of appeasement, summoning and other things that might apply when wishing to contact the dead. All were subtly different from each other, however similar seeming to the uneducated eye.

The fire sank on the hearth now, paled and began to smell of incense and moist rank soil.

Subyrus had performed the correct ritual and called the first name. He omitted from it the five inflexions that would extend the summons beyond the world, since his intent was centred on the trapped ghosts of the vase. He had also discarded the name of the king from whose tomb the vase had been taken. Occult theory suggested that such a spirit, having been recently obedient to an inaccurate summons (such as the scholar's), could thereby increase its resistance to obeying any other summons for some while after. So the name Subyrus named was a fresh one. Nor, though the ritual was perfect, was it answered.

That soul, then, had never been encaged in the vase. Subyrus erased the name from his selection, and commenced the ritual for a second.

★ ★ ★

In Vaim it was midnight, and over the hill above the magician's subculum the configurations of midnight were jewelled out in stars.

Subyrus spoke the nineteenth name.

And was answered.

The moistureless foam-clouds gathered and overspilled the vase. White bubbles and curlicues expanded on the air. From their midst flowed up a slender strand unlike the rest, which proceeded to form a recognizable shape. Presently, a foot-high figurine balanced on the air, just over the castellated lip of the vase. It was a warrior, like an intricately sculptured chess piece, whose detail was intriguing on such a scale – the minute links of the mail, the chiselled cat that crouched on the helm, the sword like a woman's pin. And all of it matt white as chalk.

'I am here,' the warrior cried in bell-like miniature tones. 'What do you want of me?'

'Tell me how you came to be imprisoned in the crystal.'

'My city was at war with another. The enemy took me in a battle, and strove to gain, by torture, knowledge of a way our defences might be breached. When I would say nothing, a magician entered. He worked spells behind a screen. Then I was slain and my ghost sucked into the vase. Next moment, the magician summoned me forth, and they asked me again, and I told them everything.'

'So,' Subyrus remarked, 'what you would not betray as a man, you revealed carelessly once you were a spirit.'

'Exactly. Which was as the magician had foretold.'

'Why? Because you were embittered at your psychic capture?'

'Not at all. But once within, human things ceased to matter to me. Old loyalties of the world, its creeds, yearnings and antipathies – these foibles are as dreams to those of us who dwell in the vase.'

'Dwell? Is there room then, inside that little sphere, to dwell?'

'It would amaze you,' said the warrior.

'No. But you may describe it.'

'That is not normally one of the questions mortals ask when they summon us. They demand directions to our sepulchres, and ways to break in and come on our hoarded gold, or what hereditary defects afflict our line, in order they may harm our descendants. Or they command us to carry out deeds of malevolence, to creep in small hidden areas and steal for them, or to frighten the nervous by our appearance.'

'You have not replied to my question.'

'Nor can I. The interior of this tiny vase houses seven thousand souls. To explain its microcosmic structure in mortal terms, even to one of the mighty Magician-Lords, would be as impossible as to describe colour to the stone-blind or music to the stone-deaf.'

'But you are content,' said Subyrus.

The warrior laughed flamboyantly. 'I am.'

'You may return,' said Subyrus, and uttered the dismissing incantation.

Subyrus progressed to a twentieth name, a twenty-first, a twenty-second. The twenty-third answered. This time a white philosopher stood in the air, his head meekly bowed, his sequin eyes whitely gleaming with the arrogance of great learning.

'Tell me how you came to be imprisoned in the crystal.'

'A Tyrant acquired this vase and its spell. He feared me and the teachings I imparted to his people. I was burned alive, the spell activated, and my ghost entered the vase. Thereafter, the Tyrant would call me forth and try to force me to enact degrading tricks to titillate him. But though we who inhabit the vase must respond to a summons, we need not obey otherwise. The Tyrant waxed disappointed. He attempted to smash the vase. At length he went mad. The next man who called me forth wished only to hear my philosophies. But I related gibberish, which troubled him.'

'Describe the interior of the vase.'

'I refuse.'

'You understand, my arts are of the kind which can retain you here as long as I desire.'

'I understand. I pine, but still refuse.'

'Go then,' and Subyrus uttered again the dismissing incantation.

It was past three o'clock. Altogether, six white apparitions had evolved from the blue vase. Subyrus had reached the fortieth name selected from the *Tabulas Mortem*. He was almost too weary to speak it.

The atmosphere was feverish and heavy with rituals observed and magics pronounced. Subyrus' thin and beautiful hands shook slightly with fatigue, and his beautiful face had grown more skull-like. To these trivialities he was almost immune, though exhaustion heightened his world-sated gravity.

He said the fortieth name, and the figure of a marvellous woman rose from the vase.

'Your death?' he asked her. She had been an empress in her day.

'My lover was slain. I had no wish to live. But the man who brought me poison brought also this vase under his cloak. When my soul was snared, he carried the vase to distant lands. He would call me up in the houses of lords, and bid me dance for his patrons. I did this, for it amused me. He received much gold. Then, one night, in a prince's palace, I lost interest in the jest. I would not dance, and the wretch was whipped. The prince appropriated the vase. When I begged leave to rest, the prince recited the incantation of dismissal, which the whipped man had revealed. Ironically, the prince was not comparably adept at the phrases of summoning, and could never draw me forth again.'

The woman smiled, and touched at the white hair which streamed about her white robe.

'Surely you miss the gorgeous mode of your earthly state?' Subyrus said.

'Not at all.'

'Your prison suits you then?'

'Wonderfully well.'

'Describe it.'

'Others have told me you asked a description of them.'

'None obliged me. Will you?'

But the woman only smiled.

Broodingly, Subyrus effected her dismissal.

He pushed the further names aside, and, taking up the stopper of rose-opal, replaced it in the vase. The fermentation stilled within.

Slowly, the fire reproduced the darkness and scents that recalled Lunaria for the magician.

The vase was proven – and ready. The promise of such a thing would flatter even Lunaria. She had had toys before. But this – perverse, oblique, its potential elusive but limitless – it resembled Lunaria herself.

As the brazen bell-clocks of Vaim struck the fourth hour of black morning, an iron bird with chalcedony eyes (fifth of the

Mechanicae) flew to the balconied windows of Lunaria's house.

The house stood at the crest of a hanging garden, on the eastern bank of the river. Here Lunaria, honouring her name, made bright the dark, turning night into day with lamplight, singing, drums, harps and rattles. Her golden windows could be seen from miles off. 'There is Lunaria's house,' insomniacs or late-abroad thieves would say, chuckling, envious and disturbed. An odour of flowers and roast meats and uncorked wines floated over the spot, and sometimes fire-crackers exploded, saffron, cinnabar and snow, above the roof and walls. But after sunrise the windows turned grey and the walls held silence, as if the house had burnt itself out during the night.

The iron bird rapped a pane with its beak.

Lunaria, heavy-eyed, opened her window. She was not astonished or dismayed. She had seen the bird before.

'My master asks when he may visit you.'

Lunaria frowned. 'He knows my fee: a gift.'

'He will pay.'

'Let it be something unheard of, and unsafe.'

'It is.'

'Tomorrow then. At sunset.'

4
Lunaria of Vaim

The sinking sun bobbed like a blazing boat on the river. Water and horizon had become a luminous scarlet stippled with copper and tangerine. A fraction higher than the tallest towers of Vaim, this holocaust gave way to a dense mulberry afterglow, next to a denser blue, and finally, in the east, a strange hollow black, littered by stars. Such a combination of colours and gems in the apparel of man or woman, or in any room of a house, would have been dubious. But in the infallible and faultless sky, they were lovely beyond belief and almost beyond bearing.

Nevertheless, the sunset's beauty was lost on Subyrus, or rather, alleviated, dulled. At a finger's snap almost, he could command the illusion of such a sunset, or, impossibly, a more glorious one. It could not therefore impress or stimulate him, even though he rode directly through its red and mulberry radiance, on the back of a dragon of brass. The sixth of the Mechanicae, the dragon was equipped with seat and jewelled harness, and with two enormous wings that beat regularly up and down in a noise of metal hinges and slashed air. It caught the last light and glittered like a fleck of the sun itself. In Vaim, presumably, citizens pointed, between admiration and terror.

A servant beat frantically on the door of Lunaria's bedchamber.

'Lady – *he* is here!'

'Who?' Lunaria inquired sleepily from within.

'The Lord Subyrus,' cried the servant, plainly appalled at her forgetfulness.

On the terrace before the house, the dragon alighted. Subyrus stilled it with a single word of power. He stepped from the jewelled harness, and contemplated the length of the hanging garden. Trees precariously leaned over under their mass of unplucked fruit, the jets of fountains pierced shadowy basins that in turn overflowed into more shadowy depths beneath. Trellised night flowers were opening and giving up their scent. In Lunaria's garden no day flowers bloomed, and no man could walk. Sometimes the gardeners, crawling about the slanted cliff of the hanging garden to tend the growth and the water courses, fell to their deaths on the thoroughfare eighty feet below. The only entrance to the house was through a secret door at the garden's foot, of whose location Lunaria informed her clients. Or from the sky.

The servant ran out on to the terrace and cast himself on his knees.

'My lady is not yet ready – but she bids you enter.'

The servant was sallow with fear.

Subyrus stepped through the terrace doors, and beheld a richly clad man in maddened flight down a stairway.

Lunaria had kept one of her customers late in order that Subyrus should see him. This was but a variation on a theme she had played before.

Near the stair foot, about to rush to a new flight – for these stairs passed right the way to the interior side of the secret door – the customer paused, and looked up in a spasm of anguish.

'You have nothing to dread from me, sir,' Subyrus remarked.

206

But the man went on with his escape, gabbling in distress.

'And I. Am I not to dread you?'

Subyrus moved about, and there Lunaria Vaimian stood, dressed in a vermilion gown that complemented one aspect of the sunset sky, her blonde hair powdered with crushed gilt.

She stared at Subyrus boldly. When he did not speak, she nodded contemptuously at the dining room.

'I am not proud,' she announced. 'I will take my fee at dinner. I am certain you will grant me that interim between my previous visitor and yourself.'

The red faded on gold salvers and crystal goblets. Lunaria was wealthy, and she had earned every vaimii.

They did not converse, she and her guest. Behind a screen, musicians performed love songs with wild and savage rhythms. Servitors came and went with skilfully prepared dishes. Lunaria selected morsels from many plates, but ate frugally. Subyrus touched nothing. Indeed, no one alive could remember ever having seen him eat, or raise more than a token cup to his lips. Occasionally, Lunaria talked, as if to a third person. For example: 'How solemn the magician is tonight. Though more solemn or less than when he came here before, I cannot say.'

Subyrus never took his eyes from her. He sat motionless, wonderful, awful, and quite frozen, like some exquisite graveyard moth, crucified by a pin.

'Are you dead?' Lunaria said to him at length. 'Come, do not grieve. I will always be yours, for a price.'

At that he stirred. He placed a casket on the table between them, murmured something. The casket was gone. The vase of blue crystal glimmered softly in the glow of the young candles.

Lunaria tapped the screen with a silver wand, and the musicians left off their music. In the quiet, they might be heard scrambling thankfully away into the house.

Lunaria and the magician were alone together, with sorcery.

'Well,' said Lunaria, 'there was a tale in the city today. A blue vase in which thousands of souls are trapped. Souls which can inform of fabulous treasures and unholy deeds of the past. Courtesans who will reveal wicked erotica from antique courts. Devotees of decadent sciences. Geniuses who will create new books and new inventions. If they can be correctly persuaded.

Providing one can call them by name.'

'I could teach you the method,' Subyrus said.

'Teach me.'

'And so buy a night of your life?' Subyrus smiled. It was a melancholy though torpid smile. 'I mean to have more than that.'

'A week of nights, for such a gift,' Lunaria said swiftly. Her eyes were wide now. 'You shall have them.'

'Yes, I shall. And more than those.'

He had got up from his chair, and now walked round the table. He halted behind Lunaria's chair, and when she would have risen, lightly he rested his long fingers against her throat. She did not try to move again.

The scents of ambergris and musk flooded from her hair.

His obsession. The growing and only motive for his existence.

Obscuring from himself his true desire – the pang of her indifference, her challenge – he saw the road before him, the box in which he might lock her up. Physically, he had possessed her frequently. Such possession no longer mattered. Possession of mind, of emotion, of soul had become everything. The joy of actual possession, the intriguing misery of never being able actually to possess her again. And his fingers tightened about the contour of her neck.

She did not struggle.

'What will you do?' she whispered.

'Presently remove the stopper of the vase. It is already primed to receive another ghost. Whoever expires now in its close vicinity will be drawn in. Into that microcosm where seven thousand dwell content. The enchanted world. They come forth haughtily and retreat gladly. It must be curious and fine. Perhaps you will be happy there.'

'I never knew you to lie, previously,' Lunaria said. 'You said the vase was a gift for me.'

'It is. It will be your new home. Your eternal home, I imagine.'

She relaxed in his grip and said no more. She remained some while like this, in a sort of limbo, before she was aware that his hands, rather than blotting out her consciousness, had unaccountably slackened.

Suddenly, to her bewilderment, Subyrus let her go.

He went away from her, about the table once more, and stopped, confronting the vase from a different vantage. An extraordinary expression had rearranged his face.

'Am I blind?' he said, so low she hardly made him out.

Youth, and, of all things, panic, seemed swirling up from the darkened closets behind his eyes. And with those, an intoxication, such as Lunaria had witnessed in him the first night he had seen her, the first night she had refused him.

She rose and said sternly: 'Will you not finish murdering me, my lord?'

He glanced at her. She was startled. He viewed her with a novel and courteous indifference. Lunaria shrank. What an ultimate threat had not accomplished, this indifference could.

'I was mistaken,' he said. 'I have been too long gazing at leaves, and missed the tree.'

'No,' she said. 'Wait,' as he walked towards the terrace doors, where the brazen dragon grew vague and greenish on a damson twilight.

'Wait? No. There is no more need of waiting.'

The vase was in his hand. Sapphire flashed, and then went out as the dusk enclosed him.

The dragon heaved itself, with brass creakings, upright and abruptly aloft. Lunaria, rooted to the ground, watched Subyrus vanish into the sky over Vaim.

5

In Solitude

Somewhere in the hollow hill, a lion roared. It was a beast of jointed electrum, the seventh of the Mechanicae, activated and set loose by Subyrus on his return. Its task: to roam the chasm of the hill, a fierce guardian should any ever come there in the future, which was unlikely. It was unlikely because Subyrus, descending, had closed and sealed off the entrance to the hill by use of the eighth mechanism. The stone pavilion had folded and collapsed in unbroken and impenetrable slabs above the place. The periodic, inexhaustible roar of the lion from below was an added, really unnecessary deterrent.

And now Subyrus sat in his darkened hall, in his quartz chair. The fire did not burn. One lamp on a bronze tripod lit up the vase of blue crystal on a small table. The stopper lay beside it, and beside that a narrow phial with a fluid in it the colour of clear water.

Subyrus picked up the phial, uncorked, and leisurely drained it. It had the taste of wine and aloes. It was the most deadly of the six deadly poisons known on earth, but its nickname was Gentleness, for it slew without pain and in gradual, tactful, not unpleasant stages.

Subyrus rested in the chair, composed, and took the rose-opal stopper in his hand, and fixed his look on the vase.

He had exhausted the possibilities of the world long since. His intellect and his body, both were sick with the sparse fare they must subsist on. There was no height he might not scale at a step, no ocean he might not dredge at a blink. No learning he had not devoured, no game he had not played. Thus, it had needed a Lunaria to hold his horrified tedium in check, something so common and so ugly as a harlot's sneer to keep him vital and alive.

When the gate had opened, he had not seen it. He had nearly bypassed it altogether. He had sought a gift for Lunaria, then he had sought to trap her in the crystal, making her irrevocably his property and denying himself of her for ever. Lunaria – he scarcely recalled her now.

Concentration on the minor issue had obscured the major. At the last instant, the truth had come to him, barely in time.

He had exhausted the world. Therefore he must find a second world of which he knew nothing. A world whose magic he had yet to learn, a world alien and unexplored, a world impossible to imagine – *the microcosm within the vase*.

Like a warm sleep, Gentleness stole over him. Primed to catch his ghost, the blue vase enigmatically waited. Perhaps nightmare crouched inside, perhaps a paradise. Even as the poison chilled it, Subyrus' blood raced with a heady excitement he had not felt for two decades and more.

In the shadows, a silver bell-clock struck a single dim note. It was the ninth of the Mechanicae, striking to mark the hour of the Magician-Lord's death.

And Subyrus sensed the moment of death come on him, as surely as he might gauge the supreme moment of love. He leaned forward to poise the rose-opal stopper above the lip of the vase.

As the breath of life coursed from him, and the soul with it, unseen, was dashed into the trap of the crystal, the stopper dropped from his fingers to shut the gate behind him.

Subyrus, to whom existence had become mechanical, the tenth of his own Mechanicae, sat dead in his chair. And in the vase –
What?

Lunaria Vaimian had climbed the hill alone.

Below, at the hill's foot, uneasily, three or four attendants huddled about a gilded palanquin, dishevelled by cool winds and sombre fancies.

Lunaria wore black, and her bright hair was veiled in black. She regarded the fallen stone of the pavilion. Her eyes were angry.

'It is foolish for me,' she said, 'to chide you that you used me. Many have done so. Foolish also to desire to curse you, for you are proof against my ill-wishing as finally you were proof against my allure. But how I hate you, hate you as I love you, as I hated and I loved you from the beginning, knowing there was but one way by which to retain your interest in me; foreknowing that I should lose you in the end, whatever my tricks, and so I have.'

Leaves were blowing from woods in the wind, like yellow papers.

Lunaria watched them settle over the stone.

'A thousand falsehoods,' she said. 'A thousand pretences. Men I compelled to visit me (how afraid they were of the Magician-Lord), only that you might behold them. Gifts I demanded, poses I upheld. To mask my love. To keep your attention. And all, now, for nothing. I would have been your slave-ghost gladly. I would have let you slay me and bind me in the vase. I would have –'

The electrum lion roared somewhere beneath her feet in the hollow hill.

'There it is,' Lunaria muttered sullenly, 'the voice of my fury and my pain that will hurt me till I die; my despair, but more adequately expressed. I need say nothing while that other says it for me.'

And she went away down the hill through the blowing leaves and the blowing of her veil, and never spoke again as long as she lived.

Pinewood

A poem written in my early twenties gave rise to this short tale.

Either from past lives or the memory of DNA, we seem to know very well emotions never yet experienced, and, glancing back at your prophecies, you may sometimes award yourself eleven out of ten.

Clear morning light slanted across her face and woke her. She turned on her side and murmured: 'David. David, darling, I think it must be awfully late –'

Receiving no answer, she opened her eyes. The other side of the bed was empty, and the little clock on his side table showed half past ten. Of course, he had woken when the alarm went off, as she never did, and left her to sleep. The clock's little round face, like cracked eggshell, ticked with a menacing reproach. She had always been certain it disliked her, in a humorous rather than a sinister manner, because she never responded to its insistent morning screams, and when David was away on business, forgot to wind it up.

Beyond the bright window the pines rubbed their black needles against the autumn wind. She shivered as she sat up in the bed. The gothic trees disturbed her, a stupid notion for a woman of thirty-seven she told herself.

Dear David. She brushed her teeth with swift meticulous strokes. He alone had never minded about her sluggish waking.

She examined her eyes and her throat in the harsh light, bravely. Not so bad. Not so bad, Pamela, for the elderly lady you are. She smiled as she ran the bath, thinking of her anxious

213

questionings, her painful jokes: 'I'm too old for you, darling, really. People will ask you at parties why you brought your mother –' in reality she was three years David's senior – and the batch of youthful snaps: 'Oh, but I look so young in these –' He was good to her, sensing the nervous, helpless steps she took toward that essentially, prematurely female precipice of age – the little line, the gray hair. He told her all the things she wanted to hear from him, all the good things, and never seemed to find her tiresome. He had always had a perfect patience and kindness toward her. And she had always known that she had been unusually lucky with this man. She might so easily have loved a fool or a boor and found out too late, as had Jane, or her sister Angela, a man with no ability to imagine how things might be for the female principal in his life – a lack of comprehension amounting to xenophobia.

Sitting in the bath she had a sudden horror that this was the day for Mrs Meadowes, the cleaning lady. A twice-weekly visitation of utter cleanliness and vigor, she nevertheless doted on David, and, naturally, bullied Pamela. Frantically Pamela toweled and scattered talc. She never seemed to know where she was with Mrs Meadowes. Her days and times of arrival seemed to be in constant flux. And now, come to think of it, Pamela remembered she was to meet David for lunch.

She grasped the phone and dialed the Meadowes' number. An incoherent child answered, presently to be replaced by a recognized contralto.

'Oh – Mrs Meadowes, Pamela Taylor here – I'm dreadfully sorry, but I simply couldn't remember – is it today you're coming? Or is it tomorrow or something?'

There was a pause, then the contralto said carefully: 'Well, dear, I can fit you in tomorrow. If you like.'

'Oh, good, then it wasn't today. Thank you so much. Sorry to have bothered you. Goodbye.'

There had been something distinctly strange about the Meadowes phone call, she thought as she ate her grapefruit. Probably something to do with that appalling child. She switched on the radio. She caught a news bulletin, as she always seemed to. Somewhere a plane had crashed, somewhere else an earthquake – she switched off. Angela had frequently told her that she should keep herself abreast of the

214

news, not bury her head in the sand. But she simply could not stand it. Papers depressed her. They came for David, and when he forgot to take them with him to the office as he always seemed to nowadays, she would push them out of sight, bury them behind cushions and under piles of magazines, afraid to glimpse some horror before she could avert her eyes. David teased her a little. 'Where's the ostrich hidden my paper today?'

As she constructed her peach-bloom cosmetic face before the mirror she thought of Angela, vigorously devouring black gospels of famine, war, and pestilence with her morning coffee. James liked her to know what she was talking about at their dinner parties. He rated a woman's intelligence by her grasp of foreign correspondents and yesterday in parliament. It was in a way rather curious. Angela had met James in the same month Pamela had met David.

She took the car with her into town, a feat she performed with some dread. David was a superb and relaxed driver, she by contrast sat in rigid anxiety at the wheel. Her fears seemed to attract near disasters. Dogs, children, and India rubber balls flew in front of her wheels as if magnetized, men in Citroëns honked and swore, and juggernauts herded her off the road. Normally she would take the bus, for David often used the car, but today it lurked in the garage, taunting her, and besides she was pushed for time. She reached the restaurant ten minutes late, and went to meet him in the bar, but he had not yet arrived. Bars were unfortunate for her, and alone she shunned them. David said she had a flair for being picked up; men who looked like mafiosi would offer her martinis, and all she seemed able to do in her paralyzed fright was apologize to them. She left the bar and went into the restaurant and ordered a sherry at her table.

The room felt rather hot and oppressive, and all the other tables were filling up, except her own. She drank her sherry down in wild gulps and the waiter leaned over her.

'Would madam care to order now?'

'Oh – no thank you. I'm sorry, you see, I'm waiting for my husband –'

She trailed off. A knowing and somber look had come over the man's face. *Oh, God, I suppose he thinks I'm a whore too.*

She took out a cigarette and smoked it in nervous bursts. She could see another waiter watching her from his post beside a pillar. *I shall wait another ten minutes and then I shall go.*

It was fifteen minutes past two when she suddenly remembered. It came over her like a lightning flash, bringing a wave of embarrassment and relief in its wake. Of course, David had told her very last thing last night that the lunch would have to be canceled. A man was coming from Kelly's – or Ryson's – and he would have to take him for a working snack at the pub. She felt an utter fool. Good heavens, was her memory going this early? She almost giggled as she threaded between the tables.

She shopped in the afternoon, and ate a cream cake with her coffee in a small teashop full of old ladies. She had bought David a novel, one of the few Graham Greenes he hadn't collected over the years. She had seen for some time that he was having trouble with his present reading – the same volume had lain beside the round-faced clock for over a month.

The journey home was relatively uneventful. At the traffic lights a boy with a rucksack leaned to her window. She thought in alarm that he was going to demand a lift, or else tell her in an American voice of how he had found Jesus in San Francisco, but, in fact, he only wanted directions to Brown's the chemists. It seemed such a harmless request it filled her with incongruous delight. Purple and ocher cloud drift was bringing on the early dusk in spasms of rain. With a surge of immeasurable compassion she offered him, after all, the lift she had been terrified of giving. David would be furious with her, she knew. It was a stupid thing to do, yet the boy looked so vulnerable in the rain, his long dark hair plastered to his skull. He was an ugly, shy, rather charming student, and she left him at the chemists after a ten-minute ride during which he thanked her seven times. It turned out his mother was Mrs Brown, and he had hitched all the way from Bristol.

After he had gone, she parked the car, and went to buy fresh cigarettes. Coming from the tobacconists, she saw the cemetery.

She had forgotten she would see the cemetery on her errand of mercy. It was foolish, she knew, to experience this 'morbid dread,' as Angela would no doubt put it. It was, nevertheless, a perfect picture of horror for her – the ranks of marble markers under the orange monochrome sky with rain falling on their plots and withered wreaths, and down through the newly turned soil to reach the wooden caskets underneath . . . She experienced a sudden swirling sickness, and ran through it to the car. Inside, the icy rain shut out, she found that she had absurdly begun to cry.

'Oh, don't be such an idiot,' she said aloud.

She turned on the car's heater, and started vigorously for home, nearly stalling. She was much later than she had meant to be.

There were no lights burning in the house, and she realized with regret that he would be late again. She coerced the unwilling car into the garage, and ran between the rustling pines. She clicked a switch in every room and resuscitated the television to reveal three children up to their eyes in some form of super sweet. Their strawberry-and-cream bedecked faces filled her with disgust. She had never liked children, and never wanted them. She paused, her hand on the door, a moment's abstracted thought catching at her mind – had she failed David in this? She could remember him saying to her as she sobbed against him: 'I only want you, you know that, and nothing else matters.'

That had been after the results of the tests. In a way she felt she had wished herself into barrenness. She thought of Angela's two sons, strapping boisterous boys, who went canoeing with their father, and brought home baskets of mangled catch from a day's fishing, and spotted trains, and bolted their food to get back to incongruous and noisy activities in their bedroom.

'A man needs sons,' Angela had once said. 'It's a sort of proof, Pamela. Why don't you see a specialist? I can give you the address.'

But then Angela and James had not slept together in any sense for ten years, Pamela thought with sudden, spiteful triumph, and it had always been a doubtful joy to them. She remembered David's arms about her and that earthy magic they made between them, an attraction that had increased rather than diminished.

The phone rang.

217

It made her jump.

'Oh, damn.'

She picked it up, and heard, with the relevance of a conjuration, her sister's cool, well managed tones.

'Oh, hullo, Angela. I don't want to be a cow, but this really is rather a bad time – I was just about to start dinner –'

'Pamela, my dear,' Angela said, her voice peculiarly solemn, 'are you all right?'

'All right? Of course I am. What on earth –'

'Pamela, I want you to listen to me. Please, my dear. I wouldn't have rung, but Jane Thomson says she saw you in Cordells at lunch time. She says, oh, my dear, she says she saw you waiting for someone.' Angela sounded unspeakably distressed. 'Pamela, who were you waiting for?'

Pamela felt a surge of panic wash over her.

'I – oh, no one. Does it matter?'

'Darling, of course it does. Was it David you were waiting for, like the last time?'

Pamela held the phone away from her ear and looked at it. There was a bee trapped in the phone, buzzing away at her. She had always been terribly afraid of bees.

'I really have to go, Angela,' she shouted at the mouthpiece.

'Oh, Pamela, Pamela,' Angela said. She seemed to be crying. 'Darling, David can't come back to you. Not now.'

'Be quiet,' Pamela said.

The bee went on buzzing.

'Pamela, listen to me. David is dead. Dead, do you hear me? He died of peritonitis last July. For God's sake, Pamela –'

Pamela dropped the phone into its receiver and the buzzing stopped.

The dinner was spoiled before she realized how late he was going to be after all. He had told her the conference might run on, and not to wait up for him. She waited, however, until midnight. Upstairs, she took the book from his bedside table and replaced it with the Graham Greene – it would surprise him when he found it.

She hated to sleep without him, but she was very tired. And she would see him in the morning.

Outside, the pines clicked and whispered, but she did not listen.

The Janfia Tree

*There are many marvellous legends of tree spirits. The
darkness of my version has to do, I think, with the fearful
danger of projection.*
Life can be what you make it. Beware.

After eight years of what is termed 'bad luck', it becomes a way of
life. One is no longer anything so dramatic as unhappy. One
achieves a sort of state of what can only be described as
de-happiness. One expects nothing, not even, actually, the worst.
A certain relaxation follows, a certain equilibrium. Not flawless,
of course. There are still moments of rage and misery. It is very
hard to give up hope, that last evil let loose from Pandora's box of
horrors. And it is always, in fact, after a bout of hope, springing
without cause, perishing not necessarily at any fresh blow but
merely from the absence of anything to sustain it, that there
comes a revulsion of the senses. A wish, not exactly for death, but
for the torturer at least to step out of the shadows, to reveal
himself, and his plans. And to this end one issues invitations,
generally very trivial ones, a door forgetfully unlocked, a stop
light driven through. Tempting fate, they call it.

'Well, you do look tired,' said Isabella, who had met me in her
car, in the town, in the white dust that veiled and covered
everything.

I agreed that perhaps I did look tired.

'I'm so sorry about –' said Isabella. She checked herself,
thankfully, on my thanks. 'I expect you've had enough of all that.
And this other thing. That's not for a while, is it?'

'Not until next month.'

'That gives you time to take a break at least.'

219

'Yes.'

It was a very minor medical matter to which she referred. Any one of millions would have been glad, I was sure, to exchange their intolerable suffering for something twice as bad. For me, it filled the quota quite adequately. I had not been sleeping very well. Isabella's offer of the villa had seemed, not like an escape, since that was impossible, yet like an island. But I wished she would talk about something else. Mind-reading, 'Look at the olives, aren't they splendid?' she said, as we hurtled up the road. I looked at the olives through the blinding sun and dust. 'And there it is, you see? Straight up there in the sky.'

The villa rose, as she said, in the hard sky above; on a crest of gilded rock curtained with cypress and pine. The building was alabaster in the sun, and, like alabaster, had a pinkish inner glow where the light exchanged itself with the shade. Below, the waves of the olives washed down to the road, shaking to silver as the breeze ruffled them. It was all very beautiful, but one comes in time to regard mortal glamours rather as the Cathars regarded them, snares of the Devil to hide the blemishes beneath, to make us love a world which will defile and betray us.

The car sped up the road and arrived on a driveway in a flaming jungle of bougainvillaea and rhododendrons.

Isabella led me between the stalks of the veranda, into the villa, with all the pride of money and goodwill. She pointed out to me, on a long immediate tour, every excellence, and showed me the views, which were exceptional, from every window and balcony.

'Marta's away down the hill at the moment, but she'll be back quite soon. She says she goes to visit her aunt, but I suspect it's a lover. But she's a dulcet girl. You can see how nicely she keeps everything here. With the woman who cooks, that's just about all, except for the gardeners, but they won't be coming again for a week. So no one will bother you.'

'That does sound good.'

'Save myself of course,' she added. 'I shall keep an eye on you. And tomorrow, remember, we want you across for dinner. Down there, beyond those pines, we're just over that spectacular ridge. Less than half a mile. Indeed, if you want to you can send us morse signals after dark from the second bathroom window. Isn't that fun? So near, so far.'

220

'Isabella, you're really too kind to me.'

'Nonsense,' she said. 'Who else would be, you pessimistic old sausage.' And she took me into her arms, and to my horror I shed tears, but not many. Isabella, wiping her own eyes, said it had done me good. But she was quite wrong.

Marta arrived as we were having drinks at the east end of the veranda. She was a pretty, sunlit creature, who looked about fourteen and was probably eighteen or so. She greeted me politely, rising from the bath of her liaison. I felt nothing very special about her, or that. Though I am often envious of the stamina, youth and health of others, I have never wanted to be any of them.

'Definitely, a lover,' said Isabella, when the girl was gone. 'My God, do you remember what it was like at her age? All those clandestine fumblings in grey city places.'

If that had been true for her, it had not been true of me, but I smiled.

'But here,' she said, 'in all this honey heat, these scents and flowers. Heaven on earth – Arcadia. Well, at least I'm here with good old Alec. And he hands me quite a few surprises, he's quite the boy now and then.'

'I've been meaning to ask you,' I said, 'that flowering tree along there, what is it?'

I had not been meaning to ask, had only just noticed the particular tree. But I was afraid of flirtatious sexual revelations. I had been denied in love-desire too long, and celibate too long, to find such a thing comfortable. But Isabella, full of intrigued interest in her own possessions, got up at once and went with me to inspect the tree.

It stood high in a white and terracotta urn, its stem and head in silhouette against a golden noon. There was a soft pervasive scent which, as I drew closer, I realized had lightly filled all the veranda like a bowl with water.

'Oh yes, the fragrance,' she said. 'It gets headier later in the day, and at night it's almost overpowering. Now what is it?' She fingered dark glossy leaves and found a tiny slender bloom, of a sombre white. 'This will open after sunset,' she said. 'Oh lord, what *is* the name?' She stared at me and her face cleared, glad to give me another gift. 'Janfia,' she said. 'Now I can tell you all about it. Janfia – it's supposed to be from the French, *Janvier*.' It was a shame to discourage her.

'January. Why? Does it start to bloom then?'

'Well, perhaps it's supposed to, although it doesn't. No. It's something to do with January, though.'

'Janus, maybe,' I said, 'two-faced god of doorways. You always plant it by a doorway or an opening into a house? A guardian tree.' I had almost said, a tree for good luck.

'That might be it. But I don't think it's protective. No, now isn't there some story . . . I do hope I can recall it. It's like the legend of the myrtle – or is it the basil? You know the one, with a spirit living in the tree.'

'That's the myrtle. Venus, or a nymph, coming out for dalliance at night, hiding in the branches by day. The basil is a severed head. The basil grows from the mouth of the head and tells the young girl her brothers have murdered her lover, whose decapitum is in the pot.'

'Yum, yum,' said Isabella. 'Well, Alec will know about the Janfia. I'll get him to tell you when you come to dinner tomorrow.'

I smiled again. Alec and I made great efforts to get along with each other, for Isabella's sake. We both found it difficult. He did not like me, and I, reciprocating, had come to dislike him in turn. Now our only bond, aside from Isabella, was natural sympathy at the irritation each endured in the presence of the other.

As I said goodbye to Isabella, I was already wondering how I could get out of the dinner.

I spent the rest of the afternoon unpacking and organizing myself for my stay, swimming all the while in amber light, pausing frequently to gaze out across the pines, the sea of olive groves. A little orange church rose in the distance, and a sprawling farm with Roman roofs. The town was already well lost in purple shadow. I began, from the sheer charm of it, to have moments of pleasure. I had dreaded their advent, but received them mutely. It was all right, it was all right to feel this mindless animal sweetness. It did not interfere with the other things, the darkness, the sword hanging by a thread. I had accepted that, that it was above me, then why trouble with it?

But I began to feel well, I began to feel all the chances were not gone. I risked red wine and ate my supper greedily, enjoying being waited on.

During the night, not thinking to sleep in the strange bed, I slept a long while. When I woke once, there was an extraordinary floating presence in the bedroom. It was the perfume of the Janfia tree, entering the open shutters from the veranda below. It must stand directly beneath my window. Mine was the open way it had been placed to favour. How deep and strangely clear was the scent.

When I woke in the morning, the scent had gone, and my stomach was full of knots of pain and ghastly nausea. The long journey, the heat, the rich food, the wine. Nevertheless, it gave me my excuse to avoid the unwanted dinner with Isabella and Alec.

I called her about eleven o'clock. She commiserated. What could she say? I must rest and take care, and we would all meet further along the week.

In the afternoon, when I was beginning to feel better, she woke me from a long hot doze with two plastic containers of local yoghurt, which would apparently do wonders for me.

'I'll only stay a moment. God, you do look pale. Haven't you got something to take for it?'

'Yes. I've taken it.'

'Well. Try the yoghurt, too.'

'As soon as I can manage anything, I'll try the yoghurt.'

'By the way,' she said, 'I can tell you the story of the Janfia now.' She stood in the bedroom window, looking out and down at it. 'It's extremely sinister. Are you up to it, I wonder?'

'Tell me, and see.'

Although I had not wanted the interruption, now it had arrived, I was oddly loth to let her go. I wished she would have stayed and had dinner with me herself, alone. Isabella had always tried to be kind to me. Then again, I was useless with people now. I could relate to no one, could not give them any quarter. I would be better off on my own.

'Well, it seems there was a poet, young and handsome, for whose verses princes would pay in gold.'

'Those were the days,' I said idly.

'Come, it was the fifteenth century. No sewers, no antibiotics, only superstition and gold could get you by.'

'You sound nostalgic, Isabella.'

'Shush now. He used to roam the countryside, the young poet, looking for inspiration, doubtless finding it with shepherdesses, or whatever they had here then. One dusk he smelled an exquisite fragrance, and, searching for its source, came on a bush of pale opening flowers. So enamoured was he of the perfume that he dug up the bush, took it home with him, and planted it in a pot on the balcony outside his room. Here it grew into a tree, and here the poet, dreaming, would sit all afternoon, and when night fell, and the moon rose, he would carry his mattress on to the balcony, and go to sleep under the moon-shade of the tree's foliage.'

Isabella broke off. Already falling into the idiom, she said, 'Am I going to write this, or are you?'

'I'm too tired to write nowadays. And anyway, I can't sell anything. You do it.'

'We'll see. After all the trouble I had with that cow of an editor over my last –'

'And meantime, finish the story, Isabella.'

Isabella beamed.

She told me, it began to be noticed that the poet was very wan, very thin, very listless. That he no longer wrote a line, and soon all he did was to sit all day and lie all night long by the tree. His companions looked in vain for him in the taverns and his patrons looked in vain for his verse. Finally a very great prince, the lord of the town, went himself to the poet's room. Here, to his dismay, he found the poet stretched out under the tree. It was close to evening, the evening star stood in the sky and the young moon, shining in through the leaves of the Janfia tree upon the poet's white face which was now little better than a beautiful skull. He seemed near to death, which the prince's physicians, being called in, confirmed. 'How,' cried the prince, in grief, 'have you come to this condition?'

Then, though it was not likely to restore him, he begged the poet to allow them to take him to some more comfortable spot. The poet refused. 'Life is nothing to me now.' he said. And he asked the prince to leave him, for the night was approaching and he wished to be alone.

The prince was at once suspicious. He sent the whole company away, and only he returned with stealth, and hid himself in the poet's room, to see what went on.

Sure enough, at midnight, when the sky was black and the

moon rode high, there came a gentle rustling in the leaves of
the Janfia. Presently there stepped forth into the moonlight a
young man, dark-haired and pale of skin, clothed in garments
that seemed woven of the foliage of the tree itself. And he,
bending over the poet, kissed him, and the poet stretched up
his arms. And what the prince then witnessed filled him with
abysmal terror, for not only was it a demon he watched, but
one which performed acts utterly proscribed by mother church.
Eventually overcome, the prince lost consciousness. When he
roused, the dawn was breaking, the tree stood scentless and
empty, and the poet, lying alone, was dead.

'So naturally,' said Isabella, with relish, 'there was a cry of
witchcraft, and the priests came and the tree was burnt to cinders.
All but for one tiny piece the prince found, to his astonishment,
he had broken off. Long after the poet had been buried, in
unhallowed ground, the prince kept this little piece of the Janfia
tree, and eventually thinking it dead, he threw it from his window
out into the garden of his palace.'

She looked at me.

'Where it grew,' I said, 'watered only by the rain, and nurtured
only by the glow of the moon by night.'

'Until an evening came,' said Isabella, 'when the prince,
overcome by a strange longing, sat brooding in his chair. And all
at once an amazing perfume filled the air, so mysterious, so
irresistible, he dared not even turn his head to see what it
portended. And as he sat thus, a shadow fell across his shoulder
on to the floor in front of him, and then a quiet, leaf-cool hand
was laid upon his neck.'

She and I burst out laughing.

'Gorgeous,' I said. 'Erotic, gothic, perverse, Wildean, Freud-
ian. Yes.'

'Now tell me you won't write it.'

I shook my head. 'No. Maybe later, sometime. If you don't.
But your story still doesn't explain the name, does it?'

'Alec said it might be something to do with Ianus being the
male form of the name Diana – the moon and the night. But it's
tenuous. Oh,' she said, 'you do look so much better.'

Thereby reminding me that I was ill, and that the sword still
hung by its hair, and that all we had shared was a derivative little
horror story from the back hills.

225

'Are you sure you can't manage dinner?' she said.

'Probably could. Then I'd regret it. No, thank you. Just for now, I'll stick to that yoghurt, or it to me, whatever it does.'

'All right. Well, I must dash. I'll call you tomorrow.'

I had come to the villa for solitude in a different climate, but learned, of course, that climate is climate, and that solitude too is always precisely and only that. In my case, the desire to be alone was simply the horror of not being so. Besides, I never was alone, dogged by the sick, discontented and unshakable companions of my body, my own restless mind.

The sun was wonderful, and the place was beautiful, but I quickly realized I did not know what to do with the sun and the beauty. I needed to translate them, perhaps, into words, certainly into feelings, but neither would respond as I wished. I kept a desultory journal, then gave it up. I read and soon found I could not control my eyes enough to get them to focus on the pages. On the third evening, I went to dinner with Isabella and Alec, did my best, watched Alec do his best, came back a little drunk, more ill in soul than in body. Disgraced myself in private by weeping.

Finally, the scent of the Janfia tree, coming in such tides into the room, drew me to the window.

I stood there, looking down at the veranda, the far away hills beyond described only by starlight, the black tree much nearer, with here and there its moonburst of smoky white, an open flower.

And I thought about the poet, and the incubus that was the spirit of the tree. It was the hour to think of that. A demon which vampirized and killed by irresistible pleasures of the flesh. What an entirely enchanting thought. After all, life itself vampirized, and ultimately killed, did it not, by a constant, equally irresistible, administration of the exact reverse of pleasure?

But since I had no longer any belief in God, I had lost all hopes of anything supernatural abroad in the universe. There was evil, naturally, in its abstract or human incarnations, but nothing artistic, no demons stepping from trees by night.

Just then, the leaves of the Janfia rustled. Some night breeze was passing through them, though not, it seemed, through any other thing which grew on the veranda.

A couple of handsome shy wild cats came and went at the villa. The woman who cooked left out scraps for them, and I had seen Marta, one morning, leaving a large bowl of water in the shade of a cypress they were wont to climb. A cat then, prowling along the veranda rail, was disturbing the tree. I tried to make out the flash of eyes. Presently, endeavouring to do this, I began to see another thing.

It was a shadow, cast from the tree, but not in the tree's shape. Nor was there light, beyond that of the stars above the hills, to fashion it. A man then, young and slender, stood below me, by the Janfia, and from a barely suggested paleness, like that of a thin half moon, it seemed he might be looking up towards my room.

A kind of instinct made me move quickly back, away from the window. It was a profound and primitive reaction, which startled me, and refreshed me. It had no place on the modern earth, and scarcely any name. A kind of panic – the pagan fear of something elemental, godlike and terrible. Caught up in it, for a second, I was no longer myself, no longer the one I dreaded most in all the world. I was no one, only a reaction to an unknown matter, more vital than sickness or pessimism, something from the days when all ills and joys were in the charge of the gods, when men need not think, but simply *were*.

And then, I did think. I thought of some intruder, something rational, and I moved into the open window again, and looked down, and there was nothing there. Just the tree against the starlight.

'Isabella,' I said to her over the telephone, 'would you mind if I had that tree carried up to my bedroom?'

'Tree?'

I laughed brightly. 'I don't mean one of the pines. The little Janfia. It's funny, but you know I hadn't been sleeping very well – the scent seems to help. I thought, actually in the room, it would be about foolproof. Non-stop inhalations of white double brandies.'

'Well, I don't see why not. Only, mightn't it give you a headache, or something? All that carbon monoxide – or is it dioxide? – plants exude at night. Didn't someone famous suffocate themselves with flowers? One of Mirabeau's mistresses, wasn't it? No, that was with a charcoal brazier –'

'The thing is,' I said, 'your two gardeners have arrived this morning after all. And between them, they shouldn't have any trouble getting the urn upstairs. I'll have it by the window. No problems with asphyxia that way.'

'Oh well, if you want, why not?' Having consented, she babbled for a moment over how I was doing, and assured me she would 'pop in' tomorrow. Alec had succumbed to some virus, and she had almost forgotten me. I doubted that I would see her for the rest of the week.

Marta scintillantly organized the gardeners. Each gave me a narrow look. But they raised the terracotta and the tree, bore them grunting up to the second floor, plonked them by the window as requested. Marta even followed this up with a can of water to sprinkle the earth. That done, she pulled two desiccated leaves off the tree with a coarse functional disregard. It was part of the indoor furnishings now, and must be cared for.

I had been possessed by a curious idea, which I called, to myself, an experiment. It was impossible that I had seen anything, any 'being', on the veranda. That was an alcoholic fantasy. But then again, I had an urge to call the bluff of the Janfia tree. Because it seemed to me responsible, in its own way, for my mirage. Perhaps the blooms were mildly hallucinogenic. If so, I meant to test them. In lieu of any other social event or creative project, an investigation of the Janfia would have to serve.

By day it gave, of course, very little scent; in the morning it had seemed to have none at all. I sat and watched it a while, then stretched out for a siesta. Falling asleep, almost immediately I dreamed that I lay bleeding in a blood-soaked bed, in the middle of a busy city pavement. People stepped around me, sometimes cursing the obstacle. No one would help me. Somebody – formless, genderless – when I caught at a sleeve, detached me with a good-natured, 'Oh, you'll be all right.'

I woke up in a sweat of horror. Not a wise measure any more, then, to sleep by day. Too hot, conducive to the nightmare . . . The dream's psychological impetus was all too obvious, the paranoia and self-pity. One was expected to be calm and well mannered in adversity. People soon got tired of you otherwise.

How not, who was exempt from distress?

I stared across the room at the Janfia tree, glossy with its health and beauty. Quite unassailable it looked. Was it a vampire? Did it suck away the life of other things to feed its own? It was welcome to mine. What a way to die. Not messily and uncouthly. But ecstatically, romantically, poignantly. They would say, they simply could not understand it, I had been a little under the weather, but *dying* – So very odd of me. And Isabella, remembering the story, would glance at the Janfia fearfully, and shakily giggle the notion aside.

I got up, and walked across.

'Why don't you?' I said. 'I'm here. I'm willing. I'd be – I'd be only too glad to die like that, in the arms of something that needed me, held, in pleasure – not from some bloody slip of a careless uncaring knife, some surgeon with a hangover, whoops, lost another patient today, oh dear what a shame. Or else to go on with this bloody awful misery, one slap in the teeth after another, nothing going right, nothing, nothing – Get out, to oblivion hopefully, or get out and start over, or if there's some bearded old damnable God, he couldn't blame me, could he? Your honour, I'd say, I was all for keeping going, suffering for another forty years, whatever your gracious will for me was. But a demon set on me. You know I didn't stand a chance. So.' I said again to the Janfia tree, 'why not?'

Did it hear? Did it attend? I reached out and touched its stems, its leaves, the fruited, tight-coiled blossoms. All of it seemed to sing, to vibrate with some colossal hidden force, like an instrument still faintly thrumming after the hand of the musician has left it, perhaps five centuries ago.

'Christ, I'm going crazy,' I said, and turned from the tree with an insulting laugh. See, the laugh said, I know all that is a lie. So, I *dare* you.

There was a writing desk in the room. Normally, when writing, I did not employ a desk, but now I sat at it and began to jot some notes on the legend of the tree. I was not particularly interested in doing this, it was only a sort of sympathetic magic. But the time went swiftly, and soon the world had reached the drinks hour, and I was able with a clear conscience to go down with thoughts of opening a bottle of white wine. The sun burned low in the cypress tree, and Marta stood beneath it, perplexed, a dish of scraps in her hand.

'Cats not hungry today?' I asked her.

She cast me a flashing look.

'No cats. Cats runs off. I am say, Where you go give you better food? Mrs Isabella like the cats. Perhaps they there. Thing scares them. They see a monster, go big eyes and then they runs.'

Surprising me with my surprise, I shivered. 'What was it? That they saw?' Marta shrugged. 'Who's know? I am see them runs. Fat tail and big eyes.'

'Where was it?'

'This minute.'

'But where? Down here?'

She shrugged a second time. 'Nothing there. They see. I am go along now. My aunt, she is waits for me.'

'Oh yes. Your aunt. Do go.'

I smiled. Marta ignored my smile, for she would only smile at me when I was serious or preoccupied, or ill. In the same way, her English deteriorated in my presence, improved in Isabella's. In some fashion, it seemed to me, she had begun to guard herself against me, sensing bad luck might rub off.

I had explained earlier to everyone that I wanted nothing very much for dinner, some cheese and fruit would suffice, such items easily accessible. And they had all then accordingly escaped, the cook, the cats and Marta. Now I was alone. Was I?

At the third glass I began to make my plans. It would be a full moon tonight. It would shine in at my bedroom window about two in the morning, casting a white clear light across the room, the desk, so that anything, coming between, would cast equally a deep shadow.

Well, I would give it every chance. The Janfia could not say I had omitted anything. The lunar orb, I at the desk my back to night and moon and tree. Waiting.

Why was I even contemplating such a foolish adolescent act? Naturally so that tomorrow, properly stood up on my date with delicious death, I could cry out loudly: The gods are dead! There is nothing left to me but *this*, the dunghill of the world.

But I ought to be fairly drunk. Yes, I owed the situation that. Drink, the opening medicine of the mind and heart, sometimes of the psyche.

The clean cheeses and green and pink fruits did not interrupt the spell of the wine. They stabilized my stomach and made it only accommodating.

Tomorrow I would regret drinking so much, but tomorrow I was going to regret everything in any case.

And so I opened a second bottle, and carried it to the bath with me, to the ritual cleansing before the assignation or the witch-craft.

I fell asleep, sitting at the desk. There was a brief sea-like afterglow, and my notes and a book and a lamp and the bottle spread before me. The perfume of the Janfia at my back seemed faint, luminous as the dying of the light. Beginning to read, quite easily, for the wine, interfering itself with vision, made it somehow less difficult to see or guess correctly the printed words, I weighed the time once or twice on my watch. Four hours, three hours, to moonrise.

When I woke, it was to an electric stillness. The oil lamp which I had been using in preference was burning low, and I reached instantly and turned down the wick. As the flame went out, all the lit darkness came in about me. The moon was in the window, climbing up behind the jet-black outline of the Janfia tree.

The scent was extraordinary. Was it my imagination – it seemed never to have smelled this way before, with this sort of aching, chiming note. Perhaps the full moon brought it out. I would not turn to look. Instead, I drew the paper to me and the pen. I wrote nothing, simply doodled on the pad, long spirals and convolutions; doubtless a psychiatrist would have found them most revealing.

My mind was a blank. A drunken, receptive, amiable blank. I was amused, but exhilarated. All things were supposed to be possible. If a black spectre could stalk me through eight years, surely then phantoms of all kinds, curses, blessings, did exist.

The shadow of the Janfia was being thrown down now all around me, on the floor, on the desk and the paper: the lacy foliage and the wide-stretched blooms.

And then, something else, a long finger of shadow, began to spill forwards, across everything. What was it? No, I must not turn to see. Probably some freak arrangement of the leaves, or even some simple element of the room's furniture, suddenly caught against the lifting moon.

My skin tingled. I sat as if turned to stone, watching the slow forward movement of the shadow which, after all, might also be that of a tall and slender man. Not a sound. The cicadas were silent. On the hills not a dog barked. And the villa was utterly dumb, empty of everything but me, and perhaps of this other thing, which itself was noiseless.

And all at once the Janfia tree gave a little whispering rustle. As if it laughed to itself. Only a breeze, of course only that, or some night insect, or a late flower unfolding –

A compound of fear and excitement held me rigid. My eyes were wide and I breathed in shallow gasps. I had ceased altogether to reason. I did not even feel. I waited. I waited in a type of delirium, for the touch of a cruel serene hand upon my neck – For truth to step at last from the shadow, with a naked blade.

And I shut my eyes, the better to experience whatever might come to me.

There was then what is known as a lacuna, a gap, something missing, and amiss. In this gap, gradually, as I sank from the heights back inside myself, I began after all to hear a sound.

It was a peculiar one. I could not make it out.

Since ordinary sense was, unwelcome, returning, I started vaguely to think, *Oh, some animal, hunting*. It had a kind of coughing, retching, whining quality, inimical and awesome, something which would have nothing to do with what basically it entailed – like the agonized female scream of the mating fox.

The noises went on for some time, driving me ever further and further back to proper awareness, until I opened my eyes, and stood up abruptly. I was cold, and felt rather sick. The scent of the Janfia tree was overpowering, nauseating, and nothing at all had happened. The shadows were all quite usual, and, rounding on the window, I saw the last of the moon's edge was in it, and the tree like a cut-out of black and white papers. Nothing more.

I swore, childishly, in rage, at all things, and myself. It served me right; fool, fool, ever to expect anything. And that long shadow, what had that been? Well. It might have been anything. Why else had I shut my eyes but to aid the delusion, afraid if I continued to look I must be undeceived.

Something horrible had occurred. The night was full of the knowledge of that. Of my idiotic invitation to demons, and my failure, their refusal.

But I really had to get out of the room, the scent of the tree was making me ill at last. How could I ever have thought it pleasant?

I took the wine-bottle, meaning to replace it in the refrigerator downstairs, and, going out into the corridor, brought on the lights. Below, I hit the other switches rapidly, one after the other, flooding the villa with hard modern glare. So much for the moon. But the smell of the Janfia was more persistent, it seemed to cling to everything – I went out on to the western veranda, to get away from it, but even here on the other side of the house the fragrance hovered.

I was trying, very firmly, to be practical. I was trying to close the door, banish the element I had summoned, for though it had not come to me, yet somehow the night clamoured with it, reeked of it. What was it? Only me, of course. My nerves were shot, and what did I do but essay stupid flirtations with the powers of the dark? Though they did not exist in their own right, they do exist inside every one of us. I had called my own demons. Let loose, they peopled the night.

All I could hope for now was to go in and make a gallon of coffee, and leaf through and through the silly magazines that lay about, and stave off sleep until the dawn came. But there was something wrong with the cypress tree. The moon, slipping over the roof now in pursuit of me, caught the cypress and showed what I thought was a broken bough.

That puzzled me. I was glad of the opportunity to go out between the bushes and take a prosaic look.

It was not any distance, and the moon came bright. All the night, all its essence, had concentrated in that spot, yet when I first looked, and first saw, my reaction was only startled astonishment. I rejected the evidence as superficial, which it was not, and looked about and found the tumbled kitchen stool, and then looked up again to be sure, quite certain, that it was Marta who hung there pendant and motionless, her engorged and terrible face twisted away from me. She had used a strong cord. And those unidentifiable sounds I had heard, I realized now, had been the noises Marta made, as she swung and kicked there, strangling to death.

The shock of what had happened was too much for Isabella, and made her unwell. She had been fond of the girl, and could not understand why Marta had not confided her troubles. Presumably her lover had thrown her over, and perhaps she was pregnant – Isabella could have helped, the girl could have had her baby under the shelter of a foreign umbrella of bank notes. But then it transpired Marta had not been pregnant, so there was no proper explanation. The woman who cooked said both she and the girl had been oppressed for days, in some way she could not or did not reveal. It was the season. And then, the girl was young and impressionable. She had gone mad. God would forgive her suicide.

I sat on the veranda of the other villa, my bags around me and a car due to arrive and take me to the town, and Alec and Isabella, both pale with convalescence, facing me over the white iron table.

'It wasn't your fault,' said Alec to Isabella. 'It's no use brooding over it. The way they are here, it's always been a mystery to me.' Then, he went in, saying he felt the heat, but he would return to wave me off.

'And poor poor you,' said Isabella, close to tears. 'I tell you to come here and rest, and this has to happen.'

I could not answer that I felt it was my fault. I could not confess that it seemed to me that I, invoking darkness, had conjured Marta's death. I did not understand the process, only the result. Nor had I told Isabella that the Janfia tree seemed to have contracted its own terminal disease. The leaves and flowers had begun to rot away, and the scent had grown acid. My vibrations had done that. Or it was because the tree had been my focus, my burning-glass. That would reveal me then as my own enemy. That powerful thing which slowly destroyed me, that stalker with a knife, it was myself. And knowing it, naming it, rather than free me of it, could only give it greater power.

'Poor little Marta,' said Isabella. She surrendered and began to sob, which would be no use to Marta at all, or to herself, maybe.

234

Then the car, cheerful in red and white, came up the dusty road, tooting merrily to us. And the driver, heaving my luggage into the boot, cried out to us in joy, 'What a beautiful day, ah, what a beautiful day!'

The Devil's Rose

I have always said I find this one of the most horrific of my own stories.

How many times it must, in some form, have happened. And, in more modern guise, still does.

One wishes to assume a strong moral stance. Yet self-denial is a wicked thing. The air is always full of first-thrown stones.

O Rose, thou art sick!
The invisible worm
That flies in the night,
In the howling storm

Has sought out thy bed
Of crimson joy:
And his dark secret love
Does thy life destroy.

William Blake

Because of a snow-drift on the line, the train pulled to an unscheduled stop at the little town of L——. Presently we passengers had debarked, and stood stamping and chafing our hands about the stove in the station-house. It was nearly midnight, but the station-master's charitable housekeeper came almost at once with steaming coffee and a bottle of spirits. A boy was also roused and sent running, apparently to wake all the town on our behalf for lodgings. We should not be able to go on for three or four days, even that depending on whether or not fresh snow were to come down. Since we had entered the great pine

237

forests outside Archaroy, we had been seeing wolves. They were thick on the ground that winter, and in the little villages and towns, we were to hear, not a carriage or sledge could go out but it would have wolf-packs running after it for mile on mile, until the lights of human habitation came again in sight.

'What a prospect!' exclaimed the estate manager who had shared my compartment from Archaroy. 'Besieged in the back of beyond by weather and wolves. Do you think, Mhikal Mhikalson, we shall ever get out?'

I said that we might, in the spring, perhaps, if not this year's, then next. But in fact, being my own creature, such unprecedented quirks of venture as this one neither dismayed nor displeased me. I had no family either behind or at journey's end to be impatient or in fear for me. My friends were used to my eccentricities and would look for me to arrive only when I did so. Additionally, in this instance, my destination was not one I hankered for. The manager, however, who had business dealings up ahead, was turning fractious. On the pretence of the errand for lodgings, I walked out of that hot room and went into the town of L——, to see what, as the isolated clocks of midnight struck, it might offer me.

It was a truly provincial backwater, such as you would expect, although the streets were mostly lit, and efforts had been made to clear the snow. There was an old market-place with a bell-tower, and close by some public gardens with tall locked gates. The houses of the prosperous ascended a hill, and those of the not so prosperous slunk down it. Some boulevards with shops all shut finished the prospect.

On a rise behind the rest was an old stuccoed house which I noticed for something Italianate in its outline, but mostly through one unprovincial lemon-yellow window burning brightly there. What poet or scholar worked late in that room when all the town slept? Something in me, which would have done the same if so placed, sent a salutation up to him.

After looking at the house, I made my way – perversely? – downhill, observing the degeneration of all the premises. The lower town fell into what might once have been the bed of some primeval river, which had carved out a bottom for itself before sinking away into the past. Over the area, the narrow streets sprawled and intertwined; it would be easy to be lost there, but for the constant marker of the hill hanging always above.

Needless to say, the snow had here been churned and frozen in mud-heaps, and the going was heavy. I was growing jaded, when, between some boarded stables and a parade of the poorest houses, I discovered an ancient church. It was of the kind you sometimes see even in the cities, crammed between newer buildings that seem to want to press the life from it and close together in its default. A hooded well stood on the snow and the cobbles near the church door which, as may still happen in the provinces, was unlocked.

The church intrigued me, perhaps only as the house had done with its window, for I sensed some life going on there. It was not an area for the wise to loiter; who knew what rough or other might not come from his hovel to demand money, or try by force to take it. Nevertheless something kept me there, and I was on the point of going nearer, when lo and behold the massive church door parted a crack. Out into the moonlight, which was now laving snow and town alike, slipped the slender, unmistakable form of a woman. It was the season when men go about garbed like bears, and she too was of course wrapped against the cold, her head mantled with a dark shawl. I recognized in her at once, even so, the thing I had sensed, the meaning of the church's 'life', or at least a portion of it. I wondered what she would do, confronted by a stranger. In these small towns mostly anyone of any consequence knows all the others. If an alien, and a man, accosted her, what then? Yet had she not put herself, alone and after midnight, into the perfect position for such an overture?

'Excuse me, young woman,' I said, as she came along the slope.

She started, quite violently. It was so very lustrous, the moon inflaming the snow, that to tell a shadow from shadows was not easy. Perhaps I had seemed to step from thin air itself.

She was so apparently startled I wondered if there were a chance I should now take her arm to steady her, tilting our faces to the moon as I did so, that she might see me, and I her. But she had already composed herself.

'What is it?' she said, in a low and urgent voice.

'The hour is very late. I wondered if you were in some difficulty. Might I assist you?'

'No, no,' she muttered. Rather than reveal herself, she

snatched her shawl about her face with her gloved hands.

'I am a stranger to your town,' I said. 'Forgive my impetuosity in speaking to you.'

'How are you here?' she said. She stood like a child who is being verbally chastised by the school-master, longing to break free into the yard where the other children are.

'How else but the train? We are snowbound, it appears.'

But who would be those other children, her companions, from whom I kept her?

Just then, far away over the edge of the town as if over a high cliff out at sea, I heard the howling of a wolf. The hair rose on my neck as it always does at the sound. The cry was too apt, it came too nicely on my cue.

But at that moment she turned up her face, as if straining to listen, and I saw her features, and her eyes.

Although the shawl hid everything but a trace of her hair, I judged it to be very dark. And her face was very white, and her eyes were so pale in that pale face they were like glass on the snow. Her mouth, in the shadow-shining moonlight, seemed dark also, damson-coloured, but the lips beautifully shaped. It was not a beautiful face, but rather an almost classical one.

'Is it safe for you to go about like this, in such weather?' I said. 'Have you never heard of starving wolves running into the streets?'

'It has been known,' she said. Her eyes, now they had met mine, did not leave me.

'Let me,' I said, 'escort you wherever you are going.'

'Up there,' she said, 'to the Italian House. But you are a stranger –'

'No, I have seen the very house. With a light burning.'

'For me,' she said, 'my beacon.'

'Will you take my arm?' I said. 'Where the snow has been left lying the way is slippery.'

She came with a swift half-furtive step, and put her black silk paw into my arm. She leaned close to me as we began to walk.

I would have liked to ask her at once what she had been doing, there in the old church, to give such an intensity to the night. Even the lamp in her room – the room of the beacon – had blazed with it. But I did not feel it was the time yet, to ask her that. In fact we said very little, but walked together familiarly up through the town. She assured me it was not a vast distance. I said I was sorry. She did not then flirt with me, or move away. She shivered, and when I drew her hand more securely into my arm, against me, she murmured obliquely, 'It is so easy to misinterpret kindness.'

'Mine in going with you, or your own in permitting me to do so?'

Then she did not answer, and we went on again in silence. All the way, we passed not a soul, but once heard a dog snarling behind a gate after wolves or the moon. Soon enough we came on to the part of the rise which ended in her house. The high walls along the street provided cover for our approach. The light still burned before us, now a huge tawdry topaz. It looked warm, but not inviting. A blind masked that upper room from curious eyes attracted to its glow.

At the foot of some steps she detached herself from me. Feeling the cold after the warmth of me, she put her hands up to her face again. Her pale eyes were steady with their question.

'As I told you, I am marooned here a day or so. May I call on you tomorrow?'

'My parents are dead. I live with my aunt. My father's sister, she is old . . . Do please call, if you wish. But –' She left a long pause, to see if I could read her thoughts. I could.

'You do not wish me to say I met you at midnight by the church.'

'No, I do not.'

She had given me by then her family name. I said, 'As it happens, Miss Lindensouth, I know some distant relations of yours, some Lindensouths, in Archaroy. Or, at any rate, I believe they may be related to you and your aunt. It will give me an excuse to look her up.'

This was a lie. If she guessed, she did not seem alarmed. Her face was without an expression of any sort. She lowered her eyes and left me suddenly, running up the icy stair with a carelessness that saved her rather than put her in the way of an accident.

I waited, briefly, across the street, to see what would happen with the light, or even if her silhouette might pass across it. But the lamp might have shone in another world mysteriously penetrating this one. Nothing disturbed it, and it did not go out.

When I reached the station-house I found the party had gone off to the inn I had seen on my perambulations. Accordingly, I took myself there.

At about six o'clock in the morning the town of L—— began to come to life. By ten o'clock, when I returned to the church, the lower streets were seething. On every corner were the expected braziers of smoking red charcoal; lamps burned now in countless windows against the leaden light of morning. Having negotiated the slop-collectors, the carts of cabbage, and the carriage-horses of some local charioteer, I gained the appropriate street, and found this scene was also changed. The well was a gossiping spot for women, who stood there in their scarves and fur hats arguing the price of butter. A wood-seller was delivering further down, and children played in the snow with little cold-bitten faces, grimly intent on their miserable game.

The church itself was active. The door stood open, and two women in black veils came out. It was plainly an hour also for business, here.

I went forward diffidently, prepared to depart again at once, but on entering the church, found it was after all now empty.

It was like the inside of a hollowed boulder, carved bare, with the half-eggshell of the dome rising above. The shrine looked decently furnished, you could say no more for it. Everything that was anything was plate. A few icons were on the screen below. I paused to glance at them; they were Byzantine in influence, but rather crude, not a form I am much drawn to.

As I was turning away, a man approached me. I had not seen him either present or entering, but probably he had slipped out from some inner place. He was about forty and had the scholars' look, a high broad forehead gaining ground, and a ledge of brows and gold-rimmed spectacles beneath.

'You are one of our trapped travellers!' he cried.

My heart sank. 'Just so.'

He gave me a name and a gloved hand. I took, and relinquished, both.

'You are interested in churches?' His manner was quietly eager.

With caution I replied, 'There is something I am a little curious about –'

'Ah,' he broke in immediately, 'that will be the famous window, I think.'

What could I say?

'Indeed.'

'Come, I will show you.'

He took me into a side arm of the church, where it was very dark. Some candles burned, but then I saw shards of red, green and mauve thrown on the plastered wall.

My scholar brought me to his prize, and directed me where to look which, unless I had been blind, I could not have missed.

The window, small and round-headed, was like an after-thought, or perhaps (as he presently informed me) it might belong to an earlier chapel, being then the oldest thing there.

The glass itself was very old, and gave a rich heavy light. Its subject was the Garden of Eden, its colour mostly of emerald, blue and purple. Distantly the white figures of the sinners stood beneath their green apple-tree, the fatal fruit in hand. They were about to eat, and God about to say to them, like every injured parent: I gave you everything! Why could you not remain as children for ever? Why is it necessary that you grow up? His coming storm was indicated by the darkling sapphires of the shadows, the thunder-wing of purple on the grass. But in the foreground was a rose-tree, and among the wine-coloured flow-ers, the serpent coiled itself, its commission seen to.

'Most unusual, such a treatment,' said the scholar.

How was it that I knew so well that she, my Miss Lindensouth, had been frozen before this window, had come out from its contemplation as if her pale skin were steeped in the transparent dyes?

'Yes?'

He quoted a supposed date of the twelfth century.

'And of course it has a name, a window like this. Probably you know it? No? Well, it has been called "Satan's Rose-Bush", in church records even, for two hundred years. Or they say simply, secretively, "The Devil's Rose". And there are all sorts of stories, to do with curses and wonders and the rest of it. The best known is the story of the Girl Who Danced. You will know that one.'

'I am afraid not.'

'How splendid. Now I have all the pleasure of telling you. You see, supposedly, if you look long enough and hard enough at the glass, here, by the rose-tree, you find another figure in the window. It is one of those freak things, the way in which angles and colours go together randomly to form another shape – or perhaps the maker of the window intended it to happen. The figure is of a dark man, Satan himself, naturally, who took a serpent's appearance to seduce Eve to wrongdoing. I must say I have looked diligently at the window quite often, but I have never been able to make it out. I am assured it is there, however. The last priest himself could see it, and even attempted to describe it for me on the glass – but it was no good. My eyes, perhaps . . . You try yourself. See, it is here and here, alongside the roses.'

Staring where he showed me, I, like the scholar, could make out nothing. I knew of course that this had not been the case with the girl.

'And the story?'

'A hundred years ago, the tale has it, one of the great landowning families had one young fair daughter. She was noted as wonderfully vivacious, and how she loved to dance all night at all the balls in the area – for in those days, you understand, sleepy L—— was quite a thriving bustling town. Well, it would seem she visited the church and saw the window, and saw the figure of Satan. She found him handsome, and, in the way of some young girls, she – I do hope you are broadminded – she fell in love with him, with the Devil himself. And she made some vow, something adolescent and messy, with blood and such things. She invited him to come in that form and claim her for a dance. And when the next ball was held, about one in the morning, a great silence fell on the house. The orchestra musicians found their hands would not move, the dancers found their feet likewise seemed turned to stone. Then the doors blew open in a gust of wind. Every light in every chandelier went out – and yet there was plenty of light, even so, to see by: it was the light of Hell, shining into the ballroom. Then a dark figure, a tall dark man, entered the room. He had come as she requested, to claim his dance. It seems he brought his own orchestra with him. They were masked, every one of them, but sitting down by the dance-floor they struck up such a waltz that no one who heard it could resist its rhythm – and yet not one in the room could move! Then he came to the landowner's daughter and bowed and asked her for the honour of partnering her. And she alone of all the company was freed from the spell. She glided into his arms. He drew her away. They turned and whirled like a thing of fire, while all the rest of the room danced in their bones to the music, unable to dance in any other way, until all their shoes, and the white dresses of the women, and the fine evening clothes of the gentlemen, were dappled inside with their blood! How gruesome!' the scholar cried. He beamed on me. 'But presently the Devil dashed his partner away through the floor. They vanished, and the demon musicians vanished, although no other there was able to regain motion until the cocks crew. As for the girl, they found her skin – her *skin*, mark you, solely that – some days later on a hill. It had been danced right off her skeleton. But on her face, such as there was of it, was fixed a grin of agonized joy.'

He paused, grasping his hands together. He said presently, 'You see, in my modest way, I employ these old stories. I am something of a writer . . .' as if that excused him.

But I too was smiling. I was thinking of the girl, but not the girl in the story. Miss Lindensouth's strangeness and her youth, the way we had met, and the hold I had instantly obtained.

'It is a fact, young girls do sometimes,' he said, 'embrace such morbid fantasies – the love of death, or the Dark Angel, the Devil. Myself, I have penned a vampire fiction on this theme –'

I looked at the window again, along the rose-tree. Nothing was there, except a slight reflection, thrown from the candles, of my own height and dark clothing and hair. These were out of scale and therefore did not fit.

The scholar offered me a glass of tea, but I explained to him I was already late for one. I told him where, to see if this might mean anything to him. But he was living in the past. He bade me a cheery regretful farewell.

I rang the bell of the Italian House, and soon enough a maid-servant ushered me in. The rooms inside were no longer remotely Italianate. They had been choked up with things, furniture, and tables of photographs of staring statue-people, bowls of petals, pianos with shut lids. The entire house-lid seemed shut. It smelled aromatically, in the crumbling way an old book does.

The aunt received me presently in an upper parlour.

'Madam Lindensouth. How very kind of you. I bring you

greetings from Archaroy, but the snow acted as Providence.'

She was a stern thin woman with a distinct look to her of the niece, the same long black brows, but these pale eyes were watery and short-sighted. She had frequent recourse to pince-nez. Her gown was proper, old-fashioned, and of good material. She wore lace mittens, too.

'And you are a Mr Mhikalson. But we have not met.'

'Until this moment.'

I approached, raised a mitten, and bowed over it. Which made me remember the Devil in the story. I smiled, but had concealed it by the time I lifted my head. She was gratified, she made no bones about that. She offered me a chair and rang for the samovar. I told her of her invented cousins in the city, concocting anecdotes, waiting for her to say, perhaps sharply, But I have never heard of these people. To which I must reply, But how odd, for they seem to have heard of you, Madam Lindensouth, and of your daughter. Thereby introducing a careful error which would then make all well, confirming we were at cross-purposes, these Lindensouths were not her Lindensouths. And getting us, besides, to the notion of a niece.

I wondered, too, how long it would be before that niece contrived to make an entrance. Had she not been listening on an upper landing for the twangle of the bell? Or had she given me up? I had not specified a time, but had come late for so eager a visitor.

Then the tea arrived, which Madam served up-country fashion, very black, with a raspberry preserve. As we were drinking it, she still had not fathomed the cousins in Archaroy. She had simply accepted them, and we had begun to steer our conversation out upon the state of the weather, a proposed wolf-hunt, literature, and the world in general.

Suddenly however the aunt lifted her head.

'Now that must be Mardya coming down. My niece, Mr Mhikalson. You must meet her, she will want to question you about the city.'

I felt a wave of relief – and of interest, having learned at last the phantom's familiar name.

I wondered how I should feel when she came in, but inevitably she had not the same personality *en famille* as she had had outside in the wolf-throated snow-night. Just then she had come from her trance before the window of the rose-snake. But now she had had all night to think of me, all morning pondering if I should come back.

She stole into the room. Nothing like her sure-footed tread, both mercurial and wanton, of the night. She bore her hands folded on her waist before her, pearl drops in her nacre ears, her eyes fixed only on the aunt.

'Here is a gentleman from Archaroy,' announced Madam. I did not correct her.

The girl Mardya dashed me off a glance. It hung scintillating in the overheated air after her eyes had once more fallen. It said, You? You are here? You are real?

'He has friends, Mardya, who claim to be related to us. It must be the fur connection, or perhaps the diamond connection.' They were suspected of being in trade, that was it – but since she did not inquire it of me, I did not hazard. Traders, evidently, she did not pretend either to know or not to know. 'Well, Mardya,' she said.

Mardya inclined her head. Her hair was piled upon it, black and silken, not wholly tidy, and so revealing it was none of it false. Her cheeks were flushing now, paling again to a perfect paper white. The earrings blinked. She was acting shy in the presence of her kin.

'Your aunt has kindly warned me,' I said, 'that you will want to know about the city. I must tell you at once, I am a frequenter of libraries. I read and do very little else.' Behold, madam, *I* am not in trade, but a beast of leisure and books.

Mardya, not speaking, stole on towards us. Taking the aunt's glass, she refilled it at the bubbling tea-pitcher.

'But no doubt you ladies spend a great deal of time with books,' I said. 'The town is very quiet. Or is that only the disaster of winter?'

'Winter or summer. Such summers we have,' said the aunt. 'The heat is intolerable. My brother had a lodge up in the hills, but we have had to get rid of it. It is no use to *us*, it was a man's place. My niece, as you say, is something of a reader. And we have our sewing and our music.'

'And do you, Miss Lindensouth,' I said briskly, 'never dance?'

She had given back the glass of tea, or I think she would have dropped it. Her whole slender shape locked rigid. Her white eyelids nailed down on her cheeks quivered and would not stop.

'I do not – I do not dance,' she said – the first thing she *had* said, in this presence.

'But I heard such a strange little story today,' I began to the aunt amiably. 'A man I met this morning, an authority on your local legends –'

'Will you not have another glass of tea?' said Mardya.

'No, thank you, Miss Lindensouth. But I was saying, the story has to do with a certain window –'

'Do have another glass,' said Mardya.

Her voice was hard with wrath, and her eyes were on me, full of tears. She expected betrayal. To have wounded her so easily gave me the anticipated little thrill. She was so vulnerable, one must protect her. She must be put behind the iron shield, defended.

'No, thank you so much. In fact I must tear myself away and leave you, Madam Lindensouth, in peace.' I rose. 'Except – I wonder if I might ask a great favour of you, madam? Might I borrow your niece for half an hour?' The long brows went up, she adjusted the pince-nez. I smiled and said, 'My sister has imposed the most wretched duty. I was to buy her a pair of gloves, and forgot in my haste of leaving. Now I shall arrive late besides, and probably will never be forgiven. But it occurred to me Miss Lindensouth, who has just the sort of hands, I see, that my sister has, might advise me. She might even do me the kindness of trying on the gloves, selecting a colour. I find this sort of task most embarrassing. I have no idea of what to look for. Which, if I am honest, is why I forgot the transaction in the first place.'

The aunt laughed, superior upon the failings of the fumbling male.

'Yes, go along with Mr Mhikalson, Mardya, and assist him with these troublesome gloves. You may place my own order while you are doing so.'

I bowed to her mitten once more. She sighed, and I caught the faint acidity of medicine on her breath.

'Perhaps, since you must remain here, you will dine with us tonight?' she said, with the grudging air that did not mask a lively curiosity she had begun to have about me.

'Why, Madam Lindensouth – to be sure of that I will go personally to shovel more snow on the line.'

She laughed heartily, and bade me get along. Her eyes of watery steel said, If I had been younger. And mine: Indeed, madam, there can be no doubt. But I am too respectful now, and besides maybe I am in search of a wife, and you see what a fine coat this is, do you? But nevertheless, I know where the fount is, the sybil. We understand one another in the way no man finds it possible to understand or to be understood by any woman under forty, and surely you are not much more?

Down in the street, Mardya Lindensouth spoke to me in a strange cold hot voice.

'I trust you rested well.'

'No. I could only lie there and think of seeing you again. I have thought of nothing else since our meeting.'

'But something delayed you.'

'Strategy. You saw how I have managed it. I am to dine.'

She would not take my arm.

'There are no gloves,' I said, 'I have no sisters.' I said, 'Run her errand later. Where can we go?'

And all at once, in an arch in one of the old walls of the street, she was leaning her spine to a door, her hands on my breast. It was a daring situation, hidden, unfrequented, yet anyone might look from an upper floor, or come by and see.

I leaned against her until her back pressed the backs of my hands into the damp wood. She was, though I could only speculate how, no stranger to kisses. Presently, engorged and breathless we pulled apart, and went on down the street. This time she took my arm.

We went to a pâtisserie along one of the boulevards. To my dismay, at one point, I saw three of my fellow travellers from the train, the estate manager among them, going by the window, hesitating at the door – and thank heaven passing on.

She did not eat anything, only sipped the scalding beverage, which was not so flavoursome as the samovar of Madam.

'I dreamed of you,' she said, 'all night. I was burning. I thought I should run out into the snow to get cool. But I should freeze there. You would come and find me and warm me in your arms. But you would never come back. I knew you at once.'

'Who am I?'

'Hush. I do not want to say your name.'

'Mardya, tell me about the church.'

'You know everything about me.'

'The window, Mardya.'

'Not here . . .'

'No one can hear, you whisper so softly, and your warm breath brushes my cheek. Tell me about the window.'

'It was quite sudden,' she said. Artless, she added, 'Two years ago, when I was fourteen.'

'Well?'

'I saw it. The same way the girl does in the story. At first, I tried not to think of it. But I began to dream – how can I tell you those dreams? – they were so terrible. I thought my heart must stop, I should die – I longed for them and I feared them.'

'Pleasure.'

'Such – such pleasure. I tried not to know. But it has been all I could think of. There is nothing here – in the town. I see no one. No one comes to her house but her friends, the Inspector of Works, the banker – everyone is old, and I am old too when I sit with them. I become like them. My hands get so stiff and my neck and my eyes ache and ache. I have nothing to live for. But now, you are here.'

'Yes, I am here.' I put my foot gently against hers under the tasselled tablecloth. Our knees almost touched, the fabric of her dress stirred against me. Her cheeks were inflamed now. All about us, human things went on with their chocolate, their tea and cake and sugar.

'Tonight she will have those two or three friends to dine with you. We will dine on chicken bones and aspic tarts. We have no money.'

'Mardya, be quiet.'

'I must tell you –'

'What? How to remain behind in the house after the others have left?'

She caught her breath.

I said, 'I remember the lamp burning and how you go about improperly at night, and I would imagine you have fooled her, she never knows. So you are clever in such matters. Shall I hide in some cupboard?'

'Not now. How can I speak of it? I shall faint.'

'If you do that, we shall attract attention.'

'Secretly then. When the darkness comes. In darkness.'

'One candle, perhaps. You must let me look at you. I want to see all your whiteness.'

'Hush,' she said again. Her eyes swam, her hands pressed on the glass of tea as if to splinter it. 'I have never –' she said.

'I know.'

'You will – care for me?'

'You will see how I will care for you.'

Neither of us could breathe particularly well. We burned with fever, our feet pressing and our hands grasping utensils of the tea-table as if to save them in a storm. But she shook so that her earrings flashed, and she could hardly hold the tea-glass any more. I took it from her, and found it difficult in turn to let go of.

Presently, I settled our account, and we left the shop and went to another, where she ordered needles for her aunt.

I escorted her up through the town, the second time, past the smoking braziers and the lamplit nothingness of other people and other things. On the rise, in the same snow-bounded stone archway, I thrust her back and crushed her to me. Her hands clutched my coat, she struggled to hold me as if drowning. We parted, and went separate ways, to scheme and wait like wolves for the night.

The dinner party – for such it was to be – was to be also all I had predicted from the picture Mardya had painted.

The Inspector of Works was there, a blown man with an overblown face, and his wife, a stubborn mouse of a woman much given to a sniff, an old maid in wife's clothing. The elderly unmarried banker had also come, perhaps an ancient flame of Madam's. But we animals were of a proper number and gender, and progressed two by two.

Madam Lindensouth came to dinner in a worn black velvet and carbuncle locket. When Mardya entered there was some life stirred up, even in the banker. She had on a dress the colour of pale fire, between soft red and softer gold, with her white throat and arms exposed. Madam did not bat an eyelash, so clearly she had not been above suggesting a choice of finery. Mardya was self-conscious, radiant. She flirted with the banker and the Inspector in a way, patently, they had never before experienced, the delicious clumsy coquettishness of an innocent and charming young girl. Only with me was she very cool and restrained. Yet as we came to the table, she did remark, 'Oh, Mr Mhikalson, I have been worrying about it. Those gloves in that particular shade of fawn. Are you quite sure that your sister will be content?'

Her daring pleased me. I said, unruffled, 'I thought they were more of a yellow tone. The very thing. But then, I told you, I have no judgement in such matters.'

All this required an explanation, that Miss Lindensouth had been in the town with me buying handwear for my relative. A knowing look passed between the banker and the Inspector's mouse.

Presumably not one of them had heard the latest news of my train. There had been a message at the inn on my return there. The line was expected after all to be clear by four the next morning. The train would depart one hour after, at five o'clock. Of course, I might be prepared to miss it. They might assume I would have no more pressing engagement than a wooing, now I was so evidently embarked.

All through the desiccated dinner, my fellow guests tried to wring from me, on Madam's behalf, the story of my life, my connections, my prospects. I remained cordially reticent, but here and there let fall a word for myself. I am a good liar, inventive and consistent, and quite enjoyed this part of the proceedings. For the meal, it was a terrible event. There was not a drop of moisture in any of it, and the wine, though wet, was fit only for just such a table, and in short supply besides.

After we had dined, the ladies permitted the men to smoke, by withdrawing.

The banker lit up and coughed prodigiously.

'These winters,' said he, 'will be my death.'

To me he added, 'How I yearn for the city. I have not been in Archaroy, let alone anywhere else, since my thirty-fifth year. Is that not a fearsome admission? Finance has been my life. I still dabble. If you were to be seeking any advice, Mr Mhikalson –'

The Inspector broke in with a merry, 'Never trust this rogue. He is still in half the deals and plots of the town. But I must say, if you were thinking of remaining a week or so, there are some horses I think you should look at, with an eye to the summer. My cousin Osseb is quite an authority. Did you know it is possible to hunt wolf here all the year round? Well, there you are. Of course,

Madam Lindensouth's brother, the father of Miss, had a lodge in the forest. But that was sold.'

'But you are not to think,' put in the banker, giving him an admonishing glance, 'that the family fortune here is on the decline. Not a bit of it. I will say, my dear friend Madam is something on the careful side, but there is quite an amount stashed away . . .'

'Tut tut,' said the Inspector. 'Can the ladies have no secrets?'

Finally we had smoked sufficiently, and went into the next room, where Madam regaled us all with some music from the piano, which, startled to find its lid had been raised, uttered a great many wrong notes.

Mardya would not play. She said that she had a chilblain on her finger. This evoked three remedies given at once by the mouse, the banker, and the Inspector. In each case, suffering the chilblain would have been preferable.

A card game then ensued, out of which Mardya pardoned herself, and I was left also to my own devices, being besides pushed to them by smiles and nods. I joined the girl by the piano, where she was searching among the sheet music for an old tune her father had been used to play.

'Come now,' I said, speaking low, 'how is it to be managed?'

'Impossible,' she said.

'Think of our stop on the hill.'

She blushed deeply, but continued to leaf through the music.

'I am afraid.'

'No. You are not afraid.'

'The Ace!' cried the banker. He added to us, over his shoulder, not having heard a word, 'Now, now.'

'Think of the apple-tree,' I said to her, 'think of the rose.'

Her hands fluttered, some of the music spilled. Her pulse raced in her throat so swiftly it looked dangerous. We bent to retrieve the music.

'Leave before the others.' She spoke crisply now though scarcely above a whisper. 'I will go down and open the door. Return almost at once and go into the side parlour below. The blinds are down, there is a large table with a lamp on it that is never lit. You must be patient then. Wait until the house is quiet. Wait until the clock in the hallway strikes eleven.'

'Where is your room?'

She told me. She was shivering, from desire or fear, both.

We had regained the music and arranged it together by the piano.

'There is the song my father used to play,' she said. But she did not play it.

It was almost thirty minutes past nine, and I suspected the festivity would be curtailed sharp at ten o'clock. After the banker had told us again to *Now*, *Now*, and the maid-servant had brought in the trusty samovar and some opaque sherry, the card game lapsed. It was a quarter to ten.

'Madam Lindensouth,' I said, 'I must return at once to the inn. I had not realized how late it has grown. There are some arrangements I shall need to make.' I left a studied pause. She would deduce I meant to give up my seat on the train. 'Thank you for your kindness and hospitality.'

'If it chances you are still here tomorrow,' she said. (The banker and the Inspector laughed, and the mouse primly sniffled.) 'We take luncheon at three o'clock. I hope you will feel able to join us.'

At the concept of another meal of sawdust and pasted aspics I almost laughed myself. Something in her eyes checked me. In holding out to me the branch of unity with her niece, a girl therefore about to taste the chance Madam had missed, there was a sudden ragged edge to her, a malevolence, which showed in a darkening of her pallid eyes, the iron smile with which she strove to underpin propriety. It was clear from this that a callous and unkind method would have sustained her treatment of Mardya from the beginning. She had never been a friend to her and never would be. Small wonder the savage innocent turned to shadows for her *Fata Morgana* of release and love. It even seemed probable in those moments that the aunt had known all along of midnight excursions to a church on the lower streets, of a flirtation with grisly legends and unsafety. Did the woman know even that this was where Mardya had met me? Did she know what plan we had (now, now) to meet in the night on the shores of lust, under her very roof? Yes, for a moment I beheld before me a co-conspirator.

When I took her hand, she said, 'Why, your hands are cold tonight, Mr Mhikalson. You must have a care of yourself.'

I uttered my farewells, got down through the house, and was

shown out into the darkness and the snow.

I went down the steps, and waited where I had done so the first night, across the way, taking no particular pains over concealment.

That light was not burning in the upper – her – room. The window was sightless, eyeless, and waiting, too. Before midnight, I should have seen the inside of that room, should have touched its objects and ornaments, invaded the air with my breath and will, my personality, perhaps a stifled cry, the heat of my sweat. I should have possessed that room, before the morning came. I did not need to see its light, now.

After about six or seven minutes, I went back. If I met anyone on the steps or in the doorway, I should say I had lost something and returned hoping it was in the house. But I met no one.

The front door was ajar, and I passed through silently, shutting it again. A muffled bickering came from above, from the dinner party.

The side parlour was as she had described, to the right of the hall, remote from the stair. It was in blackness, the table dimly shining like a pool of black water, and the unlit lamp upon it reflected vaguely, and here and there some glistening surface. I went through and seated myself on an upright chair against the wall, facing the doorway. Naturally I was quite concealed, by night, by the shapes of the furniture, best of all by being where of course I could not reasonably be.

Like the audience in the darkened theatre then, I stayed. And down the dully lighted stair they passed in due course to the hall, the banker, and the Inspector and his mouse-wife. The maid arrived with hats and sticks, and Madam waved them off from the vantage of the staircase, not descending.

All sound died away then, gradually, above. And lastly the maid came drifting along across the open door, like a ghost, to take away the final guttering lamp. Partly I was amazed she did not catch the flash of my eyes from the black interior, the eyes of the wolf in the thicket. But she did not. No one came to bother me, to make me say how I had left behind a glove, or a cigarette case, or had felt faint suddenly in the cold, and come back to find the door was open – and sat here to wait for the maid and fallen asleep. No, none of that was necessary.

At last, the clock chimed in the hall, eleven times.

Rising from my seat, I stretched myself. I walked softly from concealment to the foot of the staircase. Hardly a noise anywhere. Only the ticking of the clock, the sighing of the house itself. Beyond its carapace, snow-silence on the town of L ———, and far away, so quiet were all things now, the tinny *tink-tink* of another clock finding the hour of eleven on a slightly different plane of time than that of the Italian House.

I started to go up the stairs. The treads were dumb. I climbed them all, passing the avenues of passages, and came to a landing and a heavy curtain with a moth-ball fringe. And then, in an utter darkness, without even the starlit snow-light of the windows, her door, also standing ready for me, ajar.

I closed it with care behind me. The room was illumined only by the aqueous snow-sheen on the blind. This made a translucent mark, like ice, in turn upon the opposite wall, and between was a floating unreality, with a core of paleness.

'Ssh,' she whispered, though I had not made a sound.

I went towards her and found her by the whiteness of her nightgown on the bed. The room was all bed. It could have no other objects or adornment.

Her hands were on my face, her arms were about my neck.

'Where is the candle?' I said. 'Let me see you, Mardya.'

'No,' she pleaded. 'Not yet . . .'

My vision was, anyway, full-fed on the dark. I was beginning to see her very well.

The little buttons of her nightgown irritated my fingers, to fiddle with them almost made me sick. I lifted my face from her burning face, kissing her eyes, her lips. I pulled the nightgown up in a single movement and laid her bare in the winter water of the light, the slender girlish legs folded to a shadow at the groin, the pearl of the belly, the small waist with its trinket of starlight, and the ribcage with the two cupped breasts above it, and the nipples just hiding still in the frills of the nightgown – she was laughing noiselessly and half afraid, shuddering, pushing the heavy folds from her chin, letting them lie across her shoulders and throat as I bent to her. My hands were full of her body and my mouth full of her taste. The mass of black hair stained across the pillows, shawled over her face, got into my mouth.

I threw off my coat, what I could be rid of quickly. Her skin where it came against my skin was cool, though her lips, ears and forehead blazed, and the pits of her arms were also full of heat, and her hands, their hotness stopping mysteriously at the wrists. She was already dewy when my fingers sought between the fleshy folds of the rose. 'No,' she said. She rubbed herself against me, arching her back, shaken through every inch of her. 'No – no –'

'This will hurt you.'

'Hurt me,' she said, 'I am yours. I belong to you.'

So I broke into her, and she whined and lay for a moment like a rabbit wounded in a trap under my convulsive thrusts no longer to be considered, but at the last moment she too thrust herself up against me, crucified, with a long silent scream, a whistling of outdrawn breath, and I felt the cataclysm shake her to pieces as I was dying on her breast.

'I knew you would come to me,' she murmured. 'I knew it must happen. I called out to you and you heard me. Across miles of night and snow and stone.'

'Sometimes,' she said, 'I have seen you in a dream. Never clearly. But your eyes and your hair.'

'Are you the one?' she said. 'Are you my love? For always?'

'Always,' I said, 'how else?'

'And my death,' she said. 'Love is death. Kill me again,' she said, but not in any mannered way, though it might have been some line from some modern stage drama.

So presently, leaning over her, I 'killed' her again. This time I even pinned her arms to the bed in an enactment of violence and force. Her face in ecstasy was a mask of fire, a rose mask.

Afterwards her eyes were hollow, like those of a street whore starving in the cold.

When I began to put on my clothes, she said, 'Where are you going?'

'It will be best, I think. We might fall asleep. How would it look if the girl came in and found me here, in the frank morning light?'

'But you will come back tomorrow?'

'Your aunt has invited me to luncheon.'

'You will be here? Will you be late?'

'Of course I shall be here, of course not late.'

I kissed her, for the last time, with tenderness, seemliness. It was all spent now. I could afford to be respectful.

As I reached to open the door, she was lying like a creature of

257

the sea stranded upon a beach. Her delicate legs might have been the slim bi-part tail of a mer-girl, and the tangle of nightgown and hair only the seaweed she had brought with her to remind her of the deep.

I went down again through the house with the same lack of difficulty, and as well, for I could have no decent story to explain my presence now.

As I let myself out of the front door, and descended the steps, the air cut coldly in the icy deserts before dawn. It was almost four o'clock, but I had seen to my luggage beforehand. I need only go along to the station and there wait for the train which, because the allotted hour was now both extempore and ungodly, would doubtless leave on time.

Two doctors attended me at the point of my destination, one the man I had arranged, a month previously, to see, the other a colleague of his, a specialist in the field. Both frowned upon me, the non-specialist with the more compassion.

'From what you have said, I think you are not unaware of your condition.'

'I had hoped to be proved wrong.'

'I am afraid you are not wrong. The disease is in its primary phase. We will begin treatment at once. It is not very pleasant, as you understand, but the alternative less so. It will also take some time.'

'And I believe,' said the less sympathetic frowner, 'you comprehend you can never be perfectly sanguine. There is, as such, no cure. I can promise to save your life, you have come to us in time. But marriage will be out of the question.'

'Did I give you to suppose I intended marriage?'

'All relations,' said this man, 'are out of the question. This is what I am saying to you. The organisms of syphilis are readily transferable. You must abstain. Entirely. This is not what you, a young man, would wish to hear. But neither, I am sure, would you wish to inflict a terrible disease of this nature, involving deformity, insanity and certain death where undiagnosed, on any woman for whom you cared. Indeed, I trust, upon any woman.' He glared on me so long I felt obliged to congratulate his judgement.

The treatment began soon after in a narrow white room. It was, as they advised, unpleasant. The mercury, pumped through me like vitriol, induced me to scream, and after several repetitions I raved. One does not dwell on such matters. I bore it, and waited to escape the cage.

The ulcerous chancre, the nodulous sore, long healed, which had first alerted me in Archaroy, has a name in the parlance of the streets. They call it there the Devil's Rose.

And in that way, Satan comes out of his window, unseen, and passes through the streets. All the lights go out as he dances with the girl who vowed herself to him. And in the morning they find her skin upon the hillside.

She died insane, I heard as much some years later in another city, from the lips of those who did not know I might have an interest.

The condition was never diagnosed. Probably she had never even been told of such things. They thought she had pined and grown sick and gone mad through a failed love affair, some stranger who entered her life, and also left it, by train.

She had always been of a morbid turn, Mardya Lindensouth, obsessed by dark fancies, bad things. Unrequited love had sent her to perdition. She was unrecognizable by the hour of her death. She died howling, her limbs twisted out of shape, her features decayed, a wretched travesty of human life.

Yes, that was what dreams of love had done for her, my little Mardya. Though in the streets they call it the Devil's Rose.

Huzdra

With what glee I wrote this tale, in my late twenties, and new into the glory and pleasure of being a professional writer – at last.

As with many of my ideas, it simply came, and drove itself with simple complexity through my fingers and pen, lovely black scribble only I or my mother could read. And I have always liked justice.

It was the sunset of Midwinter's Eve. Black-haired Mirromi, the wife of Count Fedesha, sat before the eastern window of the great house, as she had sat by the same window, at the same hour, on the same day, for the past six years. The window was made up of alternating squares of blue and cochineal glass, all but the single clear pane through which Mirromi looked. This pane being, in fact, a lens of highly magnified crystal, it gave a fine and detailed view of the snowy countryside beyond the walls, and the highway which cut through it, and of any traffic that journeyed there.

And there was considerable traffic on Midwinter's Eve, everything going one way: north toward the city, for the festival. The sun was almost down, the snow darkening from white to lead, and still several carts and wagons were visible, trundling along the road, and a couple of rich men's carriages with outriders.

Countess Mirromi watched intently, just as she always watched at this moment, when the pale-crimson winter sun plunged nearer and nearer the brink of the land. The carriages galloped away, the carts vanished on their iron wheels. The road was for an instant empty. And then (Mirromi smiled) two new figures appeared. The larger was a man, walking slowly and doggedly, and he held the other, a young girl, bundled in his arms.

261

Mirromi rose. No need to watch any longer. As in the past six years, her cunning and her magic had not failed her. And though she was not surprised at her cleverness, it did her good to see the proof of it.

Countess Mirromi's hair, under its net of jewels, was black as oil; her velvet gown, under its goldwork, was blacker. And her heart and soul and mind blacker than either of them.

A track ran from the highway to the walls of the great house. This track the man and the girl he carried took without a second's hesitation, as if they had been invited, or as if they had been summoned there.

There were large gates in the wall, but they swung grindingly open as the travelers advanced, though who or what opened them remained unseen. Beyond the wall lay a grim garden, rather like a graveyard, with peculiar statuary poking from the snow, and an avenue of snow-fringed cypresses leading up toward the house. The house itself was a bizarre amalgam of tapering roofs and overhanging stories, with three gaunt towers, one of which faced directly to the east, and had a high window set in it of blue and blue-red glass.

Presently, the man and girl went on. Reaching the door, and finding this did not widen of itself, the man rapped with the knocker. It was shaped like a child's head, this knocker, with the ears of a rabbit – a silly yet rather unnerving object, especially when you saw the face of the child properly, and its malevolent grin of unherbivorous pointed teeth.

The girl rested her head on the man's shoulder, as if she were very weary. The man waited stolidly for an answer to his knock. He was quite unremarkable, except for his bigness and his obvious strength. He had an overall wind-tanned, weather-beaten look that seemed to have washed his skin and his clothes and his hair in the same brownish-grayish uncolor. His eyes were large and pallid, and appeared not as strong as the rest of him, for he stared at things in a dim, uncertain way. The girl was another matter, for though she also was clad in the drab garments of the poor, her fair skin was beautifully clear, almost transparent, like that of some rich man's daughter kept much from the sun. And her hair was a wonderful soft pale shade of reddish blond.

The door was opened abruptly.

Inside the doorway loomed a large, black-bearded man in a suit of dark scarlet velvet, with rings and chain of gold, and a pearl in his left ear. He laughed aloud at the two visitors.

'Come, don't be startled. You expected a servant, no doubt, not the master of the house. I am Count Fedesha, and you are welcome to my home on this night of Midwinter's Eve.'

'We are unlucky travelers, my lord,' said the man outside. 'We were on our way to the city for the festival, but a strange thing happened to us. As the sun turned to the west, we passed between two old dead trees on either side of the road, and no sooner had the shadow of the western tree fallen on us than our poor little horse dropped dead in the shafts. Of course, a wagon is no use without a horse to draw it, and we were forced to leave it where it stood, and come seeking help. Yours is the first dwelling we have seen on the road, and such a fine one I hardly dared approach. Yet I thought perhaps, out of your generosity, you might send a groom to aid us. My sister's a cripple, sir,' he added, almost as if in excuse; 'I have carried her all this way.'

'But tell me,' said the Count, still extraordinarily jovial, 'did no others pass you on the road who might have helped you?'

'Indeed yes,' the man replied, with a slow, puzzled air. 'Many that we called out to, though none of them stopped. Perhaps they thought us robbers, yet it seemed they never saw us, almost, you might say, as if we had grown invisible – a carriage nearly rode me down. But there's no telling. It was most odd, my lord.'

Count Fedesha laughed again, or rather, he giggled. He reached and chucked the tired beautiful cripple girl under the chin.

'Such pretty hair,' he said, 'should not be out in the cold.'

He led them inside.

Within was a vast hall, pillared in stone, and hung by tapestries that winked with gold thread in the firelight of the tall hearth; a thousand candles lit the room where the fire did not. Before the hearth lay a white bear fur with a head, and rubies in the eyes. Just beyond that, near the room's center, a mosaic was set in the floor, a curious design of circle and star, and the twelve shapes of the zodiac.

'Please, put your sister in the chair beside the fire, sir. You take the other,' cried Count Fedesha.

'My lord, you are too kind,' faltered the big man.

'Not at all. Tonight is the night of the festival, the turning away of the Old Beast, Winter. If we can't be kind to each other on such a night, why, God help us. There, put the maid down, and I'll bring you wine.' Count Fedesha waved his ringed hand at a table near the hearth. 'Will you have the white wine in the silver jug, or the rose wine in the gold? Or would you prefer the red rum of the Westlands? Or maybe some apricot cordial, in that yellow bottle there? You must be surprised that I wait on you,' added the Count, 'but it's our custom, the Countess's and mine, to send our servants away to the city on Midwinter's Eve. So they may enjoy the festival, you understand.'

The big man had placed his burden in the chair. The girl sighed, and smiled at him, and at the Count, who handed her a goblet of cordial. Her eyes, the Count observed, were an amber shade, like her hair. It really was a great pity . . . but it was foolish to speculate. Even though her innocence and grace appealed to him, there could be no leisure to dally.

Count Fedesha gave the big man rum, and made him take the other chair.

'I'm sorry we can send no one to retrieve your wagon until tomorrow, when the servants return,' the Count went on, 'but you shall be our guests tonight, eat well and sleep soft.' The big man gaped at him. They always did, and sometimes the women did too, but usually the women were more trusting than the men, and more greedy for a brief taste of good living. Some had smiled winningly at the Count, hoping to prolong their stay.

Count Fedesha watched the two of them drink from their goblets. Everything was going most smoothly, and would go more smoothly now than ever, because of the black herb Mirromi had mixed ready in the cups. But it had gone smoothly for six years. This was the seventh year, and this the seventh occasion – the last occasion, if his clever Mirromi was right, and when had she ever been wrong? – and this the seventh pair of travelers brought here by the spells Mirromi had left on the road to waylay them. Count Fedesha remembered the first time, seven years before. How afraid he had been, eaten alive with terror. But Mirromi had gone up to the Tertiary Tower, and when she had come back, she had been smiling. Before dawn of Midwinter's Eve, she had slipped out and marked the occult symbols on the two dead trees half a mile off, next, left her potent magics on the highway, the track, the walls of the house, the gates. And ever since, each year on this dreary night of Midwinter's Eve, Mirromi had reactivated the spells. Cunning, uncanny spells they were, that would select only two travelers, a man and a woman, cause them some accident – a loosened wheel, a dead horse – that would then exert a drawing influence to pull the elected two toward the great house, rendering them the while quite invisible, inaudible, intangible to any passers-by who might otherwise aid them. Indeed, Mirromi and he, thought Count Fedesha, they were an ingenious and wondrous couple; they deserved their victory.

Still, a shame this girl was so pretty; she did not look so common as the rest, not a peasant type at all, though the brother was as rough and ready as they came. The Count giggled again, softly, into his wine. Odd to recall how afraid he had been at the beginning, those seven years ago. And here he was, almost complacent.

And now came the naming of names.

Neither of his guests had offered him their names as yet, the girl too timid, the man too bemused. If they had tried, Fedesha would have forestalled them. It was important that their own names be set aside, and thus, until the moment when the atmosphere must be altered, Fedesha would give then nicknames. Having drunk the sorcerous herb, overawed in any case and eager to please, the travelers always accepted these titles. And there had been some wicked ones he had invented in the past: 'Primrose' for the woman with the sallow yellow skin, and 'Camel' for the man with the humped back, and 'Biter' for the man with but three black teeth in his head. Now the Count looked his guests over and said: 'I'm going to call you "Quick," my fellow, because you move so fast. I hope you won't mind my eccentricity.' The big man gave a slow sheepish grin. Obviously he took the point of the joke with the true yokel's lack of resentment. For the girl, the name was easy, and for once complimentary. 'The pretty lady I shall call "Amber," for her hair and her eyes.'

The girl lowered these eyes. She seemed to blush, but it might only be the firelight shining on her pale face. The Count wondered idly if she had been crippled from birth, or in some mishap. Probably her spine was weak, a frequent enough ailment among the poor, the result of childhood malnutrition.

A door opened behind a drapery.

The Count heard the step of his Countess on the mosaic floor, and turned to see her glittering there in her black-and-gold gown, and with her raven's-wing hair poured in a net of jewels. At the center of her white forehead hung a scarab beetle of black jade on a silver chain. Fedesha recollected how she had sent a demon to rob the tomb of a dead queen for it.

'Ah, the stranded travelers,' cried Mirromi. At this point no one had ever questioned, and did not now, that the Countess apparently knew everything, without having been told. 'How pleasant to have guests on this night, though with our servants all away.'

It had been very convenient that it had *been* this night, of all the nights of the year, on which the trouble had begun. What better excuse than to say their servants had been sent by a benign master and mistress to the festival in the city? When in reality, of course, their servants fled the house and neither promise of reward nor threat of pain could persuade them to remain here on Midwinter's Eve.

Suddenly, Fedesha heard the sound. Despite his complacence, what he had boasted of to himself, he became for a moment icy with returning fear. Even Mirromi stood motionless as a stone, her eyes darting. As for the big man, the man Fedesha had nicknamed Quick, he raised his shaggy slow head, and gazed about in puzzlement. Then the amber girl cried aloud.

The big man lumbered to her.

'Don't be frightened.'

The girl clung to his hand, but it was at Fedesha she stared.

'It was a fly, a great black fly.'

She had not spoken before. Her voice, Fedesha thought, was not as pleasing as the rest of her – thin and breathy, and rather flat, even in her fright.

'Oh, there are sometimes flies here, even in winter,' he coaxed her. 'They sleep in the crevices of the house, and the warmth of the fire draws them out.'

Buzz. Buzz. The fly, large as the scarab ornament Mirromi had stolen from the queen's tomb, crawled along the hearth, the flames glinting on its poison-coloured wings. It seemed oblivious of the season, the heat. Oblivious of the lunge the traveler made to stamp on it.

266

'No!' Fedesha shouted. He dragged the big man back from the hearth, and the monstrous fly droned up toward the shadowy rafters of the hall, its noise going with it.

Mirromi spoke sweetly, reasonably.

'You must forgive us. We consider it unlucky to kill flies upon Midwinter's Eve.'

When they had drunk together, the Countess and the Count, unsparing hosts, led them upstairs into another story, and into a passage where a series of splendid bedchambers were to be found behind mahogany doors.

'This room shall be yours, mistress Amber,' said the Countess, beckoning the brother to carry his sister inside.

Again, as ever at this juncture, there was fresh staring. The girl's face was full of marvel as a child's.

The fat white candles shone on the silk hangings of the bed; the coverlet was of velvet trimmed with ermines' tails. You could not see through the oval window, for it was a picture done in colored glass of a maiden plucking red fruit from a green tree – she had a disturbing girdle, like an elongated golden rat. Here and there, pomanders of blue and lavender pottery sent up a rare fragrance.

'Here is a silver basin, and the water is yet warm in it and scented with violet petals,' said the Countess. 'And here,' she flung open an upright closet, 'here is a dress that you shall wear tonight.'

Then the brother and sister saw another unlikely thing. For in the closet were hung six or seven dresses of black velvet embroidered over a thick tracery of gold. Each dress was in a different size – some would fit buxom women, and some would fit skinny ones, and one was just right for the slender cripple girl. And each dress, moreover, was an exact replica of the dress the Countess wore.

'Madam,' whispered the girl, 'it is too fine. And surely –'

'Nonsense,' said the Countess. 'As for the resemblance to my own garment, you are quite correct. You must permit us our eccentricities, my dove, really you must. And what harm will it do for you to be a Countess for one night? I will even give you my jewels to go with the gown, even my black scarab to wear on your forehead.' Though the big man had set his sister on the fur stool before the bedchamber hearth, she shivered now, but she did not

267

argue. The Countess smiled, and smiled. 'I will even dress you myself.'

'No, lady,' said the girl's brother, 'I can do it. I'm used to helping her.' He came near to the Countess and spoke low. 'She does not like others to see her. She's shy, being crippled.'

'Oh, very well,' said the Countess, granting him a vast favor. 'But don't forget, your own chamber is next door to this, and there are red velvet suits laid out there, one of which will fit you. For if your amber sister is to be a Countess for our Festival of Midwinter's Eve, then you are to be a Count.'

'Why must that be?' asked the big man, hesitantly.

'Why not, pray?' inquired Mirromi. 'Come,' she added to her husband, who had begun to giggle again. 'Give master Quick your chain and your rings, and let us leave our guests their privacy. I shall be back to fetch you to supper in one half of an hour,' she murmured, putting Fedesha's jewelry into Quick's unprotesting wooden hand.

The Count and his lady adjourned outside and closed the heavy door. At the far end of the passage a flight of fifty steps led up into another room, hung this time with black silks and with a window of blue and cochineal glass – the eastern window of the Tertiary Tower.

The Countess drew aside a silk hanging on the wall to reveal two round spy holes equipped with magnifying lenses. By means of skilfully angled tubes and the strategic mirrors placed in them, these spy holes gave a view into the rich bedchamber Countess Mirromi had allotted the cripple girl. A similar tube, once Mirromi had twisted open its amplifying valves, rendered audible any conversation which took place in the room. The Countess and the Count applied their eyes to the lenses, looked and listened.

The girl and her brother, in drugged obedience, had already dressed themselves in the velvet reproductions of their hosts' clothing. Now Amber sat on the bed in an attitude of dejection. The brother, Quick, stood before the fire.

'I'm afraid,' said the girl. 'Could we not leave, before they come back? Such a great lady, but to act this strangely. Oh, I am afraid.'

'Yes,' said the brother. 'I don't care for it. Yet, perhaps, as they said, it's merely some prank, some jest to celebrate Midwinter's Eve – though the mighty are not usually so liberal to such as we. Then, again . . . if they mean us harm, we should not get far, I having to carry you. And though I am strong, I'm not fast, my sister, nor very clever. And suppose they have guards here after all, hidden somewhere? It is a large mansion. Who knows?'

The girl buried her face in her hands, and her shoulders shook. She whispered: 'Go without me then. I know I should slow you. I would rather suffer myself than see you hurt.'

The big man knelt by her and patted her with gentle awkwardness.

'Hush, don't cry. How could I leave you? You're all my life, little sister. Besides, truly, I believe I must remain. I think we may be under a spell.'

The black action of a large fly flickered over the rooms, the corridors, the staircases of the great house, the air vibrated with its buzzing. But the Count and Countess paid it little heed as they clad themselves in homespun and rags for supper.

Quick carried Amber into the hall, preceded by the Countess, who now wore, in sharp contrast to the finery of her guests, a shapeless gray gown, rough wooden shoes and knitted stockings. Her black hair was bound in a tattered scarf. Amber's hair glowed under the net of gems the Countess had confined it in, and the black jade scarab rested on her forehead.

A long table had been set near the hearth over the design of the zodiac. At one end of the table, two places had been laid with plate of silver and fine cut-glass goblets. Close to these were a variety of generous roasts, vegetables and hot pastries, piles of costly winter fruit, candies and sweetmeats, and many jugs and bottles of liquor. At the opposite end of the table were a couple of earthenware plates and mugs, a jar of beer and an ewer of water, a loaf of coarse black bread.

The Count, in laborer's garments, waved Quick to the elegant portion of the table, seated the Countess and himself before the earthenware dishes.

'Now, no protests,' said the Count. 'This is how it is. My wife and I are able to enjoy luxury on every other night of the year. On this one night, we choose to live humbly and let our guests play our parts, don our velvets and jewels, eat of our fare and sup our wine.'

269

The brother and sister sat down. They gazed uneasily at the rich food, the laden plates. Perhaps they were pondering, if all the servants were supposedly gone to the city, who it could be who had prepared this dinner. Surely not the Countess? Despite her improverished clothes, her hands were white and her nails dyed flawless crimson. The Countess broke off a piece of the coarse bread and ate it, drank some water. She did not require cooks to provide an elaborate meal. She could summon up others who could do as well as a human cook, and better.

'Eat, drink,' encouraged the Count. He rose, carved meat for the visitors, heaped their silver platters, poured them wine. There was no pearl earring in his ear now, just a small hole where it had been.

The brother and sister began to pick at their food.

The darting of a fly, the intermittent buzz it made, had become so familiar now, it was scarcely remarkable, like the ticking of a clock. Then, abruptly, the darting buzzing stopped.

The Countess glanced up, the Count paused over his mug of beer. An instant's silence in the wide and well lit hall.

The amber girl moaned, and shrank back in her chair.

Something was hopping on the table.

It hopped between the silver salt cellars, the gold cellars of spice. It hopped into the mound of fruit, setting the apples and the peaches rolling. It was like a warty, shiny, gray-green fruit itself. It hopped, this warty fruit, into the dish of the cripple girl, and its upraised round eyes, the color of yellow sourness, glittered and glared at her. It froze to the immobility of marble, still glaring.

'It's only a toad. A pathetic harmless toad,' said the Countess. 'Surely you are not afraid of a poor ugly toad?'

'Don't strike out at it,' added Count Fedesha, somewhat nervously, to the man he called Quick. But Quick had made no move at all. Seeing this, the Count elaborated: 'There is an old legend, isn't there, that in some cases a beast slain reproduces and multiplies itself? Tread on a fly and there are two flies. The skin of the dead toad lets out two more toads.'

The toad hopped from the girl's plate. It bounded on to the knee of Quick, and then away into the shadow beyond the hearth. They heard its croaking there, and presently from another place, and then another.

The Count quaffed down his beer. For an instant he had looked afraid, and he had lost much of his blandness. The Countess Mirromi, however, was calm, and regarded the brother and sister with satisfaction. Their faces had taken on the vacant stupid expression of people half-asleep. Though they had eaten hardly any of the food, the drugs she had mixed in it were powerful ones.

Mirromi left her chair and crossed to the tall candlebranch beside the hearth. Each candle was of fractionally differing length from its fellows; the shortest was burned out, others were scarcely begun: it was a means of telling time.

'How long?' asked Count Fedesha. He giggled, but his mouth was pale and dry in the black beard.

'A little longer,' said Mirromi. 'Though I think possibly the moment has come to give our friends their proper titles.'

'Ah, yes,' said Fedesha. He seemed to recover his spirits. He got to his feet, and lifted his mug of beer, toasting the listless guests. 'Here's health to you, Count and Countess.'

'Health, Count and Countess, and a happy life,' added Mirromi, raising her own mug of water.

Fedesha and Mirromi drank.

Quick spoke thickly and falteringly, peering through his myopic eyes, obviously trying to throw off the effects of Mirromi's drug – to no avail.

'Why name us so? Count and – Countess?'

'A whim,' said Mirromi.

'A foible,' said Fedesha.

From five or six separate parts of the hall, the toad croaked. The light gleamed fitfully on its knotty skin as it shuffled and hopped, now across the mosaic floor, now along the back of a chair.

'A piece more meat, Count?' Fedesha inquired.

'A plum, Countess?' Mirromi offered.

They both laughed this time.

'Do you have it to hand?' Fedesha asked his wife.

'In my sleeve. As always.'

'This is the last year,' Fedesha said. 'Then the trouble is done with.'

'What could defeat my magic?' Mirromi said. She smiled and patted his face. 'Foolish of you ever to doubt me.'

Fedesha glanced at the crippled girl, whose gaze had grown huge with a sort of glazed anguish.

271

'A pity, though . . .'

The croaking of the toad ceased.

Fedesha gripped his wife's arm.

Quick writhed mutely in his chair, and the girl Amber whimpered.

Between the table and the hearth, something darkening on the bearskin, not smoke, not shadow. Gradually a black dog came visible. It was thin as a stick, every bone showed through its hide. Its eyes were filmed yet burning, its tongue lolled. Its body was faintly iridescent, and where its spit dripped down it flamed and then vanished.

Fedesha shook and his eyes started. Mirromi's smile became more of a snarl.

The dog did not snarl, nor growl, nor make any sound. It moved by them, along the side of the table. It sniffed at the velvet gown of the crippled girl and at her brother's velvet cuff, and then it padded away and straight through the tapestried wall as if the wall were not there.

'Now!' cried Mirromi. There was a brittle triumph in her voice. She resumed her seat, and struck the table with her white hand. The brother and sister turned to her as if she mesmerized them. 'As it is festival night,' said Mirromi, 'we will tell you a story, most worthy Count and Countess. Are you ready? Good. The story concerns a *huzdra*, which, as you may or may not know, is a kind of curse invented by the primitive folk of the Eastlands.'

'A very effective curse,' Fedesha said. He shivered and licked his lips. 'Surprisingly so.'

'But to begin at the beginning,' Mirromi said, 'for we must make certain the Count and Countess understand everything.

'It was the chill dawn of Midwinter's Eve seven years ago. The sun was just coming up, when someone commenced knocking on the gates. Occasionally I leave my bed before dawn, for there are particular herbs that can be gathered only at sunrise and on selected days in order that they retain their potency. The porter, knowing I was about, soon brought me word that a desperate peasant girl was at the gate, begging for shelter and food, offering her service at any form of work in exchange. I instructed the porter to bring the wench to me, and this he did. She was a pitiful sight indeed, filthy and ragged, half dead of the cold and almost starved. She told me her name; it was some barbaric Eastlands foolishness. I called her 'Pebble' instead, for she was aptly as dirty, as uncared-for and as common as one. She was brought nourishment and wine. I foresaw a use for her, but did not reveal to her what it was to be, saying that she must consult my husband later. I could tell she was strong, this Pebble, despite her deprivations. She kissed my hands and feet and swore she would serve me till death, but she was not so tractable afterward.

'Now you must hear, dear Count and Countess, something of my husband and myself. I am of humble stock, though you would never guess it; my husband, whose title he has given you, master Quick, wed me for my beauty, and also for certain magic powers that I possess. Accordingly, I gained the title I have given you, mistress Amber, while by my powers, my husband became a deal wealthier and more influential than before, which was to our mutual pleasure. You should realize, this magic involves traffic and trade with demons, hobgoblins and elementals. These delightful creatures will do business willingly with humankind if they are summoned correctly and paid a fee. We had learned, my spouse and I, of an ancient treasure to the north; in order to gain access to it there was one infallible demon which could aid us. And the fee this demon demands is to drink the blood of a living maiden. You will understand, then, how opportune was the arrival of Pebble. None knew her, she was a stranger from the Eastlands, dull-witted, and a maid to boot. For our servants, they would dare tell no one – they respect my gifts too much for that. So it was arranged that Pebble's blood should entice the demon, and accordingly, at sunset, I took her to the Tertiary Tower, where everything was laid out in readiness. No sooner did the wretch learn her fate, than she began to scream and struggle. I subdued her, as I am able to do. The demon was called, answered, brought us what we wished to have, and took his payment gladly. A space before midnight, when all was finished, we instructed our menials to carry Pebble away. We thought her dead, as well we might, but somehow she had clung to life, and as the servants lifted her she opened her eyes, and staring at me and at my husband, she said: 'Fine Count and fine Countess, your fine food and your fine clothes and your fine spells shall avail you nothing. I have put my *huzdra* on you both. One year beyond this night you may take your ease. But next Midwinter's Eve, look for death, and for Hell after it.' Then she did die. We witnessed her

273

buried as midnight struck and thought ourselves rid of her.

'You may suppose,' went on Mirromi, 'her puny threat would be forgotten as the year passed, but this was not the case. As the months elapsed we found we brooded more and yet more upon Pebble's words. At length, a month before Midwinter's Eve should dawn again – the anniversary of Pebble's death – I conjured one up by my magic that is wise in curses, and questioned it. And thus we discovered the nature of a *huzdra*.

'The *huzdra* is effected through some personal item belonging to whoever lays the curse. It may be something as mundane as a shoe, a scarf, a ring. Though once *huzdra* is laid on it, it assumes weird attributes – the shoe runs on its own as if a foot were in it, the scarf wriggles like a snake, the ring grows large as a noose. The object of *huzdra* is ultimately to kill those on whom the curse has been set. It is a thing of antique Eastlands sorcery, and very strong, for it is always sealed with hate. It is difficult, even for one as well versed in magic as myself, to evade this curse, for in such an instance, even the most agile demons grow uneasy. They will advise, but may not intervene. In the east, *huzdra* is feared worse than the White Plague, by simpleton and mage alike.

'As my conjuration assured me, our first concern was to find which item of Pebble's belongings had become the *huzdra*. She had brought nothing with her to the gate, all she possessed had been her rags. My husband and I were forced to go by night to the spot where we had had the girl buried, dig up the grave, and search her body. It was not difficult to recognize the *huzdra*. Little remained in the earth that was distinguishable, except for one thing: a bracelet she had worn high on her forearm, hidden by her sleeve. It was very old, the bracelet, crudely fashioned, discolored by age and by lying in the ground. The band was black copper, with seven pendants of reddish, greenish stone or black stone, chipped and dirty. I brought the bracelet to the Tower, and recalled the elemental wise in such matters, and made it tell me all I must know, though it was afraid.

'The strength of Pebble's *huzdra* was sevenfold, because of its seven pendants. Even if we could thwart the curse on the first anniversary of her death, the *huzdra* would yet be activated six more years, seven in all, and each successive year the power of it would grow. However, though the seventh year, the seventh anniversary, would be the most terrible, it would also be the last.

After that, the strength of the *huzdra* was exhausted. Though who could expect to hold off such a bane for so long?'

Mirromi glanced aside at the time-telling candles by the hearth, and broke off the story to say, 'One moment, honored Count and Countess, with your indulgence.'

Then she and Fedesha rose from their chairs and withdrew across the hall to stand beneath a tapestry of gold and ruby thread.

The brother and sister, silent all this while, lay in their chairs like discarded dolls. Only their eyes blinked and strained, and their hands twitched.

There came a sound from the fire. A hissing, spurling sound. Out of the fire bowled a bone-white wheel. It was ten feet in diameter, and though it looked solid it had no substance. It passed straight through the table, it rolled once, twice, about the cripple girl and her brother. Flames gushed from its spokes. It hurtled away into nothing and sparks faded on the air.

Mirromi said to Fedesha: 'Success, as ever. The wheel has marked them out, and not us. We have won, and this the last year of the curse.'

'My wondrous witch-wife,' Fedesha said, kissing her hand, licking his lips, which had grown red and healthy once again.

'Now I will show them,' said Mirromi. She returned to the table, and sliding something from her arm beneath her sleeve, laid it before the brother and sister on the damask cloth.

It was a bracelet of black copper, with seven pendants of greenish, reddish or black stone, chipped, grimy and very old.

'Here is the *huzdra*,' said Mirromi. 'See the little figures? First the fly; he generally appears before the rest. Next, the toad; he usually comes second. There is the dog, tonight's third visitor. And see, there the fourth thing, the fiery wheel, though its spokes are clogged with dirt. These manifestations are warnings, heralds, preparations for the ultimate terror. Whatever else, this is the final omen, this tilted pitcher. You have not seen it yet, but you shall. It will appear, as it always does, when that candle there has burned out. Then we shall have had all the warnings, and only death need come. Death is represented by these last two figures on the bracelet. Observe closely, so you shall recognize them.'

It was hardest of all to make out these last figures of the bracelet. This was the seventh occasion Mirromi had displayed them, the seventh year that two travelers, brought here by magic and drugged by occult herbs, had peered down with horror scrawled on their stupefied faces, trying to see.

One figure was of a man. In his head and on his chest little glass scintillants winked like many eyes. The second figure was female, except that below her waist her body grew into a single coiled thing, like a worm.

'It was a clever *huzdra*,' said Mirromi. 'That the demon man and the demon woman should be part of it, two for two, a man and woman as my husband and I are man and woman. Clever of that wretched Pebble; it made the curse doubly powerful. But,' said Mirromi, 'as you notice, we live. I will tell you how we cheated the *huzdra*, and how we shall cheat it tonight, the seventh and last night it can seek us.

'By my peerless spells, I have drawn to this house, each Midwinter's Eve, two wanderers from the road. Some have been brash, some sly, some foolish, though none, I think, so innocent and so stupid as you, my doves. Really the curse, while being a mighty one, is also naive. It relies upon the fear of the victim, and on his ignorance.

'The canny elemental advised me well. Never destroy the object of the *huzdra*, for to destroy it doubles its vitality, unleashing its force from the earthly materials which form it and loosing them entirely into the spirit world, where they become invincible. Destroy the bracelet, and you could never be rid of its potency. Nor must you use violence against the apparitions – the buzzing fly, the croaking toad, the black dog. They cannot be harmed, but absorb fresh energy from every blow which is dealt them. No, let them roam freely, and cherish the *huzdra*.

'Now, the *huzdra* can only match whoever works it. Though Pebble's hate was ferocious, she was an imbecile. By employment of certain incantations, runes, auras, by dressing the two strangers in our garments and our jewels, by setting before them the riches of our house, our foods and wines, by addressing them by our titles of Count and Countess, we have made them into replicas of ourselves. When Pebble hated us, she hated only the symbols – velvet clothes, silver plate, a name. And thus it is that the *huzdra* and its hate fall similarly on the appearance, the effigy, the name. In six years, twelve strangers have taken our places, become our scapegoats, and the vengeance of the *huzdra*

276

has claimed them, and we have survived royally. It is a dreadful death that comes. There are screams and raucous cries, and when midnight strikes, the hour of Pebble's burial, and we are able to return safely into the chamber, we find our jewels scattered about, and otherwise merely clean bones. For sure, too, the curse has gained strength each year. The first year the apparitions were faint, the death very swift at its predestined time. But, as the years pass, the apparitions are more solid, appear for longer periods and in a different order, though always the wheel and the pitcher are the last. The two entities which bring death have no ability to kill until the exact moment when Pebble's curse was spoken – and do not arrive before, being powerless. But even here there is a change. The shrieks of agony in the locked room are more prolonged, the bones are more thoroughly picked and drained of marrow. This is the final year, when you, my pair of ducks, are to take our place and remove the *huzdra* for ever from our house and our lives. No doubt, it will be very awful. I even ask myself if they will leave your bones intact on this occasion.

'You may ponder why I have told you all this, and in such detail. You will understand when I say that I do it to inspire you with terror. For nothing lures the *huzdra* toward you so well as your absolute fear. And now,' added Mirromi to Fedesha, 'it's time we took our guests to their chamber.'

Up the great flights of steps to the Primary Tower, to the pitch-black, dank and windowless room, whose door of stone was opened only once a year to admit terror, and to contain terror, until the stroke of midnight should end it.

Up those flights, as once every Midwinter's Eve in the past six years, two strangers dressed in velvet were propelled, their eyes running and their limbs water. This year the girl seemed to have fainted. Fedesha carried her, she felt boneless already, and escaped strands of her amber hair trailed after them on the steps. The big man stumbled forward, his hands outstretched as if he were blind.

Up to the door, the key in the brass lock. The door opened.

On the black nothingness of the tower chamber a shining pitcher had formed, tilting slowly, slowly, until from its narrow lip poured a stream of thick, red, and smoking blood.

Fedesha flung the girl into the room, thrust the big man after her. As in the past six years, he banged the stone door shut, and Mirromi locked it.

As in the past six years, Fedesha and Mirromi held their breaths, waited.

As in the past six years, there came a broken wild screaming inside the locked chamber, and then a man's screams, deeper, and without pause.

Mirromi and Fedesha smiled.

Hand in hand, like two happy children, they went smiling down toward the hall, to wait for midnight, as in the past six years.

Word gets around, even in Hell.

For six years, the *huzdra* had been negated by the stroke of midnight because the components of *huzdra* believed its victims had been claimed, the curse accomplished. Yet, as each year progressed, the knowledge that Countess Mirromi and Count Fedesha still lived, and boasted of their guile, had roused the *huzdra* to reactivate itself again upon the next Midwinter's Eve.

A curse is not a thinking thing as such. Like the spear, it homes to its target when a marksman aims it. And yet, each year cheated, each following year rewoken, and each year *stronger*, some element of the *huzdra* began to reason. The warning apparitions of the curse began to rearrange themselves, to appear for longer periods, to deviate. There was no law which bound them to materialize only in an exact order, or for any exact period. Once the sun began to sink, they were free to manifest themselves as the instinct moved them. Nor were they bound to vanish at midnight; they had merely done so from the sense that the work was completed.

And yet the work had never been completed.

Somewhere the ghost of the Eastlands girl, cruelly nicknamed Pebble for her dirt and her common, uncared-for person, somewhere that ghost roared in its limbo, unsatisfied and unappeased.

At last, the notion came aware in the midst of the unthinking but oddly reasoning entity of the curse that what deprived it of its intended victims must be a scapegoat insertion of two others, as innocent and beguiled as Pebble had been.

This, the seventh year, which brought the *huzdra* to the climax of its power, brought it also the solution to the deception.

Mirromi's magic runes on the ancient dead trees by the

highway, registering two travelers journeying in any case toward the great house, selected no others, since the Countess had no requirement for more than two, a man and a woman, to enter her doors.

The travelers were like several others of the twelve who had gone before, poor and uneducated. They had much the same tale to tell, of the dead horse, the abandoned wagon, how no one had stopped to aid them. Yes, these two travelers were very like those who had gone before, except, perhaps, more pliable than they. And even in the bedchamber, having put on the fated velvet garments, they had spoken to each other in such a desolate, pathetic way. Almost as if they had known about the hidden lenses and the amplifying tube, known that the Count and Countess would listen and watch, and had wanted to convince the Count and Countess that all was going, for the seventh time, exactly to plan . . .

It was safe to return to the tower room after midnight had struck, absolutely safe.

The only occasion when it would not have been safe would have been if, by some extraordinary oversight, two flesh-and-blood scapegoats had not been left there after all.

Count Fedesha and Countess Mirromi returned a few minutes following the stroke. The Count carried a lamp, the better to inspect what lay about. Neither he nor his Countess was squeamish. They had been inflicting negligent torture and death on innumerable droves of men and women for sufficient years that raw bones were no trouble to them. Indeed, they were rather curious, rather intrigued, to observe this last scene of the doltish *huzdra*, this last proof of their triumph.

The stone door, unlocked, swung open.

The Countess gasped, the Count grunted.

For there, quite unharmed, were the brother and his crippled sister.

A couple of heartbeats, a couple of wild inner questionings.

Then the melting of the illusion of velvet clothes and of homespun, of gem and of poverty. Of humanity.

A brown man, seeing clearly now he was naked, not only through the two large eyes in his head, but out of the several glinting eyes in his breast, which blinked, and which opened and closed, and which finally focused with great intensity. And by him, no longer a cripple who could not walk, an amber-haired woman, who reared upright from the sinuous flexible column of a serpent's tail.

Now it was the brother and sister who were smiling, with sharp, sharp teeth, while they raised their long-nailed hands as if in welcome.

And the Count and the Countess began to scream.

Three Days

I have had some interests in reincarnation, and incidents similar to this do occur.

Men like Monsieur Laurent, I hope, are very few. Of all the many and dreadful evil characters I have written of, I consider him perhaps the worst. Can there be such things as clean evil and dirty evil? If so, he exemplifies the latter. For such, perhaps, there should not be lives, but a hell of flame indeed.

The house was tall, impressive, peeling, and seemed old before its time. The only attractive thing about it, to my eyes, was the dark-lidded glance of an attic, looking out of the slope of the roof, which such houses sometimes have. The attic eye seemed to say: There is something beautiful here, after all. Or, there *could* be something beautiful, if such a thing were allowed.

Below and before, a green haze of young chestnut trees lined the street, which gave on the Bois Palais. Behind, rising above the walled gardens, were the stepped roads and blue slate caps of distant Montmoulin over the river, with, as their apparent apex, the white dome of the Sacré. All this was of course very pleasant. Yet I never come into the area now without a sense of misgiving. That is due to the house, and to what took place there.

One felt nothing extravagant could ever have issued from such a proper dwelling. And one would have been wrong. My friend (I use the term indiscriminately) Charles Laurent had issued from it. He was at that season making something of a star of himself in the legal profession, and also by way of a series of books, fictionalized, witty, rather brilliant studies of past trials and case-histories. It was in the latter capacity, the literary side, that our paths crossed. I took to him, it was difficult not to. Handsome and informed was Laurent, an easy companion, and a very entertaining one. I suppose also, the best of us may agree it is no bad thing to be on good terms with a clever lawyer. I was at this time too attempting to become engaged, and the girl's father had suddenly begun to make my way stony. After a stormy, possibly hysterical scene, worthy of the opera, my love and I had agreed we should put some physical distance between us for a while, allowing Papa's temper to cool, and relying on letters and the connivance of the mother – who liked me, and was no less than a angel – to save our hopes, and prevent our mutually going mad. It is a shabby thing for a young man to be in love with one he may not have. It puts an end to a number of solaces, without replacing them. In short, life was not at its nicest. To take up with a Charles Laurent was the ideal solution.

To say our relationship was superficial would be a perfect description; its superficiality was the shining crown of it. We knew just enough of each other as might be helpful. For the rest, food, drink, music, the arts, such as these were ably sufficient to carry us across whole continents of hours into the small ones before dawn. So it was with slight surprise that I found one day he had invited me to dine at his home.

'And well your face may fall,' he said. 'Believe me, it will be a hideous evening, I can promise you that. I'm asking you selfishly, to relieve the tedium and horror. Not that anyone conceivably could.'

Not unnaturally, I inquired after details. He told me with swift disdain that his father observed yearly the anniversary of his mother's death.

'I'm a stranger,' I said. 'At such a function I could hardly be welcome.'

'We are *all* strangers. He hates every one of us. My brother, my sister. He hated my mother, too.' He spoke frivolously. That did not stop a slight frisson of interest from going over me. 'Now I have you, I see,' said Charles. 'The writer has been woken up and is scenting the air.'

'Not at all. But you never mentioned a brother, or a sister.'

'Semery won't be there. He never comes near the house on such occasions. Honorine lives there, as I do, and has no choice.'

'Honorine, your sister?'

'My sister. Poor plain pitiful creation of an unjust God.'

I confess I did not like his way of referring to her. If it were true, I felt he should have protected, not slandered her, with that able tongue of his, to loose acquaintances such as I. He saw me frowning and said, 'Don't be afraid, my friend. We shan't try to marry her off to you. I recall too well la bonne Anette.'

I frankly thought the entire dialogue would be forgotten, but not so. The next morning an embossed invitation was delivered. A couple of nights later I found myself under the chestnut trees before that tall, unprepossessing house, and presently inside, for good or ill.

I was uneasy, that was the least of it, but also I confess extremely curious. Charles had hit home with that remark about the writer in me waking up. What was I about to see at this annual wake? Images of the American writer Mr Poe trooped across my mind: an embalmed corpse, black wreaths, a vault, a creaking black-clad aristo with long tapering hands . . . Even the daughter had assumed some importance. I think I toyed with the picture of her playing an eastern harp.

Naturally, I was far out. The family, what there was of it, seemed familiarly normal. Monsieur Laurent was a wine-faced portly maître d'affaires. He looked me up and down, found me wanting (of course), greeted me and let me pass. He reminded me but too well of that other father I had to do with, Anette's, four miles to the west, and I felt an instant depression. There was also an uncle on the premises, who stammered and was not well dressed, two deaf and short-sighted old ladies whose connection I did not quite resolve, and a florid, limping servant. I began to feel I had come among a collection of the deaf, the dumb, the halt and the lame. Charles, obviously, was not to be numbered among these. Like a firework he had exploded from the dull genetic sink, as sometimes happens. The younger brother, Semery, who after all attended, was also an exception. Good-looking, he had a makeshift air; Charles and he hailed each other heartily as rival bandits, meeting unarmed in the hills. Semery was the 'ne'er-do-well' with which so many families attempt to equip themselves. Some twist of fortune, some strain of energy, had denied the role to Charles who, I felt, might have handled it better.

The sister came late down. She did not have a harp about her, but alas, everything Charles had said seemed a fact.

The sons perhaps had taken their looks from the dead mother we were supposed to be celebrating. Poor Honorine did not even favour her father. She was that sad combination of small bones and heavy flesh that seems to indicate some mistake has been made in assembly. She ate very little, and one knew instinctively that her dumpy form and puffy features were not the results of gluttony, or even appetite. She was not ugly, but that is all that can be said. Indeed, had she been ugly, she would have possessed a greater advantage than she did. For she was unmemorable. Her small eyes, whose colour I truly do, God forgive me, forget, were downcast. Her thin hair, drawn back into a false chignon that did not exactly match, made me actually miserable. We writers sometimes postulate future states of freedom for both sexes, regardless of physical advantage. Never had one seemed so necessary. Poor wretched girl.

That her father detested her was obvious, but – as Charles had told me – Monsieur Laurent cared little for any of them. The dire lucklessness of it was that, while his sons escaped or absconded, the daughter was trapped. She had no option but to wait out, as how many do, the death of the tyrant. He was hale and hearty. It would be a long wait. How did she propose to spend it? How did she spend her days as it was?

No doubt, my remarks on Monsieur Laurent sound unduly callous. Patently, they are coloured by hindsight, but I took against him immediately, and he against me, I am sure. Yes, he resembled my own reluctant intended-father-in-law, but there was more to it than that. Lest I do myself greater injustice than I must, I will hastily reproduce some of the conversation and the events of that first, really most unglittering, dinner party.

To begin with there was some sherry, or something rather like it, but very little talk. Monsieur Laurent maintained guard across the fireplace. Aside from snapping rudely a couple of times at the old ladies and the limping servant, he only stood eyeing us all, as if we were a squadron of raw troops foisted on him at the very eve of important hostilities. Annoyance, contempt and actual exasperation were mingled in that glance, which generously included us all. I found it irritating. He knew nothing of me, as yet, to warrant such an opinion. In the case of Charles, most fathers would have been proud. We were meanwhile talking *sotto voce* and Charles said, as if reading my thoughts, 'You can see what he thinks of me, go on, can't you?'

'I assume,' I said, 'that his expression is misleading.'

'Not at all. When I won my first case, he looked at me just that way. When I foolishly spoke of it the old wretch said to me, "The stupidity of other men doesn't make *you* clever." As for the first book – well, it was a success, and I recall we met on the stairs and he had a copy. I was stunned he'd even looked at it, and said so. At which he put the book in my hand as if I'd demanded it and replied, "I suppose you'll sell this rubbish, since the majority of the populace is dustbin-brained." '

Just then the food was ready and our host marched before us into the dining salon. No pretence was made of escort or invitation. Charles conducted the two elderly ladies. Semery idled through. I looked round to offer my arm to Mademoiselle Honorine, but she was making a great fuss over the discarded sherry goblets. I sensed too exactly the dreadful embarrassment of the unlovely, and left well alone.

Needless to say I wondered how on earth, and why on earth, Charles had procured me a place at this spectre's feast. I could only conclude that Monsieur Laurent's utter disgust with humanity *en masse* did not deign to distinguish between absence or arrival. Come or go as we would, we were a source of displeasure. Perhaps even, new specimens of the loathsome breed momentarily satisfied him, bringing him as they must the unassailable proof that nothing had altered, he was still quite right about us all.

'*Sit*,' rapped Monsieur Laurent, glaring around him.

Obedient as dogs, we sat.Some kind of entrée was served and a vintage inspected. Monsieur Laurent then looked directly at me. 'The wine isn't so good, but I expect you'll put up with it.' This, as if I were some destitute who had scrounged a place at the board. A number of retorts bolted into my mind, but I curbed them, smiled politely, and had thereafter a schoolboy urge to kick Charles' shins under the table.

Whether the wine was good or not good, after a glass or two, the demon father began noticeably to brighten. I was struck by the flash of his eye, and realized that generalized contempt was about to flower into malice. I am afraid only two thoughts occurred to me at that moment. One was I regret, that this was very intriguing. The other was concerned with wondering what *I* would do if he grossly insulted me. For I could sense, the way animals scent a coming storm, how the thunder was getting up. I reasoned though I was safe, being not such fun to attack as his own. He had not had time to learn my weaknesses and wants. While the rest of them – they had been his playground from birth.

Honorine – there was no attempt at fashionable order – sat three seats away from me, with Semery and an empty chair between. Behind Honorine, above the mahogany sideboard, a large framed photograph with black ribbon on it seemed to depict the dead wife and mother. My current angle prevented any perusal of this, but to it Monsieur Laurent now ordered our attention.

'That woman,' he said, 'was a very great nuisance while she lived. I drink, as you see, to her departure. Ah, what a nasty wicked sentiment. Correction, an honest one. Besides, she has taken her revenge. Look what she saddled me with. All of you.' There was a concerted dismal rustle round the table. One of the old ladies dabbed her face with a handkerchief, but one saw it was a sort of reflex. It was plainly not the only occasion all this had been voiced. I looked surreptitiously at Charles. He was a perfect blank, composed and cool. Small wonder he could keep his head in a courtroom after being raised to the tune of this!

Beside me, however, Semery either deliberately, or uncontrollably, acted out the role of foil by snarling: 'Cher Papa. Can't you leave anything in decent peace?'

'Ah, my little Semery,' said cher Papa, smiling at him now. 'You have toiled up from the slime of your slum to say this? And how is the painting going? Sell well, do you, my boy? You came to ask . . . now what was it for? Ah, yes. For money. And I told you I would think about it, but after all what use is it to give you cash?' (Semery had gone white. I could hardly believe what I was hearing or that Semery could have given such a faultless cue for his own public castigation. It was as if he had *had* to do it.) 'You squander everything. And have such slender talent. No, I really think after all, you must do without. Tighten your belt. Or you could return and live here. My doors are always open to you.'

'I'd rather die in the gutter –' shouted Semery.

'No you wouldn't. Or why are you here?'

286

'Not to ask anything from *you*, as you well know.'

'Begging from your brother Charles, then. This afternoon's most touching scene. Such a pity I disturbed you. But Charles isn't a fool with his money if he's a fool with everything else. You won't get it from him. And I promise you, you won't get it from me.'

Semery rose. An amazing change reshaped the monster's face. It grew rock-hard, petrified. But the eyes were filled by potent electricity. 'Down,' rasped the father. The room seemed to shake at the command. Semery sank back into his chair and his trembling hands knocked over his wine-glass. Seldom have I witnessed such a display of the casual, absolute power one mortal thing may obtain over another. I felt myself as if I had received a blow in the stomach, and yet what had actually happened? To set it out here does not convey anything.

'Yes, Semery,' Monsieur Laurent now said, 'you should return under my roof, and make your name painting portraits of this beautiful sister of yours.'

Having levelled one gun-emplacement with his unerring cannon, the warmonger had turned his fire from the rout of the wounded to the demolition of the totally helpless. I could not prevent myself glancing at her, in horrid fascination, to see how she took it. Of course, she too was well used to such treatment. She cowered, her eyes down, her terrible unmatched chignon shuddering. Yet the pose was native to her. It seemed almost comfortable. Her body sagged in the lines of abjection so readily, easily.

'Compliment your coiffeur, Honorine,' said Monsieur Laurent. 'These enemies of yours have succeeded in making of you, yet again, a fright. Heaven hurry the day,' he added, drinking his wine in greedy little sips, 'when this pretence at having hair is done. A daughter who is completely bald will be a novelty. All this scraping and combing and messing. Fate intended you as a catastrophe, my child. You should accept the part. Look at you, my dear graceless lump –' At this point I put out my hand and picked up my own glass. I believe I had every intention of throwing it at his head, anything to make him stop. But thank God Charles interrupted with a (perhaps faked) gargantuan sneeze. The father turned slowly, fire duly drawn. 'And you,' he said to the recovering Charles, 'our own money-lender, the wealthy gigolo of the book stalls. What have you to say for yourself?'

Charles shrugged. 'What I always say for myself. And what you also have just said. I've a private income and you don't frighten me. You could put me out on the street tomorrow –'

'I put none of my own tribe on to the street. They put themselves there. As for your books – what are they? You plagiarize and you steal, you botch and bungle –'

'And livres pour into my hands,' said Charles.

My God, I thought, at last the razor of the father's tongue was going into a block of cork. Naturally, the confounded devil knew it. This means of hurting pride no longer worked, it seemed, or at least without evidence. Talented, loved, an egoist and lucky, Charles was not a happy target. Unerringly, the father retraced his aim.

'A pity,' he said, 'your sister has taken to reading your works. Filling her hairless skull with more pre-digested idiocy than is already in there. She puts her hat on her bald head and goes puttering off to the bookshop to discuss your successes. And so has fallen into the clutches of madwomen.'

Strangely, Honorine was moved by this to murmur quickly, 'No, Father. No, you mustn't say they are –'

'*Mustn't*? Mustn't I? You keep your mouth closed, my fat balding daughter. I say what I know. Your great friends are lunatics, and I'm considering whether or not I shall approach the police –'

'Father!' The cry now was anguished.

'What? You think they're friends of yours, hah? You, with a friend? How should you have friends, you overweighted slug? Do you think they're captivated by your prettiness and charm? Eh? It's my money they like the idea of, and your insane acquaintances from the bookshop are a fine example of a certain animal known as a charlatan.'

'I won't go there ever again,' said Honorine.

This startled me. Her voice was altered when she spoke. It had grown deeper, it was definite. By agreeing with him she had, albeit temporarily, removed the bludgeon from his grasp.

At the time, the business of the 'charlatan madwomen' and the bookshop were only a facet of an astonishing whole. I paid no particular attention. Nor do I think much more needs to be said of the dinner. Dishes came in and were taken away, and those with the heart to eat (they were few) did so. There were many and various further sallies from the indefatigable Monsieur Laurent. None were aimed at me, though I was now primed and eager for them and, I imagine, slightly drunk. In my confusion, even as I sat there, I was already mentally composing a letter to Anette, telling her everything, word for word, of this unspeakable affair. (It is from the same letter, penned fresh and with the vivid recall of insomniac indignation at two the next morning, that I am able to quote fairly accurately what I have just set down.) I also wished him dead at least twenty times. I backed the big heavy body and the thick red face for an apoplexy, yet they looked more like ebullient good health.

As soon as I could, without augmenting the casualties of that war-zone of a table by slamming out halfway through the meal, I left. I bade Charles a brisk adieu, and walked by myself beside the river until well past midnight, powerlessly on the boil. As I told Anette, my entertaining friend was out of favour now completely. I reckoned never to see him again, for it was not simple, after the fact, to forgive him this exposure to alien filial strife. I even in a wild moment suspected some joke at my expense.

However, my having ignored two notes, and a subsequent attempted visit, he finally caught me up in the gardens of the Palais. There was an argument, at least on my side, but Charles was not to be fought with if he had no mind for it.

'I can only apologize,' he said, 'in broken accents. What more can I say?'

'Why in God's name did you make me a party to the bloody affair?'

'Well, frankly, my friend, because – though you'll find it hard to credit – he is kinder to us when there is some stranger present.'

I fell silent at that, moodily staring away between the green groves of trees. Now and then Anette and I had contrived a meeting here, and the gardens filled me always with a piercing sweet sadness that tended to override other emotions. I looked at Charles, who seemed genuinely contrite, and acknowledged there might be some logic in his statement. Although the idea of Monsieur Laurent *un*kind, if such was a version of his restraint, filled one with laughing horror.

So, if you will, ends the first act.

The second act commences with a scene or two going on offstage. There had been an improvement in my own fortunes, to wit, Anette's father's deeming it necessary, in the way of business, to travel to England. This brought an unexpected lustre to the summer. It also meant that I saw very little of Charles Laurent.

Then one morning, strolling through the covered market near the cathedral, I literally bumped into Semery, and, after the usual exchanges, was invited to an apartment above a chandlers, on the left bank of the river.

Here is the area of the Mountmoulin, the medieval hill of the windmill, the namesake of which is long since gone. One hears the place referred to frequently as being of a 'picturesque quaint squalor'. Certainly, the poor do live here, and the fallen angels of the bourgeoisie perch in the garrets and studios above the twisting cobbled lanes. The smell of cabbage soup and the good coffee even the poverty-stricken sometimes manage to get hold of hangs in the air, along with the marvellous inexpressible smell of the scarlet geraniums that explode over balconies and on walls above narrow stairways, and against a sky tangled with washing and pigeons.

We got up into a suitable attic studio, and found a table already laid with cheese and bread and fruit and wine, and a fawn cat at play with an apple. A very pretty girl came from behind a curtain. She ran to kiss Semery and, her arms still round him, turned to beam at me in just the way women in love so often do when another man comes on the scene. Even in her loose blouse, I could tell she was carrying a child. Little doubt of the father, thought her hand was ringless. I remembered, with a fleeting embarrassment, Semery's supposed request for money from his brother, or Monsieur Laurent. Here might be the excuse.

There were pictures, naturally, everywhere – on the walls, on easels, stacked up, or even horizontal on the floor for the cat to sit on.

'Courage,' said Semery, seeing me glance around, 'I won't try to sell anything to you. Not at all.' This in turn reflected Charles' avowal, on first inviting me to the gruesome dinner party, that they would not try to marry Honorine off to me. It was a little thing, but it made me conscious of some strange defensiveness inherent, and probably engendered in them by their disgusting father. 'But,' added Semery, 'look if you like.' 'Of course he will like,' said the girl mischievously. 'How nice the table is, Miou,' said Semery. 'Let's have some wine.'

A very pleasant couple of hours ensued. Semery was acting at least as fine a companion as Charles; I was charmed by Miou, and by the cat, and the simple luncheon was appetizing. As for the art – I am no critic, but suppose I have some slight knowledge. While not being in the first startling rank of original genius, Semery's work seemed bright with talent. It had enormous energy, was attractive, sometimes lush, yet never too easy. Particularly, I liked two or three unusual night scenes of the city, one astonishingly lit by a flight of birds escaping from some baskets and streaming over a lamp-strung bridge.

'Yes,' he said, coming to my side, 'I call that one *Honorine*.' I was at a loss to reply. 'I don't mean to make you uncomfortable,' he said. 'But you've been bloodied, after all. You were there the last time I was.'

'Hush, Semery,' said Miou, who was rocking the cat in an armchair, practising for her baby. 'Talking of *him* makes you sick and gives you migraine.'

'True,' said Semery. He refilled our glasses with wine. 'But I can talk of Honorine? Yes? No? But I must. That poor little sack of sadness. If there were any money, I'd take her in with me, though God knows she bores me to despair. Our dear father, you understand, has stamped and trampled all the life from her. She can no longer talk. She only answers questions. So you say to her, Would you care to do this? And you get in return, Oh yes, if *you* wish. And she drops things. And she stumbles when she walks even when there's nothing to stumble over. However,' he said, with a boy's fierceness, 'there was one service I think I did her. I first took her to the bookshop on the rue Danton. And so introduced her to the three witches.'

Miou began to sing a street song, quietly but firmly disowning us.

'That's the bookshop your father objected to? And the witches?'

'Well, three old ladies, in particular one, very grey and thin, read the Tarot there in the back room. And sometimes, when the moon is full, work the planchette of a ouija board.'

'And Honorine –'

'Honorine attended a session or two. She wouldn't reveal the results, but you could tell she enjoyed every moment. When you saw her after, her cheeks would be flushed, her eyes had a light in them – Unfortunately that limping gargoyle who serves mon père found out about it all and duly informed. Now Honorine's one poor pitiful pleasure is ended. Unless she can somehow evade the spies, and our confounded father –'

'Sur la chatte, le chat,
Et sur la reine le roi . . .'

naughtily sang Miou to the cat-baby.

'On the other hand,' Semery added, now with great nonchalance, 'I did visit the shop today and one of the eldritch sisters – good lord, I must paint them – no rush, they're each about three hundred years old and will outlive us all – well, Miou-who-has-stopped-singing-and-is-all-ears-and-eyes, well, one of them gave me a note to give to Honorine. Something the spirit guides had revealed which my sister apparently desired to know –' And from his jacket, Semery produced a piece of paper, unsealed, merely folded in the middle, which he held aloft, quizzically. 'I wonder what it can be?'

'You shouldn't have brought it here,' said Miou. She crossed herself between fawn paws. 'Magic. Ghosts.'

'Where else, then? Papa is out tomorrow afternoon and I can take it to the house. But I could hardly do so today, could I now? One foot on the threshold, and he'd have seized me in his jaws –'

'Well,' said Miou. 'Put it away somewhere.'

'Don't you think I should read it? Secret communications to my little sister . . .' He looked back at me. 'Actually, I did. Here, what do you make of this?'

And he opened the paper and put it in my hand.

I admit, I was curious. There seemed no harm in it, and I have always had a quiet disrespect for 'supernatural' things.

On the paper from the mysterious bookshop were these words as follows:

As we have told you, she is to be found as a minor character in some of the history books, and there has also been at least one novel written about her. The name is correct, Lucie Belmains. She did indeed die as a result of hanging herself. The date of her death is the morning of 8 April 1760.

'Fascinating, isn't it?' said Semery. 'What does it mean? Who is Lucie Belmains?'

Miou and the cat were already peering between our shoulders at the paper.

'Lucie Belmains,' said Miou, 'was a minor aristocrat, very beautiful and very wicked. She would drink and ride a horse and swear better – or worse – than a man. She was the mistress of several princes and ducs. She once dressed as a bandit and waylaid the king on some road, and was his mistress, too, perhaps, till she became bored with all the riches he lavished on her. Then she fell in love with a man five years her junior. He loved her too, to distraction, and when he was killed in a duel over her, Lucie gave a great party, like a Roman empress, and in the morning she hanged herself like Antigone from a crimson cord.'

Semery and I stood amazed until Miou stopped, breathless and in triumph.

'It seems,' said Semery then, 'there is indeed one novel, and you have read it.'

'Yes. When I was a little girl,' said Miou, all of seventeen now. 'I remember my sister and I read the book aloud to each other when we were supposed to be asleep. And how we giggled. And we dressed up in lace curtains and our mother's hats and raised glasses of water pretending they were champagne and said: I am Lucie and you are my slave! And fought like cats because neither of us would *be* a slave. And then one day Adèle hung her doll up by the neck from a red ribbon and we had a funeral party. Maman found us and we were both beaten.'

'Quite right. These are most corrupting activities for a future wife of France's leading painter, and the mother of his heir.' At which Miou smiled and laid her head on his shoulder. 'But even so,' said Semery, stroking her hair, 'what has all this got to do with Honorine?'

I said, 'She's making a study of this woman, or the period?'

'No. She has no interests any more.'

Later, towards evening, we strolled along the river bank. The levelling rays of the sun flashed over the water. I had arranged to buy the picture of the escaping birds for Anette. I knew she would like it, as indeed she did – we have it still, and since

Semery's name is now not unknown, it is worth rather a deal more than I paid for it. But there was some argument with Semery at the time, who thought I was patronizing him, or trying to pay for my luncheon. Thank God, all that had been settled, however, by the hour we emerged on the street, Miou in her light shawl and straw bonnet with cherries. When we reached the Pont Nouveau and I was about to cross over, Semery said to me, 'You see, that business with the paper – belle Lucie Belmains. Something about it worries me. Perhaps I shouldn't let Honorine have it. Would that be dishonourable?'

'Yes.'

'Or prudent?'

'Maybe that too. But as you don't know –'

'I think perhaps I do. The purpose of the witches' ouija has often to do with reincarnation – the passage of the soul through many lives and many bodies.'

We had all paused in mutual revelation.

'Do you mean your sister is being told she lived a previous life in which . . .'

'In which she was beautiful and notorious, kings slobbered at her feet, and duels were organized for her favours.'

We looked at the river, the womb and fount of the city, glittering with sun, all sequins, which on the dark days of winter seems like lead.

'Well,' Semery said at last, 'why not? If it makes her happy for a moment. If it gives her something nice to think about. There's nothing now. What has she got? What can she hope to have? If she can say to herself, just one time in every day, *once* I was beautiful, *once* I was free, and crazy and lavish and adored, and loved.'

I looked at him. His eyes were wet, and he was pale, as if at the onset of a headache. Impulsively I clasped his hand.

'Why not?' I said. 'Yes, Semery, why *not*?'

Miou let me kiss her blossomy cheek as a reward.

I went over the bridge with the strangest feeling on me imaginable. I find no name for it even now. It seemed for a moment I had glimpsed the rickety façade of all things and the boundless restless terrible truth beyond. But it faded, and I was glad of it.

★ ★ ★

As the glorious summer drew to its close, intimations of winter and discontent appeared. The birds and golden leaves began to be displaced by emptiness in the trees of the Bois; Anette's father returned, foul-tempered, and shut his house like a castle under siege against all comers, particularly one.

It was nearly three months since my chance meeting with Semery. We had met deliberately a couple of times since: I had even been invited to his wedding, the thought of which now made me rather melancholy. As for Charles Laurent, I was sitting at a café table one morning, curiously enough reading a review of his latest book – as usual a success – when I happened to look up and saw two women seating themselves a few tables away. I was struck at once by a sense of confusion, such as comes when one is accosted by an old acquaintance whose name one forgets. But it was not that a name had been forgotten, for frankly I was not familiar with either of these women. It must be, then, that they put me in mind of others with whom I was. Because of this, I studied them surreptitiously over my newspaper.

The nearer woman, with her back to me now, was apparently a maid or companion, and a withered specimen at that. She seemed ill at ease, full of humble, insistent protestation. No, I did not know her at all. The other, who sat facing me, was not particularly remarkable. Not tall, quite slim, and plainly dressed, her fine brown hair had been cut daringly short and she was hatless. Two little silver earrings flickered attractively in her ear-lobes. That was all. Her skin was sallow, her features ordinary. Then the waiter came and I was struck again, this time by a quality of fearlessness, *boldness*, out of all proportion to what she did, which was merely to order a pot of chocolate. There was something gallant in this minor action, such as you sometimes find in invalids taking their first convalescent stroll, or the blind listening to music.

Quite suddenly I realized who she was. It was the graceful bravery, though I had never seen her exhibit it previously, that gave her away. Honorine, of course.

I resolved immediately I would not go over. I had no real wish to, heaven knows. Memories of her wounded social clumsiness did not inspire me. I could only be a ghastly reminder of a hideous event. Let her enjoy her chocolate in peace, while I stayed here, keeping stealthy watch from my covert of news-paper.

So I kept watch, true to my profession, taking rapid mental notes the while. Surely, she was not as I recalled. It was small wonder I had not recognized her at once. She had lost a great deal of weight, yet here she sat eating gâteau, drinking chocolate, with the accustomed appetite of a famished child. And there truly was about her a gracefulness, of gesture, of attitude. And a strange air of laughter, mischievous and essentially womanly, that despite myself began to entice me to her vicinity. In the end I gave in, rose, walked across and stood before her.

'Mademoiselle Laurent. Can I hope you remember me?'

Her eyes came up. Those eyes not large nor bright – but they were altered. They shone, they were alive – The oddest thing happened now. The loud blush of shyness, which one might have expected, rushed over her face. It was the order of blush well known to the adolescent, which makes physically uncomfortable with its heat, the drumming in the ears, the feeling the brain may explode under its pressure. All is instant panic and surrender to panic. What is there to be said or done when such a mark of shame is branded on one's forehead? But the eyes of Honorine Laurent did not fall. She drew in a long breath and said, calmly, as if blood and body did not belong to each other, 'Why, monsieur, of course I remember you. My brother's friend. Please, will you sit down? We have greedily eaten all the cake, but there's some chocolate left.' And she smiled. As she did so the red blush went out, defeated. Her smile was open, friendly, not afraid – nor false. And her eyes sparkled so they were pretty, just as the smile was pretty. One writes of auras. Honorine had just such an aura. I knew in that moment that I was in the presence of a woman who found her own lack of beauty no disadvantage, who therefore would not use pain or sullenness as a weapon, who believed that in the end she herself was all that she required, although others were quietly welcomed should they come close to warm themselves in the light. In short the look of a confident woman, a woman who has known great love, and awaits, without impatience or aggression, some future, unhurried, certain joy.

As if I had been hypnotized, I drew out a chair and sat down. I had only just breakfasted, but I drank the chocolate which was poured for me in a daze. Presently the withered lady companion, fretting like a horse for hay, was thankfully dispatched to collect some cotton, and arm in arm Mademoiselle Honorine and I turned towards the gravelled paths of the Bois Palais. I had offered to see her to her door, and she had said, 'Yes, do. Charles is home in a filthy temper – one bad review, I think, of his excellent book. He'll be delighted to see you. And my father is . . . out.' And there was that mischief again. She did not then hate Monsieur Laurent, this elfin woman with her slim hand so lightly through my arm. She did not hate me for being witness to his humiliation of her. And she was used to escorts, she was used to friends.

I recall she asked me about Anette, very graciously and tactfully, and abruptly all my cares came flooding out in a torrent of words that astonished me, so in the end we sat down by the fountain with the nymphs as I made my complaints to life and heaven. Sometimes Honorine patted my arm gently. 'Oh, yes,' she said, 'ah, no?' with such unflurried kindness and sympathy – *she* with all her woes, so tender towards mine – and at the finish I remember too, she said, 'You have a sound literary reputation and I would say your prospects are fine. Besides, you and she love each other. Could you perhaps,' and those eyes of hers flashed like her earrings, like the summer river, 'run away together?' I realized, even at the time, that this last piece of advice came straight from the idiomatic guide-book of Lucie Belmains.

For that, naturally, was the one I had beside me, there on that bench: Lucie Belmains, who had died on the eighth of April, 1760. Lucie Belmains, but at her softest, sweetest – who knew love, and love's fulfilment, and touched my hand from her greater knowledge, ready to listen, and to reassure me. Even to suggest a madcap means of how to win the age-old game. The means *she*, more daring than I, might have taken.

Why not? Semery had said. Why not let that poor little dumpy bundle of a sister, that sack of sadness, creation of an unjust God, think of some better chance she had been given, once, if it could make her glad? And, *Why not?* I had magnanimously echoed. My God, why not indeed, if this exquisite person was to be the result . . . No, I did not believe in her reincarnation. But her *alteration – this* I believed. How could I avoid belief? The living proof sat with limpid laughing eyes beside me. As tyrants are changed by faith to flawless saints, so faith of her own kind had changed this human failure to a glowing being. There was a loveliness about her, yes, loveliness. Some latent charm, extant in her brothers, formerly lost in her, had evolved and possessed her, perfectly. And that smile, those eyes – And her walk. Her carriage. Years have gone by since that day, to dim the vista. I loved Anette then, I love her still, and no woman in the world, in my eyes, can equal Anette. And yet I look back to this Honorine I had the happiness to find that far off morning, and I must set down the truth as it seemed to me then, and seems to me now, older, wiser and less innocent as I am. I have never, save for my wife, met any woman who enchanted me so thoroughly. For she was beautiful. Her beauty lay all around us on the air. And even if I did not credit the transference of the soul, yet the soul I did credit. And it was the soul of Honorine that brought the loveliness and the beauty and the enchantment. For you see, she was then completely those things so few of us ever are, and if we are, so briefly: at peace, joyful, *sure*.

We reached the house, that dire house, and even this seemed less awful by her light. She was no longer afraid of it. She went up the steps and beckoned me in as if I might be comfortable there, and so I, too, felt no foreboding.

Charles was in the drawing room and jumped up when he saw me out of a snowfall of papers. Having brought us together, she was gone. I stared after her, and then at the closed door. Presently, Charles left off talking of his book, and said, 'Well, what do you think of *her*?'

She had made me skittish, too. I said, no doubt rudely, 'This is not the same sister.'

Charles nodded vigorously. 'It can't be, can it? Isn't she a jewel?' He was proud of her. 'If she keeps this up, we'll get her married to a rich potentate in half a year. You've seen Semery, and know the cause, I understand?'

'Yes.'

He gazed at me, and said, mock-seriously, 'Of course, it's a form of madness. If she killed someone, I could get her off on a plea of this. My client reckons she is actually a lady who is dead.'

'Surely, she reckons she has *been*, not is, Lucie Belmains.'

'Hair-splitting worthy of the bar. But it's a miracle. If she's gone a little mad, so nicely, why not?'

And thus the third culpable party added his careless *why not?* to Semery's and mine.

'But does she,' I said, 'know that you –'

'She knows Semery and I – though not you, cher ami – are in on it. But she doesn't review the matter with us, nor we with her. Then again, considering the extravagance of the idea, not to mention results, she's very serene about it all. I don't think she's even read anything, no history of this woman. Save the smallest outline in some encyclopaedia. On the other hand I suspect her of writing about her feelings. I gather a diary has been started. But she only revealed that to me because I caught sight of the article on her vanité. She's said nothing else. After all, she knows we're a bunch of vile sceptics. As for Father – well, no whisper must reach *his* ears. And you can guess, all this of hers has thrown him off balance. She eats more and grows more slight, she cuts off her hair and buys earrings. But you should see her with him. Stay and lunch with us and you will.'

The prospect of encountering Monsieur Laurent again brought me to with a jolt.

'Unfortunately, I must be elsewhere.'

'And anywhere but here? Well, you'll be missing a treat. And by the way, have you seen what this devil in the *Journal* has the wretched audacity to say about my book –?'

Half an hour later, just as I got out into the hall, the limping servant hobbled by me and flung open the street door. And there stood Monsieur Laurent, his horrible puce face thrust forward, seeing me at once, before Charles and all things else. I felt like a seven year old boy caught stealing fruit in someone's orchard. I had been so determined to avoid the monster. Nor had I heard any summons to warn me of this collision; the sinister limper seemed to have known of his master's arrival by telepathic means alone.

'Good day,' said the maître to me, advancing into his domain. 'Hoping for lunch?'

I writhed to utter as I wanted, but did not.

'No, monsieur. I am lunching with friends.'

'I thought my plagiarist son was your friend. Or have you grown wise to him, seen through him? I note,' he added, directing his attention now to Charles, 'one critic at least has had the wit to penetrate your sham nonsense. I must send him my congratulations.'

Charles, touchy over the review (for which his father must truly have scoured the journals), was plainly for once caught on the raw spot. Without looking at him, I saw his anger reflected in the momentary pleasure of Monsieur Laurent's little eyes.

'And where's your beauteous sister? I've some news for her.'

'Here I am,' said a voice from the stairs.

Monsieur Laurent gave vent to that toneless noisy amusement generally called a guffaw. 'Yes, there you are. What plenteous abundance of hair! Where is it? Have I gone blind? Do you still go out on the street like that, and make yourself a laughing stock?'

Turned to stone, my eyes only on the shut front door, I waited. And I heard her gentle voice say, casually, light as down, 'Yes, Papa, I'm afraid I do.'

'You silly sheep. Look at you. Well, I suppose it's generous of you to give everyone, complete strangers, such a good laugh. But do I permit you to draw money to buy earrings, and make yourself resemble a circus monkey?'

'No, Papa, the earrings were purchased from the small allowance Mother left me. But if they worry you, I'll take them off.'

'Worry me? *You* worry me. You brainless thing, flapping about the house, scribbling, mooning. What's wrong with you?'

'I am very well, thank you, Papa.'

'That damnable fool, your female parent, what a curse she left me. A snivelling profligate dunce and a literary jackal for sons. An idiot daughter.'

She was down the stairs now, I heard the rustle of her gown. She seemed to bring a coolness with her, a freshness, like open air, escape from the trap.

She said, 'Come and see the new sherry, Papa. I took your advice on the business of wines and have been trying to improve my knowledge. I'd like you to taste this latest bottle and see what you think.'

'If you chose the stuff, it must be worthless muck,' said this charming father.

'Not necessarily,' replied Honorine, for all the world as if she were talking to a sane and rational human being instead of to a thing from the Pit. 'I've tried, in my choice, to apply all you told

300

me the other day. But if you think the sherry is poor and I'm mistaken again, of course I shall want you to correct me. How can I benefit from your superior understanding in these matters, if you're lenient?'

What could he say, the beast? She had him, as seldom have I heard any so had. What had gone on – I can only conclude she had begun to take an interest in the ordering of the cellar, as La Belmains would certainly have done, and Monsieur, true to himself as always, had insulted her and attempted to belittle her over it, as over all else. Whereupon she must have assumed the attitude that she was being given an altruistic lesson for her own benefit, which notion she here continued. I have done just as you said, she informed him now. But if I am wrong – for naturally, I do not for a moment deny you are more clever than I am – you must let me know. And *do* be as harsh, as discourteous as you can be. I shall regard it as a mark of your concern and patronage. My God! I nearly laughed aloud. Whatever revolting abuse he threw at her now, came with her awarded licence. She would sit meekly before him, nodding as he ranted, presently thanking him for the tutorial. I was, despite everything, after all tempted to stay for lunch.

I compromised then, and indicated to Charles I would remain long enough to try the new sherry. And when the monster eyed me and made some remark about there being no luckier club for a minor writer than the free one of somebody else's house, I snatched a leaf from her book, grinned wildly at him, and cried, 'And such an entertaining club, too.'

It goes without saying he hated the sherry, which was a discerning one. But he said not much about it, save it was ditchwater. Honorine promised to bear this in mind. It was at this point that he recollected the news he wanted to tell her.

'Your hags of the Tarot have gone,' he said. 'Did you know? An end to clandestine sorties to the bookshop and table-tappings at my expense. Perhaps an end to the silliness you've been parading these last months, eh?'

'Ever since you showed such displeasure,' said Honorine placidly, 'I've not visited the shop.'

'No. But things have come here from there. From your faker parasites. Bits of paper brought by your ugly maid. Or by dear Semery when I'm out – you thought I wasn't aware? There's not much I miss. I've read some of these secret notes, billets-doux. Let me see. What did they say?'

We had all turned very silent. Honorine was pale and she put down her glass. From the erratic glitter of those delightful earrings of hers I could learn the quick erratic motion of her pulse.

Monsieur Laurent made a great drama over recalling. He, like the soulless evil he was, had sound instincts for a victim's shrinking and fear. Yet, if he had got hold of any communications from Honorine's three witches, it seemed to me they would probably mean nothing to him. His was a sly mind, but not an intellectual slyness. He pulled the wings from insects to agonize them and prevent their flight, not to study the complexity of their pain and flightlessness. But the information of the ouija board, ridiculous as it might be, was also intensely personal. He had, no doubt, always been in the habit of opening his children's private correspondence, and taunting them with its closest passages.

Eventually, his head tilted back in a sort of cold dry ecstasy, he announced: 'Lucie Belmains. Born at Troy-la-Dianne in April 1729. Hanged dead on April eighth 1760. Now do I quote that as it should be? Hah? And do I have *this* right – that you, my dollop of dough, unlovely, loveless, hopeless wreck that you are, are the reborn Lucie, so beautiful, kings paid ransoms for her company, and duels were fought to the death?'

There was a long terrible pause, with no noises in it save a patter of leafy rain on to the road outside.

I did not look at her. I do not know how she seemed, but I can conjure it. Who needs to be told? This was her sacrement, holy, and hidden. And now he had it in his fangs, mauling and maiming it, before us all. He had only been waiting, only *seeming* muzzled. But how could he be? All the servants were in his thrall. And her diary, maybe he had even got a grip on that, this savage rabid dog. Yes, so he must have done, to come at the roots of her dream, the beautiful, abnormal structure that had made bearable her life. But it was not to be bearable. *He* could not bear that. She should not spring up from the crushing. He would pile on another weight.

I suppose seconds went by, no more, while I thought this, and suffered for her, and yearned again to kill him.

Then she spoke, and my head cleared of the black cloud,

because her voice was steady – self-possessed. She had made a virtue of passivity. She gave no resistance now, since it would only lead the torturer on. She said, 'Yes, Papa. Isn't it absurd? For me to imagine, even for an instant, I might have been such a person. But you seem to have discovered that I do imagine it. And I do. While, truly, thinking it every bit as unlikely and preposterous as you do yourself.'

The cold ecstasy left him at that. Temper came instead. For a moment I thought he would strike her, but physical blows were not what he enjoyed.

'And what gives you to think such errant twaddle? This salivatory drivel from what? A *ouija board?* Fakers and schemers – they take your money – *my* money – and tell you anything you like to hear.'

'No, Father. They never asked a sou from me.'

'So you say. You *say*. But no doubt you make donations? Eh? And you've done their dubious reputation good, I expect, babbling to those you know of the *accomplishments* of this hocus-pocus. Lucie Belmains. *Lucie Belmains*. Does she even exist? Tell me that, you dunce. You'd swallow anything to make you out not the clod you are.'

I could hold myself no longer. I regret it, but I think in the long term it made no difference. He was on the trail, this bloody dog. He would have found it all at length, whatever was done or said or omitted.

'Monsieur. Lucie Belmains most decidedly did exist. I'm surprised, sir, with your exceptional bent for knowing everything and missing nothing, that you've never heard of her.'

'*Ah,*' he said, turning his gaze on me. 'So we're to be paid for our sherry with information. This is not,' he said, 'your concern. You may leave my house.' And he smiled.

'I can think of nowhere, off-hand, I could leave with greater pleasure.'

'Brave words for a sponger,' he said. 'Or did you steal something while my back was turned?'

'In the sight of God!' shouted Charles.

But I, at the reckless, heedless spur of immaturity, answered, 'Steal from you, monsieur? I'd be more fastidious.'

'Would you?' he said. 'From Anette Dupleys, then, that fine plump dowry of hers and her property in the south that goes with it. Indeed, a much juicier theft than anything the poor Laurents could offer you.'

It seems he had done me the honour of finding out something about my circumstances, also. And what he had found out, of course, was the thing set to cut me to the bone. I forget what I said or anything at all, until I got out, burning as if in flames and in an icy sweat, on to the street. Unfortunately, whatever I did in my passion, I did not seize a fire iron and murder him.

Charles came flying after me and grabbed my shoulder as I reached the Bois.

'In God's name – what can I say – Oh my God – Forgive me.'

I had chilled in the fire-following ice by then and said stiffly, 'There's nothing to forgive you. I stayed when I was aware I should not. As for Anette's money, who doesn't know? That is all the argument between her father and myself. I am a fortune-hunter. Naturally.'

We quarrelled about all this for a while, aimless and appalled. Finally I accused him of leaving Honorine to face horror alone. 'No, no,' he said, 'it was she sent me after you. She was quite calm still. He hasn't broken her. I thought he had. But she's talking to him so delicately, saying yes, she agrees with every-thing he says, but there it is.'

I thought of her grey face. I said, 'Now he has the name of her hopes in front of him, he'll go on until he has destroyed them all.'

'How? She believes exactly what her witch-ladies told her. He can't touch that.'

'He'll find some way,' I said.

As I walked alone back along the leaf-lit paths I had travelled with Honorine, through the sombre dusk of a coming storm, I knew my premonition was a true one.

The week before Semery's wedding to Miou, the two brothers and I dined in a good restaurant on the Boulevard du Pays. Charles seemed vaguely troubled at the outset, but he neither explained nor made a burden of it, the wine flowed, and soon enough there were no troubles in the world.

I judge it was about midnight when a written message was brought to Charles at the table. He read it, and went very white.

'What?' said Semery. But a sense of dread and dismay had passed unsounded between them, not by any mystical means, but from old habit, a boyhood terror that came back whenever some dark shadow proceeded from their father.

I put down my glass and sat in silence.

Presently, Charles covered his eyes with his hand.

'We must go to the house,' he said.

'Very well,' said Semery, his bright tipsiness all gone. 'But why?'

Charles took his hand from his eyes. He looked at me.

'This isn't your affair. There's no need for you to be caught up in it.'

'If you prefer,' I said. It had had echoes of his father's words in showing me the door.

'No, no, I don't mean to offend you – Oh my God, my God.' He stumbled to his feet and the chair clattered over. He did not even seem to see the obstacle as he avoided it.

In a few minutes we were out in the autumn night, still without an answer. Only a pall of black disaster hung about us, sure as the smell of death. It needed no name. In some degree, each of us knew.

I think he told us on the way to the house. I am not positive. It may have been on the very threshold. Or perhaps he did not tell us at all, was not required to. It seems to me now he never did say, in words. Yet I remember later, when we were in a room downstairs, lighted only by a lamp, and cold, he took up the open book left lying on a table, and directed me to the place. I remember I read it and for a moment it made no sense, and then I fathomed the sense and my heart sank through me, leaden and afraid, for her sake.

To piece it together now will, perhaps, be better. What use is there, after all, to hesitate? As I had known, Monsieur Laurent must destroy her dream, and so he had, by the very simple expedient of doing what she had not. Honorine had taken her enlightenment almost solely from her ladies of the bookshop. What she had already read of Lucie Belmains had not been, presumably, specific in the matter of dates.

Honorine had trusted her mediums implicitly. She had believed what she had been told. Every fragment of it. But every fragment rested on every other. It was not a house of stone, not even of cards, but glass, that whole harmless shining starry edifice, and it shattered at a tiny mortal blow. How gratified he must have been, that demon, the weapon so easily come by, and so sharp.

They had told her, I had myself witnessed it, that Honorine's former self, her belle Lucie, had hanged herself, and died on the eighth of April 1760. But if they were wrong in this, then the entire codex must be mistaken, a lie. And so it was proved. For this date was in error. Lucie Belmains, as history has recorded, as that very book Charles handed to me had recorded, had hanged herself on the morning of the fifth of April, and being cut down, was buried on the evening of the seventh, for the summer was forward that year. Of the eighth of April there was, and needed to be, no mention.

Three days out. Only that. Three days.

Monsieur Laurent had been at pains to tell her, and to show her, no doubt. I can envisage the scene that passed between them, father and daughter, there in that dank fireless room, as *we* dined on the Boulevard du Pays. I have seen it often in my mind's eye, and listened to it over and over in those half dreams that come between sleep and waking when one is unhappy or very tired.

So she was rid of her fantasy and her madness. So he gave her back the single and only life she had, that dreary, pointless, loathing life, and her own former self, he gave her that, too. He widowed her of beauty and of love, love which had been, love which might yet come, if not as Honorine then in some future when she might be born once more another Lucie. And worse than all that, he throttled the sweet dignity and charm of what she was becoming, had become. God damn him. I do not ask for lives, but for a hell of fire and shrieking where he may burn and scream for all eternity.

After he had instructed her, Monsieur Laurent went out to his own gentlemen's club. And Honorine, climbing up to that attic room whose window I had first admired, swallowed a dose of some poison kept for rats. She died in convulsions about an hour after we arrived.

She had written none of those parting notes so common in such cases. I do not think her wish was to instill in anyone feelings of guilt. In her father, the prime offender, it would have been impossible. I gather, though I never met him again, that his attitude remained consistent towards her, even after her death.

She was a fool who had always displeased him, and displeased him only a fraction more by dying so violently under his roof. He was used to say, I believe, that if she had desired an end so greatly, she should have drowned herself in the river, and thereby saved them all the fuss and the expense her domestic suicide entailed. And of course there was fuss and expense. The newspapers carried the story in a riot. This did Charles no good, but it was the shocking death itself, I am sure, which wore him down, and eventually changed the pattern of his life, as is generally reckoned to its detriment. He left the bar less than a year after. His elegant and carefree wit, which had long deserted him, began to return in a strange little lay community attached to a monastery of the Languedoc. Occasionally we correspond; I do not presume to understand his present existence, nor to approve or disapprove of it, but he apparently does some good for himself and for those around him. Other than these messages to me or to Semery, he writes nothing now.

Semery himself, who in his way had already broken off the chains of a false life, was not fundamentally altered, but his grief and his remorse were awesome. Though the marriage went forward on the day assigned, he faltered through it all barely coherent and blind with tears. Later, I gather, he made some attempt to destroy his canvases, but fortunately friends arrived and prevented it. Miou helped as only she could, by her persevering tenderness, until in the end some care of her and of their approaching child brought him to his senses.

But none of us was untouched.

Honorine, as I said, surely did not intend this torrent of guilt. That guilt should be experienced was unavoidable. Yet she, she was in that last hour so isolate, I would say she thought of no other, either to long for their comfort or to wish them ill. She must have climbed those stairs up through the house in an utter darkness of heart and mind, and soulless too, for her soul had been wrenched from her, as in the myths it is, by the Devil. Her imaginings, or rather the black void within her – one shrinks from its contemplation.

However, though she left no concrete parting gift of bitterness in the form of a letter, there is that journal of hers, which Semery now possesses, and which he has allowed me to see. She wrote nothing in it of despair. It was all joy, from start to finish. The finish being where she had left it off in the midst of a sentence, probably because she had been told her father required her downstairs. It is the joy, of course, which is unbearable. It is the unfinished sentence that fills one with terror as if reading the order for an execution. What breaks the heart is the motto she has written just inside the cover: *Je suis parce que j'ai été.**

For none of us were untouched.

At six o'clock on the morning after her death, not having slept or shaved, nor completely in my right mind, I hurried westward across the city. The dawn was beginning to wash stealthily in along the dry riverbeds of the streets, and I remember I met a flock of sheep being ushered into the Faubourg St Marie. When I reached the house of the Dupleys I woke it, and its neighbours, by hammering on the door.

What was said and performed was madness, and I can recollect only fragments of it now, that to this day have the power to embarrass me, or sometimes to make me laugh. Suffice it to relate, I fought my way by means of shouted threats through several servants, and eventually through Anette's father himself (who thought me dangerously insane), all the way to Anette's mother (who thought much as he did, but with more compassion). And so to Anette herself who, whatever she thought, did not love me less. There in a corner of a room, her good kind mother outside the door, as our protector, the father in the hall roaring that the police should be called, I said nothing of what had happened, only perpetrated yet one more scene worthy of the opera, crying in Anette's arms, and then seizing her hands and asking her to get dressed and come away with me at once. There was the briefest addendum to this plea. It concerned her trusting me, it concerned our being married by the quickest means the law allowed, it concerned my ability to support her, that she was of age but would lose all her money and inheritance. That maybe we should live without pecuniary margin for ever. That she should bring warm clothing, and whatever else she might need, and her pet kitten. And that I could not swear not to attack her father if he interfered any further. To all of which she listened gravely, then said that I must go away at once, and that she would then meet me, with her mother's help, complete with

* *I am because I was*

one small valise and the kitten, in an hour's time in the Bois Palais. At first I argued. Not because I thought she was putting me off – wretch that I was I had every right to think that she might be – but simply because I was so shaken and wild I could not bear to leave her. Nevertheless, in the end she persuaded me. I went, while Monsieur Dupleys, standing on his steps in his dressing-gown, with the manservant, waved a purportedly loaded pistol at my back. And in just over an hour, mother, daughter and kitten appeared in the Bois, and we and the fountains wept, and the little cat wailed in astonishment, and God alone knows what the early strollers made of it all.

As it turned out, there was a later reconciliation, and Anette lost nothing by her elopment. We were, though, a year married by then, and my own financial prospects had taken a soaring turn towards fortune. I like to suppose that even if they had not, we could still have possessed the great happiness we had from the commencement, and still share together. I am now received by Monsieur Dupleys, who pompously and placatingly, and also out of a need to make me uncomfortable, sometimes refers to that tempestuous morning, as if it were some game we all played. But it was nothing of the sort. Or, if so, it was Honorine's – Lucie's.

For it was because of Honorine that I risked, as I did, our chances. This I have since explained to my wife. Not only through the upheaval of that ghastly suicide. No, more because of those ephemeral moments of a woman's *life*, in which I had partici-pated. I had been trying, desperately, to make at least one iota of the dream be true. *Could you perhaps run away together?* she had said to me. Lucie's scheme, brave, beautiful, reckless Lucie. Lucie gracious enough to assume Anette's money meant nothing to me, in which assumption she and Anette have been, probably quite alone. And so I honoured Lucie. I went to my love and asked her to run away with me, and she consented. I shall be grateful for that, to Honorine, until the day of my death.

The last act is now concluded, and yet there remains something in the way of an epilogue. I have said I have no leanings to superstition, or to esoteric occult ideas, and part of me clamours here to leave well alone. After all if, as I believe, it proves nothing, then the circumstances I have outlined turn only darker, and they are surely dark enough. On the other hand, the inveterate story-teller finds it hard to reject such a gem. For gem it is, of a sort.

Some years had passed; the great-grandchildren of Anette's first cat were playing with two children of our own across the floors of our house. Researching in an area that had nothing whatever to do with Lucie Belmains, I suddenly came across a strange reference to her. It dealt, as did the rest of the rather obscure material I was examining, with the negligence, connivance, and ineptitude of some doctors, when presented with various classic but misleading symptoms. There was, for instance, a case of hysteria amusingly and dreadfully diagnosed as la rage, and a nastier affair of the same rabid condition, genuine, thought to be lycanthropy. Then came an interim paragraph, and next a name (Lucie's) that caught me unawares and made me start. Some wounds, though they heal, retain a life-long capacity for hurt.

'Lucie Belmains,' went on my material, after a token biography, 'having slain herself on the morning of the fifth of April, was medically certified as mortal, and buried swiftly, due to the extreme and unusual heat of the season. Readers who have scanned the novel *La Prise En Geste* will be familiar with the following quotation from it.' The quotation does indeed follow, but I will omit it here. It was from a flowery work, the very one I am sure Miou and her sister had giggled over under the covers, and as a result of which their poor doll was hanged on a ribbon. The substance of the quotation was this: that on the sixth of April, one of Lucie's living admirers, having entered the bedroom where the body was laid out, and kneeling by the bed in a transport of grief, was abruptly terrified to see the dead woman's left hand flutter as if beckoning to him. Hastening to uncover her face, however, he found only the discolouration and popping eyes such a corpse would exhibit, and, running out of the room, he fainted.

'What is not widely known,' the material went on, 'is that this incident is a fact, and not merely a flight of fancy on the part of a romantic author. There are two other facts, even more slenderly recorded, and not utilized by the writer of *La Prise En Geste*. Firstly, that Belmains' maid, on the evening of the seventh, the actual night of burial, found disturbed the veil which covered the cadaver's face, it being partly pushed or drawn in between the

310

lips. Secondly, that several comments were made on the suppleness of the limbs. This was put down to the hot weather. While the whole affair was meanwhile thought so scandalous, its sequels were largely rushed and overall camouflaged, to the point that for several years even the Duc de M——, who had been for so long the lady's intimate protector, thought she had died by accidental choking.'

The conclusion my material evolved from all this is a fairly obvious one. That though Lucie had sufficiently strangled herself as to induce a kind of catalepsy, she was not dead, and did not die until the injury of a mainly collapsed windpipe was augmented by the disadvantages of the grave. Not the material, but I myself, venture to suggest she could not, in this state, have lingered very much longer. No doubt only until the morning of the eighth of April.